Elizabeth Carver frowned at herself in the mirror. Without the fichu, the dress could be worn low enough to show her breasts. She tugged the dress down, forcing her breasts higher. She was always being told what to do, what to wear, what was proper. She felt hemmed in tighter than any stays or corsets ever were. She couldn't breathe.

Elizabeth began to descend the stairs. At any moment she felt she was going to burst free of the silk completely. Her face showing not a trace of the turmoil within, she took the first step and stopped. There was a man seated in the entry hall. He was handsome, in a rugged sort of way, fierce, like a buccaneer. He wasn't at all the sort of person she was used to seeing in her father's house. . . .

Michael never knew what it was that made him look up, but ever after he knew it was the most fateful moment of his life. From that instant nothing was as it was before, nor ever could be again.

THE FALLON BLOOD—
a novel of history, adventure, and passion.

THE FALLON BLOOD

REAGAN O'NEAL

POPHAM PRESS
An Imprint of Ace Books
A Division of Charter Communications Inc.
A GROSSET & DUNLAP COMPANY
360 Park Avenue South
New York, New York 10010

THE FALLON BLOOD

A Popham Press Original

First Printing: February 1980

2 4 6 8 0 9 7 5 3 1
Manufactured in the United States of America

To Harriet,
who pulled hen's teeth.

1

The English wind blew the dust of the road in Michael Fallon's face, as it had for miles past, and cut through his thin shirt and his flesh as well. He'd given up wishing he still had a coat. That had gone two days before for a stale loaf of bread and a small mug of beer. He had been lucky to get that much, and knew it. In this country there was more likely to be a kick and a curse for an Irishman than any sort of kindness.

Perhaps, he thought, he should have sold the contents of the bag he carried. Sold it long ago. He hugged the long, narrow sack tighter and grinned mirthlessly. It gave him a piratical look, with the high cheekbones and hook nose a long ago Spanish ancestor had bequeathed him. Only startlingly blue eyes kept him from being one of the Black Irish, those other descendants of storm-tossed Spanish Armada survivors. His grin faded. The selling would have changed nothing. Some things were fated to be, and he had the feeling he had been fated to walk this endless English road, fated from the day he was born.

Ahead, around a bend in the road, an inn appeared. The brightly painted sign swung violently in the wind, but he could still make it out. A man knelt in front of a huge figure wearing a crown and holding a scepter. Below, in neat letters, it said "The King's Man." It was the place he had been seeking.

He leaned against the rough stone fence along the side of the road. Frowning, he turned up his foot to examine the hole in his left boot, and the blister that had formed at it. He was stalling. He'd seen that blister fifty times before. This was the place he'd sought, but now, in sight of it, he wondered if he had the right to involve anyone else in his troubles, even for an hour.

The man bustling out of the inn shielded his broad face from the wind with one hand and headed for the barn, muttering to himself about eggs. He gave a casual glance up the road and slowly came to a halt. He stared hard at the dark-haired traveler.

"It can't be," he whispered. A smile spread across his face. "Michael! Michael Shane Fallon! Is it you, or is it your ghost I'm seeing?"

"It's me, Timothy Cavanaugh, me or what's left of me. I'd heard about the sign, but I didn't quite believe it. Have you become a good Englishman, then, bowing and scraping to their fat German king?"

"Don't be talking like that where people might be hearing you." Cavanaugh glanced around nervously, though there was no one in sight. "Come inside before you get the both of us arrested for sedition."

At the door Michael stopped for a last look down the road. His resolve hardened. If they came, let them come, and be damned to them. He turned and strode inside.

A dozen tables stood on a well-scrubbed floor, with chairs instead of benches at every one. The only other occupant was a barmaid, a pretty girl with coppery hair. And remarkable breasts, Michael noted. At their entrance she began industriously scrubbing at the bar with a rag.

"Out with you, girl," Timothy said. "Gather those eggs before I take a switch to you. And don't come back till it's time for the custom to come."

She trotted out, with an interested smile for Michael. He shook his head; he was sorry for that interest.

While Timothy drew two mugs of ale he laid his bag on the table. A quick tug at the drawstring revealed the hilt of a sword. He pulled two pistols to where they, too, lay just inside the opening.

Cavanaugh set the mugs and a plate of meat and cheese on the table, ignoring the bag and its contents. "Sit, man. Sit. Is it on your way back to the old country you are? I remember you were always talking about going back after we were mustered out."

"I've been there and left," Michael said, dropping heavily to a chair. He tried to keep his hand steady as he popped the first piece of ham into his mouth. And the second. God, but it was good.

"And how is it there now?"

"As it's always been. What the English haven't stolen already, they soon will."

Cavanaugh looked at him in surprise, then eyed the sword and pistols. "Tell me. I've heard tell of some men in Ireland, now. The Whiteboys, they call themselves. You wouldn't be having anything to do with them, now would you?"

Michael's back stiffened, and he kept a rein on his temper with difficulty. "Do you think I'd be riding around burning barns and harrying poor farmers while prattling about how I'm fighting the English?"

"No, lad. No, of course not." Cavanaugh sketched a line across the table top with one hand and gave a short laugh. "I mind me the first time I saw you. Not even beginning to shave, you were. Come to seek fame and fortune in King George's German war with a sword as old as my grandfather and a musket that must have been on the Ark. You remember? Riding all over hell and gone, never knowing who we'd face next. Austrians, Poles, French, Russians. And you, thinking it was such grand fun."

"I was young then."

"Eh? Yes. Yes, you were. So were we all. But tell me. Do you remember cutting your way into Freiholm to save my hide? A fine day. Three hundred pounds sterling a man from that paychest we took, and promotions all around. Aye, Captain Fallon?"

"The King of Prussia's Irish Hussars were long ago, Timothy."

Timothy sighed. "But it provided the money for your farm."

"Maybe it would've been better if I'd never gone. I said I've nothing to do with the Whiteboys, and that's true, but I'm still here under false pretenses, after a manner of speaking. But then, I think you've guessed I'm not carrying that sword to spit cabbages."

"I did think just that," Timothy replied, "and the pistols

for shooting flies.'' The words were light, but his tone was forced and his face long.

Michael kept his eyes on the table as he began. ''I went back after we were mustered out, as I said I would. I should have stayed away like you did, bought a tavern somewhere. But I'd that idea of getting a piece of Irish ground, of starting the land and the Fallon name. I got it, all right.''

''Good land, was it, Michael?''

''Beautiful land, Timothy. Not a mile from where I was born, just a short walk from the River Shannon. It was a fine life, for a while, quiet and calm. With the money I had, the rackrents couldn't pull me down. The first crop was mine, free and clear, with a second on the way. There were families in the village who remembered mine kindly. I even went up in a party with some of them to the fair at Ballinasloe.''

He fell silent, and Timothy waited before prodding him on. ''What happened, lad? What changed it?''

''There was a girl. No, Timothy, not what you're thinking. She was pretty enough, but I'd never looked at her twice until the day she walked past my door. An Englishman, a colonel staying at the big house above the village with the Fitzhuberts, was riding past the other way. He stopped her as if to ask directions. I saw it all from my cottage. The next I knew he was down off his horse, laughing and putting his hands all over her, and she was beating at him and screaming she was a good girl.''

''And was she?''

''Would it have mattered?'' He didn't wait for an answer. ''I did the only thing I could. I went out and knocked him down. That was bad enough, I suppose, him being who he was, but he wouldn't let it end with that. He drew his saber.'' The man across the table shifted uneasily. ''If I hadn't been a hussar, if I'd still been just a farmboy, I'd have grabbed the girl by the hand and ran away, to keep from being split like a sheep. But you see, by instinct, not even thinking about it, I'd grabbed up my own sword as I ran out.''

''Oh, God, no, Michael.''

A snarl twisted his mouth. ''He said the Irish were only

good for two things. He'd demonstrate the first by killing me, then show the girl what the other was. He might have been fine at hacking at poor peasants with the thing from horseback, but the King of Prussia's Irish Hussars would've thrown him out for a butcher's apprentice. I ran him through on the second pass. I tell you, Timothy, I never meant to kill him, not even after we crossed swords, but I was that mad I could hardly see straight, and when he left himself open, I did it. The work of a second, and I couldn't call it back if I had a thousand years. Not that I'd want to. He deserved it, and likely more. But there I was, with him dead, and his horse off and running back toward the village, and the girl so white-faced scared she looked ready to drop dead on the spot. It's a charge of murder, no matter that he had a sword in his hand.''

Cavanaugh puffed out his cheeks and nodded vigorously. ''That it is. Murder for killing a man. Murder for killing an Englishman. Murder for killing an English colonel. Lord, man, they'd hang you three times over for it.''

''So I knew. I started running, and I've not stopped or slowed till now.'' He paused, then went on quickly. ''Hell, I'd best tell all of it. The flyers are out on me already, saying I killed him from behind, to rob him.''

''So they'll hang you four times, do they catch you. Now, what can I do to make sure they don't?''

Michael's throat thickened. ''Always ready for the troubles, aren't you?''

''Ah, lad, we went through a lot together. Now, what?''

''The name of a smuggler who'll let me work my way to the Continent. A meal. A place in the barn for the night. No, that's all, Timothy. If I'm discovered, you didn't know I was there, and you don't know who I am. I'll not be taking you down with me.''

Cavanaugh studied the tabletop for a moment, his lips moving as if planning his words carefully. Finally he looked up.

''So you intend trying for the Continent, then. You'll be safe enough from the English law there. Of course, you'll have to stay away from the German principalities. There are still British soldiers there, I understand. And in the ports there'll be marines. Him being a colonel, they might have those flyers out to the Navy.'' Cavanaugh eyed him, and went on in an off-hand manner. ''Of course, there's always the colonies. America.''

''Do you still believe the stories about gold to be picked up off the ground there?'' Michael laughed. ''I remember that fat Brunswicker telling you those tales, and you lapping them up like cream and buying him more ale the while.''

''I'm serious, lad,'' the other said quietly.

Michael regarded him soberly. ''God's blood, Timothy! How do I get there? Have you asked yourself that? Everything I own, now, wouldn't stretch to cover a passage to America. And if it could, I'd certainly need more than my share of wits to prosper without two pence to rub together.''

''There's a way, if you'll listen.''

''I'll listen to anything.''

Cavanaugh leaned over the table intently. ''I know a man in Liverpool who's signing indentured servants for the colonies.''

''Indentured—.'' Michael leaped to his feet, knocking his chair spinning. ''That's your idea? Selling myself as a slave to some Englishman?''

''It's not like that, Michael.''

''They're close enough to making slaves of us in our own country. I'll not cross the ocean to let them do the same to me there. Better to go fight for the French, or the Russians or Swedes. I'd still be my own man!''

Cavanaugh's hand slammed flat on the table. ''Will you sit down, Michael Fallon? You promised to listen. Will you go back on your word?''

Michael glared at him, then slowly bent to set the chair back on its feet with a thump. He sat down rigidly, and fixed the other man with a tight look. ''I'm listening.''

Cavanaugh eyed him uncertainly. Fallon could still react like a boy, he knew, if he didn't approach this correctly. ''It's not like you're thinking at all. It's more like being an apprentice, almost.'' Michael scowled; Cavanaugh hurried on.

"Your passage is paid, and you agree to work for the man who pays it for three years, or five. The jobs are clerk and bookkeeper and carpenter and brickmason and the like. I've seen the advertising for them. I've talked with men who've done it and gotten their freedom as promised. Now then, does that sound like slavery to you?"

"Perhaps not," Michael said grudgingly, "but even so, I've none of those skills."

"But you can read, lad, and write and figure. And you acted as quartermaster for our company that one whole year and did a better job of it than any we ever hired. If that's not clerking, then what is it?"

"Yes, but—."

"And the capper, lad, the capper to it is when you finish your service, you get land, forty or fifty acres of it, sometimes more, and every inch of it yours free and clear. Was what you had in Ireland as good as that, for all the rackrents you paid?"

"No. Not half so much."

"That's not the whole of it, either. I said I've heard of men rising. Well, some of those men began as indentured servants, and some of them became, not just men of property and substance, but men of wealth."

"And how many drinks did you buy for the hearing of those tales?"

Cavanaugh rose. "Not a one, lad. Not a one. But let me be getting us two more. These have gone and disappeared."

"You're not thinking of making me drunk enough to go to Liverpool, are you?" Michael asked with a quick grin. "I always could drink you down and carry you home after."

"Say you so?"

The second round went quickly, as did those that followed, until the barmaid returned to get ready for the first of the evening's regulars. She watched them navigate the stairs to Cavanaugh's private room with a shake of her head.

Cavanaugh rambled while Michael thought. America. The colonies were huge, stretching deep into an unexplored continent larger than all of Europe. It could indeed be a place for a man to grow and build, a land where there was such room.

Land of his own. That was no more than a dream to a man from Ireland. There he'd been lucky to rent a tiny patch from Murphy, who'd rented a larger piece from an absentee English landlord. If he could own land, his land, with no rents to be paid, no landlords to be beholden to, then he could do anything. He could build an empire. He could found a dynasty. By dark he was roaring the same toast over and over again.

"The American colonies and the Fallons, for a thousand years to come."

When the last customer had gone, more than one complaining of the drunken noise from above, the barmaid came up to help them to their beds.

She pushed Timothy into his room, barely waiting to see where he fell before hurrying Michael down the hall to another chamber. She was staggering herself by the time she had him seated on the bed. With a sigh of relief she pushed a strand of silken hair off her forehead and began pulling his shirt off over his head.

"A thousand years," he said fuzzily.

"Yes, love." She folded his shirt over the back of a chair, then started on his breeches buttons.

"Will you stop that, girl? I can do for myself."

She sat back on her heels and waited skeptically. Unsteadily he got to his feet and fumbled the buttons open. In one move he pushed the breeches down to his ankles and dropped back onto the bed.

Kneeling at his feet she finished removing the pants, first tugging off his boots. "A shame to waste all that," she said hopefully.

Michael blinked away the fog and peered unashamedly down the front of her blouse. Rounded breasts with just a light sprinkling of freckles across the tops jiggled pleasantly every time she moved. She gave a startled squeal as he snatched her to his lap.

"You can't get a Fallon too drunk for that, lass." He tipped her back, his mouth coming down demandingly on hers, her tongue answering his.

Suddenly she sat bolt upright on his lap. "What are you doing? Do you think I'm a strumpet, to let any man as comes by give me a green dress?" He hugged her to his hard-muscled chest.

"I think you're an armful of the best. But you can go this minute if you've a mind to. I'll play no villain with you."

She gazed into his fierce blue eyes. "I'll stay." He smiled lazily, and pulled loose the strings of her blouse. Her breasts were free; he pulled her to him, his teeth catching a thick, brown nipple, tongue caressing it. Her fingers ran through his hair, pulling his head tighter against her. The hardness in his groin brushed against her thigh.

"Hurry," she moaned. "Hurry."

He rolled her down onto the bed, his hard body moving over hers. She groaned as he entered her, and her legs whipped tightly around him. He tangled his hands in her hair and rained kisses on her upturned face. Her arms and legs held to the flexing of his back and buttocks and thighs.

Small, breathy whimpers started in her throat, in time to the creaking of the bed's rope underpinnings, growing louder and louder. Her teeth sank into the side of his neck to stifle her cries. With a scream she couldn't fight back, she came. And then his breath rasped past her ear as he, too, reached release.

For just a moment he let his weight rest on her, then rolled over, pulling her over on top of him. He smoothed away damp hair from her forehead. "You've an angel's talent for making a man happy, lass. What's your name?"

She smiled against his chest. "Bess, sir. And if I may say so, you have a talent for making a woman happy."

Michael chuckled deep in his throat. "Well, I thank you, Bess. Did I by any chance ask you about going to America? And if I did, what was it you answered?"

"Oh, I don't want to go there, sir. They say the savages cuts off people's heads."

Michael signed and settled deeper in the pillows. "Too pretty a head to be cut off. Still, could be, could be rich in America." His voice drifted drowsily. "Ought to come. Ought to—."

The words trailed away, and she lifted up on his chest to look at him. His eyes were closed, and he breathed the long, regular breaths of a deep sleep.

She pushed at his shoulder, without much hope of success. He slept on. With a regretful sigh she clambered off him and shrugged back into her clothes. On impulse she gently kissed his lips. Then she pulled a blanket over him and tiptoed out, softly closing the door behind her.

Light shining through the window finally wakened Michael. He lay still for a minute, wondering which hurt more, the sun burning through his eyelids or his head reminding him of the night before. With an effort he pushed himself up. The mirror showed him in remarkably fine shape for a man who knew himself at least half dead. As he stared in the glass he realized he'd found a decision in the ale, and that decision still held.

Splashing water in his face he hurriedly dressed, wondering vaguely how he'd managed to fold his shirt so neatly and yet leave his pants in a heap on the floor. Then, pitcher in hand, he walked down the hall to his friend's room. Timothy lay sprawled on his back, fully clothed and snoring loud enough to rattle the windows. Michael held the pitcher over his head and slowly turned it upside down.

Timothy jerked erect, choking and sputtering. "I'll kill you. Friend or not, I'll break your head."

"I'm going to America, Timothy."

"I'll tear off your limbs one by one. And then—. What was that you said?"

"I'm going to America."

"Praise be. Some sense at last. When?"

"As soon as you stop wallowing about there and tell me how to find this man of yours in Liverpool."

"Wallowing about, is it? I—. Forget about telling you. I'll take you myself." He reared up out of the bed. "What are you waiting for? The horse won't hitch himself."

Fifteen minutes later they were on the road to Liverpool.

2

The *Rose*, bound from Liverpool, England, for Charlestown, in His Majesty's colony of South Carolina, was far from looking like her namesake. Eighty feet long and thirty in the beam, full-sided and deep, she was made to cram the largest amount of cargo possible into the smallest amount of space, a cargo largely of indentured men and women.

The *Rose* made landfall on a brisk, January morning in 1765. A shadowy line appeared, like mist on the horizon. Slowly that faint darkness grew more substantial, until a continent reared up out of the sea to lie before them, sweeping across the whole of their vision as if it were the whole world brought together. America.

The closer the ship came to land, the more the crew resembled a stirred ant heap. They bustled around at jobs Michael now recognized, but some things he didn't know at all. One clambered out on the bowsprit, legs wrapped around the slim spar, hands clutching the jibstay, eyes fastened to the waters ahead. Another scrambled to the topmast cap of the foremast, one hand holding him against the sway of the mast while the other shaded his eyes to search their path.

Andrew Toomey, a young ship's officer with whom Michael had spent many an hour, passed by. He was frowning: Michael caught his arm. "What's happening, Andrew? Why the extra lookouts?"

Toomey looked quickly to the quarterdeck to see if the captain was watching. "He's going through the Swash."

"Is that so dangerous, then?"

The young man hesitated. "Mr. Reed, the first mate, has made this approach a dozen times. There's been talk of building a lighthouse, he says, but there's none yet. So we take a bearing on two points of land and steer straight for a small river mouth. That'll put us fairly in the Swash. The lookouts will watch for the water to change color over the Charlestown Bar and keep us squarely in the channel.''

"I've a feeling there's more," Michael said quietly.

"There is," Toomey said with a short nod. "Just inside the Swash there's another small bar. Even before we clear the Swash we must bear away from the harbor mouth to clear it. And then we'll tack back up. There's little room in the channel, and it's an awfully sharp tack. If we go in irons we'll strike the Bar, or drift into the shallows and break up in the surf.''

"Well, those are certainly joyous alternatives. I take it this isn't the normal way to enter this harbor. There'd not be this excitement if it was.''

Toomey took another look for the captain. "A vessel this size would usually lie outside the Bar until a good part of her cargo had been lightered ashore, then go in through the Eight Foot Channel. But Captain Harding says the lightermen are all thieves and will pilfer the cargo before it gets to shore. As he's responsible for it until it does get to shore, not so much as a packet of needles will be allowed over the side before he's safely tied up.''

The man was going to risk all their lives to prevent a few pounds of theft? "Is he drunk, or a madman?''

"Sir, it's his command. He can do with it as he wishes. There's an old saying that at sea the captain and God rank in that order.''

"Mr. Toomey!" Captain Harding's shout brought the same galvanized leap from the young man that it always did. The captain leaned over the quarterdeck rail and bawled his words for the whole ship to hear. "Why is it, Mr. Toomey, that every time I look for you, you're talking to that damned Irishman? I don't like my officers fraternizing with the cargo. Perhaps if you study the question from the foretop you can come up with an answer. Now, Mr. Toomey. Right this minute.''

With an apologetic glance at Michael, Toomey turned and trotted to the foremast shrouds. He went up like a spider, feet nimble on the ratlines, swinging out on the futtock shrouds, almost upside down, to climb precariously over the outside edge of the top.

Harding had bent back over a fistful of manifests with Mr. Reed. He appeared to have forgotten Toomey as soon as he finished shouting.

As shouts began to come down from the lookouts, Harding kept his eyes on the papers, refusing to show any of the agitation that gripped the rest of the crew. Reed attempted to do the same, albeit nervously. Seamen went about their jobs tensely, ears cocked for the shuddering crack of the keel breaking on the Bar. The other passengers noted none of it. Their attention was all on the shore, so startlingly green— and so low to the water.

"It's flat!" Gale cried. "A high tide'll cover it."

"It is a judgment from God that we are put down in such a land," Mrs. Hanna intoned. "We must pray to Him to receive our souls."

The ship's head dropped away, toward the south. Michael watched the sails. If disaster came the first warning would be there.

"Do you think they'd set us ashore in a marsh, Mr. Fallon?" Hanna wrung his hands, ignoring his wife's furious looks and the finger she kept jabbing in his side. "Savages, Mr. Fallon. How will we protect ourselves against savages?"

Michael pulled his attention back to the deck. "Savages, is it? I don't know much about savages, but I've seen half a dozen ports in Europe that show no more to the sea than this." The sails were all slack, the foreyards not yet turned. He glanced toward the shore, but at the water, not the land. From where the breakers began they had only a few hundred yards before they'd be in the shallows. "No, I don't think it's savages should worry you at all."

"I say it's a wilderness," Gale said stoutly, "and wildernesses have savages."

"It is God's judgment." Mrs. Hanna's voice was like a funeral bell.

Abruptly the wind caught in the sails all at the same time, and the mass of canvas cracked like God's whip to chastise the wicked. The same thought seemed to strike Mrs. Hanna, for she looked to the sky, whitefaced and trembling, quiet for the first time since coming on board.

Michael looked to the breaker line, less than a hundred yards from the ship. "You're a lucky man, Gale. You don't even begin to know how lucky. Why, with no more luck than you've got right now, I expect you'll live to a rancid old age."

Gale blinked uncertainly, and the rest fell to arguing over whether it was an insult or not, and if so, how much of one. Hanna's wife stood stiffly, eyes closed and mouth moving in silent prayer.

Michael kept his eyes ahead, running the low, sandy beaches and the scrub pine forests toward the point they'd round into the harbor. The *Rose* moved slowly into the wind, creeping past the point and on out beyond the middle of the harbor mouth before turning in. As it did, he smiled, a smile of delighted surprise.

The harbor mouth was two miles and more across, and inside it widened and ran deep. Down the length of it were anchored over a hundred sail, ships of every size from coasting schooners, little more than decked-over longboats, to vessels more than twice the size of the *Rose*, as big as frigates. Lighters and barges and small sloops snuggled in close to many of them, while barrels and crates were swung out on booms and onto larger vessels, or they themselves were loaded for the trip to shore or upriver.

A host of smaller craft flitted across the water like mayflies, fishing boats under patched sail with crews of two or three black men, large dories rowed by four or six with a steersman and a passenger attired in the height of fashion, even dugouts made from roughly hollowed tree trunks and paddled by roughly dressed men who could have passed for savages had it not been for their white skins and European features.

Michael knew now how the Vikings had felt, sailing into

the mouth of some Irish river and seeing for the first time the land they meant to have. This is mine, each had said, and known inside that he would have the land or die on it. He smiled now as they had smiled then, like the sea-wolf staking his claim. "This is mine," he said softly. "This is mine."

Two rivers came down to form the harbor, and on the peninsula between them the city was built. Charlestown. It wasn't so large as London, but it could hold its own against all but a handful of towns in England. Two tall steeples towered over the spread of it, stretching from river to river. As they wended through the pack of the harbor details began to appear. Buildings of brick were everywhere, prominent dwellings of the sort built by men of wealth. The streets bustled and flowed with traffic in a continuous and purposeful stream. The reverberations of a church bell pealing the hour floated out over the harbor. With a crash the anchor fell free, and the *Rose* swung at her place in the river.

3

A scraping along the ship's side drew Michael to the rail. Bobbing alongside was a boat rowed by a weathered black man. He swung his oars in, and stood to grab a deadeye and steady the boat for his passenger to scramble over the rail. The passenger moved with a seaman's nimbleness, easily timing his leap to the rise of the swells, but his clothes were those of a clerk, an unadorned black tricorn, a somber gray suit, and shoes with plain steel buckles. Once on deck he headed quickly for the quarterdeck, looking neither left nor right.

"Hold there," Harding shouted. "Not the owner himself boards this ship without permission. Who the devil might you be?"

The man hastily made a leg, sweeping his hat before him with a flourish. He had a wide grin on his long, narrow face. "Sure and you must remember me, Captain Harding. Christopher Byrne, sir, at your service. It's in the employ of Mr. Thomas Carver I am. It's to him a good bit of your cargo is consigned, or so I'm told."

"Back over the side, Mr. Byrne. Mr. Carver will have to wait until I'm tied to the wharf before I unload one bale. He knows my way. If he wanted his goods lightered ashore he should have used his own ship."

"You're mistaking my purpose, captain. I'm not after the cargo. That's to be landed at the bridge, as agreed. Mr. Carver sent me out most particularly to fetch back an indentured man you're supposed to have for him. A clerk, he is."

Harding thrust out his hand, and Reed had the list ready to put in it. Some of the bound men stepped forward eagerly. The captain looked up sharply. "Which one of you is Michael Fallon?"

Michael straightened from the rail. "I am."

Harding's mouth tightened. "You, is it? I'll be glad enough to get rid of this one, Mr. Byrne. He is a pest, taking up my officers' time when they should be about their duties. All right, then. Into the boat with you."

"I've some belongings below——."

"Then get them. Get them and get over the side." He turned away.

It took only moments for Michael to gather his few possessions and stuff them into the same bag he'd carried to the King's Man. Another pair of breeches, two extra shirts, some small clothes, that was the sum of it. In the bottom, though, wrapped in a rag, was the money he'd gotten for one pair of officer's pistols with set triggers, chased with silver, and one sword, finely balanced and engraved on the blade in German.

Little enough it was, too. The man who bought them thought they were stolen, brought in as they were by a ragged Irishman, and paid accordingly. Michael had been in no position to haggle. It was a small foundation for an empire, he thought, but it was a beginning.

Byrne was waiting astride the railing when Michael went back on deck. "Over the side with you, lad," he said with a quick grin. "We've not much time to get where we're going."

Michael nodded, and climbed down to the boat as smoothly as he could.

It was of overlapping planks, and pointed at both ends. The oarsman sat amidships, one calloused foot braced against the seat in front of him. He eyed Michael expressionlessly as the Irishman took his seat. Michael studied him as well. He knew they had black slaves in the colonies, but he'd thought of them as ragged men, laboring dolefully. The boatman's clothes might be faded, but they were far from rags. And despite his impassive face he appeared more satisfied than sad.

The boat rocked as Byrne entered, and the boatman greeted him with a smile. "Carver's Bridge, Daniel. Quick as you can."

"No time at all, Mr. Byrne. No time at all." The oarsman pushed them away from the *Rose* with one oar, then fitted both in the locks and began long, powerful strokes that took in his whole body from braced foot to broad shoulders. The boat literally skipped across the water.

"This bridge, now," Michael said. "What kind of bridge would a man be owning? Is it a toll bridge of some kind?"

Daniel chuckled and nearly missed a stroke. Byrne threw back his head and laughed. "No, no, it's not that kind of bridge at all. It's a custom around here to call a wharf a bridge. So, Mr. Carver's bridge is really Mr. Carver's wharf. Is there any other question you might be wanting to ask?"

"There is." Michael jerked his head at the boatman. "Is he one of those slaves I've heard tell of?"

"Daniel? Lord no, man. Daniel's a free man. Aren't you, Daniel?"

The black man nodded. "Yes sir, Mr. Byrne. I'm a free man, like my daddy was before me. Now his daddy was a slave to Mr. Perroneau Tristam, till he saved Mr. Tristam from drowning in the Stono Inlet. Mr. Tristam gave him his freedom, ten pounds currency, a boat, and a new suit of clothes every year till the day he died. We been boatmen ever since, and I reckon we always will be."

"I apologize, Daniel," Michael said, "if I offended you."

This time the boatman missed a stroke, and sat all the way up before remembering to take it up again. "No, sir. You didn't offend me none."

"He's got something in common with you, Daniel," Byrne said. "In a manner of speaking, that is. He's a Black Irishman."

Daniel looked from the red-headed Irishman to the dark-haired one. "He don't look no kind of black to me."

"None the less, he is. He has the mark of it. Tell me, Fallon, have you done much clerking?"

"A goodly bit."

Byrne nodded, still eyeing Michael shrewdly. "Times be, looks tell a false tale, I've no doubt."

Michael's eyes flickered. "And you? Are you a clerk?"

"A clerk! God save me. I'm second mate on the *Annalee*, one of Mr. Carver's own."

"A fine position, that."

Byrne's irritation had faded to a kind of seriousness. "A little advice for you, Fallon. There aren't many will accept an indentured man who acts as though he's as good as they are. When I boarded the *Rose*, I could pick out the other bound men. But you, now, lounging against the rail. Man, I thought you were a paying passenger, maybe even in the captain's cabin. You'll have to watch that."

"I'll show respect where it's due, but I'll truckle to no man."

"I did not speak of truckling," Byrne said sharply. "I just said watch yourself. Many consider a bound man no better than a slave, and they'll do you harm if they think you're getting above yourself."

"You give much advice, and freely."

"I know what it takes to survive as a bound man. I was one."

Michael looked up in surprise and started to speak, but the other's attention was on grabbing a ladder as they slid in beside a wharf. Daniel rose quickly, taking hold of the ladder himself, and Byrne disappeared up it.

"It was a smooth trip, Daniel," Michael said, "and a fast one." He clambered up the ladder, his possessions clutched precariously under his arm.

The bustle of the harbor seemed belied on the wharf. A few men desultorily rolled barrels across the rough, uneven planks. Another leaned on a large broom, frowning at it as if wondering what to do with it. Crates and bales and barrels were stacked everywhere, often with only narrow walkways between the mounds; they might have been shipped in yesterday, or leaving tomorrow, or they might have been there a twelvemonth. Against a piling, throwing stones at the water, slouched two soldiers.

Their red coats were a flare to Michael. The dark blue facings and breeches were unfamiliar, but they were British

regulars, surely enough. If the flyers had already been abroad
in England at his coming, might they not in the weeks since
have made it here on a packet? He began to regret selling the
weapons.

"Our protectors," Byrne said sourly, noting Michael's
gaze. "The 60th Foot. The Royal Americans. Royal hooligans would be more like it. Always getting drunk, they are,
starting fights, mistaking decent women for tavern sluts."
He spat. "Come. We're keeping Mr. Carver waiting."

Michael followed him the length of the wharf, past the
bulk of the warehouse at the foot of it, to a large, open
carriage in the street, shining black with tall, gilded wheels.
A coachman in blue and white livery, himself nearly as black
as the carriage, waited on the driver's perch. At their
footsteps he looked around, and grinned widely when he saw
Byrne.

"A quick trip, Mr. Byrne, sir." He gave a little bow as he
spoke. "A pleasant one, I hope, sir."

"It was that, at any rate, Samuel." Byrne leaned closer to
Michael. "You were wanting to see a slave. Well, Samuel,
here, is one." He climbed into the coach and sat with his
back to the driver. "The Church Street house, Samuel."

Michael entered the carriage slowly and sat where he could
watch the driver. It was strange. The man seemed happy.
How could a man be a slave and not rage against it? How
could he not feel his chains every minute? Samuel cracked
his whip over the horses, and the carriage started slowly
down the street.

Peddlers thronged the way. Most were fishmongers,
hawking piles of fish in a myriad of sizes and shapes from
stands or from baskets carried on their heads. Oxcarts,
loaded high with barrels, each guided by a black walking
alongside with a long switch, plodded toward the wharves
lining the river side of the street. Samuel wove his way
skillfully through the crush.

At a wide boulevard they turned toward the center of the
city, away from the river, but if anything the press increased.
The peddlers were there in even greater numbers, men push-

ing barrows, women with baskets selling a thousand small
things. Fine carriages vied for right of way with wagons
driven by sallow, withdrawn men who seemed a breed apart
from the cheerful folk of the city. Craftsmen dodged and
wove their way through the traffic, followed closely by
slaves carrying toolchests on their shoulders.

For a time they moved toward a great, white steeple that
towered over everything. That was Saint Michael's, Christopher said. Newer than Saint Philip's, the city's other
Anglican church, Byrne told him, it was the most important
church in the city. The State House was across the way from
it, and the beef market, with its vultures circling overhead.

Short of the church they turned down the peninsula again.
The houses now were almost uniformly large, some of two
stories, but most of three. Some were of brick and some of
wood, and all were set flush with the street, or with only a
small garden before the front door. If Carver lived in one of
those, Michael thought, he must be a man of some wealth. Of
course, he did own a wharf and at least one ship. In Ireland or
England that would argue for position and substance, but in
these colonies who could tell?

The carriage drew to a halt, and Byrne leaped down.
Michael stepped out more slowly and stood looking at the
house. Three stories high, white with dark green shutters, it
stood with one end to the street. Down the left side ran two
long verandas, on the first and second floors. Dormer windows and dark roof tiles glinted in the sun. Through
wrought-iron gates in the brick wall to the left he could see a
graveled carriage path leading back into gardens, and just a
glimpse of stables at the rear.

As Samuel opened the gates, Byrne tugged at the bell-pull,
the looked around for Michael. "Come. We have to see Mr.
Carver now. You'll have time to gawk later." He frowned.
"Maybe."

When Michael reached the door it was being held open by
a white-haired slave with a dignified air. Byrne took Michael
by the arm, pulled him onto the veranda and down to the door
leading inside the house.

"Mr. Carver's a busy man, Fallon. If you're going to be in his service, you'd best learn not to keep him waiting. If." His ready smile disappeared, and he bounced on his toes. "Yes. Wait here. Seth, tell Mr. Carver I'm here."

"He's been expecting you, sir," the butler said. "He said you was to go right on in. He's in the study."

With a deep breath and an unreadable look at Michael, Byrne went to the tall door to the left of the hall and tapped. To a murmured reply he slipped through, pulling it shut behind him.

The butler bowed and gestured to a high-backed chair against the paneled wall.

"Would you care for a seat, sir?"

"Thank you, Seth."

"May I get you something to drink?"

"No, thank you."

"Then if you'll excuse me, sir, I have duties."

Michael barely noticed his going. He sat with his belongings in his lap and studied the hall, the fine wainscotting and the sweep of the stairs. The lowboy across the hall and the very chair he sat in, he had seen their like before. Chippendale, the style was called.

Elizabeth Carver frowned at herself in the mirror. Without the fichu folded over her shoulders the dress could be worn low enough to show her breasts, the way Alicia said women did at the court of France. She took a deep breath. They were certainly large enough and round enough to belie her sixteen years, but it still didn't work the way Alicia said it was supposed to. She was supposed to look womanly, even sultry, but her face destroyed it all. Heart-shaped, surrounded by raven ringlets, it spoke of innocence. It screamed infant at her.

Her dark blue, almost purple, eyes grew petulant. Papa wouldn't let her wear it anyway. If she went to visit Alicia, she might be able to, but he'd hear of it eventually. Angrily she tugged it lower still, forcing her breasts even higher. Pink nipples peeked over the top of her bodice. If she wore it like that, they'd never even look at her face.

A slave woman in a dark brown dress entered quietly. Her mouth fell open when she saw the girl. "Miss Elizabeth!"

With a tiny shriek Elizabeth whirled, pulling the dress up with one hand and pushing herself back into it with the other. When she saw the black woman her mouth tightened. Defiantly she pulled the dress back down where it had been.

"Don't you ever come up on me like that again, Samantha. Not ever. Why, I nearly died. I thought it was Papa."

"Your father see you wearing that dress like that, Miss Elizabeth, he make you wish you had died."

"That's quite enough, Samantha." Elizabeth turned back to the mirror, twisting this way and that.

"Enough! Huh! Ain't *near* enough."

"Anyway, Papa won't ever find out."

"And what going to stop him?"

Elizabeth rounded suddenly, eyes flashing. "He'd better never find out, or I'll know who to hold responsible."

Samantha drew a deep, long-suffering breath. "Miss Elizabeth, you know——."

"I know what?"

"You keep parading around like that, he bound to find out. He could've walked in here his own self." Her face took on a determined look. "And you know that's true."

It was true, and that made it worse. She was always being told things. What to do. What to wear. What was proper. She felt hemmed in tighter than any stays or corsets ever were. She couldn't breathe. Those women in Paris weren't hemmed in by strictures. They did what they wanted, when they wanted.

"I think I'll take some air, Samantha."

"Yes, miss. You wear the brown——"

"I'll wear this," the girl said, and before the slave woman could move she swept out of the room.

Samantha hurried after her, darting round her like a pilot fish. Elizabeth's doubts were already beginning to gather; at the staircase they began to congeal. At any moment she was going to burst free of the violet silk completely. Desperately she wanted to pull it up, just a little, but not with Samantha to crow over her. She couldn't.

Samantha's steady drone decreased in volume flight by flight as they descended the stairs. Elizabeth began to perspire. What had she trapped herself into? If she went outside, anyone who saw her would rush to her father with the tale. She wasn't certain what he'd do, but it certainly wouldn't be pleasant. But if she didn't go, it would be the same as backing down to Samantha. What could she do? What should she do?

Her face showing not a trace of the turmoil inside, she turned to descend the final flight. Her hand trembled on the bannister. At the first step she stopped. There was a man seated in the entry hall. He was handsome, in a rugged sort of way, like a gypsy, only fairer. No, he looked fiercer than that, more like a buccaneer. But he was dressed like a laborer, for all his looks, in rough shirt and breeches, with scuffed boots that some gentleman must have given him. He wasn't at all the sort of person she was used to seeing in her father's house.

Michael never knew what it was that made him look up, but ever after he knew it was the most fateful moment of his life. From that instant nothing was as it was before, nor ever could be again.

He saw her. From the head of the stairs, a child-angel's face peered down at him over the openly displayed breasts of a wanton. The pure innocence of that face, combined with the sensual carnality of the body, clutched at his gut like a fist and brought an almost painful tightness to his groin. Yet it went beyond that. Already there was a hint about her of the allure to come. Bewitchment was in her eyes, eyes a man could get lost in. They reached out and laid hold of him and put a spell on him. In that moment he knew he'd never be entirely free of her again.

The door to the study slid open, and Christopher emerged, preceded by an older man, graying and slightly stooped. He'd an air of worry about him, but there was strength in his blue eyes, despite the lines at their corners, and a forcefulness to his walk. He started for Michael, looking as he did to see what the young man was staring at.

"Elizabeth!" he roared. "Cover yourself!"

Elizabeth jumped back, wide-eyed. A blush, starting at her breasts, raced up her white throat and flooded her face. She began tugging the dress higher, desperately hoping he hadn't noticed just how low it'd been. "It's the latest fashion in Paris, at the court, Papa. I want to wear it to the Fourriers' ball next week. Please say that I may. It'll be all the rage. Please?"

"We don't live in France, child," he snapped. "If you wear that in public you'll be the subject of sermons at Saint Michael's and Saint Philip's, both, for the next month. Even the Presbyterians would preach about it. Now go back to your room and put on something more suitable. Samantha, go with her and help her choose something proper."

Elizabeth dropped a deep curtsey, casting a baleful glare at Samantha as if she were to blame for it all. "Very well, Father."

The old man watched her stalk upstairs and shook his head. He spoke softly, as if he'd forgotten anyone else was there. "Perhaps I'm trying to keep her a child too long, but she wants to grow up so fast."

She'd already made it, Michael thought, no matter her age. Before her father could say anything more that might lie between them as a future embarrassment he rose, scuffling his feet to draw attention. Carver wheeled on him, and he shifted uneasily. He hoped Carver hadn't seen him staring at Elizabeth.

"Christopher's right," Carver said suddenly. "You don't look like a clerk. You're more like a pirate. Are you one?"

"I am, sir," Michael said firmly. "A clerk, that is."

"Irish." It was a flat statement, expressionless. "Papist?"

He'd been a child the last time he'd been to either confession or mass, or more than seen the inside of a church, but something made him stubbornly refuse to deny it now. "I was born in the Mother Church."

"You'll get along better if you convert to Anglican." He said it as if it was of no real importance. "Christopher here did, and more than one of your countrymen." Michael mur-

mured something noncommital. "All right, Christopher.
You can go now. I'll send for you if he needs to go back."

"Yes, sir." Byrne let himself out, with a friendly glance at
Michael.

Carver turned abruptly back toward his study. "Come
with me."

Michael followed. Go back? Could Carver mean to send
him back to England? Never. He'd run first, find another
place for his new beginning.

The study covered the width of the house, with windows
stretching nearly from floor to ceiling. Opposite the veranda,
a fireplace took up almost the entire side of the room. A large
globe stood in one corner, and a Turkey carpet covered the
floor. Carver sat down behind his desk and scribbled furiously on a piece of paper. He motioned vaguely toward a
chair facing the desk.

"Your name is Fallon?"

Michael rested tensely on the chair's edge. "Yes, sir.
Michael Shane Fallon."

"Um? Oh, yes." He held out the paper and quill. "Here.
Copy the sentences at the top in the space below them. Do the
sums, then write your name at the bottom." It was plain on
his face he expected little, if anything.

Michael put down his bag and took the paper. He read it
quickly, then looked sharp at the merchant. There were three
sentences, simple things a schoolmaster might set down for
children to practice their penmanship. Below that were two
columns of figures to be added, with two numbers to be
subtracted from each in turn. Sums for babes to do. Carver
stared back at him blandly, still proffering the pen. There had
to be a trick.

Taking the quill he leaned over the edge of the desk for a
place to write. He took great care, making sure it was in his
best hand. The columns of figures were quickly done, but he
went over them twice, still certain there was a hidden hook.
He could find nothing.

Be damned to it, then, he thought, and signed his name in
bold strokes across the bottom. He looked for the sand, and

Carver, whose interest had perked when Michael began to write, handed him the shaker. He dusted the paper lightly, waited for the sand to absorb the excess ink, then poured it into the box set by the inkwell for that purpose.

"There, sir."

Carver read slowly, making a sound in his throat from time to time. Michael couldn't tell if he was pleased or displeased, and he wasn't sure he cared. This was no time to be playing games.

Finally the old merchant gave a vigorous nod. "This is well enough, though it's no real test, of course." He paused, stroking his chin. "In the last year I've bought the indentures of one master baker who couldn't bake, one master cobbler who couldn't sew leather, and one master carpenter who didn't know a hammer from a saw. It didn't seem too far fetched that I might be sent a clerk who couldn't write or do sums, especially when he looks as if he'd never spent a day behind a desk in his life." He paused; Michael kept silent. "Well. I suppose the thing to do now is see how you do with a full set of books. What is that thing?" he added when Michael picked up his bag.

"My belongings, sir." A quick grin flashed on his face. "You might say it's all my worldly goods, at the moment."

A look of compassion appeared in the old man's eyes. It was a pitifully small bundle, even for a bound man. "Come along, then."

Seth appeared in the hall the instant they did, with a hat and walking stick for Mr. Carver. Michael took the chance for a surreptitious glance at the top of the stairs. But the landing was empty.

Outside, the carriage waited, Samuel as still as a statue. As they reached the front steps another equipage pulled up, and a young man in satin and velvet climbed down.

He was Michael's age, but taller by a good three inches, and swarthy with the dark eyes that'd passed Michael by. There was a spring to his walk, not quite a strut, but more the assurance that the world would get out of his way.

"Good day, sir." There was a touch of arrogance in his

voice, even speaking to Mr. Carver. "Is Miss Carver receiving?" He struck a pose, a fist on his hip pushing back his coat to better display his waistcoat.

Michael suppressed a smile. A popinjay, he thought. Then he saw the eyes. They were obsidian, and not only in color, but in coldness, as well. No, a vulture.

"I'm certain she is, Justin," Carver said. "Seth will give you some refreshment until she comes down. Justin, this is my new clerk, Michael Fallon. Michael, Justin Fourrier."

Justin eyed Michael's clothes with cool contempt, extending a reluctant hand. "Fallon? I don't recall any family of that name."

"There may be none," Michael said grimly. "Yet. I'm just arrived from Ireland. Mr. Carver has my indentures."

Fourrier jerked back his hand as if he'd picked up offal. "Indentured? And a clerk? Well, it's none of my affair, of course, Mr. Carver." He turned slightly. Michael had suddenly become invisible. "If you'll pardon me, sir, I'll go in to Miss Carver." He sketched a bow toward the older man, then rushed up the stairs, nearly running Michael down.

Michael glared at the door, shaking with wanting to go after the man. Just five minutes to teach him a man didn't become transparent.

"He's not such a stickler as he seems," Carver said. Better, he knew, to smooth ruffled feathers at the moment than to tell the truth. He climbed into the carriage, then added, "He wants to marry Elizabeth." His tone was curiously flat.

Those words hit Michael hard, and the fact that they did stunned him even more. Had he really thought of her in terms of marriage? An indentured man and a merchant's daughter? It was madness. It'd be years before he could offer for her like. As well to have the thought killed before it grew. Then why wouldn't it die?

He sat across from the old man, his back to the driver. "He seemed surprised at my being your clerk, sir."

"Shipping houses don't have bound men as clerks, Michael. Those positions are reserved for the sons of the house's best customers, so they can learn enough to set up for themselves and do without the house that gave them their start. It's an exchange, the trade you lose later for the trade you gain now.''

''Then, if I might ask, sir, why is it you're taking me into this position instead of one of your customers' sons? Young Fourrier, for instance?''

''Justin's not interested in entering trade to get money, though—.'' He bit off the end of his remark. ''As to why, the last clerk I had was the son of a good customer, a man of good birth and upbringing. But he not only spent more time drinking and wenching than in my warehouse, he gambled incessantly.'' His lips pursed as if at a bad taste. ''He had to flee the colony, at last, and left the records he was keeping in complete disarray. That, I decided, was the last of the young gentlemen for me.''

''I'll do my best, sir,'' Michael said, and meant it as a promise.

''I'm sure you will, Michael.'' Carver looked at the sun and frowned, then consulted a fat pocket watch. ''Drive on, Samuel. The bridge.''

The carriage lurched off, and Michael watched the house recede. He was just studying it again, he told himself, as he'd done on arrival. He kept thinking that. The windows remained empty of a girl with raven curls.

4

Michael settled quickly into his new life. His room above the stables was spacious, and he didn't mind the faint smell of horses that permeated the air. It was little enough to a country man. The furniture, for the most part cast off from the main house, was sturdy. In fact, and the thought always brought a grin, it was finer than that he'd had in Ireland.

A large bed, set opposite the door, had a feather mattress and goosedown pillows. On one side a large clothespress held the plain suits Mr. Carver insisted on buying, saying he couldn't have a clerk who looked like a dock idler. On the other a lowboy, with a mirror over it, contained the rest of his possessions. By the windows was a table, where he ate meals fetched from the kitchens. It wouldn't have been a bad life, except for one thing, and he'd begun leaving early to avoid that.

He hurriedly tugged his stock straight and shrugged into his coat. For two months he'd maintained his early schedule, only to sleep late now. Clapping on his hat, he ran down the steps and started for the street. Almost immediately he skidded to a halt. Damn. He was too late. Elizabeth was already in the garden, taking her morning stroll.

She floated down the paths calmly, fingers occasionally touching a white blossom on a low dogwood branch. His eyes followed her with an ancient hunger. Her skin would be softer beneath his fingers than those four-petaled flowers. He bowed to hide his stark look, but she swept past unheeding of his presence. When she was safely gone he straightened and took a deep breath. It was to flee that throat-parching desire at the sight of her that he'd taken to leaving early. He would not, he vowed, be late again.

He was on the carriage path when Mr. Carver called to him from the veranda.

"So there you are, Michael. I was beginning to think you'd taken to sleeping at the bridge."

No, Michael thought, but I burn for your daughter, and if I am much in her presence the desire will be writ plain on my face. "I want to straighten up those books, sir. Young Wynfrey left it all in a bigger mare's nest than I believe even you suspected."

"I must say you're a pleasant surprise, Michael. And I'm aware you've been working longer hours than I ask. Take this afternoon off. You've earned it. You may use my library, if you wish to read. I've just finished Salmon's *Abridgement and Review of the State Trials*. You might find that interesting."

"I thank you, sir, and I would like to read. Only—," he hesitated, "—I did happen to notice you had Thomas Phipp's treatise on growing rice and the Frenchman Mieraux's journal of trade with the West Indies. If I could borrow those instead?"

Carver's eyes widened in surprise, and he nodded slowly. "Yes, of course, if that's what you want."

"It is. Was there something else you were wanting me for, sir?"

"Uh? No, nothing else."

"Then, if you'll excuse me, the day is high already, and I'm behind time. And thank you, sir." He sketched a leg and went on into the street.

Carver watched him go, tapping absently on the bannister. So there was ambition there, too. It would be interesting to see where it led.

Michael commonly took the roundabout way to the bridge, heading first away from the wharves toward King Street. There he turned up the peninsula till he came to the Printing House, just below Broad Street, where Peter Timothy published the weekly *South-Carolina Gazette*. Next to Dillon's Tavern, it was the best place in the city for finding out what was going on, not only from the handbills posted around but from the loungers outside. But today he couldn't seem to see the advertisements of rice and indigo, ships and slaves. He left quickly and headed down Broad for the Bay, not pausing at Saint Michael's or the State House for a gossip. He couldn't have taken anything in even if he'd heard it. Softer than dogwood petals she'd be.

Jepson, the Scots wharfman in charge of loading and unloading ships at the bridge, was waiting for him just inside the warehouse door. "Do you know what Mr. Carver intends about the purchase from Mr. Soule, si—? Mr—? Do you know what Mr. Carver intends?"

The wharfman still had difficulty deciding exactly where Michael fit in the scheme of things, a bound man giving orders to free men. When he was irritated his burr became more pronounced; if he talked to Michael long, he became nearly unintelligible.

"Keep it," Michael said.

"But there's no more than three hundredweight of good rice to a tierce," the wharfman said thickly. "All the rest is midlings and small rice."

"Bring in men with sieves," Michael explained patiently. "Have them separate it and barrel it according to kind."

"Aye. But I dinna like it. Paying top price for a mess of midlings and stock feed, while he goes on his way."

"He won't go for long. Bring the wharfmen here from the other wharves, a few at a time. Let them see what you're doing, and let them know why."

Jepson grinned slowly. "Aye. Aye. The story'll be all over town in a day. Soule'll have to open every barrel he sells, to prove it's rice."

Michael left him chortling to himself and climbed the narrow stairs to his box-like office. Light from the outside window spread over his desk, from which he could see through the inside window that opened to the warehouse. From the shelf he took ledgers and boxes of loose papers and set to work, forgetting Jepson, trying to forget Elizabeth.

Slowly the pile of sales and transactions scribbled on

scraps of paper decreased. He'd just put one receipt aside when something made him pick it up again. Two hundred tierces of rice delivered by the coasting schooner *Santee Pride*, with a scribbled note in Wynfrey's crabbed hand that ten barrels had been ruined by wetting. That was unusual. Those barrels were tight enough to be used as water casks, and sometimes were. Something began hammering at the back of his mind.

He ruffled through the ledgers until he found it. Ten barrels of damaged rice sold, the same day, to Matthew Titus and Company for animal feed. The same barrels? If so, it was a very quick sale. Besides, unless he was badly mistaken, Titus and Company handled only first quality rice.

Maybe it was Soule's attempted deception that made his mind wander that way, but he wondered what the difference between ten barrels of first quality rice and ten barrels of stock feed would cover in the way of gambling losses. The conviction settled on him slowly, but it settled firmly. If anything was to be proven against Wynfrey, though, he'd need more than supposition and a single receipt.

The door swinging open to bang against the end of the desk brought him erect. Byrne stuck his head in with a grin.

"Are you burying yourself in the work, then, Michael? It's a fine, bright day outside. Very fine for March. Not a cloud in the sky. I tell you, man, it's a day to be drinking cold sangaree, or snuggling a hot wench."

Michael laughed and leaned back in his chair. "That's all very well for the likes of you, but there's some of us have a job of work to be done."

"Since when did you start living your life by the Book? Come down to Dillon's with me. I'll stand you a pint of beer or two. Besides, Mr. Carver told me himself he gave you the afternoon off, and it's close enough to noon for any but the English."

"All right, then. Let me put this away, and I'll go."

Dillon's was crowded at that hour, with every table full and men on benches out front. As they entered, the tapster pushed a staggering redcoat out the door. He followed them back in, dusting his hands. "Come in here soused as a fishwife dunked in a pickling barrel," he said. "When I said this was a respectable place as don't serve drunks, he called me a damned colonial nit and wanted to fight. I showed him colonial nit."

"That you did," Christopher said, "and right enough, too. Would Tim Grogan or Henry Anslow be around?"

The tapster nodded, with a sharp look for Michael. "They're in the back corner, where they always be."

"Then come along, Michael. We'll get us a pipe and see what they have to say."

Michael took a clay churchwarden from the public rack and broke off an inch of the stem to get a fresh mouthpiece. The tobacco was a thick twist, heavily flavored with rum, that had to be shaved and broken up in the hands. Christopher used tongs to hold a coal for their lighting.

Puffing, they strolled back through the tavern. From the murmurs of greeting, the number of tankards raised in his direction, Christopher was well known. He returned all salutations with a nod, but he didn't stop.

Between the depth of the tavern and the tobacco smoke, the back of the room would have been dark except for the wrought iron sconces on the walls and the lamps hanging from the ceiling. Even so, the ceiling was dim with haze.

The table where Christopher finally stopped was separated from the others, though still in the common room. Four men sat there, coatless, two playing put and two watching. The players continued their game, slapping the cards down with a grunt, stopping only to rake in the wager and deal again. The watchers looked up immediately.

"It's all right," Christopher said. "He's a friend." The two men slid warily aside to make room, and they sat down. "The two who're so interested in the cards are Henry Anslow and Tom Milner," he went on. One of the players waved a hand before slapping his next card down. "These others are Robert Gosnell and Martin Hill. Cousins, God bless them."

The card player who hadn't waved spoke without lifting his sharp nose from his cards. "Now that you've told him our names, Byrne, maybe you'll tell us his."

"Michael Fallon, Anslow. And I said he's a friend."
Christopher grabbed a passing barmaid by the skirt. "I'll
have a bowl of sangaree for this table, Sally." As she turned
away he flipped up her dress for a look at her ankles, and she
snatched it away angrily. "But they're so lovely," he called
after her.

"Sangaree," Anslow said sourly. "Honest beer not good
enough for you?"

"You don't have to drink any if you don't want it." He
smiled suddenly and leaned back complacently. "I won
thirty pounds Saturday last betting Mr. Milford's Dancer to
beat that Georgia bay."

Gosnell's goggle eyes grew even larger above his fat
cheeks. "Thirty pounds! That's betting deep."

"Deep? There were fine gentlemen there betting ten times
as much, and more. Besides, I never lose."

Hill had been engrossed in rueful study of the cards and the
heap of winnings in front of Anslow, but at that he snickered.
"When did that start? Just the other day I watched you play at
loo with some of those fine gentlemen and never win a
hand."

"A trick of the eyes, lad. I've the touch of gold in my
fingertips."

"Brass, more like it," Hill snorted.

"Jealousy. Pure jealousy. Ah, here she is." The barmaid
set the punchbowl on the table, eyeing Christopher's hands
warily, and he began ladling out the dark mixture of iced and
sweetened wines with bits of nutmeg floating on top. "Speak
now, if your principles keep you from drinking. There'll just
be more for the rest of us." No one spoke, and he passed a
mug to Michael.

"Dia's Muire Ihuit," Byrne toasted Michael. God and
Mary with you.

Surprised, Michael replied automatically. "Dia's Muire
Ihuit agus Padraig." God and Mary and Patrick.

The other men all drank deep, but as soon as the mugs hit
the table the four turned their eyes to Michael.

"Now," the sharp-faced Anslow said, "it's time for some
questions."

Hill idly flipped over cards from the deck. "Are you a loyal subject of your King, Fallon?"

Michael's ears pricked. He'd sensed something as soon as he sat down, but only now did he have a suspicion what, and he didn't like it. Conspiracy. "That's a strange question to be asking."

"These are strange times," Anslow snapped. "And you haven't answered the question."

Four pairs of hot eyes glared at him, and he glared back. He was damned if he'd answer, not knowing who was asking, or why.

Christopher broke the silence. "Ease up, lads. He's Irish."

Hill's mouth fell open in surprise. "What in hell's that got to do with anything?"

"You'd better not let Grogan hear you ask that. You know how he feels about it." Byrne sighed and leaned forward. "Look you, man, have you ever heard of an Irishman who was loyal to an English King?"

"I'd rather hear it from him." They all looked at Michael expectantly.

He chose his words carefully. "I'm as loyal as most Irish, you could say. As loyal as Christopher here. And I'll say no more on it till I know who I'm talking to."

Christopher slapped the table. "And a good answer it is, too."

Anslow frowned. "You can trust to his blood, Byrne, but the rest of us would rather know where he stands. Will you tell us that, Fallon?"

"Stand on what? God's teeth, I don't know what you're talking about."

"Taxation without representation." Anslow smacked his lips over the phrase. "How do you feel about that?"

Michael looked at them in bewilderment. Christopher stepped in quickly. "He's new in the colonies, lads. It means, Michael, being taxed by a government in which you've no say, no one to represent you."

"Then I'd say I was against it."

Anslow pounded the table with his fist, and the others murmured approval. "That's the ticket. And that's just what we have here. The folk in England elect their Parliament, and they're taxed by it. That's right enough, only they're not satisfied with that. They have to go and lay taxes on us. They don't tax your Ireland, but they tax us."

"Well, Ireland has its own Parliament, feeble as it may be," Michael said, "and its own taxes."

"And so do we. So do we." Anslow looked around for disagreement. "We've our Assemblies and the like, and they lay taxes, too. But the English Parliament still taxes us."

"Last year," Christopher said intently, "having nothing else to do, they passed the Currency Act and the American Revenue Act. Anti-American Revenue Act, they ought to call it."

"Now wait a minute," Michael said. "I know something of that. It barely touches us here. It's the New Englanders who trade in molasses and rum. They're the ones it hurts."

"Hurt one, hurt all," Gosnell said, but Hill barked, "Damn blue-nosed New Englanders. They're worse than the bloody lobsters." He subsided under his companions' glares, and Christopher went on.

"It's the principle of the thing, Michael, lad. We're taxed by a Parliament we'd no hand in selecting, where no man speaks for us. If there are taxes to be raised, let it be done by our own Assembly right here in Charlestown. And Robert has the right of it. If it hurts one colony, then it hurts us all."

"What's this other thing you mentioned? The Currency Act?"

"There's no big to-do about that one, now. It seems Virginia was issuing more paper money than the colony could back, so now no colony can issue a single note more than's already in circulation. Actually, we violate it every time we use a bill of credit as currency."

Michael frowned. "That's more serious than a tax on molasses."

"Taxation without representation," Anslow muttered into his mug.

Christopher leaned back, thoughtfully studying Michael.
"Now why would you say that?"

"Well, it's obvious, isn't it? As the old paper money
wears out, there's less to go around, less to pay men for their
hire, less to buy things. And of course the men who can't be
hired can't buy anything at all. It all builds up like a snow-
ball, you see. I suppose, too, if you look at it like that, the
taxes hurt us, too." Anslow and the others stared at him,
open-mouthed.

"Go on," Christopher said quietly.

Michael began to warm to the subject. "The less of the
paper money you have, the more important it becomes to
have some money that doesn't wear out, gold or silver. But
the taxes, the customs, have to be paid in specie, and it all
goes to England, so it means we've got less and less of that,
too. God's teeth, you know how hard it is to get coin, even
now. We could end up having to barter like savages. The
English merchants would have us in their coat pockets.
There's your real problem, not this representation thing."

"Michael, you're a wonder."

"And why's that?"

Rather than answering Christopher tossed his pipe on the
table and rose. "Gentlemen, Mr. Fallon and I must leave
you, now." He pulled Michael up by the arm.

The others barely noticed their going for the argument that
had broken out. Words like currency and specie flew back
and forth across the table.

"Christopher, why the hurry?"

Byrne kept a slow pace toward the street, and a hand on
Michael's sleeve. He spoke low, beneath the buzz from the
tables. "Those lads are eager enough, but they've only three
brains between the four of them. Some things it's best not to
talk about in front of them."

Michael sighed. He knew he'd let himself get carried
away, but he couldn't stop yet. Christopher had brought him
there deliberately, and he had to know why. "Things such
as?"

"There are men in the various colonies, lad, who like to

keep up with the news elsewhere. So, they write to one another. I saw a letter from one of them in Boston, John Adams, saying exactly what you said back there, only he was so confounded oratorical about it you had to think three times over every word to puzzle out his meaning.''

"And what does that have to do with me?" He stopped short of asking where Christopher had seen the letter.

"You can't use a letter like that, or a man like him that wrote it, to explain the ins and outs of things to men like Anslow and Gosnell. You have to have something to grab hold of them, fire them up. That's why we use slogans and catch phrases like taxation without representation.''

"We?" Michael followed Christopher through the door to the street.

"I saw a young lawyer last year in Virginia, by the name of Patrick Henry. Now he could get you fired up and breathing smoke over the weather on a fine spring day. But we don't have anybody like him, and lacking that we need someone who can explain what this is all about in language plain enough for those types to understand.''

Michael felt a sinking sensation. "You don't mean me? What about you? They know you. They'd listen.''

"But I get carried away when I talk about it. The first thing you know I'd be challenging somebody in the crowd to fisticuffs, and devil take the speechifying.

I just get caught up in the thing. What do you say? How'd you like to stand up and tell people the same things you said back there? No haranguing. Just a plain talk.''

Michael shook his head. How could he explain that he didn't dare get up in front of a crowd? Being recognized, especially by soldiers, meant being sent back to England to hang. "I'm no talker, man. I'm not a politician.''

"Listen, Michael. I brought you here today because you seemed a handy man for a rough and tumble. But I listened to you, and I watched you think on the move. You could do it.''

"I can't. I can't explain why, but I just can't.''

Christopher sighed. "Think on it, man. It's important.''

"I'll think, but I won't change my mind.''

Christopher gestured as if to say what happened, happened. Michael turned away from him, toward Church Street. But after all, what could it harm? And there he was arguing Christopher's side. It could do a great harm. Men under arrest made no fortunes.

Suddenly he realized a squad of redcoats was bearing down on him. He leaped back out of the way, and his back hit something soft. A squeal and thud spun him around. A girl sprawled at his feet, glaring at him, her basket overturned to spill out a dozen small packages. The dust from the passing soldiers settled on his coat as he went to one knee and began gathering her bundles.

"It's sorrier than I can say that I am, miss. There's no excuse for failing to see a girl as pretty as yourself." He set the basket upright and took his first good look at her. She really was pretty, with full lips and merry brown eyes.

Her anger had already gone. She stared at him with her mouth open, running one hand up and down the neck of her well-filled, low-cut blouse. At last she seemed to find her tongue. "It's all very well, picking up my marketing, but what about me?"

Michael got to his feet and held down a hand to her. She took it in both of hers and pulled herself up. "Maybe I'd better be carrying this basket home for you, lass. No doubt you shouldn't be lifting any weight for a time after such a nasty spill."

She dusted her skirts, head down, but her eye took him in from head to toe. "I don't know that I should be accepting favors from strange gentlemen. It could be dangerous."

He took hold of her chin and lifted her face. There was a tigerish light in his eyes. "A pretty little sweetmeat like you," he said softly, "I'm liable to gobble her all up."

She caught the tip of her tongue between her teeth and wrinkled her nose at him. "It's a long walk, sir. All the way up the Bay above Vanderhorst Creek."

"All the more reason you shouldn't carry this load." He held out his arm gallantly. "Shall we go, then?"

Smiling, she dusted off her hands on the back of her skirt

and took his arm. For the space of a block she walked well away from him, her fingertips resting on the inside of his arm, maintaining a dignified, frosty silence. He watched, amused, as she slowly drifted closer. When they reached the Bay she was clutching his arm tightly, her breast pressed softly against it. Every time he looked down at her his eye was caught by the shimmering valley between those lightly tanned mounds.

"What work do you do?" she asked as her silence failed as well. "I see you on a ship, somehow. You look—. Oh, I don't know." She shivered, and the front of her blouse quaked interestingly. "You look like one of those freebooters who carry girls off."

"Gladly would I carry you off, had I a ship. But I'm only a clerk, as yet, working for Mr. Thomas Carver."

"A clerk! That's almost a gentleman." She felt his arm tighten and looked up. "Did I say something?"

"No," he said shortly. He lightened his tone. "You didn't say anything wrong. It's just there are those think it doesn't make a man any better, being a so-called gentleman."

She hugged his arm again and giggled. "You sound like my master. He's always talking about the mechanics, silversmiths and carpenters and the like, and how they're as good men as the ones who run the colony. He says most of them have better sense."

"Sounds like a dangerous man," Michael chuckled. "I'll wager the Assembly is fond of him, if they know of it. Who is he?"

"Mr. Christopher Gadsden is who he is, and he's not dangerous, neither."

The name gave him pause. Of course the Assembly knew of it. Gadsden was in the Assembly, as well as being a reputable merchant and planter. "I just meant it's a new idea, different from what most people think. New ideas are always dangerous. I never thought of an Assemblyman to talk like that."

"Well, he does. He says the common people have to have a say in their, their destiny." She nodded for emphasis. "He says they must have a part in making the laws they live by and the taxes they pay. He says taxation without representation is no better than stealing.''

Michael stopped in the street. "What was that?"

"What was what?"

"Those words. Taxation without representation. Did he use those words?"

"Why, yes, he did. But what of it?"

"Nothing, lass. Nothing." Gentlemen who wrote other gentlemen to let them know what was happening. A gentleman who uncharacteristically championed the mechanics. Four men in a tavern, not even mechanics, no craftsmen they, but spouting a phrase as if it was memorized, and that the same phrase used by the gentleman. It was too much for coincidence. "Has Christopher Byrne ever come to visit Mr. Gadsden?"

"Cook would have my hide if I went prating who was visiting the master."

"It's no never mind. Come. I'll carry your basket on home for you."

She shook her head, suddenly diffident. "There's no need. It's only over there." She pointed to a house much like Carver's, a single-house it was called.

He brushed some hair back from her cheek. "The dust those soldiers kicked up is all over my coat. Do you think you could brush it off, back in your room?"

She frowned down at the street. "I don't even know your name."

"Nor I yours, lass."

"It's Mary. Mary Billings."

"Michael Shane Fallon."

"Oh, that's a fine name." She bit her lip and glanced away, watching him from the corner of her eye.

He ran a finger lightly across the top of her breasts. "Will you let me in, Mary?"

She shivered at the extra meaning in his words. Wordlessly she took his hand, holding it in the small of her back with both of hers, his knuckles just brushing the swell of her buttocks, and led him down the carriage path beside the house to the outbuildings behind. Not till she closed the door to her small room did she let go, and then he pulled her to him, his mouth fastening on hers.

He quickly tugged her blouse loose at the waist and ran his hands up the bare skin of her back. His arms tightened, crushing her against his chest.

She pulled her lips free breathlessly. "Clothes," she whispered.

In one motion he pulled the blouse up over her head and off. She backed away, one arm covering her bare, firm breasts, then, smiling, let it drop. She spun, skirt flaring slightly, hands busy at her waist. At the second spin the skirt swirled to the floor. In shoes and stockings she flaunted herself at him.

In seconds his clothes joined hers on the floor. He reached for her, but she sank to her haunches out of his grasp. Her hands trailed down after her, across his chest and flanks.

"So hard," she murmured. "So strong." She planted a light kiss on each of his thighs, then her mouth fastened on him.

He hissed and jerked at the shock and the sudden warmth of it. His hands tangled in her hair. For only a minute he stood it, then pulled her roughly to her feet. "Much more of that," he said hoarsely, "and there'll be no need of going on."

"We can't have that," she breathed. She leaned against him, whispering into his chest. "The bed. Please. Hurry."

He cupped her buttocks and lifted her, carrying her still clutching his shoulders, her head buried beneath his chin. Gently he laid her on the coverlet. She fumbled between them, lifting her heels to rest on his buttocks, and he thrust into her.

"Darling Michael. So good."

He smiled and kissed her down the line of her chin. She began to sigh, to make low cries deep in her throat as he moved within her. Her eyes fluttered shut, and he kissed the lids. Lovely brown eyes. Violet eyes. No, brown eyes.

Fiercely he ground his mouth down on hers. This was

Mary he held in his arms, not Elizabeth. Mary who was grinding her body against his. Mary who dug her fingernails into the muscles of his back. She stiffened against him, screaming into his throat, and he covered her mouth with his as he came, as much to cut off his own cry as hers. Elizabeth!

She stretched, cat-like, as he brusquely put on his breeches and sat back on the edge of the bed to do his stockings. "So good," she said dreamily. His silence reached her, and she touched his arm. "There's nothing the matter, is there, Michael?"

He reached back to pat her hip. "No, sweetling, there's nothing wrong. You're as much pleasure to bed as a man could bear."

She giggled, content, and rolled back on the bed. "You pleasured me, too. But it's just as well you're going." She twisted around and began rummaging under the corner of the bed for her shoes. "There's work waiting for me in the kitchens."

He straightened his stock in a scrap of mirror on the wall, and pulled on his coat. "If you stay like that, it's me who'll keep you from it."

She dimpled and sat up cross-legged on the bed. "Michael? I will see you again, won't I? I don't mean to entangle you, but you are as sweet as honey."

He looked at her sitting there and had to take a deep breath. "I'll be back. Most certainly. But if I don't leave now, I may not leave at all." Blowing her a kiss, he ducked out the door.

There was a bounce to his step as he walked down the path. Elizabeth had managed to creep into his mind even in the arms of another woman, it was true, but he could think of her now, if only for a time, without the gut-wrenching lust that had consumed him since he'd first seen her. It might not be fair to Mary, but he would see her again, and forget Elizabeth in her caress.

5

For two months Michael kept to his way, passing civil words and little else with the mechanics who drank in the common room of Dillon's, passing warm and often exhausting hours in Mary's bed. Byrne eased his pressure for Michael to join the movement, whatever it might be, and though Elizabeth's presence still lit fires in him, she no longer haunted his dreams at night. Or, at least, seldom. Life in Charlestown was becoming familiar; he was beginning to relax into it.

The scent of early May roses was in the air when he slid from Mary's bed and began to dress in the somber black he had worn as suitable for Sunday. He hadn't stayed the entire night before this. Briefly he wondered if he had time to return to Church Street for fresh linen before going to the bridge, but decided against it. The sun was already well up, and most honest folk were at work long ago.

Mary sat up with the covers around her breasts and watched him dress with a slight smile of approval for the muscular body disappearing beneath black wool and white lawn. Not until he finished buttoning his waistcoat did she speak.

"Michael?"

"You're too late, little cabbage," he said absently, tugging on his coat. "I'm dressed already. Besides, I have work to do, and so do you. It's Monday morning, and the day is already high."

"Michael, who is she?"

His fingers, tying the ribbon to hold his hair pulled back, slowed almost to a stop. "She? She who?" His eyes met hers in the piece of mirror, and she looked away with a careless toss of her head.

45

"It doesn't matter. I make no claims on you." She smiled. "Just a lovely tumble and tickle. That's what we have, and that's what I want. But I can't help wondering."

"About what?"

She tipped her head to one side. "Well, sometimes when we're together it's different. Sometimes you come in like you're full of lightning bolts." She laughed suddenly. "It's what every woman wishes for, then wonders if she'll survive it when it comes. Only, it's not me you're making love to, those times."

He picked up his cocked hat and twisted it slowly round in his hands, then set it down again and sighed. Had he been so transparent, then? "Do you want to end it?"

"Oh, no." She bounced out of bed and ran to press against him. "I don't want to know about her. Honestly I don't. Do you think I'd risk another hiding if I didn't want you?" A hand flew to her mouth as she realized what she'd said.

"Another hiding? What are you talking about, Mary?" He took her by the shoulders and pushed her back where he could look at her, but she kept her head down. "Has someone been after you because of me? Answer me. The truth, now."

She nodded slowly without looking up. "Cook. She saw you leaving one afternoon two weeks ago. Thank God she just thought you'd been visiting. There's no telling what she'd have done if she'd known what we were really doing." She stifled a short giggle. "She'd never think of people doing that in the daylight, though."

"And she beat you for that? Damn it, you're not a slave. You have rights. Stand up for them."

She looked up at him then, a wry look on her face. "You and your fine talk of rights. If I tried standing up for my rights, cook would see to it I stood up all year long for not being able to sit down. Besides, beast that you are, you'd likely have enjoyed seeing it. Me, bent over the back of her tall chair with my skirts around my ears, yelping and kicking my heels in the air like a three years' child, while she wore out my bum with a willow switch."

He laughed and pulled her against him. "The part about

your skirts around your ears I like, but if I want to make you yelp and kick your heels I think I'll use something other than a switch.'' She laughed in her throat, but the smile faded from his face as a serious thought came to him. ''Poplet, I've no wish to be earning more trouble for you.''

''There's no need to worry. After the way I blubbered she's convinced I learned my lesson.''

She snuggled against him contentedly, rubbing her thigh against his. Her fingers began to creep up into his hair. ''You're worth ten times the risk.''

Michael pushed her gently away. ''You're likely late in the kitchens already, and she may be coming to look for you any minute. It's after eight o'clock.''

''Lord!'' She leaped back, eyes wide. ''Bloody blue hell!'' Whirling, she dove for her clothes, and began scrambling into them, trying to put on all of her petticoats at once. Her voice came muffled through layers of cotton. ''Please don't let anyone see you leaving. Please?'' Her head popped out for a quick, pleading look. ''Just because I'll risk a whipping doesn't mean I want one.''

''I'll be careful,'' he said, but she was engrossed in pulling her stockings on, a task that should have been done before the petticoats, and muttering distractedly to herself. Smiling, he let himself out, and left her to her hurry.

Outside the light was beginning to fade despite the morning hour. The sky was ominous, dark purple clouds rolling in from the west across the Ashley River. Grumbling thunder sounded in the distance, but in the garden all was still. In the foreshadowing silence not a leaf stirred, and the smoke from the kitchen chimney rose in a thin reed wisping into nothingness.

The broken oyster shells that paved the drive cracked and snapped beneath Michael's feet, loudly it seemed to him, but no one came. He walked faster. There was no one to see after all.

He reached the gate and skidded to a halt. A closed carriage stood in front of the house, with slaves swarming around it. The coachman was fastening his buttons with one hand and wiping stray dust off the rig with the other. Three small black stableboys tugged and pulled at the straps and buckles of the harness. The groom, his sweaty face glistening like polished coal, danced around them, alternating screaming that they were doing it all wrong and pushing them aside to do it himself.

Michael frowned and moved back behind an oak. He'd promised to take care. If it took skulking in the bushes like a footpad, he'd do it. But what, he wondered, were they doing in the street? All of this bustle spoke of singular haste. But where would Mr. Gadsden be going in such hurry of a lowering Monday morning?

The door to the house opened, and two men came out. Peter Timothy, publisher of the *South-Carolina Gazette*, hurried along beside Christopher Gadsden, who seemed to overshadow the smaller, darker man, not so much by size as by the force and power of his presence. Gadsden was barely above medium height, with a prominent chin and a high forehead. His eyes gave the first sign of his magnetism. They were mesmeric.

"This is ridiculous," Gadsden stormed. "For what does the Assembly have an agent in London? What is Garth doing there, gambling in the hells or looking out for the interests of the colony? He was sent the strictest instructions. He was to join the other colonial agents in opposing this, this monstrosity even being proposed. Yet the next we hear, it's not only proposed, it's passed. And we don't even hear it from him." He wheeled on Timothy. "You are certain of all this? The information is correct?"

"It's correct, sir," Timothy said wearily. "What shall we do?"

Gadsden's face darkened. "Even you must agree the last chance of peaceful persuasion is gone."

Timothy was silent.

"If we can't change it, we'll make use of it. We'll build a bonfire with that paper to burn the throne itself."

Timothy looked around wildly. "For God's sake, sir. This is a public street."

Taking the smaller man by the sleeve, Gadsden drew him toward the carriage. "All right. We'll talk in the safety of my carriage. But the whole world will know soon enough."

The groom and stableboys scrambled out of the way, barely finished with their tasks. The coachman climbed to his perch, fumbling with the last button on his waistcoat. Heads together in close conversation Gadsden and Timothy climbed into the carriage, and a rap on the roof from inside sent it lurching off down the street.

Michael waited until the stable workers had gone back up the drive before he came out, and then he did so slowly, thoughtfully. Burning the throne? Something had passed in London. An act of Parliament? Well, whatever it was, he knew where to find out. He'd have a stop at Dillon's before going on to the bridge.

The darkened sky finally split open, letting loose a downpour left over from April, driving the fishmongers and peddlers to shelter in doorways and under eaves, hurrying mechanics on their way. A private of the 60th Foot lay against the side of a building, snoring, oblivious to the rain pouring in his face, or the whore hurriedly rifling his pockets for a stray coin that might have escaped the tapster's hand. She looked up as Michael passed, but didn't slow her fingers' probing.

A train of high-wheeled wagons, each drawn by a six-horse hitch, creaked past him, splashing mud at every puddle. The harness bells clanked dolorously in the wet. The upcountry drivers sat hunched on the seats, hats pulled low, and even the dogs that usually ran ahead of the train trudged drearily.

By the time he reached Broad Street Michael was sodden, and mud had oozed up over his shoes. But the light and warmth of the tavern beckoned him the length of the street, and he picked up his pace.

Outside the tavern two slaves huddled miserably by a sedan chair. Michael eyed them curiously as he turned in. The few men who used a chair generally treated their bearers well. They certainly weren't left out in the rain.

Looking at the bearers, he didn't see the cloaked shape that cannoned out of the tavern and crashed into him. Startled, he fought for balance, muddy shoes slipping on rain-slick cobblestones, and crashed to the pavement.

Justin Fourrier regarded him indifferently from beneath a dripping tricorn. "Watch for your betters, man," he snapped, and climbed into the sedan chair. The bearers were on their feet before he was inside, and no sooner was the door shut than they started up the street at an easy gait.

With a strangled roar Michael surged to his feet. Before he could take a step Christopher darted into the rain and threw his arms around him in a bearhug. He struggled as the other man pulled him into the tavern. Benches scraped as men turned to see what was going on.

"Easy Michael, easy with you." Christopher stopped just inside the door, but he didn't release his grip.

"That's the second time he's done that. He acted as if I was no more than a clump of dirt. Let me go. I won't stand for it."

"You have to stand for it, man. At least, for now. What would you do if you caught him? You're a bound man. If you so much as strike him he can have you up before a magistrate and flogged. It's a fool's game you're thinking of. You can't win."

Michael went rigidly still. With an effort he forced himself to relax. "All right, then. I can't win today. Drink with me to tomorrow."

Christopher spread his hands with a rueful smile. "I would that, were I not flat. The cards desert me for the moment."

"And you talk to me of fools' games. Well, never mind. I'll buy, if you can stand to drink beer for a change. Tapster, two pints of beer, if you please."

"I'll drink anything that's free, except water."

Michael took the tankards, turning serious as he handed the redhead his. "Christopher, you're a man as hears things. What's occurred of late?"

"Such as?"

"Such as an act of Parliament that Charles Garth was

supposed to try to stop. Only, he failed, and it's been proposed and passed without so much as a word from him about it. I gather it's something to do with paper. And trouble likely over it.''

Christopher stared at him with his mug half tilted. ''For a man wanting information, you know an awful lot.''

''You know about it, then?''

Christopher hesitated before nodding. ''Hell, the whole city will know before the day's down. Come to the back.''

Anslow was at the table alone, reading a letter that he folded and pocketed when Michael sat down. ''What's he doing here?'' he asked Christopher. ''He's not one of us.''

''Us?'' Michael said.

''Just a few lads who think the right way,'' Christopher replied easily. ''We've banded together to make our opinions known.'' He turned to Anslow. ''There's nobody born a member of the Liberty Boys. They have to be recruited. Now bring out the letter and let Michael here know of this Stamp Act our gracious sovereign has given us.''

''It's the Parliament, not the King, that's—,'' Anslow began.

Christopher waved his protests aside. ''The letter, man. The letter.''

Reluctantly Anslow laid the pages on the table and smoothed them out. ''It's called the Stamp Act.'' He spoke as if he begrudged every word. ''Come the first of November, 1765, no legal papers can be served or given, no warrants or summons, no clearance papers for ships, unless it has a stamp on it. Have to have the stamp for newspapers and broadsides and pamphlets, even for packages of playing cards and dice. It's a wonder they're not requiring it for musket wadding.''

''There's been stamped paper required in England for years,'' Michael said.

''This ain't England,'' Anslow snapped.

''There are some differences, Michael,'' Christopher said smoothly. ''Tell him what Benjamin Franklin said, Anslow.''

Michael looked at him in surprise. "Benjamin Franklin? Him that's the deputy postmaster for the colonies? What's he got to do with this?"

"He's also the London agent for the Pennsylvania colony."

"And he used to be a partner in Mr. Timothy's paper," Anslow added. "He spoke up to Mr. Grenville, the Prime Minister, he did, when all the colonial agents were called in to give their views. They say he told him straight: the money should be raised by the colonial assemblies. That would make it an affair of the people who must pay it, it being what he calls an internal tax, one that you've got no choice but to pay. The Parliament, he said, could levy external taxes, the kind you can avoid paying by not buying the taxed item, tariffs and such, but not internal taxes, as the colonies aren't represented in Parliament." He nodded sharply to emphasize the words.

Michael took a long pull at his tankard before speaking. Taxation without representation again. On the other hand, this man Franklin had reason with him. "It sounds as if the money's to be raised for some special purpose."

"Yes. Oh, yes." Anslow ruffled the pages, but barely looked at the one that came to the top. He sounded as if he had it memorized. "The money raised by the Stamp Act is to be used to reimburse the crown partially for the expense of keeping members of His Majesty's armed forces in His Majesty's North American colonies for the preservation of the lives and property of His Majesty's subjects there and the protection of England's trade with those colonies." He twisted his face and spat on the floor. "Protection. Preservation. There's been no trouble with the Indians in four years, none with the Spanish in three, and none likely since Florida was ceded to the crown. Just what is it we need these soldiers for? I'll tell you. To drink and start fights and harass decent women in the streets. And the officers are as bad or worse."

"But what can you do about it? It's passed. It's done with."

He was greeted by silence, embarrassed on Christopher's

part, suspicious on Anslow's. Something was afoot. His
curiosity was pricked, but he was damned if he'd show it.

The drumming on the roof tiles had faded away, and a
quick glance down the length of the common room showed
the sun coming out in the street. He tossed back the last of his
beer. "I'll be leaving now. I must shift these wet clothes and
get on to the bridge."

Christopher reached out as if to stop him. "Michael, I—."

"I do have to go, Christopher. We'll talk later."

As he walked out into the sunny street a thought struck
him. How many of those men in there, drinking so quietly,
were Liberty Boys? And what were they planning?

He turned up the drive of the Church Street house hurriedly. He still had to change, but with luck he'd be no more than
an hour late. Half-way past the house he saw Mr. Carver on
the veranda, talking to a dignified man with a broad face and
a prominent nose. With a start he recognized Henry Laurens,
one of the most influential merchants and planters in the
Carolinas. And, more importantly in light of what he'd heard
and seen that morning, Christopher Gadsden's foremost
opponent in the Assembly.

Mr. Carver saw him at the same moment. "Michael, what
are you doing back at this hour? Has something happened at
the bridge?"

"No, sir. I was caught in the rain, and I came back to
change."

"It's just as well. I've something for you to do. I was
going to send for you." He turned to Laurens. "Henry, this
is the young clerk I told you about. Michael Fallon. Michael,
this is Mr. Henry Laurens."

Michael bowed. "I recognize Mr. Laurens, sir. It is an
honor to make your acquaintance."

Laurens returned the bow courteously. "Thank you,
Michael."

Michael was seized by an impulse. What would Laurens
say to his news? "Mr. Carver."

"Eh? Yes, Michael?"

"There's some news in the city, sir. You may not have

heard, yet. Parliament's passed a stamp act for the colonies.''

Carver and Laurens looked at each other, frowning. ''Damn,'' said Laurens heatedly.

''Now, Henry—.''

''Don't 'now, Henry' me, Thomas. They've gone right ahead, ignoring our advice and our pleas alike.''

''Nevertheless, it is the law now.''

''I didn't say it wasn't the law. I merely say it's a bad law. We tried to stop it and failed. Now we must try to repeal it.''

''Pray God it can be done before the hotheads have a chance to profit on it.'' Carver's voice was bleak.

Laurens nodded grimly. ''Yes. I must go now, Thomas. We'll meet again this afternoon.'' He nodded to Michael. ''And good day to you, too, Mr. Fallon. I've heard considerable of your abilities from Mr. Carver.''

''Thank you, sir,'' Michael replied, and made a leg, but Laurens was already heading for the street, a preoccupied frown on his face.

Michael's own face was carefully blank, but his mind was hot. Gadsden and the Liberty Boys, Thomas Carver and Henry Laurens.

Carver's voice pulled him out of his reverie. ''Come inside, Michael.'' As Carver closed the study door behind them, he was lost in his own thoughts. ''I'll have to get hold of the Middletons, if they're in the city,'' he murmured. ''And the Draytons, and young Rutledge.'' He started suddenly as he remembered he wasn't alone. ''Yes, Michael. Come over to the desk and look at this map.'' He unrolled it over the desktop, setting the inkpot to hold one end and the sand sifter to hold the other.

Michael bent over it. It covered a part of the province south of Charlestown, with all of the rivers and roads marked. Names of plantations, or in some cases of their owners, had been written in. One, on the Combahee River, had been circled. Mallaton.

''I've bought a rice plantation,'' Carver said. His finger

came to rest on the circled name. "George Mallaton, the owner, spent one summer too many there instead of coming to the coast as he should have." He shook his head and sighed. "Yellow fever. His heirs have no interest in planting and were happy to sell, but I don't know what condition the place has fallen into since his death. It was a matter of buy quickly or not at all. That's where you come in. I want you to look over the plantation's books, and the operation of the place. Let me know what it's going to take to put everything to rights and be ready for next year's growing season. It's too late for this year, of course." He tapped a fingernail on the spot on the Combahee and spoke half to himself. "Elizabeth deserves as much." He nodded slowly.

Michael looked up from the map sharply. Elizabeth? What did she have to do with buying a rice plantation? A bitter answer came almost immediately. Fourrier was a planter's son. What better wedding gift for Fourrier and Elizabeth than a rice plantation? "I'll need a boat to get there," he said slowly.

"What? Oh, yes. I've arranged for a boatman."

"All right, sir," Michael said. "I'll see that everything is arranged properly." He'd see it was the best wedding present a woman ever received, damn Fourrier's eyes. "When do I meet the boatman, and where?"

Carver tugged out his pocket watch and checked it against the clock on the mantel. "He should be reaching the bridge any minute now. By the time you get some clothes together, two or three days' worth, and get back to the Bay, he should be ready to leave." He noticed Michael staring fixedly at the map. "Is something the matter?"

"What? No, sir. Nothing. If you'll excuse me, sir?"

He left Carver studying the map again himself, finger once more resting on that circled name.

The sun was bright outside, but the air was still damp with a heavy mugginess that told forbodingly of summer to come. He tramped back to the stable, casting glances over his shoulder at the house, at the windows of Elizabeth's room. There was no sign of her, no swirl of curtains, no movement.

It would have been fitting, he thought, if she'd been there to see him go, considering the nature of his journey.

He changed his clothes quickly, toweling off with a rough square of osnaburg, packed two suits of clothing in his drawstring bag, and kicked the door shut behind him. As he clattered down the stairs, he resolved not to look up to her room again. Until the last instant he kept it. Then, when the next step would take him where he could no longer see her window, he looked. Not even a sign of life. He hurried on, castigating himself for a lack of will. Damn the girl, anyway.

Most of the wharves were busy along the Bay. It was a peak rice shipping period, barrels crowding everywhere, along with deerskins, indigo, and pitch and other naval stores. At the end of Carver's Bridge a large, double-ended skiff with a jury-rigged tiller was lashed to the ladder that led to the water. There was something familiar about the black boatman's weathered face, Michael thought. A minute's study brought it to him. It was Daniel, who'd rowed him ashore his first day in Charlestown. He slapped his thigh in recognition, and Daniel looked up.

"Do you be my fare, sir? The gentleman I'm to take to the Mallaton plantation on the Combahee?"

"That I am, Daniel. Catch." He dropped the bag to the boatman and scrambled down the ladder after it. Daniel was regarding him questioningly. "You don't remember me, do you?"

"No, sir. I'm afraid I don't."

"Michael Fallon's the name." He stuck out his hand, and the boatman looked at it in surprise for a minute before taking it. "In January you fetched me from Captain Harding's *Rose*. The Black Irishman."

A wide grin split the boatman's face. "Yes, sir. I remember now. You surely have changed."

"Just the outside, Daniel." Michael looked at the boat and shook his head. "I remember you row a fine fast clip. How many days do you expect it to take us?"

"No days at all," Daniel laughed. He kicked some canvas-wrapped poles lying the length of the boat. "I got me this. Leg-o'-mutton sail. Shouldn't take more than five or six hours. Luck be with us, I have you there by three o'clock this afternoon.''

"Then let's be off.''

The patched, brown leg-o'-mutton pulled them down the Cooper River quickly and round the tip of the peninsula, cutting across the spit of White Point where a deeper vessel could not go. They had to beat back up the Ashley, but once the skiff made the turn into Wappo Creek, directly west of the city, the wind pushed them at a brisk clip, the marsh gliding past as fast as a man could run, down the creek and out into the Stono River, running down the coast. An occasional heron, flapping across the river, and a snowy crane standing on one leg in the marsh grasses were the only signs of life.

The plantations were not many along the coastal rivers. Most were inland, along the drainage of the great tidal rivers that ran to the sea. Some were there, though, great houses, of wood or brick, each with a dozen outbuildings.

"They're sure fine-looking places, ain't they?'' Daniel said.

"They are that.'' Such a place would be heaven for any man, he thought, that and a good wife beside him. He said as much to Daniel.

"A wife? Oh no, sir. I don't want no wife. Comes time for me to settle down, I'll buy me a nice looking girl, and I won't free her none neither.''

"But why not a wife, Daniel? You wouldn't have to pay to buy her.''

"True, sir. But a slave girl, I be the boss; a wife, she be the boss.''

Michael fell back in the boat laughing.

The Combahee River curved back on itself time and again. Michael held the tiller while Daniel continually retrimmed the frayed lines to the triangular sail. Then, as they rounded a bend, Michael saw the dikes of a rice plantation. High earthen mounds running for hundreds of yards along the river, they were meant to keep the water level over the rice constant, trapping the water behind them, keeping excess out. On top of the dike slaves hurried along with buckets carried on yokes across their shoulders, periodically disappearing down the far side of the embankment.

Daniel climbed back over the seats to take the tiller. "I said we'd make it. By the sun it isn't much later than three." He pointed the boat in at a small dock. A grassy slope ran up from the river to a two-story white house with porticos across the front.

"Are you certain this is the right place, Daniel?"

"This the Mallaton plantation, all right."

Michael climbed up on the dock and headed down the riverbank. A dirt ramp led up to the top of the dike. Some of the slaves with yokes and buckets eyed him curiously as he passed, but they hurried on, saying nothing.

The interior of the field was divided into long rectangles by dikes just like the one by the river. Some rectangles were already shallowly flooded. In others, stooped blacks worked with hoes, making trenches about three feet apart. In these runs the rice seed would be planted. Then the section would be flooded. A man rode to meet him, dismounting to walk the last part of the way.

"I'm looking for the Mallaton plantation," Michael said.

"This is it," the man said, and stuck out his hand. "Are you the new owner's representative?"

Michael took the hand and nodded. "Yes, Mr. Carver sent me to look things over. I'm Michael Fallon."

"Peter Harris." He waved a hand at the activity in the field. "I see you didn't expect this."

"No. With Mr. Mallaton dead I expected the fields to be lying fallow. So did Mr. Carver."

"I thought the new owner would want a crop, so I went ahead with the planting." He caught the unspoken question in Michael's glance. "I was Mr. Mallaton's manager."

"Quite a surprise. A happy one for Mr. Carver." Michael smiled. "Mr. Carver has asked me to go over the plantation's books, see what sort of profit and expense it has." They started along the dike toward the house, something nagging at the back of Michael's mind. He looked back over his shoulder, but he couldn't seem to put his finger on what it was.

"It's not there," Harris said. "The reservoir, I mean. That's what you're looking for, isn't it?"

Michael turned to take a good look. There *wasn't* any reservoir. The water for flooding the fields wasn't there. "But, how—."

"We use the tidal system. With the sluice gates we use the river to flood the fields. No worry about drought, like the inland plantations."

"Mr. Harris, I have a boatman with me. He'll be taking me back as well, so he'll need a place to stay and some food."

"I'll have him put up in the quarters."

Michael nodded slowly. Daniel would probably be more comfortable there than he would sitting alone in the big house with no one to talk to. "He's free, Harris, not a slave. I wouldn't want any misunderstanding."

"I'll make certain it's known."

The plantation house was the kind called a double-house, like two of Mr. Carver's house put together with a large hall running the length of the building. Every piece of the furnishings spoke of imported elegance, from English furniture to Turkish rugs to crystal chandeliers. Michael settled in what had been George Mallaton's study with the plantation's records, while Harris went to arrange for Daniel.

It was Michael's first chance to examine the actual workings of a rice plantation, and he made the most of it. At once it became clear that a steady profit had been made, even with constant expenditures by Mallaton for racehorses and fighting cocks—and the betting that would have to go with them, Michael thought. His eyebrows went up as he checked the figures. With only the smallest amount of prudence Mallaton could have doubled his acreage every three years. Double in only three years, and that with all the expense of his imported gewgaws. No wonder the rice planters could live like grandees.

He bent back over the table, scribbling furiously, stopping only to dip his pen or trim a new one. One set of papers was for Mr. Carver, a straightforward report on the plantation's finances. Another he made for himself; it was a detailed transcript of the costs involved in setting up the plantation. There was no telling when it might come in handy. By the time Harris returned he had two stacks of finely covered foolscap.

"I thought you might want to wash up for supper," he said.

Michael sat up and worked his neck to loosen the kinks. Shadows through the window lengthened with the setting sun. "Thank you, I will. Is there time for me to stretch my legs outside for a moment?"

"Oh, certainly. Plenty of time. I didn't want to rush you at the last minute." He stopped, visibly indecisive. "See here, Fallon, I think I'd better be straight with you. I put in the crop for more than just making sure the new owner was off to a good start. I like the job I have here, and I'd like to keep it."

"Well, I'll put in a word for you," Michael said slowly, "mention the work you've done. But I think it's only fair to tell you I've reason to believe Mr. Carver bought this as a wedding gift for his daughter. Since her intended is a planter himself he'll want to manage himself, or perhaps bring in his own people."

Harris breathed softly, "Damn. I'd hoped he was another merchant climbing the ladder."

"Ladder? What ladder?"

"The ladder to the aristocracy. More than one merchant has bought rice or indigo land to get the status of being a planter."

"Added status? Man, some of the most important men in the colony are merchants. Henry Laurens. Gabriel Manigault. Christopher Gadsden. I could go on with a dozen more."

"They're merchants, but they're important because they're planters, too. It's from that they get their place. You're not long in the province, are you?" Michael nodded. "In England, it's lords and such. Here it's planters. Only our aristocracy isn't rigid, like theirs. If you become a planter, and you're reasonably pleasant, then you're accepted into the ruling class. It doesn't matter if the money that started you was inherited or earned in trade or won on horseraces, so long as it was honestly come by. So, merchants buy plantations and become aristocrats. It happens all the time."

Michael nodded thoughtfully. He gathered the papers together and rose. "Now, if you don't mind, I think I'll take that turn outside."

The sun was a glowing red ball sinking on the horizon. Long lines of slaves wound their way down the dikes, the day's work done and supper waiting in the quarters. Those coming from the upriver fields were indistinct, their faces in darkness, their shadows stretching out long in front of them. The waters of the fields glinted in the deepening twilight.

A creaking board heralded Daniel's arrival. He watched silently. Michael spoke, finally. "Are you comfortable, now, in the quarters?"

"Yes, sir. It's right fine there, and they happy folk."

"Happy? As slaves?" He shook his head. "I don't see how they can be."

"It ain't being slaves they happy with, sir. Just being treated good and fed plenty. That's all most folks want, I guess."

"And freedom? What about that?"

"Most of them be scared of it do you give it to them. Anyways, they know they ain't going to get it. They ain't going to risk running away and getting caught, and they know ain't nobody going to bankrupt hisself by setting them all free, so they happy right where they be." Michael nodded in the darkness, understanding, yet not understanding. "Mr. Fallon, we leaving here tomorrow?"

"No, Daniel. I'll need most of tomorrow here. The day after, I think."

"Oh, that be fine." Daniel grinned suddenly. "There a gal down to the quarters thinks a boatman from the big, wicked city is something. I have one more day, I going to show her just how wicked it be." They laughed together easily. "Good night, Mr. Fallon."

"Good night, Daniel." With a last look at the silver river Michael turned and went back inside.

6

Charlestown simmered as the last cool of spring gave way to the heat of summer. So did Charlestown tempers. Companions who'd drunk together for years suddenly erupted in blows across the table, and shouts of "Gutter trash Liberty Boy!" and "Gutless King's cotquean." Men muttered in corners, and friends spoke guardedly, listening for hidden meaning.

Daniel was sitting on an upturned bucket beside a warehouse, puzzling out the words on a broadside. Three soldiers of the 60th Foot, weskits undone, facings stained, saw him at the same time Michael did. They lurched toward the boatman.

"What you doing there, darkie? You can't read."

Daniel's head jerked up. "I can read, some, sir," he said. "And I can puzzle out the rest."

"He can read, he says," the spokesman chortled. He had an unpleasant, gap-toothed grin and a nose that had been broken more than once. His companions cackled drunkenly. "This bloody colony," he snarled. "Won't give no credit for a few drinks to His Majesty's troops, but they got niggers sitting in the street, lording it over folks, pretending they can read." Suddenly he snatched the broadside from Daniel's hands, and the boatman rose, his back to the wall. "Admit you can't read, damn you. Admit it, or we'll skin you right here."

They were inching forward when Michael stepped up behind them. "Back away there," he snapped, and on sudden inspiration, "Stand at attention, damn you."

The voice of command snapped them as rigidly upright as only a drunk can stand. As Daniel slid along the wall toward Michael, one soldier followed the boatman with a wavering gaze until his eyes fell on Michael. His mouth fell open.

"You ain't—. You ain't no officer," he managed, and the other two jerked around.

The bent-nosed leader advanced, head and fists thrust forward. "Bloody civilian."

Michael's fist crunched into the lobster's nose, and he felt a thrill of satisfaction. The man rolled backwards on the ground. He straightened groggily and felt for his once-more broken beak. "Kill you," he muttered, and struggled to his feet, tugging out his bayonet. His companions fumbled for theirs.

Michael set himself, looking around for a weapon. With even a stick he might have a chance, but there was nothing. Suddenly the three soldiers froze. There was a scuffle of feet behind Michael. He risked a glance over his shoulder. Spread out behind him were a dozen men, warehousemen and dock idlers, barrel staves and maul handles in their hands. They stood quietly, eyes fixed on the soldiers.

The redcoat Michael had hit rubbed at his nose, winced, and shook his fist. "We'll settle you yet." His two companions pulled him away down the street.

Michael turned to thank his rescuers, but they were already drifting away, seeming to avoid one another's eyes as well as his.

One glanced back at Michael as he left. "Don't think I'm one of those damned Liberty Boys. I just can't abide the lobsters." He suddenly looked around to see who was listening and quickened his step.

Michael picked up the broadside, dropped by the soldier, and smoothed it out. "Are you all right, Daniel?"

The boatman nodded. "Yes, sir. Thanks to you. What they want to do something like that for? I never seen any of them before in my life."

"Scavengers. You were handy." He frowned at the broadside. "What is this thing, Daniel? Where'd you get it?"

"From a ship in the harbor, just down from New York. Man seemed real excited about it. He said it was about something the folks up in Virginia done, but I hadn't got it all worked out fore them soldiers come.''

Michael scanned the first line, and a name leaped out at him. Patrick Henry. Christopher's fire-eating young lawyer. Now, it seemed, a member of the Virginia House of Burgesses. Hastily he read the sheet. It hadn't taken Henry long to create a stir. He'd proposed a set of resolves on the Stamp Act; the true strangeness was that they had passed.

The first four resolves were innocuous statements that colonists in America had certain rights which had been recognized by the Crown long before this. But the fifth had meat to it, and teeth.

RESOLVED, that the General Assembly of this colony have the sole and only exclusive right and power to lay taxes and impositions upon the inhabitants of this colony and that every attempt to vest such power in any other person or persons whatsoever other than the General Assembly aforesaid has a manifest tendency to destroy British as well as American freedom.

He read that one over again. God's teeth, they'd as much as told the British Parliament to pack up and go home.

"You're lucky that soldier couldn't read what he had, Daniel, else he'd likely be frogmarching you off to the Provost for treason.''

"Trea—? Lord God Almighty, Mr. Fallon. What's in that thing?''

A faint smile appeared on Michael's face. "A man getting people fired up over the weather on a fine spring day.''

And in Charlestown bubbles began rising to the top.

The August heat was at its worst, and there wasn't so much as a breath of air to dispel it, despite the open windows. Elizabeth sat at the vanity, drumming her fingers while Samantha worked at arranging her hair.

"Can't you hurry? Am I supposed to sit here until I'm as sweated as a fishwife?''

"I'm almost done, Miss Elizabeth.'' The slave woman

pushed the last bone pin in place and patted the curl it held.
"There."

"About time. You're as ham-fisted as a field hand." She
studied the effect in the mirror. It actually wasn't a bad job,
she grudged, but only to herself. There was no need to give
Samantha a swelled head. "Have you told Samuel to bring
the coach around?"

"No, Miss Elizabeth. I was just going to when you told me
the red slippers wouldn't do and get the gold ones, and
then—."

"Well, go, go. Do you expect me to sit here all day? Or am
I supposed to walk to the shops?"

Samantha sighed in exasperation and pursed her lips.
"Very well, Miss Elizabeth. I'll tell him."

With its high, lace-trimmed modesty piece Elizabeth's
Watteau sack dress was perfectly proper. For girls and old
ladies, she thought, but not for a young woman. She rose to
follow Samantha downstairs, with a final look in the mirror
from the door. Papa was paying so much attention to her
gowns lately that she had to be extremely careful. It was
really too awful.

Outside her father's study she carefully arranged her face
in the half-pout that always brought men around, including
her father. Well, sometimes brought Papa around. She entered without knocking.

Her father didn't even look up. He was behind his desk,
perusing a map, in deep discussion with that clerk of his.
What was his name? Talon? Fallon, that was it. They seemed
to have their heads together often of late.

"Agreed, Michael. Harris will stay at Mallaton." Carver
was looking pleased.

"Papa?"

The two men looked up, startled, Carver with a smile
spreading on his face, Michael with a tightness coming into
his eyes.

"What can I do for you, daughter?"

"I'm going shopping, Papa. I'm taking Samuel and the
carriage, and Samantha, of course. Oh, yes, and one of the

liveryboys to carry my purchases.''

Carver hesitated. ''I'd rather you didn't go out just now.''

Elizabeth's careful expression slipped for an instant. ''Why on earth not?''

''Child, there are rowdies in the streets today, waiting to see how the Assembly votes on sending delegates to the Stamp Congress in New York. If the vote is to send no one, or if the delegates aren't approved of, there will be trouble.''

Elizabeth shook her head and sniffed. ''Bother. I'll have Samuel with me, and besides, not the meanest layabout would dare raise his hands to me on a public street.''

''These aren't ordinary dock idlers I'm talking about. They're primed and set for trouble, looking for it.'' He sighed as her chin jutted out. ''Oh, very well. But you'll need more protection than Samuel.'' He eyed Michael, studiously looking out the window. ''Mr. Fallon will go with you. Anyone will think twice before starting trouble with him.''

Michael turned stiffly from the window, his mouth open to protest. It stayed that way. What the devil could he say? What reason could he give? That he couldn't be her protection because he very much feared if they were alone together for long she might need protection from him? He stood speechless. Elizabeth was under no such handicap.

''Really, Father, this is too much—''

''That's enough, Elizabeth,'' Carver said sharply. ''You have your choice. Mr. Fallon attends you, or you stay at home. Which will it be?''

So suddenly that both Michael and her father stared in bewilderment, Elizabeth's frown turned to a smile. ''Very well,'' she said sweetly. ''He can come with me, if you insist, but I won't be crowded in the carriage. If he comes, there's no need for the liveryboy. He can carry my parcels.''

Michael found his voice then, but before he could use it, Carver nodded and said, ''I'm sure Mr. Fallon won't mind. Will you, Michael?''

He was trapped. ''Of course not, sir.''

Elizabeth was a trifle disconcerted. She'd expected protest. Well, at least her father hadn't stopped her altogether.

She busied herself with her fingerless, dark lace mitts. "Come along, then. I'll be back shortly, papa."

"Take care, child."

Michael put his tricorn under his arm and followed her out onto the portico. Samantha was at the steps with Elizabeth's parasol and fan, a young black lad in livery at her side. Elizabeth dismissed the boy, ignoring Samantha's startled look, opened the parasol and headed for the carriage. Samantha, looking after her, at Michael, at the boy retreating up the carriage path, shaking her head, followed slowly. Michael trailed along behind.

Elizabeth fanned herself slowly as the carriage wound its way through gradually thickening traffic. The fan did little to dispel the heat, and the motion of the carriage was too slow to generate even a slight breeze. She tried to take her mind off the torrid weather by thinking of what laces and lawns the modistes might have, eyeing the garments of ladies passing in the crush.

Michael watched the street with a different eye. The throng was as heavy as ever, but this was a crowd to be watched. The solitary redcoat, out on the town, the knot of two or three, half drunk or more, were gone. But three times in the space of ten minutes Michael caught sight of a squad marching, each man tensely alert, bayonets fixed on their shouldered muskets, led by a sergeant with his halberd. Some in the crowd watched the soldiers closely— determined, ragged men with barrel staves, or sailors carrying belaying pins. And passersby and peddlers made haste away from both.

At the first shop he held the door for Elizabeth. She took it as his duty and swept by without acknowledgment. He followed her in with a wry smile. She didn't know him from a fencepost; that changed nothing.

The dressmaker and her assistant, with smiles and curtseys, covered the counters with bolts of English lawn, boxes of dutch lace, and piles of Italian fans. Immediately Elizabeth was engrossed. The assistant was not so engrossed, however. She patted her yellow hair for the handsome

Irishman, and gave him a wicked smile. Michael returned her smile with interest.

"Mr. Fallon."

Michael stiffened as Elizabeth snapped at him. Had she seen the girl smiling at him? And if she had, why should it bother her?

"Hold out your arms. That's it. Straight out to the sides."

Uncertain, Michael did as he was bid. She took two lengths of lace and tossed one over each arm, straightening them neatly for study. He gritted his teeth till he was certain they could hear the grinding. He quivered with barely suppressed anger. Unconcerned, Elizabeth held a piece of this cloth and a swatch of that up to the lace to see how they looked together.

The dressmaker's assistant, amused, grinned at him, twitching her hips once at the same time. This time the modiste saw her, and gave her a sharp rap across the wrist with her measuring stick. Her yelp drew Elizabeth's attention, but the two women met her look with bland smiles.

Elizabeth turned back to the decision at hand. The Brussels lace with the blue silk. That was it.

She left the shop feeling quite satisfied. Michael, embarrassed by the parcels he carried, viewed the street with a jaundiced eye. The riffraff were still in evidence among the ordinary passersby, and the marching soldiers, too.

"Any change, Samuel?" he asked quietly as he tucked the bundles under the carriage seat.

"No, sir, Mr. Fallon." The coachman jerked his head fearfully up the street toward the State House. "I sure wish they'd hurry whatever they going to do. Things is getting more boisterous all the time."

"Be quiet, Samuel," Elizabeth said inattentively. She took her parasol and fan from Samantha and settled herself beside the black woman. "Drive on."

The next shop was much like the first, with the modiste and her assistant rushing to curtsey and spread their wares for inspection. Here, too, the assistant seemed distracted from her work. In this case, it was the street outside that drew her attention from the fabrics. "I wonder if they've chosen yet," she mused.

Both Elizabeth and the dressmaker looked at her sharply, and Elizabeth threw down the fan she had been examining. "I did not come here for political discussion," she said icily. "If I cannot make a purchase without being told the events of the day, I will not make one. And I will tell my friends to do the same."

The modiste, seeing a large part of her custom slipping away, stammered in her haste to soothe. "I'm very sorry, Miss Carver. It won't happen again. I assure you."

"See that it does not." And Elizabeth marched out of the shop. Michael, wondering at her temper, was barely in time to open the door for her.

When he turned from the door he found that she had not returned to the carriage. Instead she stood talking to Justin Fourrier, one hand resting lightly on his arm.

"Please, Justin," she said, "whatever you say, don't mention congresses or stamps or delegates. Promise me."

"I promise," he said, obviously surprised by the request. "A pack of fools, playing at treason."

"Not another word about it, Justin. Neither for nor against. Shopgirls moon over that stupid congress. My coachman seems terrified. My father even insisted I bring his clerk for protection. All of it because of this silly stamp thing."

Fourrier raised an eyebrow at Michael, the corner of his mouth curling up. He was on ground he was surer of, now. "His clerk?" He stepped back and swept a courtly bow. "If it please you, let me be your guardian, so that you may, indeed, have a guardian."

Michael bristled. He was more protection with a switch than this jack-o'dandy with a sword.

Elizabeth smiled up at the dark Huguenot. The day might go better than she'd thought. "Mr. Fourrier, you do me honor." She tucked her hand under his arm. "Mr. Fallon, go back to the house. Tell my father that Justin will protect me, if there's any need."

"Your father told me to accompany you," Michael said.
"I cannot leave you, even with Mr. Fourrier." Justin handed
her into the carriage. "I said, your father—"

"You are dismissed, Mr. Fallon. Drive on, Samuel."

The coachman rolled his eyes helplessly at Michael, then
cracked his whip over the horses. The carriage lurched ahead
down the street.

Michael glared after them. Elizabeth and Fourrier. How
much pleasure it would have been to knock the popinjay
sprawling. And that was senseless. They were betrothed, or
as much as.

In gloom he started back to Church Street. Then, before
he'd gone half a block, he saw a man he had been needing for
a week or more. "Mr. Drayton! Sir! Mr. John Drayton!"

Drayton turned at last and waited impatiently, tapping his
walking stick on the cobblestones. He had a high, sloping
forehead and a pointed nose and chin. A member of the
Governor's Council, he was a staunch King's man, and one
of the party that sought more power for the Council. He hated
Gadsden as much for his insistence that the Council remain
weak as for his radical views.

At that moment Drayton was wearing a frown. "Yes, yes.
What is it?"

"I'm Michael Fallon, Mr. Drayton. Mr. Thomas Carver's
clerk."

"Yes. I've heard him speak of you. What is it you want?"

"It seems possible," Michael said carefully, "that
Jonathon Wynfrey, Mr. Carver's last clerk, may have made
some errors in recording exactly how much rice was bought
from you."

Drayton eyed him shrewdly. "Errors, eh? Go on."

"If you might have your secretary make a listing of what
we purchased from you the last three seasons, and what was
paid, it would help immensely."

"Very well. I'll have such a list made and sent to you. We
can't allow, uh, errors to go uncaught."

"No, sir." Quickly Michael cast around for something to
change the subject. Any minute the planter would be asking

openly how much had been stolen. "Do you know, Mr. Drayton, if the Assembly's voted on the delegate question, yet?"

The other man jerked erect. "You're not one of Gadsden's men, are you?!"

"Gadsden's men?" Michael said. "I've never met him, sir."

Drayton relaxed slightly. "They voted to send representatives, and without so much as a by-your-leave to the Council. Christopher Gadsden, Thomas Lynch, and John Rutledge. Those are the men they're sending. I'd have thought Lynch and young Rutledge would have better sense. As for Gadsden of course, well, one can expect anything from Gadsden."

"Did I hear my name mentioned?" Approaching unseen, the slender Gadsden leaned on his cane and watched their surprise with amusement. "You're well, I hope, John. And you, sir, are Michael Fallon, I believe?"

Before Michael could open his mouth, Drayton drew himself up indignantly. "And I believe you said you did not know Mr. Gadsden. Good day to you both."

"Sir!" Michael called after him, to set the matter straight, but realized it was impossible. Even Gadsden's word in support would do more to convince him he was right than to dissuade him. Drayton turned. Michael opened his mouth again. "Will you still have that list sent?"

"I said I would. I do what I say." He turned on his heel and stalked away.

"I hope I haven't caused you trouble," Gadsden said. Michael failed to see the twinkle in his eye.

"No. No, I don't think so." Still, Michael frowned at Drayton's retreating back. It wasn't pleasant to be taken for a liar. "If you don't mind, sir, I'd like to be knowing just how you know my name."

"I heard it mentioned, as the name of one who might be useful to the cause of liberty."

"Heard it mentioned, along with enough of a description to pick me out on the street." Michael grinned, and Gadsden smiled in return.

"Well, perhaps more than mentioned. It's said you have a good head on your shoulders, and you think the right way about the cause. You could be a valuable man, a prominent man, even."

Michael shook his head. "I've no desire for politicking, sir. And as for the way I think, I think the American colonies have a bad bargain, which is the usual way of it when you deal with the British. From that I'd say your cause is likely a good one, but there are ten thousand good causes. A man could spend every minute of his life on them and not touch the hundredth part."

"Um. Well." Gadsden looked down at the paving stones, pursing his lips thoughtfully. "And the Virginia Resolves," he said suddenly. "What of them?"

"What of them? Well, they seem the right way to go if you want to stop this Stamp Tax. To my mind we must deny the English the right of any taxes at all. If they've the right for one, then they've the right for all, and no matter about external or internal."

"Then you might be interested in this. It was passed just before the delegates were elected. It is what we will present in New York."

Michael took the paper Gadsden pulled from his coat pocket and unfolded it. He scanned it quickly, but one section held his eye.

RESOLVED, that the only representatives of the people of this province are persons chosen therein by themselves, and that no taxes ever have been or can be constitutionally imposed on them, but by the legislature of this province.

"Mr. Fallon, those ten thousand good causes you spoke of are scattered all over the world. This one's in your own yard. Think of it. Good day."

With a bow Gadsden disappeared into the swirl of traffic, leaving Michael to see Christopher Byrne, staring after Gadsden.

"Wasn't that Christopher Gadsden, lad?"

"It was. Don't you know him?"

Byrne's head jerked around, and his smile faded. "Know him? No, No. I've had him pointed out to me, is all. I was a little surprised to see you talking to him so friendly like. You're coming up in the world, making the acquaintance of the muckety-mucks."

"Just trade," Michael said, and wondered why he lied. "Will you tip a glass with me? For a change, I've news."

"And I've a piece of news or two as well. 'Tis said the stamp agents for South Carolina will be George Saxby and Caleb Lloyd."

"They've been talking that in the streets for a week, now. Come on. Let's prime you with some of Dillon's beer and see if we can't get something fresher out."

Byrne paused at the mention of Dillon's "Ah, listen, Michael. Would you mind walking yourself up to Queen Street, to Shepheard's? There's a tab at Dillon's—a pound or two. You understand."

"You haven't been gambling again? I thought you'd sworn off."

"You can't expect a man to be in London without trying his hand at one or two of the hells," Christopher said sheepishly.

"All right, then," Michael said with a smile, "Shepheard's it is." And he wondered when Christopher had given his name to Gadsden, and why Gadsden had chosen today to approach him.

7

The delegates sailed for New York, and Charlestown waited uneasily for the arrival of the stamped paper. Summer passed into autumn; tempers grew hotter.

Michael was tying up a bundle of papers when he heard the commotion in the warehouse. He opened the window and stuck his head out. Jepson, in the entrance, was thick in a jabbering knot of warehousemen and dock-idlers. The Scot looked up at Michael's halloo, mouth working and burr thick. "It's the *Planter's Adventure*, with the paper. She's anchored under the guns of Fort Johnson."

The paper. Less than a fortnight was left before the act went into effect. Just the same, he'd been hoping by some miracle the cursed stuff would never arrive. Now there was no telling what would happen. He'd better get back to Church Street now, and take both his own news and the colony's with him.

By the time he reached the house he was running. Angry bunches of men were jabbering on street corners, gathering numbers despite the approach of evening. He took the steps two at a time, tucked his tricorn under his arm, and knocked on the study door.

"Come." Carver was seated behind his desk. "Ah, Michael. You look as if you've been running. Sit down and cool yourself. What brings you here in such a hurry?"

Michael laid the papers on the desk, away from Carver's reach. "The *Planter's Adventure* made port this afternoon."

"Damn." Carver's voice grated angrily. "We've tried every single thing there is to try. Henry Laurens, for one, still thinks we can find a way out, but I'm no longer sure."

"You know what this means, sir."

Carver snorted. "I know quite well. Gadsden may be in

New York, but his mob will still be in the streets over this.
Liberty Boys. Killcows and bellswaggers, that's what they
are.''

"Yes, sir." Michael was leaning forward intently. "But if
they stop the stamped paper, not a ship will be able to clear
the harbor. We must get every cargo we can shipped and
gone, else, come the first, you'll likely have a full warehouse
and nowhere to send it.''

"Yes, Michael. Step up the loadings.'' He hesitated.
"You don't see the full impact of it, do you? It goes beyond
the customs collector not giving clearances except on
stamped paper. Some will try to close the courts on the same
grounds. No stamped paper, no official business transacted.
No sales bigger than buying a fish in the market. No contracts.''

"Sir, I thought you were opposed to the stamps. You
sound as if you want to use them.''

Carver eyed Michael speculatively. "I've heard many
dock workers attend the Liberty Boys' meetings. And clerks.
You're mixed up in it?''

"That I am not,'' Michael said forcefully. "I've seen the
mob before, in Ireland and other places, and I've no wish to
be part of one, no matter the cause they cry.''

"Then I advise you to stay in this evening. There'll be
trouble. If any approach you, remember, good law or bad
law, it is the law. And all laws, good or bad, must be obeyed
until they're changed.''

"Yes, sir.'' Did the old man think he was one to run with
that pack, he wondered, or was he talking to convince himself? It was time to tell him his own news. He touched
the bundle of papers on the corner of the desk. "About
these—.''

The merchant reached out to pick them up.

"It's about your former clerk, Jonathon Wynfrey.''

Carver's hand stopped as if the bundle had turned into a
snake. Slowly he pulled it back. He sat without speaking,
watching and waiting.

Michael frowned and went on. "Wynfrey was a thief.

More than fifteen hundred pounds he stole, current money.
Over two hundred pounds sterling.''

Carver drummed his fingers on the desk. ''You can prove
all of this?''

Michael nodded. ''I can. Every bale of your goods he sold
on his own account. Every time he ordered a hundred barrels
and wrote that he'd ordered a hundred and ten. It's all there,
every shilling of it.''

The old man touched the bundle, reluctantly. ''I'll take
these. Mention it to no one.''

Michael frowned. This didn't make sense. ''Did you know
this, sir?''

''No, Michael.'' Carver growled tiredly. ''I suspected,
but I didn't know.''

''You suspected,'' Michael said blankly. Then it came to
him. ''You won't use it, will you? You'll not use a page of
it!''

Carver tried to look away, but Michael's eyes held him.
''No. No, I won't use a page of it.''

''Why? Mary, Joseph and Jesus, why? They'd hang a poor
man in a minute for touching the thousandth part of that. Are
you going to let him go free because he's a rich man's son?''

''In a way, Michael. Yes.''

''And what about that law we've got to obey, good or bad?
What about that?''

''It's not right, is it?'' He picked up the offending papers
and turned them over in his hands. ''If I made the use of these
you want me to, what would happen? Tell me that.''

''Why, once the charges against Wynfrey were laid before
a magistrate, a warrant would be issued.''

''And beyond that? I'll tell you. Nothing.'' He tossed the
bundle back on the desk. ''As far as young Wynfrey is
concerned the charges may as well not exist. Nothing can
make him come back here and face them. He might never
even hear of them. But I would be here. To face the planters.''

''You're not saying there'd be feeling against you for it?
Well, his father, of course, but—''

"Yes, his father, and his father's friends, and more than one planter that barely knew either of them. This isn't a little thing like trying to slip in poor quality rice as premium. That's almost a game, to some of them. This is theft. A planter's son, one of their own, no better than a common cutpurse, a figman with his hand in another man's pocket. It would embarrass them, more than you can imagine, and every time they dealt with me they'd be reminded of it. I'd find myself shipping little more than my own rice. And for what? For laying a charge that's useless."

By then Michael had sat back in his chair. He felt dazed. He shook his head to clear it, but that only made the fog swirl more. "I should be old enough by now to know the way of the world." He pushed up out of his chair. "I'll go to my room, now, I think."

"Michael?"

"Sir?" He stopped at the door without turning. Sparks of anger were rekindling in him, but the fog still clouded the flames.

"Don't—" The merchant halted, then finished lamely. "Don't forget to stay in tonight."

Michael smiled bitterly. "You've no need to worry, sir. All the Irish rebels are dead, long ago."

He left then, quickly, before he said more than he should. He seethed. For a false charge of murder and a trumped-up charge of stealing, he'd hang, did they ever catch him. Wynfrey would never even have the charge laid, not with the evidence of his stealing written on the walls for the world to see. And murder? Would wealth and position be a shield against that? Wealth and position. Without them a man was less than nothing, not so much as a bump in a rich man's road.

The garden behind the house was laid with formal walks paved with large squares of slate that absorbed the sound of his footsteps. Stalking between tall banks of roses and olean-der, he saw nothing until he rounded the corner where an ancient oak spread limbs as thick as a man.

Elizabeth sat on the stone bench at the base of the tree, face upturned, laughing. Through the gall of his thoughts desire seized him. Someone else was there, the someone who caused those smiles and laughs, who had that face upturned to him as if captivated. Justin Fourrier.

The planter's son, his coat off, postured for her with a small-sword, attacking low-hanging twigs furiously. Elizabeth clapped delightedly, applauding every sally as if he'd dispatched a dozen desperate villains. Michael moved to leave, and a twig cracked beneath his foot like a pistol shot.

Justin looked up at the sound and smiled, flipping back the lace at his wrists. "Here's what I need. You there, Irishman, whatever your name is, come down here."

"Excuse—" Michael began civilly.

"I said come here. I can't say I think much of your father's servants, Elizabeth. He should have gotten a Dutchman, or a German. They can at least obey. These Irish are too stupid to even understand what they're being told."

"Oh, Justin," the girl laughed. "Come, Mr. Fallon. Mr. Fourrier is a guest of this house. Come along, now."

Justin flexed his knees and presented the sword in the guard position. "Mr. Fallon? You'll have him above himself, Elizabeth."

"He's an indentured servant, Justin, not a slave, after all."

"Be better if he was. All they're good for, anyway." He launched a long thrust into the air. "Well, man, are you going to do as you're told or not?"

Michael walked slowly to the bench, still in a haze. When Fourrier produced another sword and pushed it into his hands he stared at it blankly. The point was bare. There was no button. Idly he wondered if Fourrier actually intended them to fence with unguarded swords. It didn't seem important; he let the thought drift away.

Elizabeth's eyes followed Justin; he strutted in front of her like a peacock. "Now I can really show you what I meant. Hold the thing up, man. He's probably afraid I'll hurt him. Come on. Hold it up."

Michael raised the sword slowly, stiffly. Justin took a stance in front of him, flexing and posturing still, slashing his blade from side to side. His feet are too far apart, Michael thought absently. Fourrier smiled at Elizabeth and, without warning, lunged, a sneer already forming in anticipation of the Irishman's fear. Nothing of Michael moved except his awkwardly held blade, and that just enough to deflect the other wide of the mark.

Justin straightened angrily, not quite certain what had happened. "I didn't tell you to move about. Stand still there." Again he took a stance and lunged. Again Michael's blade moved just far enough to force it aside.

Elizabeth looked from one man to the other in confusion. There was an unnerving undercurrent to this she could barely catch. It made her feel strange.

Michael remained a statue, looking straight ahead, barely seeing the rage that suffused Justin's face, or the obsidian glitter in his eyes. He was panting.

"Stand still this time," he breathed. "Still. Don't move. Not a muscle. I command it."

Michael watched the circling point in front of him and the baleful smile behind it as if they were part of another world. The blade flashed toward him. On instinct he twisted, parrying in full.

For an instant they froze in a twisted tableau. Michael studied the extension of Justin's blade disinterestedly. Half a foot or more would have gone into his chest, had he stood as ordered. He raised his eyes to Fourrier's. Sullen anger met him. Purposeful anger. So there was an answer to it. Murder would be allowed, for a man of the proper position.

Elizabeth had gone rigid, one hand half raised to her mouth, a scream frozen in her throat. Her eyes were unnaturally bright, and her breasts felt painfully tight. "Justin, that looked dangerous." There was a tension in her voice that didn't come from fear.

Fourrier belatedly jumped back, sword raised as if to defend, though Michael made no move to follow. "You Irish bastard," he spat. "I'll have no more of your insolence."

The flames of anger flared in Michael, and the last of the fog burned away. His eyes blazed like sapphire. Words flowed out of him. "You have no grace with the sword, bucko, nor any style, either."

"What?"

"In fact, you use it like a tailor's apprentice cutting cloth. Mr. Fourrier. Sir."

Justin seemed to swell. The color went out of his face. He quivered all over. "I'll have you—."

A wolfish smile came to Michael's lips. "You choke the sword. A sword's like a woman. If you hold her tight, strangle her, she'll always be disobeying you and trying to escape. You must cradle her gently, like a bird in your palm. Like so." He brought his blade up in a manner that would have graced any *salle d'armes* on the Continent. Disbelief warred with the anger on Fourrier's face. "Then she'll obey you, and protect you, and fight for you. Like this."

In one smooth motion Michael's blade whipped around Justin's, point coming to rest a scant inch from Justin's gold-embroidered vest. Justin stumbled back, certain his death was intended. When he realized that it wasn't, that the blade had been halted short on purpose, a blind rage came over him. He would be done with the Irish scum, once and for all.

With a cry he rushed to the attack. Almost immediately the blade was at his chest again. He beat it aside, and in some fashion the other blade spiraled around his to threaten him again. Heedless, he pressed on, and once more the Irishman's blade found its place at his chest. Slowly it dawned on him that that point was coming closer at each pass. The first had ended with it an inch away. Now it was half an inch. Sweat began to run down his face. He took a step back. And another.

Coolly Michael followed, each move precise and surgical. Riposte, parry, counter. His entire body moved in rhythm, his breath was even, and at every step he came that much closer to killing Fourrier. The slight smile was still there on an otherwise expressionless face. He had forgotten expression, forgotten everything save a spot on Justin's waistcoat, directly over the heart.

Fourrier thrust high, desperately, and Michael beat the sword down. His left hand shot out to grasp the blade and tear it from Justin's grip. Point to the other's throat, he forced him back, till his back was against the wall and skin began to dimple around the steel.

All the while Elizabeth sat watching, mouth open, panting as if she herself was taking part. She hugged herself, shivering, but she felt strangely warm, all over. A faint perspiration misted her face and throat, and beads of sweat ran down between her breasts. She waited, for something, but she didn't know what for.

The corner of her eye caught a movement.

"The sword, Michael. Give it to me." Carver had stepped seemingly out of nowhere to put his arm between the two men. His voice was almost gentle. "Please."

Michael looked at him, and moments later saw him. He let out a long, shuddering breath. The tension ran out of him like water, leaving a loose, rubbery feeling behind. He laid the sword in the old man's hand in formal surrender. The other dropped to the ground, stained red along the blade.

Justin, too, let out a long breath, and its leaving brought back his tongue. "He attacked me. Your servant attacked me. I want him——."

"I saw it, Justin," Carver said coolly. "If it's taken to a magistrate, I must testify, of course."

Fourrier stared at him, his expression unreadable. "He'll believe me," he said flatly.

Carver's face tightened. "Few men have ever questioned my veracity." His voice hardened. "I find it especially strange in one who wants to marry my daughter."

Justin started. "I—I didn't mean it in that way, sir."

"I don't see any other way to mean it."

"If I gave any offense, sir, it was unintentional, I assure you."

Carver sighed. Perhaps it really was just a slip of the tongue. He wanted to believe that. "Very well, Justin. Make your apology to my daughter, and then you'd better leave."

"Of course, sir." Composing his face quickly, Justin swept a bow to Elizabeth. "My dear Miss Carver, pray accept my humblest apologies for this incident." His voice rolled on in oily solicitude.

Elizabeth barely noticed he was there. Why had she never noticed how blue Michael's eyes were, and the way his hair seemed to defy brush and comb? It was savage, like himself. The way it nestled around his ears made her want to stroke them with her fingers.

"Elizabeth. Elizabeth?"

Her father's voice broke her trance; vaguely she saw Justin go. "Yes, father?"

"Child, I regret that you witnessed this . . . outrage. Go to your room. Have Samantha put a cold compress on your forehead."

"Yes, father," she said. As she rose she cast a glance at Michael. How strong his hands looked, broad and capable. She shivered as if one of his fingers had run down her spine.

Her father watched her walk away, concern etched on his face. Then, abruptly, he said, "Michael, I'll see you inside."

He started off before Michael had a chance to speak. He followed slowly. His temper had done it again, pushed him beyond the limits of decency. A part of him shouted that the limits were too small, but he pushed it back. The last time he'd fled to America. Where could he go now?

In the study Carver went straight to the sideboard near the window. "Let me see that hand."

"It's nothing, sir."

He clenched it into a fist, but the older man pulled it up into the light and forced it open. A deep gash ran across the whole width of the palm. The clenched fist had kept the gash shut, but now it began to bleed again.

"Nothing, is it? Seth will fetch bandages."

"I've a clean hankerchief in my pocket. I'd as lief use that."

"Very well, but first—" The old man moved the hand over a tray and, before Michael saw, splashed a dollop of brandy over it.

"God preserve us!" Michael jerked free, shaking the hand in the air. Awkwardly he tied the handkerchief over the gash, stinging now more from the brandy than it had when cut. "And that's a waste of good liquor."

He froze as Carver thrust a glass at him. Hesitantly he took it. Brandy was not a bound man's drink. It slid over his tongue with a remembered smoothness.

"Sir, I apologize. I forgot myself."

Carver waved the apology away. "She'll survive it better than you might suppose. I don't like it, but she'll survive it, and there's no more to be done about it. What worries me now is you, Michael."

"Me?"

The old man hesitated, choosing words carefully. "That was quite a display. I doubt there's a fencing master in the city could duplicate it. Were you a fencing master?"

The question hung between them.

"I was not," he said finally.

Carver was relentless. "Then what? When you first came I didn't press you. I needed a clerk, and you were a good one. Competent, more than competent. Still, I detected something in you I couldn't quite put my finger on, a hidden energy, a purpose. Now, I must know. Who are you, Michael Fallon? What are you?"

Michael, summoned a smile. "I'm Michael Shane Fallon, a clerk and an indentured servant, with two years, two months, and some days left on my time." And a man under a charge of murder.

"That's not what I mean, and you well know it. The truth, Michael, and no worming your way round it. The sword. Begin with that."

He gulped the rest of the brandy. It exploded warmly in his

stomach. "Ah, the sword, now. Well, I was a soldier for a time. A time. Seven years of it. Fifteen, I was when I began. There was a fellow, Timothy Cavanaugh, took an interest in me. It was him taught me the sword, drumming it into me till I was ready to collapse."

"Cavanaugh?"

"Aye. He was a soldier before I was born, and lucky for me he was. He kept me alive until I learned enough of soldiering to do it for myself. He's out of it now, with a tavern below Liverpool." He was saying too much. "This is fine brandy. I'm out of the habit of drinking it."

"Why come here? Why sign indentures? I'd think a man with your drive could make something of himself in his home country."

Michael laughed or perhaps it was a snarl. "Home country, is it? No Irishman has a home in Ireland, One of your slaves could get his own piece of land as easy as an Irishman in Ireland."

"And that's all you want? A piece of land?"

"Once it was. Not now, though, or rather, that and more. I intend building something. I'll plant crops on my own land, ship them in my own bottoms. That's my dream." His face grew hard. "I'll be able to buy and sell men like Mr. Justin Fourrier."

"He could have killed you, you know."

"He would have tried. Hell, he did try."

"And would you have killed him?"

Michael studied the pattern on the rug before answering. "No. No, I would not." His mouth contorted. "It takes a man of power to kill another man and get away with it."

Carver sighed. The answer disturbed him. So much bitterness in the man. He had the sudden feeling that it must not grow. Michael Fallon, he decided, should not be allowed to destroy himself.

"And how will you go about this building? How do you mean to start?"

"I've a few pounds I brought with me. When my time to you is done, sir, it'll be trade for me."

The old man frowned at his desk. "You know it's illegal for a bound man to engage in trade?"

"I do." Michael grinned suddenly. Some of the gall seemed to wash away. "Else I'd have begun the first evening I arrived."

"There's a fine of triple the amount of the goods traded, payable by the man you trade with to the man who holds your indenture. Of course, if the man you trade with is the man who holds your indenture, then he must pay the fine to himself."

Michael blinked. "Sir?" His head was spinning, and only partly from brandy. Was Carver saying—?

"If you're willing to take the risks of the trade, the losses as well as the gains, you can trade through my accounts. Just add your order to mine. No one will question it. You ship on my vessels, and your goods will be sold in lot with mine." He paused. "Well?"

Michael closed his eyes. " 'Willing?' God, it's more than willing I am, sir. More than—"

"Enough, Michael," the old man smiled. He sniffed suddenly and rubbed his hands together. "Tell me. Do you play the game of chess? I know many military men do."

"Chess?" Michael was off his guard. "Why, yes, I do. But," he added with a smile, "I'm a military man no longer. I'm a merchant."

Carver smiled back at him. "And so you are." He took out a wooden chessboard. "One merchant to another, would you oblige me with a game?"

Elizabeth rose from her crouch by the door and retreated toward the stairs. Her knees ached; the nagging fear of discovery was on her. She had the feeling that if her father saw her he would know immediately she'd had her ear to the keyhole. She darted up the steps, skirts held high, and didn't stop until she was safe behind her bedroom door.

She threw herself into the windowseat, staring out at the evening shadows in the garden, seeing nothing. A soldier, and as a boy, too. Idly she wrapped a curl around her finger, twisting and untwisting it. Why would a boy become a soldier? He was Irish. Could he have been a rebel? The thought raised goosebumps. A rebel would dare things. Things other men wouldn't.

Angrily she released the curl. Justin dared nothing. Everyone assumed they'd marry, eventually. Her father assumed it. Justin assumed it. But he was so, so stiff. All the time. Even when he was having fun, doing something that made her laugh, she had the feeling that only part of him was involved. A small part. He was certainly no impetuous lover.

Her breath caught in her throat. Lover. She wrapped her arms around herself, crushing her breasts. That could be a man's hands doing that. It could be Michael Fallon's hands. She squeezed harder, as if the warm pressure could make him appear.

It was suddenly too hot in the room. Her clothes felt tight. The air seemed heavy. Even to think of him was madness. He was a servant, a bound man. And yet, her father had offered to set him in trade. He'd never done that before. He was even playing chess with him, and there were only three or four men with whom he would do that. Possibly, just possibly, he might countenance a small flirtation, if it was no more than that. She smiled. Or if he thought it was no more.

She twisted the thought this way and that, peering at it from all sides. It would have to be very discreet, certainly. None could be allowed to know she was involved with a servant. But if Justin should suspect, that should wipe away his complacency and his punctilio. Jealousy would transform him into a lover. Her face took on a satisfied, vulpine cast. And in the meanwhile, there would be Michael.

8

Michael spent the night in a restless half-sleep, just below the edge of consciousness, where dreams were known for dreams yet took on an air of bewildering reality. Columns of figures ran by with increasing rapidity. Six months trading. A year. Pounds. Shillings. Pence. And behind them, unbidden, violet eyes. A tiny Michael Fallon ran among the figures, shouting for the eyes to go away, trying to keep from falling into them and drowning, trying to keep from wanting to. He began to climb, up the figures, up. He had to get away. Suddenly the figures were stacked barrels of rice and indigo, barrels marked, Ship for Fallon. They shifted underfoot. The stacks began to collapse. And he was falling, falling forever into those violet eyes.

He sat up with a start. Cold sweat ran down his body. It took a minute to realize he was in his room over the stables. It was light outside. He put his feet over the side of the bed. And he remembered the dream.

It was insanity. The trade was fine, but not the girl. One thing had nothing to do with the other. Her father might well help him enter the trade, but he would not welcome attentions to his daughter. Far from it. He'd send for the constables to haul him away, and rightly so. The chasm was still there, between them, and if it might narrow in the future, it was impassable now. What matter that he felt cousin to a moonstruck calf?

He sighed and got to his feet. There was water in the pitcher on the lowboy. He splashed some into the bowl to wash. She had her future planned. She would marry Justin Fourrier, the rich planter's son of old Huguenot stock, not the struggling, impecunious Irishman. Not a bound man. His hand slammed into the wall, making the mirror dance. Justin Fourrier.

Mr. Carver never required more than half a day on Saturday, unusual among the merchants in the city. Sometimes he didn't even require that. This, the nineteenth of October, 1765, was one of those days. But there was work for Michael to do, work for himself. And it must be done before the mob moved against the paper.

As Michael walked toward the bridge a strangeness about the street impressed itself on him. Except for the muffled bells of Saint Michael's, there was an almost deadly quiet. To the last man passersby were on edge, nervous, as if waiting for something they feared. Even the gutter rats had lost their swagger of the past few months. With a start he realized that almost no women were abroad, save a few of the lowest sort. Something else was missing, as well. Uniforms. The soldiers were gone, not only the lone drunks, but the marching squads as well. There wasn't a whiff of a redcoat anywhere.

Hard by Saint Michael's he stopped again. Behind the tall, white columns small knots of tradesmen whispered urgently, scanning the street for hostile ears. Across the way, at the State House, a slow stream of men went in. Each, watchful, wore a frown. None came out. Even the beef market had caught the fever. The usual loud haggling was muted; customers were few and hurried. The vultures that lined the roof of the market were restless today. Few scraps were being thrown out for them; they were hungry.

Slowly Michael started on. Then he saw the gallows. Where Broad Street and Church Street met it stood, in the middle of the intersection, as tall as a two-story house. And on it hung a figure, swaying slightly in the breeze.

His steps faltered. Hangings took place down at White Point, near the low water mark. And there was no hanging scheduled. Oh, God. It couldn't be the Liberty Boys. They couldn't have hung some poor bastard.

As Michael hurried closer he could make out a sign hanging around the figure's neck. *Stamp Collector*, it said. That was impossible, he thought. Saxby was in England and Lloyd was holed up in Fort Johnson. Then, suddenly, he realized it wasn't a man. It was a dummy. He heaved a sigh of relief. A bundle of old clothes. An effigy. Or rather, three of them. The stamp collector was in the middle, with a devil on the right and a boot with a head stuck on it on the left. Across the bottom, in large letters, a sign said *Liberty and No Stamp Act*.

Periodically Dillon's spewed out men, mugs in hand, who laughed and toasted the gallows and laughed some more. Few of those scurrying past in the street seemed amused; they quickened their pace, eyes to the ground.

Michael started as a hand touched his shoulder, his fists half clenching. It was a smiling Byrne. "Admiring our handiwork, are you now?"

"Your work, you say? The Liberty Boys?"

"Mine among others, Michael, lad. Mine among others." He ignored the second question. His tense smile grew wider by the minute.

"I'd not be admitting it, were I you. The magistrates will no doubt be wanting to clap the lot of you in irons. There's nothing they'd like better than a public confession."

"Michael," Byrne scoffed, "You've not been paying close attention to what's happening. Half the magistrates are with us, and the other half don't matter." He shot a hand toward the scaffold. "That's been standing there for hours. Where are your constables to tear it down? Tell me that, now."

Michael shook his head. "Waiting for you all to come out in the open, so they can hang you."

"They'll have to hang the whole Assembly," Christopher said in a patronizing tone. He started for Dillon's, turning half-way there for one last crow. "The whole Assembly, lad."

Michael took a deep breath, and looked up at the gallows. All hell was about to break loose. No doubt of it. A fine time to be starting in trade.

At the bridge and the warehouse, trade was just beginning

to get under way again after the summer slowdown. The first of the year's rice crop was now reaching Charlestown, and the sudden deluge of goods, outgoing and incoming, hadn't yet been absorbed. The men still hustled about trying to catch up.

He wasted no time finding Jepson, who was overseeing the lading of six ships tied to the wharf. "Has the *Two Sisters* finished loading yet?"

"No, si—. No, it has not."

"Then load an extra three barrels of rice with Mr. Carver's consignment."

"Three barrels?" The Scots burr thickened. "Three barrels?"

"Yes, three barrels. Can't you do it?"

"Well, no, I mean, yes, I can. But I never heard of changing a shipment by only three barrels."

"Well, you've heard it now. And find Mr. Hollister for me. He's usually around the wharves this time of day."

Jepson sniffed. "Aye. Find Mr. Hollister and load three whole barrels."

Michael climbed to his office. He took the wrapped packet of instructions for the *Two Sisters'* captain from the desk and undid the string. He pulled one out and laid it on the desk. Proceeds from sixty tierces of rice to be reinvested in fine Bohea tea at the best price the captain could find. Carefully he copied it over again, adding three more barrels.

Once it had been done he felt a queer excitement. It was begun. He took out a small ledger and opened it to the first page. His hand shook slightly as he dipped the pen. October 19, 1765. Three barrels rice. To Liverpool, England on the *Two Sisters*. For a time he simply looked at the entry. The first.

A rap came at the door. He slipped the ledger into a drawer. "Come in."

Peter Hollister pushed open the door and lumped his bulk down in a chair with a wheeze. "Jepson said you wanted to see me. Mr. Carver wants to buy, eh? Jepson's burr was so strong all I could make out was three barrels, or what sounded like it. What got him so upset?"

"Mr. Carver does want to buy," Michael said carefully. "Three barrels of rice."

"Three barrels?" Except for the burr Hollister duplicated Jepson's tone exactly. He peered at Michael over the tops of his spectacles. "How can I make a profit on three barrels?"

Michael found it hard not to laugh. Hollister made his living as a middleman, buying from small planters who needed ready money but weren't willing to hire transport down to Charlestown. Where merchants of note dealt in hundreds of barrels, or even thousands, Hollister sold perhaps fifty or sixty at a time. And for the prices he paid he could have made a profit giving it away.

"Mr. Carver's one of your best customers, perhaps your very best, for indigo and tobacco as well as rice."

"All the same, three barrels. Why I'd lose all my profit just on cartage to get it here. There'd have to be a premium over the going price."

"It has to be first quality, mind you," Michael said as if he hadn't heard. "We want no seconds or thirds."

Hollister puffed up. "My rice is always first quality. All of it."

"We've been finding barrels of midlings, and even small rice, in what you bring lately."

"Impossible. I check every barrel myself." The thought of Hollister heaving his fat around to check for quality made Michael's mouth twitch. The same thought seemed to strike Hollister. "Well, most of them," he admitted grudgingly.

"We'll not pay full market for seconds or thirds."

"I tell you I deliver first quality only. I guarantee it. And I won't take a shilling less than the full market price."

"Very well, then," Michael said as if conceding the point. He stuck his hand out. "Full market price it is."

Hollister grasped the outstretched hand with a sharp nod. "Done." Suddenly it dawned on him that he'd forgotten all about the premium. He deflated in his chair. "You may be an Irishman, but I still say Carver got a Shylock when he got you."

"No need to be unpleasant," Michael said mildly. "A glass of wine on the bargain?"

"It's probably the only profit I'll make on this," Hollister grumbled.

Hollister took the offered glass, gulped the wine down, and held it out for more. Michael obligingly filled it again, then corked the bottle and put it away before the other drank it all.

"You'll have it here this afternoon, then?"

"Umph. What? This afternoon? Why so quickly? There must be two or three thousand barrels in this warehouse right now." He set the glass back on the desk and pushed it hopefully toward Michael.

Michael picked it up and set it aside with his own, ignoring Hollister's sigh. "I want it now. From the looks of things this morning the stamp trouble could blow up at any minute."

"Oh, it'll be a rare show, all right," Hollister said absently, his attention on the wine cabinet.

"Rare show? They'll be bringing the redcoats down from the barracks if they don't watch out."

"Soldiers?" That brought the fat man's attention round. "You don't think the soldiers would actually come out?"

Michael stared at him in surprise. "Perhaps, and perhaps not. I said it might."

Hollister rubbed the back of his hand over slack lips. "I'd better be going," he muttered.

"The rice. This afternoon?"

"What? Oh, yes, yes. This afternoon." He bolted out of his chair and waddled hurriedly down the stairs.

Michael watched him leave from the window. From the way he kept rubbing at his mouth it was plain he wanted a drink in the worst way possible. Why did I have to mention soldiers, Michael thought. And why should Hollister be so afraid of them?

Michael got out the bottle again and poured himself another glass. Let Hollister cringe. Michael Fallon was on his way. In a few short months his small stock of money would be doubled, then doubled again. There was nothing could stop him now.

As long as he was there, he decided, he might as well work

on the tangle Wynfrey had made. The first he opened bore evidence of the previous clerk's theft. He hesitated; made the correcting entries; and kept no separate record. There was nothing to be done about Wynfrey. He pressed on with the balancing, heedless of forenoon turning into sultry afternoon.

"Last chance 'fore dark! Snappers! Groupers!"

The fishmonger's cry pulled him up out of the ledgers. It was growing dim outside, and he noticed that his eyes hurt from working in the fading light. The rumbles and thumps of the warehouse were stilled. He might well be the last man there. He'd worked through dinner, and if he didn't hurry he might miss supper as well.

Lost in his own thoughts about the price of tea in Liverpool, he was almost to Church Street before he realized he was forcing his way through an ever-thickening crowd.

There were no merchants, he saw immediately, no planters. A few artisans dotted the crowd, men dressed well enough, but with printer's ink on their hands or the smell of glue or woodshavings about them. The rest were the worst sort, dock-idlers and gutter sweepings, layabouts and alley trash, sailors off ships in the harbor full of rum and itch, backcountry wagoneers passing around the product of their stills, men with hard, eager eyes. The gallows still stood in the intersection. Low murmurs filled the air.

Then a half-dozen men, soberly dressed and respectable appearing, climbed over the gallows. Silence fell. They loosened ropes and eased down the figures, the scaffold creaking under their feet. The crowd parted slightly to let a six-horse team pull a wagon to the gallows, closing again behind it as it passed.

Michael watched as the six, now in the wagon, set the figures up on poles. The "Liberty and No Stamp Act" banner was shifted next, set up high over the dummies. A palpable anticipation hung in the air. Michael started pushing back the way he had come.

It was harder going back than going in. More people had arrived after him, and more were arriving every minute.

Late-comers jostled for room as if afraid they might miss something. There was laughter in the crowd now, but laughter with an edge to it. They had the air of a crowd at a carnival, or at a hanging. He didn't intend to stay long enough to see which it was. He pushed free of the press and hurried through the verge.

"Hey, you!"

In an instant a semi-circle of half-crouching men formed in front of him, half grinning drunkenly, the other half deadly grim. He glanced over his shoulder, and there was another group behind him.

A long-nosed man in a dirty coat, with a deep scar across his nose and cheek and the lower half of his left ear gone, pushed himself forward with a swagger. "And where might you be going in such a hurry, me fine swell? Huh?"

Michael shifted for a firmer footing on the cobblestones and watched warily for the first sign of a rush. "I forgot some papers for my master," he said firmly. "I was just going back for them."

Lop-ear spat. "Ain't taking part in the festivities, eh?"

"Seemed to be leaving in an awful hurry just to be going for some papers," somebody in the pack shouted. "Maybe he don't want to take part."

A shaven-headed hulk with the burn scars of a blacksmith on his forearms shook a heavy fist. "Let me squeeze the truth out of him."

"Maybe he's a stamp collector."

Michael waited for someone to laugh, but no laugh came. Were they blind? They knew who the collectors were, and they knew what they looked like. They couldn't be that drunk, but even the boozy grins faded into grim bleakness. They inched closer, like a hyena pack almost certain of its victim. Suddenly he saw Hollister pass by with a bottle in his hand.

"He knows me," he said quickly. "Hollister! Peter Hollister!"

One of the men caught the fat trader by the arm and pulled him into the circle. "Do you know this man?" lop-ear asked.

Hollister peered at Michael blearily. Closing one eye he pushed his head forward as if to get a better look, then nodded vigorously. "Know him. Wants it all put down with troops. Soldiers in the city. Heard him." He nodded again, and nearly fell. Lop-ear grabbed him to keep him up.

"He's in his cups," Michael said. "He doesn't know what he's saying. Look at him."

The pack shuffled closer. "You picked him," Lop-ear snarled. Michael set himself.

Suddenly there was a break in the circle, and Christopher Byrne forced his way through. He threw himself in front of Michael and whirled to face the motley crew. "Easy, lads, easy. You all know me."

"We know you, Byrne," Lop-ear growled, "but he's a stamp collector."

"A stamp collector!" Christopher turned and looked Michael over from head to foot. He threw back his head and laughed. "A stamp collector dressed like that? Since when would they be making a stamp collector out of a clerk?" The laugh cut off short. He glared at the lop-eared man.

Lop-ear shifted uncomfortably. "Well, he wants us should be put down with troops. Hollister here heard him say it."

Christopher rounded on the fat drunk. "Did you now, Hollister? Can't you men see he's too drunk to recognize his own mother?" An edge of doubt appeared in some of the faces, a thin one. "You there, Hollister." The trader looked around, blearily, until one of the circle turned him in the right direction. "Do you know me, Hollister?"

Hollister stared at him unsteadily. "I, I do." He blinked uncertainly and looked around as if for a clue. Finally he took a deep breath and straightened with saturated dignity. "You are Isaac Morton, the silversmith."

Hoots of laughter ran around the circle. Christopher threw back his head and roared. Even Michael had to smile. "Isaac Morton, is it?" Christopher crowed. "And him no more than five foot three and bald as a baby's bottom, to boot."

Before the laughter had a chance to fade Byrne turned to

Michael, his voice low. "Say you want to march with them. Say it, man. Be quick."

Michael hesitated only a moment. Christopher had just saved his life. Of that he was sure. He might be doing it again. "Gentlemen," he said loudly, and the laughter faded as they stopped to listen. "Gentlemen, I'd admire to march with you, if you'll have me."

The men cheered. "Welcome," Lop'ear roared, "to the cause of liberty!"

The wagon with its effigies began to move through the crowd, who split to let it by and fell in behind it. Waiting was over. They were full of vigor and liberally laced with alcohol and jovial shouts. Placards appeared, proclaiming Liberty, or the Rights of Englishmen, or Damnation to the Stamp Act. Here and there, onimously, torches flared into light, and cutlasses were taken from beneath coats. With gathering strength they marched down Broad Street to the Bay.

Michael leaned over to speak for Christopher's ear alone. "As soon as we've gone a little way I'll slip off. Thanks. I owe you my life."

Christopher glanced quickly around before answering. "You do, and we'll neither of us escape the tar and feathers. Look you. There are hundreds round us. If you want to repay me, see this thing through." He straightened and marched along as solemnly as the rest.

Michael took his own look round. There *were* hundreds, and more joining as they went. And Lop-ear and blacksmith seemed as occupied with Byrne and Fallon as with shouting and sign-waving. It might be his imagination, and Christopher's too, but it was no time to find out. He marched.

The jostling men, flooding the street from side to side, turned down the Bay behind the wagon. The church bells kept their muffled knell. Householders doused their lights as the seething torchlit mob approached.

When the men crowded onto Tradd Street, doubling back toward the center of the city, Michael began to wonder. They seemed to be moving with a purpose. "Where are we bound?'' he called to Christopher over the tumult.

A gap-toothed ruffian with one eye answered him in a drunken shout. "Saxby's house!"

"Saxby? What in God's name for? He's in England."

Instantly Lop-ear and the blacksmith appeared. From somewhere Lop-ear had acquired a cutless, and the other had a bludgeon as long as his arm. "Question is, are you with us, or against us?" Around them men turned to hear his answer.

"I'm here, aren't I," he snapped. Most of them read the heat in his voice as fervor and turned away. Lop-ear, though, gave him a sharp look before melting back into the mob.

The wagon stopped in front of a house set flush with the street. The halt was disorderly, those at the rear trying to push their way forward, pressing to be at the front. Michael was jammed between the one-eyed man and two drunken sailors, with not even room to lift a hand. Slowly, with shouts of "Quit pushing, damn you," and "Stop shoving or I'll carve your guts," the churning ceased. An eerie silence fell over them all.

The men from the wagon stalked to the house door, two dozen bullyboys hard at their heels. "Open! Open! Deliver the paper! Open!"

Finally the door opened a crack, and they poured through, slamming it back against the wall. Shouts drifted out into the silent evening, and the sound of furniture overturning and glass breaking. A woman screamed, and the echo of it stayed in the air long after the cry was gone.

The mob fed on it, gorged on it. A low, animal growl ran down the street. The hair on the back of Michael's neck began to rise. Axes were brandished in the air, and iron bars. The sailors pressed against him managed to raise belaying pins. And all the while they growled, a deep, gutteral sound that came from a level less than human.

Those who had gone inside came out, and stood in silhouette against the lighted hall.

"There's no stamped paper here."

A moan, almost of disappointment, answered.

"Burn it!" came a scream.

"There's no paper!"

The sober-dressed men moved into the crowd, soothing, quieting. Here one clapped a man on the shoulder and spoke in another's ear. There one pushed down a raised club, speaking quietly and quickly. Bit by bit the mob began to change. Smiles broke out. They had something else to focus on, now.

He looked for Christopher. Byrne was smiling, as if all was as it should be. The way he knew it would be. He was talking quietly to the men around him, turning their scowls to anticipatory smiles.

From the wagon the leaders produced a coffin, and lifted it on their shoulders like pallbearers. *American Liberty*, it said on the side in big letters. As if by signal the church bells began a slow toll. And the march fell in, in funeral time. Every man put on a solemn expression, or tried to; but laughter, quickly hushed, kept breaking over the slow footsteps of the crowd.

Michael looked back. The door still stood open, light streaming into the street, onto the marchers as they passed. Their faces seemed fixed, gargoyles in the night. The door remained open until long after the last of them was gone.

Up the peninsula they turned, up the length of the city, clutching their torches, fingering their cutlasses and clubs. Street by street the cortege grew, and the newcomers had no somber air. At every corner they joined, apprentices and tavern girls, laborers and blowses. They came singing and laughing and passing bottles of wine, and their festive air began to infect the entire march.

The mob pressed on. Suddenly Michael realized where they were going. The barracks where the redcoats were. The march was heading straight for them.

If the soldiers were forted inside the barracks, meaning to fire their muskets through the windows, there might be a chance to survive. If they were waiting in the darkness, however, waiting to move in on a fire-and-advance-by-ranks, it was likely to be the end for hundreds.

They rounded onto the green before the barracks, the soldier's drillfield. Michael held back, keeping to the edge, waiting. The windows of the barracks were dark. There was no spark of light, no reflection off a gunbarrel or bayonet, nothing. It had to be the fire-and-advance, then.

The men with torches moved in the dark, and bonfires, laid beforehand, suddenly flared high. One by one the effigies were taken from the wagon and tossed to the flames. Ever louder shouts greeted each one. The last, the stamp collector, drew a howl Michael could feel in his bones. The mob shrieked, faces contorted, flushed with more than the heat of the fires. Then Michael saw a head at a barracks window, and then another, and a dozen more. Just short of taking cover he stopped. There wasn't a musket in sight. They were just watching.

Now the leaders began directing men in digging a hole. One of them brandished a prayer book. The rest brought the coffin closer. It appeared they would hold a funeral for Liberty.

Out of the corner of his eye Michael saw Byrne slipping by. He caught hold of his arm. "Christopher, you knew there was no stamped paper at Saxby's. You knew before a man went inside."

Byrne drew himself up, and smiled wryly. "All right, Michael. I knew. Saxby's not even back from England yet. What of it?"

"What of it? Why? That's what of it. Why break into a house, tear it half apart, terrify the people in it?"

"Power, that's the reason. No, not what you're thinking. Not just the power of the mob running wild. Tonight we entered the house of a prominent King's man. We built bonfires where they toast a barracks full of redcoats. They didn't stop us, Michael. They didn't even try. They couldn't. We'll do it again. And they still won't be able to stop us. Soon or late, the English will come to realize that it's us who are running things here. Not William Bull in the State House, and not their redcoat soldiers, either. Us. The people."

"And what do you do then? What do you do when the soldiers don't stay in their barracks, and the Royal Navy drops anchor in the harbor? What then?"

A familiar, mocking smile flitted over Christopher's face. "Why as to that, ask Mr. Gadsden, or perhaps Mr. Timothy, at the *Gazette*. What you want is not for the likes of me to be knowing."

Michael backed away from him. He felt cold inside, and angry, and the noise from around the fires seemed to fade. "Good God! You're wanting it, aren't you? You're talking rebellion. Man, don't you know any better? You're Irish. You should know what rebellion brings in your bones, win or lose. And it's seldom win, now, is it?"

"Hsst, Michael." Christopher looked around them quickly. "You're talking things that should be left unsaid. See Gadsden." He moved deeper into the darkness. His voice came, deadly serious. "There's a tidal wave coming, Michael. You must ride it out, or be swept away."

Rebellion. Michael stalked away. These fools ran toward it, dancing over the precipice with never an inkling. You knew what it meant, in Ireland. You sucked it in with the milk at your mother's breast. Families lost. Land lost. Hope lost. Raging fires in the long twilight before an endless night, that was rebellion's harvest.

When he passed through Carver's gates on Church Street his weary steps dragged on the carriage path toward the stables. A rustle in the shrubbery brought his head up. Mr. Carver stepped out of the shadows. They looked at each other silently. Finally the older man spoke.

"There was trouble tonight, Michael. Were you part of it?"

"I was there. I wasn't part of it."

"Come inside." He sounded tired as well, or perhaps sad.

Michael followed him noiselessly into the study. A pool of candlelight caught the front edge of the desk. Carver sat behind it, his face in shadows. The light lay like a barrier between them.

"What happened?"

Slowly at first, as he skirted around Christopher's involvement, then in quicker, sharper tones, Michael told of George Saxby's house and the bonfires, until the feel of the mob was in the room and their howls seemed to echo behind the walls. He stopped abruptly, and they both seemed poised for a moment, listening to fading cries of anger.

"So, it has begun. I had hoped—." Carver's voice stopped.

Michael felt a strange desire to reassure him. "They're hooligans, sir. A mob. Just a mob."

"It always begins with a mob, Michael," the old man said softly.

"It does, and often enough, when it's all over, it ends with one, too."

Carver made a sound in the darkness. "My father used to tell me when I was a boy that next year will not be like this year." He shook his head. "It's faster now. Tomorrow won't be like today. No, more than that. The next hour will not be like this hour. At times I expect the earth to open momentarily and swallow everything I know."

"A tidal wave. Someone said tonight that it's a tidal wave, and we must ride it out or be swept away."

The old man nodded. "And who can ride a tidal wave? No mortal man. We can only continue to live our lives as best we can." Carver shifted in his chair. "I'm having a reception next Thursday evening. I had some thought of canceling it, given what's happened, but I won't. My daughter informs me that I am most particularly to invite you."

"Sir?" Michael's head came up in the darkness. "Of course, I must refuse."

"You will come, Michael. Times are changing. Faster than we can catch hold of, perhaps. You'll come. You'll be my guest."

"Then it will be my pleasure, sir," Michael said levelly.

Carver rose and leaned into the light, his hand outstretched. "Until the wave catches us."

Michael stepped into the light and took the hand firmly.

For the first time since he had met him the merchant looked his age, and more. "Until the wave catches us."

"Good night, Michael."

"Good night, sir."

It was cool outside. Michael stood gazing into the darkness. He had begun in trade and, even more of a wonder, Elizabeth had taken notice of him. Two parts of his dream, both happening on the same day, both happening long before he had any right to expect. And yet, they might have come too late. He looked up to her window, but the house was a dark mass looming against the night.

A tidal wave, and they would all be swept away.

9

When Michael returned to his room the afternoon of the party, Christopher Byrne was waiting for him.

"There's been talk about you, lad. You shouldn't be avoiding us."

Michael took his best black suit from the clothes press. It was true; he'd avoided Byrne, and the daily street crowds, and even Dillon's. "What kind of talk?"

"You should be with us, Michael." Christopher swung his feet down off the table with a thump. "It's a time for choosing sides. There'll be no neutrals in this."

"I should be with you? Like last night? For God's sake, man, Henry Laurens is as much against the stamps as you, even though he is against Gadsden's mob."

"I'd nothing to do with that," Christopher said swiftly.

"It was your crowd, just the same. Forcing their way into his house with lampblacked faces, disguised as sailors. When he started calling names in spite of it, they were quick enough to leave. A sham and a farce. A member of the Assembly, and treated so."

Christopher shifted uncomfortably. "Perhaps it was an excess. Michael, listen to me."

Michael threw the suit on the bed and whirled to face him. "No, you listen. I'm not in this, not on either side. I've my own life to lead, and it doesn't include being pulled down for a rebellion, no matter how grand and glorious it seems on the surface. I'm not in it, and that's that."

"Well." Christopher rose slowly, and paused at the door. "There's more to this than paper, lad. More than a cutpurse mob. You know it, and I know it. I said there'll be no neutrals, and there won't. Choose a side before it's chosen for you."

The door closed quietly behind him. Michael began to brush his suit. They wouldn't be content with silence. Now they must come after him. Well, he was no part of it, nor would be. He brushed harder. No part of it.

Critically Elizabeth examined herself in the drawing-room mirror. Blue velvet always gave her eyes a vivid color, and it was cut just low enough, no longer a child's high neck, nor yet as low as half those that would be worn to the party. Not low enough to excite her father, but low enough for what was to be done. At the thought she tingled with anticipation.

Tonight she'd be a woman, though a youthful, innocent one. Innocent enough to pique this Michael Fallon's interest, but woman enough not to put him off. Instinct told her that innocence was more the way with this man than flaunting. She'd make him want to protect her. Elizabeth smiled.

Her father came in, nodding at the flower arrangements and the gleaming brass. "Excellent, Elizabeth. The room couldn't look better." His gaze took in her dress, and he hesitated.

She caught the hesitation; before he could speak she was straightening his collar, though it didn't need it. Nothing, she knew, made a man feel at once the center of attention and yet off balance so well as having a woman straighten his clothes. "There. We mustn't have you disarrayed when the guests will be arriving any minute."

"What? Yes, of course." He'd lost the moment, he realized, without knowing quite how. Still, it was just as well. She was becoming a woman, and it wasn't too soon for her to dress it. She could well be married within a year. "That reminds me. Mr. Fourrier sent a note. He and young Justin may arrive quite late."

"Justin," she said blankly.

"Yes, child. Justin. What's the matter?"

"Nothing. It's just—well, after what happened I thought he would absent himself."

"Not come? Don't you want him here, Elizabeth?"

"Of course I do, Papa," she said quickly. "Don't be

silly." The bell rang, and Seth passed on his way to answer it. "Come, we must greet them."

He gave her his arm with a frown. It wouldn't disappoint him greatly if she turned from Justin Fourrier. But they'd been as much as betrothed for years. Elizabeth had seemed at least content with it, sometimes eager. How could she grow so cool, so fast?

The first guests entered. He covered his thoughts with a smile and a greeting.

Michael waited till well after dark before leaving his room. He'd arrive fashionably late, neither the first to come nor the last, and he'd arrive by the front door. If Carver wanted a guest, not a servant, that was what Michael would give him.

When Seth opened the door, he gaped at Michael for an instant; then he took his hat with a broad grin and led him in. He made the announcement in a ringing voice. "Mr. Michael Shane Fallon."

A number of the guests turned. Some stared on recognizing him; others simply examined his clothing critically. He was, he knew, a crow among peacocks. More than one woman, though, fluttering her fan a little more rapidly, thought him a hawk among jays. A buzz started as they asked who he might be, a shocked buzz when they were told.

Carver came to greet him immediately. "Michael. I'm glad you came."

"My pleasure, sir."

Elizabeth laid her hand on her father's wrist. "I'm sure you know my daughter, Elizabeth," he said, a twinkle in his eye.

Michael made an elegant leg to her. "I have had the pleasure of meeting your charming and beautiful daughter, sir. Miss Elizabeth."

"Perhaps you'd be so kind as to get me a glass of punch, Mr. Fallon," she said, smiling. From the corner of her eye she saw her father's surprise. "We must make him feel at home, Papa."

"Indeed. For now I leave him to you."

Elizabeth smiled up at him after her father had gone. "You heard my father, Mr. Fallon. You're in my care."

"I believe it's customarily the other way round, Miss Elizabeth. I'll fetch you the punch, now."

She held out her hand. "I'll go with you."

Hesitating just a second, he took it on his arm. Her touch was like a flame. He ladled punch for both of them, hardly able to think; she was standing so close. "It's a lovely party," he said, and cursed the inanity of it.

"Thank you." She eyed him over the cup rim. "May I call you Michael?"

"If you wish, Miss Elizabeth."

"Done, then, Michael," she said with a laugh that showed her perfect small teeth. "Now you must call me Elizabeth."

"That I will not. 'Tis a thing for intimates and family. So would your father think, and rightly."

She wrinkled her nose. "Poo. It's no such thing. If you don't, I'll, I'll call you Poo. So there."

It was Michael's turn to laugh. "A dire fate. Very well. I surrender. Elizabeth."

"Mr. Jean-Baptiste Fourrier and Mr. Justin Fourrier of Les Chenes."

Many eyes turned to the door, Michael's among them. He'd never seen the elder Fourrier. What sort of man had produced Justin?

In any company it would have been Justin who drew the eye first, but Jean-Baptiste who kept it. To his son's satins, he was plainly dressed in black velvets. At first glance he seemed a shorter, gaunter copy, Justin with every spare inch and ounce boiled away, but the second left no doubt which was the original. There was power to him. Cold, dark power. And if Justin's eyes were vulture's, his were viper's. They looked for no weak prey, but took the strong as well.

With a start Michael realized that Jean-Baptiste was headed for him, Justin trailing behind. Elizabeth had disappeared from his side. He straightened himself.

Carver had seen the Fourriers' direction, and moved to cut them off. Now he stepped in front of them. His voice was hearty. "It has been long since you've been in my house, Jean-Baptiste. It's good to have you here."

Jean-Baptiste motioned toward Michael. "That is the one. There could not be two to fit that description. What does he do here?"

Carver stiffened. "He is a guest, Jean-Baptiste." Steel crept into his voice. "My guest, as you are."

The planter's eyes flicked coolly from Michael to the merchant. "He is a servant."

"And he is my guest."

Jean-Baptiste's lips thinned. "Your—guest—attacked my son with a sword. For striking a free man, the penalty is twenty-one lashes with a cat-o'-nine-tails. So? For attempted murder, how much?" The eyes weighed carefully. "Five hundred lashes, perhaps more. I wish no death for an attempt. But, a lesson must be learned. Perhaps seven hundred."

"No," Carver said calmly. "I would be called to testify, my friend."

"You would testify against a gentleman, for such a one as this?" His voice was suddenly expressionless.

Michael felt as though he was hiding behind Carver. He had to speak. "I've no fear of an honest hearing before an honest magistrate."

Jean-Baptiste eyed him unblinkingly. Slowly he turned to Carver. Once more for a Fourrier Michael had ceased to exist. "I will speak to you of this later, Carver." The Fourriers turned, and strolled across the room.

It took an iron effort of will for Michael to keep still. The muscle in his cheek jumped with the force of his rage.

"I'm glad to see you can control that temper upon occasion," Carver said.

"Upon occasion, sir."

"Yes." The merchant hid a smile. "Now, Michael, there are men here you must meet. Young Rutledge first—"

Michael was led away, hearing no more than half of what was said. Where had Elizabeth gone? She'd asked for him, and called him Michael. And run away without a word!

He roused himself; John Rutledge was saying "—and Bull announced this morning that all the stamped paper's been off-loaded at Fort Johnson."

"Then it's all been for nothing," Michael said softly.

Rutledge halted his glass halfway to his mouth, surprise on his patrician face. Just Michael's age, the lawyer was already spoken of as a man to watch in the colony's politics. He looked at Michael now as if seeing him for the first time. "Exactly, Mr. Fallon," he said finally. "For nothing. This time."

Most of the talk was inconsequential chatter, though; the Middletons sternly kept to social fripperies. After half a dozen conversations and twice that many cups, he slipped outside to the veranda. Elizabeth. Elizabeth. The wine didn't help.

He leaned on the bannister and breathed the dark night air deeply. It helped sweep away the wine fumes. A faint noise drew his eye to the end of the veranda, on the edge of the moonlight. He could barely make out a woman. It almost looked like—yes, it was Elizabeth. He started down the porch toward her.

Elizabeth smiled to herself. When he'd not seen her, she'd had to kick the bannister. Now she fanned herself slowly and moved down into the garden, careful that her steps were slower than his. When his first step crunched on the shell path behind her, she whirled as if startled.

"Why, why, Michael. You surprised me."

He stopped short. Why could this girl make him feel awkward when no woman ever had? "I'm sorry. I didn't mean to. I'll leave you."

She put a hand on his arm. "There's no need for that. I would enjoy your company."

She tucked her arm in his with the casual assurance that he'd do as she wanted. He walked beside her, breathing in her scent, aware of the moonlight on her shoulders, dappled through the leaves. But Elizabeth was Carver's daughter.

"This is wrong, Elizabeth. You, walking alone in the dark with a man."

"Poo."

He sighed. "It could be dangerous."

She turned to him, eyes luminous. "Would you be dangerous?" she asked ingenuously.

"I—" He looked down at her almost in a trance. Those half-parted lips, so soft, so inviting. He swept her into his arms and kissed her fiercely, long and deep. Suddenly he pushed her away. "Oh, God," he said thickly. "That dangerous."

Lavender lynx eyes regarded him for a minute, then her arms were around him, her face buried in his coat. "Don't say that. Don't." She trembled. His kiss had been more than she'd expected, more than she'd dreamed. She tingled down to her toes; her lips felt swollen.

Gently he smoothed her hair. "You don't know, child. I'll take you inside."

"But I'm not a child, Michael. I'm a woman. I have a woman's feelings. For you." She let her voice drop plaintively. "You do have some feeling for me, don't you?" She held her breath.

His face twisted painfully, and his hands felt suddenly helpless. "I love you, girl," he said at last. "God help me, I love you. But it cannot be. Your father likes me well enough, but I'm scarcely what he'd want in a suitor. He'd set the constables on me as soon as he found out."

Elizabeth smiled to herself and sighed in relief. Thank goodness he'd brought it up. She hadn't been sure how to. "Then he mustn't find out."

"Elizabeth, I can't—"

"For me? Please?"

And then he had her in his arms again, kissing her. And she was kissing him back. And he was drowning. Drowning. Thank God for kind Mary. Lightning bolts indeed.

The next evening the *Carolina Packet,* under Captain Robson, dropped anchor. Rumors flashed that more stamped paper was on board, that George Saxby was among the passengers, a hundred wilder things. Men howled against the stamps and all who supported them. Then delegations from the Assembly and the Liberty Boys were invited on board the ship by Robson. There were no stamps. There was no George Saxby. There was news, however. Saxby was on the *Heart of Oak*, Captain Gunn, that had sailed on the hour with the *Packet*. She must make Charlestown soon. The speechmakers withdrew, the gatherings dispersed to wait.

After a weekend of secluded corners with Elizabeth and nights with Mary, Michael came late to the warehouse door on Monday. Catching hold of a boy running by, he pressed twopence on him. "A pot of coffee, Sam, hot and black, as soon as you can get it here. The rest is yours." As Sam darted off he shouted, "And strong enough to float a spoon." There was much to be done if the ships were to clear before the first.

He climbed to his office, but for once he couldn't fix his mind on the trade, not even after half Sam's coffee was gone. He was uncomfortable over Elizabeth.

He didn't like it, going behind her father's back like that. And that was ridiculous. He'd tumbled many a girl behind her father's back, or under his nose, if need be. But he respected Thomas Carver, and, more, liked him. And Elizabeth was no tumble in the hay.

He made a noise at even thinking of her so. She was a goddess, a virgin goddess, and he'd keep her so. He meant to marry her, when he was a merchant and not a penniless bondsman. He'd marry the girl, and he'd not besmirch her honor in the meanwhile, neither by allowing their snugglings to be known nor by allowing them to go too far.

Faith of the Lord, but it was hard, though. In her innocence the girl did things, letting her hands wander where they shouldn't. And her kisses were enough to turn a man upsidedown and crosseyed. Three little days, and he couldn't have made it sane without Mary.

She'd marked it, had Mary, with a catty remark that earned her a smack on the bottom. And then there'd been a spell of making up. A long spell.

When Christopher barged in at mid-morning Michael shook his head. "Not a word. I've work to be done, no time to do it."

"Too much time between some mort's legs. You should keep your women in their place, and that's not interfering with your politics, even in a roundabout way. Tell the tart to leave over."

"Watch your mouth, man. She's no tart." He stopped; he hadn't meant to snap like that. "A gentleman," he said in a lighter tone, "never talks about his lady."

"But we're neither of us gentlemen, lad. We're Irish." He whooped at his own humor. "Look you, now. Since Saxby's back—."

"Saxby's back? When?"

Christopher dropped into the extra chair. "Lord, man. Did she keep you that wrapped up, then, that you don't know what's happened? Saxby's ship arrived two days ago. He knew the temper of the town, and came ashore at Fort Johnson, to hole up with Lloyd. Then, yesterday afternoon, this made the rounds." He tossed a folded broadside on the desk. "Surely you heard the celebration, the church bells ringing?"

"I took it for more of your lot carrying on." The sheet purported to be a free and voluntary statement of George Saxby and Caleb Lloyd. Because their office had proven so odious and disagreeable to the people, it said, they would not carry out the duties of it until the question could be decided in England.

"Is this legitimate?"

"Aye, man. They had it rowed across to the city yesterday before services. It's real enough. Come down the Bay at the foot of Broad, and you'll see. Saxby and Lloyd should be here soon."

Michael snatched his hat and followed.

The streets were packed from side to side when they arrived and they had to force their way an inch at a time. The crowd was even bigger than on the night of the gallows, Michael saw. It was the same crowd, too—sailors and alley sweepings, doxies and tosspots, mixed with mechanics and artisans. This time the mob was definitely festive. He refused more than one proffered bottle, but there wasn't a hint of anger at it. The drinkers were happy.

"The mob as usual, Christopher?" Michael asked wryly.

"Look you to the balconies, man, and the windows."

Every window above the crowd was filled, the balconies packed tight—crammed with silk-coated men. He recognized several of them, planters and merchants. Including, he was surprised to see, Mr. Carver.

The merchant saw him at the same instant, and also seemed surprised. Michael frowned. Did Carver think he was in the cause? Perhaps he took his presence here for proof. After a moment Carver nodded and returned to watching the river through a spyglass.

A boat was making its way to shore, a Union Jack at the head of it. Then a puff of air spread the flag slightly; the word Liberty was stitched boldly across the center. A shout went up along the river. Silence fell as two men were helped ashore. The welcoming delegation, their friends who had arranged this, formed nervously around them. A way opened before them, a path to a platform built on the back of a wagon.

After a moment's hesitation the escort moved toward the improvised stage. The men inside their circle seemed calmer than they. Michael recognized the spare features of Caleb Lloyd. The other, prosperously portly, must be George Saxby.

It was Saxby who was first to mount the platform. For a moment he surveyed the throng. Taking a deep breath he held aloft a rolled parchment.

"This," he said loudly, "is my sworn declaration." In the quiet his words carried to the furthest reaches of the press. "Until the united application of the several colonies for the repeal of the Stamp Act is received, and until it is known whether the Parliament will still determine to enforce that act, I will not exercise the office of Stamp Agent. This I do solemnly declare and protest before God Almighty."

The street exploded in shouts and cheers. Saxby solemnly handed the written copy of his pledge to his escort and left the platform to be replaced by Lloyd. Once more silence fell and once more the pledge was made.

At his final word a solid mass of noise rose. It seemed

every man in the street was shouting at the top of his lungs.
Church bells began to ring, just a few at first, then more and
more, till every bell in the city was pealing. Drums appeared,
and fiddles, horns, and hautboys, playing a score of tunes
that merged into the pandemonium. Over it all cannon from
the Artillery Company and ships at anchor sounded their own
salute.

Someone had fetched the Liberty flag from the boat, and
with it in the fore the two men were paraded down the street,
Saxby looking overwhelmed, Lloyd relieved.

With a start Michael realized that Christopher was shouting at him. "What?"

"They're taking them to Dillon's," the other shouted.
"Will you come with us?"

Michael thought of Mr. Carver and shook his head. "No,
you go on. I must see someone."

The flow swept Christopher away. As Michael struggled
against it, toward the house where he'd seen Carver, Justin
Fourrier came out on the steps. There were others of his ilk
with him, finely dressed planter's sons, casually arrogant. It
was Fourrier who caught Michael's eye.

Justin inspected the passing crush as if sniffing a bad odor.
"It's treason," he said to friends loudly. "Damnable
treason, and there should be hanging for it."

"Words to get a fancy rooster plucked," somebody called
from the crowd.

Fourrier bristled and glared. "They should send in troops
and hang the lot of you rabble," he shouted.

His friends quickly closed ranks, but the crowd only
jeered, those who took any notice at all. It was a day of
victory.

As Michael pushed out of the crowd and started up the
steps, Mr. Carver came through the door. "Sir, I wanted to
talk to you about—."

"Oh, Michael. I saw you with Christopher. I'm afraid
those rumors about him are right."

Michael could only stare blankly. "Rumors, sir? What
rumors?"

"I'm afraid he's one of the Liberty Boys."

"Because he was here? Mr. Carver, I was here, and a thousand others who're never a member of the Liberty Boys."

Carver shook his head. "No, he's one of them, all right."

Michael phrased his words carefully. "Will he lose his position should he be?"

"What? Oh, no. He's a good officer. Besides—" he lowered his voice"—the time may come when it's well to know someone in the radical camp." The crowd had thinned enough for them to move, and he led away from the direction they'd gone.

"Sir?" Michael couldn't believe his ears.

"It seems they've won today. The Liberty Boys, I mean. They've stopped the stamps—for the moment. But if it's to be stopped for good, we merchants will have to do it."

"Merchants! Do you mean to ally yourselves with Gadsden?"

"Come, Michael." Carver sighed patiently. "Merchants can't function when there's riot and anarchy. We need peace and law for trade to go on, contracts to be risked. And not law enforced by bayonets. We can't get it except by ending the Stamp Act."

"But how? You're scarcely one to march in the street, with the rabble here. Will you petition the King, sir?"

"Not the King. Our brother merchants in England. Colonial merchants owe hundreds of thousands of pounds to English merchants. However, we will say, due to the unrest and disorder brought on by the Stamp Act, we are unable to pay a farthing on what we owe. How long do you think it'll take them to start pounding on the doors of Parliament? I'll tell you, Michael, they may prate of rights at meetings of the Liberty Boys, but this battle will be fought and won, and open rebellion averted, for the value of trade."

On the first day of November, as Thomas Carver had predicted, the courts closed their doors, the Customs ceased issuing clearances, and the port of Charlestown closed.

Michael closed the door to Mr. Carver's study behind him

and walked over to warm his hands at the fire. "These March days may be warm enough, but the nights still think it's winter."

Carver finished bundling some papers and tied a cord around them. "It is unsafe to go to the bridge so late. Footpads took three last night. They grow bolder daily."

"In daylight, sir, I'd have to crack more sailors' heads. They blame the merchant houses for closing the port, and for their troubles with the soldiers."

Carver nodded. There were more than a thousand ships in the harbor, and not a one could stir from anchor. The sailors were ashore with no place to go, no work to do, and no money to spend. The soldiers said the sailors stole to finance their drinking; the sailors said they couldn't walk the street without being hauled off to the Provost. It was an explosive mixture, and someone was always striking sparks.

"Shipments from Mueller and Corwin are due any day," Michael went on. "Even leaving your own rice at the plantation, I'll have the devil's own time figuring where to put it." He turned suddenly. "It's going on for four months, sir, that nothing's gone out."

Carver rubbed his face with both hands. "Governments work slowly, Michael. We've been patient four months; we'll be patient four more, and four beyond that, if need be." He rose and took up his hat and stick.

"Are you going out, too, sir?"

"Yes. Another no doubt futile meeting at William Bull's house with the men who could stop all this, if they would. But Bull won't forget he's the lieutenant governor, and governor till another's appointed. Egerton Leigh won't forget he's a judge, and a representative of the law. And Gadsden won't forget he's Gadsden. Well, we must try, before this city stews to death in its own juice."

Michael thought about that as he made his way to the Bay. They must try. God's teeth, every man in Charlestown was trying for something different. Christopher Gadsden wanted rebellion. Thomas Carver wanted peace. Michael Fallon would settle for a resumption of trade.

Suddenly light flare in the darkness ahead as an alehouse door burst open, a soldier backpedalling out to fall in the dust. Even as the redcoat hit the ground two sailors in canvas pants and striped shirts were on him, pummeling him as he lay. Fool, Michael thought, to go into a sailors' tavern. A small knot of soldiers, coming around the corner, fell on the sailors instantly. Their arrival was a trigger, though. The alehouse suddenly disgorged a score of seamen swinging bottles and broken stools. Someone began shouting for the watch, till the shout was cut off by the thud of cudgel on flesh. Another squad of redcoats came down the street at the double and waded into the melee, rifle butts rising and falling.

Michael went on by. It wasn't the first such tonight, nor would it be the last.

The Bay was dark just below the Bridge. A scrape of shoe-leather against stone pulled him up. At first he saw nothing. Then something moved in the deep shadows. Clouds shifted, and revealed the shape in a gentleman's cloak. The man lifted his head.

"Mr. Gadsden!"

The man took a step toward Michael. "Fallon, isn't it? You're surprised to see me, I take it."

"It's been a dangerous place in the night, of late."

"I haven't found it so. I come here often. There are those who'd load a ship and sneak it out under cover of darkness if there wasn't an eye to watch. Though it may help that I let it be known I carry these." He hefted a stout stick and opened his cloak to show a brace of pistols. "It's the last night of it, though. Tomorrow they'll be allowed to sail, and no one will try to stop them."

"How can you be sure? Tonight's meeting can't be more than just getting under way."

"I know, Mr. Fallon. I know. I will arrive late, just as they're deadlocked and going hoarse from argument. Then I'll come to my senses, see that all this isn't doing any good. I'll throw my weight behind Thomas Carver and Henry Laurens. With us together Bull will come around, and the clearances will be given. Without the stamps, of course. By this time I think they'll swallow that without a murmur.''

"But why, then?" Michael asked. "Some say all this is to punish England, but I didn't think you were—."

He cut off short, and Gadsden chuckled. "That stupid, you were going to say?" He went on over Michael's protest. "No, it's not for England, all this. That fight's being fought by our merchants."

"Then there's no reason for it! It's hurting none but ourselves."

"And that's the reason for it, man! No, let me finish. If we won this without strain, we'd never be ready to fight when the price was clear, especially if the gains weren't clearly ours. Now, though, when the next fight comes, they'll all remember how damned old England forced our ships to stay in harbor and choked our trade. Oh yes, that's how they'll remember it. And they'll remember, too, how they stood shoulder to shoulder to fight it. Such are men's minds. Well, I'd better be going to that meeting."

"Mr. Gadsden, why are you telling me all this? And what in the devil's name is it you're after? Sir?"

Gadsden smiled and pulled his cloak around him. A few steps down the street, once more just a shape in the shadows, he turned.

"Your friends speak well of you, Mr. Fallon," he said. And he was gone.

10

Justin walked his horse through the icy fog on Broad Street. Pompey, who'd been waiting for his return home, dashed out to take the reins. Justin swept by, intent on the fire inside.

His father was in the study when he entered, bent over his desk reading a letter. Without speaking Justin poked fitfully at the fire. Perhaps he ought to have another log put on.

"Have you any news?" came Jean-Baptiste's dry voice.

"News?" He kept peering at the fire. "No. The canaille are gathered on the street corners despite the fog, if you call that news."

"The fog will burn off, and the rabble will have sun to celebrate in. If you had more years you would have listened, and you would know what it is they celebrate."

Justin's mouth twisted. "It's of no importance. A loutish lot; the whip would settle them."

"The day is coming when this foolishness of the herd in power will be ended. The power can and will fall to us."

Justin nodded. "Yes, but—."

"I have the skill, but I am too old. The grasping of power in the times to come will be a young man's work. Your brothers are too young, though, too inexperienced. I will send Henri and Louis to England for schooling this year. I hope there will be time for a year or two on the Continent as well before they must be brought back. Even so, they will still be too inexperienced for what must be done. Your sister? A woman." He gestured expressively. "Gabrielle will marry eventually, for the benefit of the family. Nothing more can be expected."

"And that leaves me."

Jean-Baptiste eyed him coldly. "Yes, you, who still does

not know that information is more powerful than the whip, or cannon. It is the man with information who orders the cannon.''

"Very well, Father. What information should I have heard?''

"The Stamp Act has been repealed.''

"Repealed!'' He slammed his fist into the cypress mantel. "So those treasonous dogs have their way. But there's the end to it.''

"No! It will lead them to do more.'' Jean-Baptiste watched the light dawn for his son. It came so slowly; would God had given him a worthier heir. "Exactly. They will do more, and it will hasten the day. Remember, the foolishness will end. After, there will be a new order. Or perhaps I should say a return to an old one. The Carolinas will be possibly a duchy. Such a plum will go, of course, to a favorite from England. For those of unquestioned loyalty, those who have been of great service, there will be other plums. A barony, perhaps. It is a thing to be considered.'' He stroked his chin reflectively, watching his son rise to this glittering bait, and draw back sullenly. The young found it so difficult to think beyond today to tomorrow. "What is it, Justin?''

Justin looked up. "Elizabeth,'' he said.

"Ah, Elizabeth.'' Jean-Baptiste shook his head. "That a woman can distract you so. Still, I suppose you consider the man, Michael Fallon, as well.''

"Who? Fallon? You mean that insolent Irish jackanapes? I've realized it's beneath me to even consider a quarrel with a servant. I've wiped him from my mind.''

"He will be a dangerous man,'' his father said drily.

"Dangerous?'' Justin laughed.

"He is allowed to trade through Carver's accounts, so my sources tell me. That took a certain daring, however he managed it. His dealings also show a willingness to take risks and a certain intelligence. They prosper. He will grow, and he will one day be dangerous.'' Could not the boy think? God, there was Fallon with the brains and daring to be a proper son, while his own son could not see beyond a guinea or a wench. The Irish gutter trash was a better man than a Fourrier. God curse the bastard.

Justin swallowed. Despite his words he couldn't think of Fallon without burning. "If he's so dangerous, or will be, perhaps he should be killed." He bared his teeth in a smile.

Jean-Baptiste's hand clenched on the desk. "No." Would this foolish youth never learn? "Hear me. You will not yourself make any attempt on this Fallon's life, nor will you allow anyone else to do so. None of your hirelings, you understand. He is by no means worth the risk at present. It is understood?"

"It is understood," Justin said slowly. Something was digging at the back of his mind. And then he had it. "As soon as I mentioned Elizabeth, you brought up Fallon. Why? What connection is there between them?"

"It seems," his father said carefully, "that she frequents secluded parts of the Carver garden in his company."

"What are you saying?"

"I am saying nothing. She may yet be the mother of Fourrier sons. Still, she is a girl, not even a woman. She may, innocently, be led by one who thinks to work his way to the Carver fortune."

"You call this nothing?" Justin cried.

"You will control yourself." Jean-Baptiste waited until Justin quieted before going on. "There is no danger. Thomas Carver may be a foolish merchant, but he will not allow his daughter to marry a servant. If he should, you will marry one of the Pinckney girls."

Justin drew breath. "You seem to forget that Elizabeth is Carver's sole heir, while the Pinckney fortune will be split many ways, and little of it to the daughters."

He sighed ruefully. "If you must have this girl, get her with child. Then she must marry you, and quickly. Just be certain you are the first. In any case, go now. I have more important things to do than talk to a son who does not listen." He turned back to his letter from London. The stirrings in Parliament were of interest.

Justin glared at him. He hadn't meant to go to his father for advice nor for information. Elizabeth! She was so beautiful he'd almost be willing to marry her without her father's money. And she was his, damn it. His!

God rot Fallon, luring her into the garden. He might try to put his hands on her. He might—.

With an oath Justin rushed out, toward the stable. He looked around furiously. "My horse! Where's my Arab? Pomp! Simpy! Get Arab out here, you black simpletons!"

Elizabeth sat in the upstairs sitting room intermittently watching the fog-shrouded street and reading *The History of Count Olandro*. Her father's disapproval of romances was usually enough to ensure their enjoyment, but today her mind drifted from the words. And Samantha puttering around didn't help, either.

"Samantha, that is all. You may go."

"Yes, Miss Elizabeth."

"And close the door behind you. I don't want to be disturbed."

She waited till the slave woman left, then tossed the book aside. How could she interest herself in pale fiction when she had vivid reality to compare with? Just thinking about Michael's kisses made her go shivery. But how long before he was affected as she was? Oh, it was delightful, even wonderful, as it was, but he always managed to stop, saying they shouldn't or they mustn't, and leaving her all hot and itchy feeling, as though she were hanging in air.

Her hand crept up to her breast. That time a few weeks back when her breast had somehow been loosed from her bodice. He'd hesitated for just a second, as if he wanted to stop. But then his head had bent, and he had kissed her pale skin, his tongue sending wine along her veins. It was heaven. Each time since then she'd managed to tempt him, he'd hesitated less, till now there was no pause at all. Soon she'd offer both breasts, and then—.

She caught her breath and clasped both hands tightly on the arms of the chair. She had to keep herself in hand. She had to be discreet. In a year, perhaps two, it would have to end.

She'd marry Justin, probably. There must be no breath of scandal to threaten that proper marriage—or a better, should one present itself.

On the whole she thought she'd wed Justin. He was the most eligible of her suitors, certainly. And it had been assumed they'd marry for so long most people thought they were betrothed. Yes, she must be nicer to Justin; she had been offish lately. So often thinking of Michael Fallon, his lips, his hands . . .

A clatter of hooves in the street drew her attention; Justin was tying his horse to the hitching post. She smiled. There was no time like the present. Rising, she carefully smoothed her dress and checked her hair in the mirror; he would be announced in a moment. The minutes stretched, and her smile faded. She went to the hall and listened down the stairwell. Silence. He must have come to see her father, not her. The thought irritated her. Very well. She'd wait, and catch him as if by accident when he came out.

Thomas Carver sadly poured a glass of Madeira. News of the repeal was overcast by the means of its coming. It'd been brought ashore by survivors of the *Rose*, broken on the Charlestown Bar in the morning fog. Michael had gone to join the search, along with a hundred other men, but there was faint chance of finding anyone this time. The fog was still thick, and the sea was rising.

"Sir, Mr. Justin Fourrier is here."

Thomas Carver turned as Seth spoke. "To see me?"

"Yes, sir."

"Well, show him in." He waited in front of the study fireplace and was surprised when Justin made a formal leg.

"Your servant, sir."

"And yours, Justin. But why this bowing and scraping?"

"Sir, the nature of my visit impels formality." Justin hesitated. "Because of the—understanding—between your daughter and myself I am somewhat more protective than would otherwise be proper."

"Indeed," Carver said drily. "And just what is Elizabeth to be protected from?" He motioned to the Madeira with a questioning look.

"No, thank you. She must be protected from her own innocence. A young girl such as Elizabeth—and I think I may claim the right to call her by her given name—a young girl may, in her innocence, be led to give her friendship unwisely, never realizing that others will use and abuse that friendship."

"And who will abuse her friendship? Not you, I trust?"

Justin looked at him sharply, then decided it was an attempt at levity. He smiled dutifully. "Certainly not. There is in your house the Irish serving man, Michael Fallon. It's come to my attention that he is chivvying himself into Elizabeth's confidence. Clearly, his purpose is to use her, since no relationship is proper between them. You're a wealthy man, sir. He may be trying to insinuate himself into your notice. I realize this is the same man I had that, that bit of trouble with, but believe me, I've forgotten that long since."

"How did this, ah, come to your attention?"

"It was—it was rumored—"

"Rumored?" Carver's voice was cutting. "Street gossip? You come to me with rumor? That is the act of neither a suitor nor a gentleman." Justin's mouth thinned, and his ears seemed to lie back. "I am well able to school my own daughter and keep order in my own house. You've been a guest here often, and will be again, I hope. Now, sir, I bid you good day."

Justin made a tight-lipped apology before hurrying out, but Carver barely heard. He clasped his hands behind him to still their trembling. How dare Justin come there with whisper and innuendo? But what if it was more? He sat down to consider the possibility.

Elizabeth had seemed content with Justin, so he had made himself content as well. Justin was certainly more than eligible, and certainly sought after. The amiable jealousy of Elizabeth's friends made that clear. She didn't see what he saw, that Justin's avarice seemed at times more engaged than his heart. She'd remained fixed on him. But what if she wasn't? What if she'd begun to look at Michael Fallon?

Fallon was a well-set-up young man, presentable, with a solid head on his shoulders. Against him was that he was still bound. Still, he had ambition. After he'd been free a year or two he could be taken into the firm as a junior. No one would comment if Elizabeth married Michael Fallon, partner in Carver and Fallon.

Let their feelings develop on their own, if they would. In the meantime, put Michael in the way of better trade. If marriage came, good. If not, he might still be a man for the firm. And it might be well to get Michael out of Justin's way for a day or two. Yes, it would be well.

Elizabeth was waiting when Justin came out of the study. "Why, Justin, wherever did you come from? Don't tell me you're leaving. . . ."

Justin turned stiffly. "I'm sorry, Elizabeth. I came to see your father, and—. No. No, of course I wouldn't leave without speaking to you."

She'd never seen him so flustered. "Come into the drawing room and tell me what's troubling you." She closed the door behind them and turned to regard him. He'd thrown his tricorn on the table and was frowning at it. "Come. I'll ring for some refreshment."

"Elizabeth, what is this Fallon man to you?"

She froze with her hand at the bell-pull. In an instant she turned with a slightly questioning smile. "Mr. Fallon? Why he's the most amusing servant we've ever had. He tells the drollest stories."

"That's all he is? A servant who tells amusing stories?"

"Of course," she laughed. "What else could he be?" She moved closer, smoothing his lapels with both hands. "Don't tell me you're jealous of a servant?"

"Of course not," he said indignantly. "It doesn't take jealousy for me to want to protect you."

She tilted up her face, opened her eyes wide, let her lips

part slightly. He was slow to take the hint. She was nearly on tip-toe before he took her in his arms.

She examined his kiss dispassionately. Michael's made her feel like warm honey inside; this didn't even bring a tingle. He let her down, and she pressed her face against his waistcoat. "Oh, Justin," she said breathlessly. "Justin."

"I don't know what came over me," he said thickly. But his father's admonition, get her with child, came back to him, and his grip tightened. She looked up at him from under her lashes. He picked her up again and kissed her even more thoroughly than before. At last she drew back, saying "Justin, my father might come in."

"Yes." He released her, breathing hard. "Yes, we wouldn't want that. I'll go now, but I'll return and we'll continue." There'd be no Irishman's stories once he got her properly alone.

He leaned forward for another kiss, but she glanced anxiously toward the door.

She hurried the good-byes as much as she could, and when he was gone dropped into a chair. Drat it all. No. Damn it all. Now some of the time she wanted to spend enticing Michael would have to be given to Justin. It'd take forever to seduce the Irishman.

Michael walked up the steps with his sodden coat over his shoulder, and left his shoes and stockings on Carver's veranda before going inside.

When the merchant saw him he leaped to his feet. "Good Lord, Michael. What happened?"

"We overturned off Cummins Point." He stood close to the fire, baking the chill from his bones. "Instead of finding survivors of the *Rose*, we needed rescue ourselves."

"You found no more, then?"

"None alive," Michael replied bleakly. "Two dead. A nameless seaman. And a young officer named Andrew Toomey."

Carver put a brandy in his hand. "Here. Drink this straight down. I'm sorry. You knew the man?"

"He was my first friend in this country." He gulped the brandy down. "If you don't mind, sir, I'd like to go to my room."

"I'm afraid I need you, Michael. I want you to take another look at that Santee property before I buy. I'm beginning to think there's something wrong there, and I need to know before the papers are signed."

Michael looked at the merchant in surprise. He was plainly exhausted, and Carver had never been one to ask for more than was due. Surely Carver knew the plantation was an excellent buy; he and Michael had discussed it several times. "May I leave in the morning, sir? There's no hope of getting there tonight, and—."

"No, Michael." Carver shook his head and avoided looking at the soaked and weary Irishman. Any danger to Fallon would come before Justin's temper had a chance to cool. "I've already sent a message to Daniel, and had your things packed. All you need to do is change and go. I need this report, Michael. I wouldn't ask it else."

"It's all right, sir. I'm on my way."

The first thing Michael saw when he reached the bridge was Christopher, sitting alone on top of a piling, taking long, thoughtful pulls from a bottle.

"A mighty lonely celebration of repeal."

Christopher peered at him blearily. "You think I should be celebrating, do you? Why? You tell me that."

"Why, you've won, you and your Liberty Boys."

"Won, have we? That's what those fools think, dancing around like drunken idiots. We won nothing. Here, read this." He pulled a wadded-up paper from his coat. "Something else the *Rose* brought us."

Michael smoothed out the sheet. "An Act for the Better Securing the Dependency of His Majesty's Dominions in America upon the Crown and Parliament of Great Britain. That sounds familiar, somehow."

"Oh, it should, lad. It should." Christopher took another pull at the bottle. "Change a word. America to Ireland. Do you recognize it now? The Irish Declaratory Act, near word

for word." He wiped his mouth and leaned forward to point.
"Read it right there. Yes, right there."

"All resolutions, votes, orders, and proceedings in any of
the said colonies or plantations, whereby the power and
authority of the Parliament of Great Britain to make laws is
denied or drawn in question, are hereby declared to be utterly
null and void to all intents and purposes whatsoever."

Michael stuffed the paper back in Christopher's pocket.
"And what did you expect them to say? That we can pass our
own laws now, and they'll sit by and watch us?"

"I don't know. Don't know what I expected. Not this,
though." He tilted the bottle up, and the level went down
another inch.

"Listen, I must go. Are you all right? Can you get home by
yourself?"

Christopher sat erect with the bottle held on his knee. "An
Irishman can't get drunk, lad. Go on with you. I'll be all
right, me and my bottle."

Michael went on to the end of the wharf, where Daniel
waited, his boat tied to the foot of the ladder. "He going to be
all right, Mr Fallon?" the boatman asked.

"I should likely help him back to his rooms," Michael
said, glancing back down the dock. Christopher threw the
empty bottle spinning into the river and fished another from
his coat pocket. "I'd have to fight him, though. He'll be all
right."

Michael and the boatman climbed down and pushed the
skiff out into the river.

"You going to look for more cypress swamp, Mr. Fallon?
I expect you already know most every piece in the Lowcoun-
try ain't already planted."

"Maybe tomorrow, Daniel. Tonight we go as far as we
can and find a good place to camp." He looked back at the
solitary drinker on the dock. "I expect we'll have a better
night than some."

11

The day of his freedom dawned briskly in January of 1768. Michael dressed with special care. Three years to the day since he'd set foot in Charlestown, and he had reason to wonder if the man in the mirror was anything like the man who'd stepped ashore that day. That man was alone, and wanted it so. This man had friends in Thomas Carver and Christopher Byrne, and others. That man was as near penniless as makes no never mind. This man had five hundred pounds sterling and would have more. That man had no future but dreams. This man had a woman he would marry and a future clear and bright. Hardly the same man at all.

The walk to the house fit the day. Elizabeth blew him a kiss from her window before ducking back out of sight. Seth met him at the door with a deeper bow than ever before and a murmured, "Congratulations, sir." And in the study Mr. Carver was waiting.

On the desk were two glasses of brandy, and between them a rolled paper. Carver picked up the paper and handed it to Michael with a smile. "Perhaps you'd like to do the honors." He gestured to the fireplace.

Michael unrolled it a little way. 'I, Michael Shane Fallon, do hereby swear and pledge my service in indenture—.' Carefully he laid it on the burning logs. As it flared the merchant handed him a glass."

"A toast, Michael. To freedom and trade."

"To freedom and trade."

Carver filled the glasses again. "What are your plans now? I've a reason for asking."

"I'll put most of my money in rice, and hold it. Then I'll use that to back bills of credit to buy more, and so on until I can go no further."

Carver chose his words carefully. "For your first independent dealing you've chosen dangerously. Why?"

"You, sir." Michael flashed a grin. "You, and Mr. Laurens, and two or three gentlemen of your acquaintance. Early this month you all stopped shipping rice. You're still buying, all you can get your hands on, but you're not selling. Something's going to happen. I don't know what, but I'll wager it'll put the price of rice up. Am I right?" He sipped his brandy casually while the merchant regarded him with amusement.

"There are fifty men in this city who should have noticed what you did. Not one did. You're going to make a fortune, one day. I'll give you a hint. The exemption on rice as an enumerated good is due to expire."

"And you've discovered it won't," Michael said quickly. "Once it's discovered we can still ship south of Cape Finisterre without going to England first, it'll go through the roof."

"Exactly. And as that's the case, there's nothing more for me to say but go out and spend the rest of the day celebrating. You may find your friend Byrne out as well. I've given him command of the *Annalee*."

Michael couldn't find Christopher, not at Dillon's or Shepheard's or Poinsett's although he lightly sampled their wares. By the time he came on Daniel, laughing with a circle of black boatmen, he was beginning to feel it was indeed a celebration. The boatmen all left politely as soon as he appeared, hats in hand, watching him from the corners of their eyes. He apologized to Daniel for running off his company.

"It don't matter, sir. We just swapping stories."

"Stories, is it? From the way you were all laughing that last must have been a ringer."

Daniel laughed weakly and looked away. "It just a boatman story." Suddenly he looked up at Michael intently. "You wouldn't tell it, sir, you promise?"

"Promise? I'll swear it, by whatever honor a Black Irish can have. I'll never tell a soul."

The boatman grinned. "It be about Mr. Peter Cranwell, sir."

"Him they call Flayflint? Lord, Jepson says the man's cheap enough to raise mice for their hides and boil the carcasses for tallow."

"That be the one, sir. He buy him a boat for to bring his rice and such to Charlestown. That old boat Mr. Milton was going to break up, 'bout sixty ton burden. Sort of big for the river, but Mr. Cranwell, he buy it. When he get it to his place he load all the rice it can hold. Then he start to load the deck. Pitch and turpentine and some hogsheads tobacco he buy up the country. Lord knows what all. When they try to warp her out from the dock, she sitting in the mud on the bottom."

"I'll bet Cranwell was fit to boil," Michael roared.

"But that ain't the whole, yet. He won't let them unload nothing. He make them take out a anchor in the boat and kedge her out to the channel. The folk he hire to sail her, they say she too full, but he say go, so they go. They go fine, too, till they get to St. Helena Sound. They not out the river good fore they hit a floating log. Boat that size, it shouldn't matter. But Mr. Cranwell, he don't spend no money to make repairs when he buy her. That log crack open two, three rotten planks. That boat go down like they cut the bottom out. The crew don't have time to do more than get in the dinghy they towing. So, they row to Charlestown, where they supposed to meet Mr. Cranwell. He down to the dock when they row up. He see them, he start to shout and jump up and down and get red in the face. He lace them up one side and down the other. He say they ain't going to get no pay, and he see they never get no work again. Then he ask them where the boat go down."

Michael was laughing. "Then? *Then* he asked them?"

"Indeed he did, sir," Daniel laughed. "And they say it happen so fast they never get no fix, never see no marks. He got nothing left to threaten them with. They go off and tell everybody on the waterfront where the boat be, and Mr. Cranwell, he sit and sweat and wish he knew."

Michael's laughter slowly died, and he squeezed his eyes

shut, trying to clear the alcohol. It came to him. "Daniel," he said urgently, "how much longer before the water seeps in and ruins that rice?"

"Three, four, maybe five more days."

"And you know where it is? I mean, you can find the general area?"

"Yes, sir. But—."

He could feel the excitement building in him. "Get five or six more boatmen who can swim. You can swim, can't you? Then get five or six more, and promise them double, no, triple the daily wage for as long as they work for me. Now, where's Cranwell, do you know?"

"I see him go in down to Dillon's 'bout an hour ago. But Mr. Fallon, you promise you wouldn't tell."

"Hell, I'm not going to tell him. I'm going to snaffle the teeth out of his head before he knows they're gone." And he was off and running down the street.

Sixty tons burden. That meant two hundred and forty tierces of rice, normally. At the current fifty shillings a hundredweight—. He laughed as he dashed into Dillon's. Christopher snagged him by the arm as he went by.

"Where away so fast, lad? Come, sit with a captain. I buy for all my friends."

"You're a captain with a full cargo aboard, from the looks of you," Michael laughed. "I've no time for the drink now, but I need you. You know the *Edisto Packet*, about a hundred tons burden? Go to Mr. Carver and ask him if I can hire it for a week."

Christopher stared, with his mouth hanging open. "Are you daft, man? Hire a ship? What do you need with a ship? And what could you do with it in one week?"

"Make my fortune. Go broke. A hundred things. Will you do it or no?"

Christopher downed the last of his drink and struggled to his feet. "Never let it be said one Irishman wouldn't help another just because he was daft," he said, and wove his way out the door.

Michael took a deep breath and went in search of the

barkeeper. If someone else had gotten the same idea—"I'm looking for Mr. Peter Cranwell. I was told he's here."

"Aye, he is that," the tapster said around a straw. "He's upstairs with a bottle and his miseries for company, and I don't reckon he wants more."

"This is business, innkeep."

The man fielded the crown Michael tossed him and jerked his head toward the stairs. "The Red Room. Third on the left. But I never told you." A clamor broke out at the tables. "All right. I'm coming. I'm coming."

Michael went up the stairs, making an effort to go slowly. He felt as if he were moving very fast, and everyone else barely moved at all. It was the way he'd felt as a youth, before his first battles. Well, this was likely to mean more to him than all the battles put together. He knocked on the door of the third room on the left.

"What do you want?"

Michael opened the door and went in. "My name is Michael Fallon, sir."

The man behind the table had a large, red-veined nose. He glared at Michael over it with mean little eyes. "And what do you want, Michael Fallon sir?"

"I've come about the boat you lost in St. Helena Sound."

"You know where it is?"

"No, I don't."

Cranwell dropped back in his seat and picked up his mug. "If this is some kind of joke—."

"It's no joke. I want to buy the salvage rights from you."

"Salvage rights?" Cranwell's eyes lit up, and he became almost pleasant. "Surely. Surely. Let me see. There were five hundred tierces of rice and—."

"On a sixty-ton ship? Faith and the sides must have stretched a mite." It took an effort to laugh in the man's face.

Cranwell's mouth twisted, and his eyes grew mean again. "Never you mind how big it was. Just you make me an offer, and I'll see if that's big enough."

Michael made as if he was considering. "A hundred pounds."

"A hundr—." Cranwell fell on his face on the table, his shoulders shaking with laughter. The laughter faded into a choking fit. When it ended he raised up, his face suffused. "A hundred pounds sterling wouldn't cover the cordage and anchors."

"Well, I don't know about that. But you see, in the first place, it's not the ship I'm interested in, it's the cargo. In the second place, the cargo isn't on a dock. I have to go out and hunt for it. You might say I'm buying nothing at all from you. And in the last place, it isn't a hundred pounds sterling. It's a hundred pounds currency."

Cranwell swelled like a toad. "Get out. I don't like jokes."

"Think on it, Mr. Cranwell. Right now you've nothing. A hundred pounds is better than nothing, even if it is currency."

The struggle between anger and avarice was clear on the planter's face. "All right, damn you. A hundred pounds. When do I get it?"

"Within the hour." He had to keep calm, or the man would see something was up. "I'll fetch pen and paper from below and draw an agreement—."

"Don't need any paper. My word's my bond. No one questions my word." He grinned piggishly, his chin wet from the liquor.

Michael hesitated. It wouldn't be easy to do business after questioning the man's honesty, but—

"His word will do." Both Michael and Cranwell started as John Rutledge stepped through the still open door. The young lawyer was followed by his friends till the wall looked like a patchwork quilt for the colors of their coats. "Mr. Fallon, isn't it? I hope we're not intruding. We were walking past and thought we might be able to help. If you don't mind."

"Not at all, Mr. Rutledge. You're quite welcome. I'm sure Mr. Cranwell feels the same." Cranwell grunted sourly into his mug.

Rutledge smiled. "Yes. As to Mr. Cranwell's word, my

friends and I will attest that it's good. In point of fact, we'll even testify to it.'' He smiled again as Cranwell choked.

Michael had to stifle his own grin. ''Sir, there was never a doubt in my mind as to Mr. Cranwell's word. The paper would've been solely for his protection.''

Rutledge burst out laughing, and this time Michael couldn't stop himself from joining. In an instant the others were roaring as well, with only Cranwell sitting in the corner a..d glowering.

''Come, Mr. Fallon. Will you drink with us?''

''I will, Mr. Rutledge, and be pleasured to. But only a short one. I must go to my harvest in St. Helena Sound.''

The third day in St. Helena Sound went as slowly and as futilely as the first two. Michael stood at the rail of the *Edisto Packet* and watched the boats returning through the failing light, their improvised grappling hooks already inboard. Daniel's was the first to touch, and he tied off and climbed aboard tiredly. He stood indecisively before speaking.

''This the right place, Mr. Fallon. I know this be the right place.''

''I don't doubt it is, Daniel. But it's a lot of water out there, and it's a small ship, after all. Go on and get yourself something to eat. It'll be a long day tomorrow.''

''We find it.'' The boatman turned slowly for the galley. ''We find it.''

Michael watched the ship's shadow on the water fade into indistinct darkness. Yes, they'd find it, if he had to swim out there himself with a grapple in his teeth. He took one last look before going below. They'd find it.

They damn well had to.

The boats were out early on the fourth morning, well before there was light enough to see. When the first hint of sun appeared on the ocean horizon, they were already beginning their patterns.

They rowed side by side with no more than ten yards between. From the rear of each boat a V of rope ran down into the water. Across the ends of that was a bar, and from

each bar hung large hooks, pieces of iron, even small anchors. They were towed high enough not to snag the bottom,
but low enough, Michael hoped, to catch in the rigging of a
sunken boat. He hoped.

The boats made their sweeps continuously through the
morning, back and forth across the area, up and down, like
waterbugs doing a dance. At intervals one would jerk out of
line and halt, and the other boatmen would rest on their oars
while the man on the hooked boat dove. Time and again a
dejected black face, glistening damply, popped back to the
surface. A log floating submerged. A huge mass of seaweed.
A hump in the ocean floor. And the search went on.

Shortly after noon they all hauled their grapples aboard
and headed for the *Edisto Packet* and the midday meal. One,
in a bigger hurry than the rest, didn't wait to take in the bar.
He simply swung out of line and rowed for the ship as fast as
he could. Half-way there his boat jerked to a halt, the ropes at
the stern taut. The other boatmen passed him, laughing and
jeering, as he went over the side. Before they made it to the
ship he was back on the surface, whooping and shouting.

Michael ran back to where the captain, a big-nosed,
broad-faced man named Grooms, peered through a spyglass.
"What's the matter out there? Is it a shark?"

"Not from the way he's grinning," the captain said.

The boatman in the water waved both hands over his head.
"The boat! I hooked on the boat!"

Michael leaned against the rail weakly while the ship
exploded into activity around him. Thank God. He'd almost
begun to   . No, he'd never doubted, not really. And that
boatman. He'd double his wages for a bonus. Sure and he
deserved it.

The capstan creaked as the anchor was hauled in, and
enough sails shook loose to move the hundred yards to the
wreck. When the anchor went back down, right by the
snagged boat, and the boatmen swarmed aboard, it was as if
they'd found a shipload of gold, not rice. They laughed and
slapped one another on the back, and the ship's crew raised
three cheers. One of them even started a tune on a tin whistle.

Michael passed among them while the meal was being given out. "Eat light," he warned. "Remember you're diving."

The warning was hardly necessary. The same excitement that made him pick at his food was on the rest as well. More than one half-filled plate sat on the deck when the first diver splashed into the water.

On the deck was a flurry, too. Hatch covers were swung off, braced yards rigged as booms to lower nets over the side. The first of the heavy rope nets sank beneath the surface, and everyone held their breath. Divers surfaced and waved, and the first load, four barrels, was hauled up and swung on board.

Michael hurried forward with a prybar as one of the tierces was rolled clear of the net. Taking a deep breath he forced open the end of the barrel. With a grin he plunged his hand into the rice. "Dry as bone," he announced, and another cheer went up. "Come on, now. Get this closed up and below. There's plenty more to come on board. Move along, now."

The nets began swinging up with regularity, each time bringing three, four, or even five barrels. The first edge of excitement was gone, now, and everything was workmanlike. The barrels were swayed directly into the hold. The boatmen dove again.

One of the nets swung in with a single huge hogshead. A seaman puzzled out the brands on the barrelhead. "It's tobacco."

"Check it. If it's dry, put it below. If not, empty it over the side."

The stream continued. More rice. Another hogshead of tobacco. Two, almost as big and even heavier, of turpentine. Some small barrels of pitch. More rice.

By the rail Michael noticed two barrels set aside. "What's the matter with them?"

"Too light," was the answer. "Must have got water in somehow."

Lighter? Rice didn't get lighter when it was wet. It

swelled, got heavier. Michael picked up the prybar.

There was a brand on the barrelhead, CPRI. A queer excitement came over him. It couldn't be. Cranwell wouldn't have sold if—. Seamen crowded around us he hurriedly pried it open. The barrel was filled to the top with flat, coppery two-inch squares. Indigo.

The stuff rich dyes were made from was the most expensive cargo shipped from the Americas. From any British colony.

Michael picked up one of the cakes and broke it. The grain was tight, the color brilliant. And the cake felt light in the hand. That was good. He ground the two pieces together to make a small pile on the deck. Someone ran to get a lit splinter from the galley. When the flame touched the piled powder, it flared and burned brightly, leaving almost no ash. The brand didn't lie. It was copper indigo, the best. At twenty-five shillings currency to the pound, three shillings sixpence sterling, and three hundred fifty pounds in a cask—.

"Are there any more below?" he asked finally.

"Yes, sir," one of the divers answered. He was staring at the indigo almost reverently. "They spilled all over the bottom like they was deck cargo. You can tell they too light for rice, even under the water."

"How many?"

"Fifty, maybe sixty, maybe more."

Michael closed his eyes. Fifty, sixty, maybe more. Here he was sweating over the bringing up of the rice, and all the while, right there, was enough indigo to make the whole of the rice less than pocket change. He could forget the rice and the rest and still be a rich man.

"All right," he said firmly. "We'll get the rice and tobacco and such later. Bring up the light barrels first."

His excitement communicated itself to the others. The divers dove as if they were being paid for speed; the sailors handled each barrel as if it were their own. The number of casks with the CPRI brand mounted. Thirty, forty, fifty. And still more came.

Suddenly Michael realized he hadn't seen Daniel for some

time. He wasn't with the men resting on the rail. Heads popped up in the water and went below, more heads, and still no Daniel.

"Have you seen Daniel?" he called down. "Daniel! Have you seen him."

A diver pointed. "He be over toward the bow last I see."

"How long?"

The diver shrugged.

With a curse Michael kicked off his shoes and mounted the rail. He took a deep breath as he dove, and clove the water cleanly. He stroked and kicked deeper in the gray-green murk, deeper, deeper. There was something in front of him. He grabbed it, felt along it. A spar, the bowsprit. Daniel must be close by, but where?

He circled out from the bow. Little light filtered down that far, and bottom mud seemed suspended in the water, drifting in tendrils. Already his chest was feeling tight. Not much time left.

There. A shape off to the right. Something that moved with the water, but more solid than the clouds of mud. He swam toward it. The shape became clearer. A man, Daniel. Unconscious. One of the huge hogsheads, tobacco or turpentine, had slid over to catch his foot against two of the small casks.

Michael pushed at the small ones. They wouldn't move. They were wedged too tightly against the bottom. It'd have to be the big one. A ton, it would weigh, or more. On land he'd have had no hope. Even here, where the water bore a part of it—. He braced his feet against a small barrel, his back against the large one, and shoved with all his might. Nothing moved. He shoved harder. His chest burned with need for air. There was a tightening band round his throat. Move, damn it. Move.

Suddenly the hogshead jerked. An inch. Another. With incredible slowness it tilted over, fell away, raising a spreading cloud of silt. Daniel began drifting away. Michael's chest heaved. The body demanded he breathe, and only his will kept the mouth shut.

He grabbed at Daniel, caught a handful of shirt. With his feet he pushed off for the surface. The burning was not only in his chest, now. Every limb felt like a flame. His eyes were closed, and he worked on the memory of what air was like. The murk of the water drifted into his brain. He knew he was fading. Stroke, you Black Irish bastard he screamed at himself. Stroke, damn you. The free arm wasn't working as it should. It pawed at the water. The fingers weren't even cupped. Oh, hell. It was a damned good try, anyway. He opened his mouth and filled it with fresh sea air.

He opened his eyes and stared around at the ship, the sky, the faces peering anxiously down. Divers joined him in the water, towing both him and Daniel to the ship. They tried to lift him up first, but he wouldn't go till they'd taken Daniel.

"He's dead," they told him on deck.

"Get him over a barrel," he said gasping still. "The sea took one from me, but I'll take this one back."

They looked at him and at one another as if he were crazy, but they brought a barrel and draped Daniel over it. They rolled him back and forth assiduously, kneading his back, chafing his limbs. Michael's eye fixed any who shirked.

Suddenly Daniel shook, and then coughed. In a long retch he spewed up a gallon of water, then hung limply. He looked slowly around the circle of men, stopping at Michael's dripping form. "You."

Michael shrugged. "Somebody had to stop you from dozing off down there." Daniel grinned weakly, and he went on as an idea grew. "I think I ought to have you where I can keep an eye on you. How'd you like to be patroon at a plantation, in charge of all the boats and barges and such?"

"I never think of it before," Daniel said simply.

"Well, you think of it now. And I won't take no for an answer." He got to his feet and stared at the men standing around them. Every seaman and diver was in the circle. "What are you all doing? The indigo's dissolving down there. The water's getting to the rice. Get to work, all of you."

When the *Edisto Packet* sailed into Charlestown harbor

the story was already known. A piraqua had happened by the first afternoon of salvage, and a planter's barge the next morning. To tell anyone who might not have heard, all the boatmen except Daniel rowed ashore as soon as they passed the first wharves. Even so, trouble didn't come until they were half unloaded.

Peter Cranwell came trotting his way down the wharf like a pig in a black suit, followed by two men with constable's staves. He leveled a finger dramatically at the ship. "That is my cargo."

Michael took a deep breath. "I've been expecting you to try this, Cranwell. You know full well I bought the salvage."

One of the constables made his way forward, hat in hand. "Begging your pardon, Mr. Fallon, but Mr. Cranwell claims, that is, he says—."

"Don't be so touchy," Cranwell snapped. "He's not a gentleman."

The constable shifted uneasily. To his mind this Fallon looked more like a gentleman than Cranwell. "Ah, yes, sir. Well, Mr. Cranwell, he says that you, sir, by way of a joke, like, offered to buy the cargo of his boat what was sunk for a hundred pounds. Then he, also by way of a joke, and you both knowing it, accepted."

"Exactly," Cranwell broke in. "Who ever heard of selling a cargo like this for a hundred pounds?"

"I have, for one," John Rutledge said, "and there were others there, too." He leaned lazily on his walking stick. "I heard you were coming in today, Mr. Fallon. Tolerable good luck with your fishing, I see."

"Tolerable, Mr. Rutledge."

The two constables looked from Cranwell to Rutledge to Fallon to each other.

"Now listen—" Cranwell began.

"Ah, Mr. Cranwell," Rutledge said. "I remember you so well. From Dillon's Tavern, for instance. Others remember you, too. Like young Middleton. Of course you remember us all, don't you? And now, if this little joke of yours is over, perhaps we could let these constables go."

"I—."

"It is a joke, isn't it? Because, if it isn't, I believe Mr. Fallon could bring an action for defamation of character. I'd be happy to represent him."

Cranwell's mouth twitched twice before he spoke. "I, I suppose it was a joke."

Rutledge smiled. "Good. In that case I expect you'll be going, Mr. Cranwell. And of course you two gentlemen can go as well. If there's a fine I'm certain he'll pay without question. He's a man who doesn't mind paying for his jokes."

With a strangled grunt Cranwell scurried away, the two constables hard in his wake.

"Do you think they'll fine him?" Michael asked.

"I doubt it, but he'll fret at it, till he comes down with a mania. It's no more than he deserves."

"I must thank you, Mr. Rutledge. For the second time you arrived in the nick."

"I know Cranwell." He looked at Michael a moment, then gestured to the ship. "If you don't mind my asking, what are your plans now?"

"I've given thought to becoming a planter," Michael replied, and watched for a reaction.

Rutledge's was to offer his hand. "I'm delighted, sir. May I be the first to drink to that—a bowl of sangaree at Dillon's, or perhaps a bottle of Madeira?"

"You may, sir. Captain Grooms, Mr. Jepson will help with the rest of the unloading. If you'll lead on, Mr. Rutledge."

"A planter!" Mr. Carver said. He leaned back in his chair and shook his head. "Why not put the profits into the rice market?"

Michael set his glass on the mantel and turned from the study fire. "Sir, I gave some thought to that, but it's as a planter I'll begin. When I can afford to ship my own crop in my own bottoms, then I'll expand into trade."

"That's the reverse of what most do. It's a big undertaking, this planting. To find a good piece of land—"

Michael strode to the cabinet and in a minute had Carver's map of the province on the desk. "Here, on the Santee. Not far from the land you purchased. Two thousand acres for a good price, with enough cypress swamp to put eight hundred acres in rice. I'll start with two hundred for next season."

Carver was caught up. "Next season! Well, perhaps you can. But for two hundred acres you'll need, oh, seventy prime slaves. That'll be a vast expense."

"Yes. The slaves." Michael straightened and breathed heavily. "There are some who'd think me strange for it, but I intend to hold them as bound men. After eight years service I'll give them their freedom, same as you gave me mine."

"That, will be strange," Carver said slowly. "If you've objection to owning slaves, Michael, perhaps you should consider indigo. You don't need nearly so many as for rice."

"Truth to tell, sir, indigo is too big a gamble."

"A gamble? Indigo? The price goes higher every year. There's never been a firmer market for anything."

"So long as we've the bounty. Two more years at sixpence a pound, then down to fourpence a pound for seven more years. After that, nothing. And what do you think the market'll be with no bounty?"

"There'll be a bounty," the merchant said. "The whole purpose of it is to keep hard money from leaving English hands for French and Spanish indigo. They'll never drop it."

"I'll gamble on my skill with cards, sir, or the speed of a horse, but never on what fools in a government will do."

Carver laughed. "Well, Michael Fallon, planter, what now?"

"For me it's back to my room to freshen up, then off to see the owner of the Santee property."

In his room, though, he found Elizabeth sitting on his bed, hands primly folded. They didn't stay that way. She rushed to him and threw her arms around him. When he could finish kissing her he pushed her back.

"Girl, are you insane? What if someone saw you coming here? Or sees you going?"

"Bother! I had to see you." She studied at twisting a
button off his waistcoat. "Ever since you went off on that
silly boat I haven't had a moment alone with you." He pulled
her close again, and she wet her lips for the expected kiss.

Instead he just looked down at her tenderly. "You little
goose. You don't even know what that silly boat means to us,
do you? It means I'm becoming a planter. In a year I'll be
asking for your hand. We'll sneak behind the bushes no
longer. I see it surprised you it can come so soon."

Elizabeth wasn't surprised, she was shocked. Marriage?
To a bond servant? Of course, he wasn't bound any more;
still. . . . But a planter, with his dashing good looks, his
hands that brought ecstasy? "Darling." She leaned closer
for a kiss.

"My puppet, I can spend the afternoon here kissing you,
or I can go and meet the man who's going to sell me my land.
You choose."

With a sigh she straightened. Lord, but even that devilish
grin of his made her—. No. "You go." She put a quick kiss
on his chin. "For luck. Now go."

She watched him down the carriage path from the window.
What a fine figure of a man. If his plans for a plantation
worked out—. If only they did.

12

Christopher stopped his horse by the tall, stone gateposts with their heavy gates. Tir Alainn, a brass plate on one post said. Beautiful Land. Of course Fallon would name the place in the old tongue. He wondered if anything about him was changed in a year.

The way up to the house, on top of a hill that sloped down to the river, was lined with new-set oaks a dozen feet high. Oaks, now. They took a long time to grow. Planting for generations to come, it was called.

Beyond the house was Michael on horseback, down on the dikes by the river. As he rode closer the smell of the rice blossoms drifted to him like the delicate scent of a woman's perfume. In the fields slaves waded among the flowers, picking something out of the water and stuffing it into sacks.

"What are they doing, Michael?"

A happy smile lit Michael's face. "Christopher! God, and it's good to see you. Don't you know? Crayfish. Crayfish by the hundreds. They'll strip a field clean, do you let them. This is one task the hands enjoy, though. They'll boil the creatures up tonight for supper. It's a tasty dish, the way Esther cooks it. You'll see."

"Lord, but haven't you turned into the planter for sure, bossing your blacks and eating crayfish?"

"Away with you. Come up to the house, we'll share a cool drink and tell each other lies."

From up close it seemed incredible that the house had gone up in less than a year. It was three stories, with columned porticos on the second and third floors and a mansard roof of dark, Charlestown tiles. A double stair, edged by wrought iron railings, led to the portico on the second level. Inside it was repeated, this time by a curving, free-standing double stair rising from the entry hall.

"It's a hell of a place for an Irish farmboy to be living," Christopher said once he'd caught his breath.

"Oak and cypress throughout." He slid open the door to his study and chased out a workman fitting wainscotting. "What'll you have? I've some fine Irish whiskey here."

"Lord, yes, I'll take the whiskey." He lifted the glass Michael handed him. *"Dia's Muire Ihuit."*

"Dia's Muire Ihuit agus Padraig."

"Ah, it's angel's milk. You've no idea what they're calling whiskey these days."

Michael sipped, then set his glass on the desk. "I'm thinking you didn't come here to complement my house or my whiskey, nor to speak the old tongue, neither. You'll see I'm being direct. After all, it's been a year, and I've not seen a hair of you."

Byrne sighed. "I could say I was feared you'd be big headed with your fine plantation was why I didn't come, but it wouldn't be true. No, I've just been lazy, lad. Too lazy to get on a horse and come."

Michael sank into a wing chair and gestured for Christopher to take the other. "Yes. And now something's put you on your horse. What?"

Byrne grimaced. There wasn't going to be an easy way to get to it. "Gadsden's gotten the Charlestown merchants to agree to non-importation, you know. He's heading the committee to enforce it."

"So. It's politics again, is it?"

"Yes. If you've seen the non-import you'll recall there was a list of exemptions."

"A few," Michael said drily. "Everything a planter needs to operate."

Christopher grimaced. "Well, it was the only way we could bring you planters to agree, and it wouldn't have gone without you."

"Who's we, Christopher?" Michael's voice was quiet,

but his gaze was firm. "Gadsden? Timothy? Who? You ask an awful lot, but you don't tell much."

Christopher hesitated. "All right, then. Yes, they're in it, and others you wouldn't expect. Your fine friend John Rutledge, for one, and Henry Laurens, ever since he twisted the customs inspector's nose on the Bay. Do you want more names?"

"No." Damn it, these weren't just the cream of the colony. They were his friends. "What is it you want?"

"We want a tighter agreement, a real agreement, to shut down the imports entirely till those damned Townshend duties are gone. But we need more backing from the planters. Talk to them, man. You can't turn me down this time."

"Damn it, man, it doesn't make sense. How can we do without paper, or glass, or lead, or any one of the other things on the list? Be reasonable. They're even taxing tea!"

"For God's sake, don't you see that's why we have to stop them now?" Byrne's eyes blazed. "If we let this get by, they won't stop. And they'll add more till there's never a hope of us stopping them. God's teeth, Michael, you know the English. They won't even slow till they've got us by the throat, making us pay for the air we breathe."

Michael sighed. Christopher was right. He didn't want to mix in politics, but—. "I'll think about it. I'll be wagering you have a list of the planters you need swayed?"

Christopher did. A long list of men, along with what Michael should offer this one, but only if he had to, and what he should on no account say to that one; exactly what kind of backing he should try for; and how to get letters to a safe place in Charlestown.

With that Michael threw up his hands. "Enough, Christopher. I'll talk with these men, and that's all. That's all, I say. No secret letters, nor any of that. I'm not a spy, for God's sake. Now, we'll talk of something else. You. How is it with you?"

"I'm saving my money, keeping away from the cards. In four years, I reckon, I'll be owning my own ship. And maybe taking a wife."

"A wife! Have you a girl to mind?"

"It's early days for that, yet. I'm still trying to find that little serving girl you were tumbling. I know you were. There's no need denying. But I haven't seen her anywhere."

"She married a shoemaker."

"A shoemaker! Ah, the pity. And you. Have you thoughts of bringing a wife to this palace?"

Michael looked around the room as if seeing it for the first time. "It does seem empty without a woman, doesn't it? Almost as if it's waiting for her."

"Any particular one, lad?"

Michael produced a laugh. "No, of course not. But even I'll not stay a bachelor forever. Look, can you stay a few days? We've more than one night's talking to do. I'll have Daniel row us upriver this afternoon for some fishing."

In September of 1769, Michael began his first harvest. The straw was still green, the grain waving high above the water before the sluices were opened and the fields drained. The hands moved down into the impoundments, crossing in stooped rows, sickles flashing. The grain was left lying on the stubble to cure. When the last field was done, it was time to go back to the first and carry the grain to be cleaned, first by hands with flails on a large circular floor, then by one of the new cog machines driven by a pair of oxen.

Present through the entire harvest were the rice birds. They were lean when they came in their streaked winter feathers, but they fattened quickly. Michael laid aside fowling pieces for slaves who did nothing from dawn to dusk but stand at the fields and shoot, but the thousands that fell made not a dent in their greedy numbers. But they were toothsome, made sweeter, perhaps, for having gorged on his rice.

With the end of the harvest came no rest. Hogs and sheep were slaughtered, and cattle, too, and put up for the winter. The corn and potatoes and beans had to be sorted, the best kept aside for the spring planting and the rest put away. There was more land to clear, and boards and scantlings sawed for the outbuildings yet to be finished. Shingles had to be made, and staves and oaken hoops cut for the coopering of rice barrels. It was close on to Christmas before Michael could make the trip to Charlestown. And to the reward he sought for all his labor.

Once installed in rooms at Dillon's, he hurried to the Church Street house, pausing only briefly before he knocked at Mr. Carver's study door.

"Come in." Carver, deep in piled papers, broke into a smile as soon as he saw his guest. He popped to his feet. "Michael, you've no idea how good it is to see you. Your visits have been all too few.

"There's always work to be done, sir, and I've no mind to hire an overseer."

"And it prospers?"

"It'll make four tierces the acre, for sure."

"Excellent, excellent. What am I thinking of? Here I haven't even offered you a drink. Will you have brandy? Or Madeira?"

Michael took a deep breath. Strange, how some things could make a man feel like a footling boy. "Sir, I've come to you on a matter of some importance."

At the formal tone Carver set the brandy back down. "And that is?"

"I wish to ask for the right to pay court to your daughter, Miss Elizabeth."

"Indeed." The older man suppressed a smile. "And have you spoken to my daughter about this?"

"Well, sir, in a manner of speaking. . . ." Michael realized with rage he was blushing.

"On, Michael, Michael." Carver was chuckling at his discomfiture. "I can think of no man to whom I'd rather give the right. Will you have that wine now, in celebration?"

"No, thank you, sir. Eliz—. Miss Elizabeth is waiting." Confound it! He colored like a boy again. "Excuse me, sir."

When he slid the door shut behind him, Elizabeth was there. Except for a certain brightness of eye she didn't seem excited at all, bored almost. He decided women just took such things more matter of factly.

"He said yes."

She tucked her arm in his and led him into the drawing room. "Of course he did. But Michael, I wish you'd asked him for my hand."

"A forward little baggage it is!" he laughed, and pulled her into the triumphant circle of his arms.

Elizabeth was not yet satisfied. "You have your plantation. What more can you be waiting for?" She stiffened. "There isn't another woman, is there?"

"Lord, no. You know you're the only one." He carefully blanked a certain Santee widow from his mind and kissed her thoroughly and often as he spoke. "I want everything for you. The very best. I want a nice, conventional courtship, and a properly long betrothal. And a proper wedding. We'll have no more behind-the-bushes in our lives. I love you." He drew back. "For the moment, I'm afraid, I have to go out. Business. No, I mean it." He gave her one more kiss for a goodbye, and then another. Then, as good as his word, he left.

It was all very well, Elizabeth thought breathlessly, for him to kiss her like that. But to traipse off that way! Business? She knew what business that was. He'd another woman somewhere. He'd kiss her and caress her till she lay awake all night, then go out and enjoy himself in the arms of another woman. Well, they'd have their proper marriage, and it wouldn't be after any long courtship and betrothal. She'd see to that.

Michael's business took him up the Bay, to a house he'd visited often before. Or at least the rooms behind. This time he climbed the front stoop and knocked on Christopher Gadsden's door.

In the drawing room the curtains were drawn and the lights low. Gadsden was there, and Peter Timothy and Christopher Byrne and others he recognized but didn't know by name. Gadsden rose to greet him. "Welcome, Mr. Fallon, to my home, and to the cause."

"I thank you, for the first, but not the last, Mr. Gadsden. I've done as I said I would among the planters, though with precious little result, but I'm no joiner of causes, yours or anyone else's.''

Gadsden eyed him sharply. "We'll accept your reluctance along with your aid. For the time, at least. Now tell me. You say you had little success with the planters? Do they not favor our cause?''

"I didn't talk causes." He glanced at Byrne, who shifted uncomfortably. "I thought you knew that. What I did was talk taxes, the duties and what they add to the cost of running a plantation. All agree they're an unfair burden, but they'll not let their land lie fallow and their livelihoods go to ruin to fight it.''

"But if you had talked cause," Timothy broke in, "they would have seen. God, must our rights and liberties depend on not endangering planters' livelihoods? Let them put their livelihoods, and their land, and their blood, if need be, into the fight. The cause of freedom is a holy one.''

"Come, Peter," Gadsden said restlessly. "It no longer matters. You see, sir, we've decided we can do quite well with the agreement we have.''

A slow burn began in Michael. "You mean to say I've run around talking men into something you don't need? You could've put Christopher back on his horse and sent him to tell me.''

Gadsden spread his hands blandly. "Mr. Fallon, we trust you, but we aren't fools. As you say, you're not a joiner.''

Michael's jaw tightened. "All right then. I've done as I said, and there's an end to it.''

"Please, I didn't mean to anger you. Stay and join the conversation. Tonight we talk of Mr. John Wilkes, and the money the Assembly voted to his aid.''

"Mr. Wilkes?''

"Yes, Mr. Fallon," Gadsden said. "Mr. Wilkes. Three times imprisoned and expelled from the House of Commons for his attack on George III in the forty-fifth issue of his paper, the *North Briton*. Three times re-elected from prison by the people. The cry in London is, Wilkes and Liberty. Now, if only William Pitt could forget he's Earl of Chatham and remember he was once the Great Commoner, we'd have two great voices raised for our liberties.''

The conversation became general, and everyone took a chair. How much opinions had changed, Michael thought, in a few short years. Once they were all loyal subjects of the King, and it was the Parliament that ravaged their rights and destroyed their liberties. Now the Assembly could send ten thousand pounds to pay Wilkes' debts, and him a man whose preoccupation was twisting the King's tail. The waters were getting deeper.

13

Thomas Carver studied the reports on his desk. Non-Importation was ridiculous in that summer of 1770. A merchant would be accused of importing prohibited items. He'd say it was ordered before the agreements, the Committee would say it didn't matter, and the goods would be stored under bond. Carver snorted. It wasn't coincidence that the stored goods were always the sort that wouldn't be damaged by long storage. It was enough to make him regret his own adherence.

On the other hand most merchants were adhering to the agreements, including many of the smaller ones who would be ruined if they continued. The trouble was the Committee made up for its leniency on the few with severity against the many. There was the case of Ann Matthews, for instance. A widow, she had no money to pay storage on goods ordered before the agreements. On finding they were being damaged by the weather, she broke open the cases and sold the goods. The Committee promptly published her name as a violator. On pain of displeasure of the Committee, and of having their own names published, no one could do business with her.

The widow hadn't given up, though, and the new *South Carolina and American General Gazette* had risked giving her a hearing. She'd named the names of men who had cases similar to hers, but who weren't proscribed. Mr. Edwards. Mr. Lightwood. And Mr. Edward Rutledge, John's brother. Still the Committee refused to relent.

He must do something for her. Discreetly. The Liberty hotheads turned on anyone who showed open disagreement with them, whether he violated the agreements or not. They'd managed to run William Henry Drayton out of town. Of course, he'd persisted in attacking them with letters to the

Gazette, sneering letters, openly contemptuous of what he called the vulgar herd.

His daughter's entrance gave him a start. He watched her cross the room, lit by the July sun, and wondered again, as he often did of late, how the little girl had been so suddenly replaced by this regally beautiful woman. "You come to talk to me seldom of late, my dear. I assume you are in want?"

She opened her fan with a practiced snap. "Why, Papa," she said with a smile, "you know I am a dutiful daughter. Though if you really wanted to do something for me, you could make them stop this embargo. There's not a scrap of lace in the shops, nor a hat I'd be willing to give to Samantha."

He laughed. "I wave my hands and it all vanishes. Oh, dutiful daughter, the Committee isn't so easily disposed of."

"Oh, bother the Committee! They're just a bunch of horrid men, shipping a gentleman like Mr. Drayton off like that."

"He left in a cabin he paid for," Carver said slowly. "Listing him among returned cargo was simply the Committee's idea of further ridiculing him." He stopped suddenly. This wasn't like Elizabeth. She hated politics; it was the quickest way to lose her attention.

She hurried on. "Isn't it wonderful about the new fish market at the foot of Queen Street? It's said they're going to clear the streets of fishmongers."

"Elizabeth," he broke in, "you don't care one iota about the Non-Importation Committee or William Henry Drayton, and you have as much interest in fishmongers and fishmarkets as you do in Cathay. Out with it."

She worked her fan and studied the toe of her slipper. "Louisa Forbes just returned from her honeymoon. She's Louisa Richardson, now. She's invited me to Fairhope for a visit." Her father shifted in his chair, she hurried on.

"It's very cool there this time of year, and there hasn't been a single case of fever. There've been three in Charlestown, already. Papa, you know I don't like admitting I'm afraid, but between the fever and the heat, well,—." She opened her eyes very wide and turned a pitiful face to him.

He didn't believe this talk of fear. People could have been dropping in the streets, and she'd have fought tooth and nail against leaving, had she wanted to say. Fairhope? It was less than an hour's ride from Tir Alainn. He didn't mind at all. In fact, he was beginning to look forward to Fallon as a son-in-law.

"All right," he said. "You'll take Samuel and the closed coach. We can spare a livery boy as well as Samantha. Now when is this visit to take place?"

Elizabeth stared at him, her next set of arguments tumbling over the tip of her tongue. It took a moment to shift them. "Samantha will be enough." She thought furiously about her wardrobe—the new dresses being made, the furbelows her green needed. "My invitation is for Saturday. Oh, thank you, papa!" She would have to add an order with Madame Marie today.

When she closed the bedroom door behind her, she was shaking. She'd been so clumsy. But then, this was so important. Thank God her father didn't know how important.

As the carriage swept into the drive at Fairhope Elizabeth worked her fan doggedly against the heat. The leather curtains had had to be lowered against the dust kicked up by the horses. It'd been a choice of swelter or choke to death in the dust. Lord, how she hated travel.

There was Louisa, now, running down the steps followed by a train of slaves for the baggage. "Elizabeth! Dear Elizabeth! How good to see you!"

Elizabeth embraced her briefly for the heat. "Dear Louisa. It's been so long." Still the same too-slender girl with a face more pixieish than pretty, she thought. What ever had Henry Richardson seen in her?

"Do come in. I'll have Mandy bring us some cool ratafia. And you'll want a chance to freshen."

"You can't imagine how wonderful that sounds. The roads are miserable. How pretty everything looks." And it did. Large and in the double-house style, the house had a broad front stair and wrought-iron work at the windows. Flower beds wrapped it in color.

"Henry has wonderful taste, has he not? To think this was my wedding gift. And he let me choose all the furnishings. He's such a dear." Every time she spoke of her husband her face made it clear she was deeply in love.

Besotted, Elizabeth thought. The fool. But then, given Louisa's looks, Henry had only to be polite for her to tumble into marriage.

Louisa called to Mandy for the ratafia, then showed Elizabeth to cool water to bathe her hands and face. All the while she chattered of her honeymoon in London and Paris, the noble palaces, the rustic ruins, the styles, the balls.

Elizabeth answered for the most part in monosyllables, relaxing in the relative coolness of the house. As she sank into a drawing-room chair and took a glass of the cool fruit and almond liqueur, though, she realized Louisa had switched topics to gossip of the neighborhood. A name pricked her ears. "Fallon?" she asked with studied casualness. "Is that Michael Fallon?"

"His name is Michael. Do you know him?"

"Why, yes. He was in my father's business for a time."

Louisa dismissed Mandy with a wave of her hand, leaned conspiratorially. "Mrs. Hopkins would just eat him up, my dear. Every last scrap of him. If she could."

Elizabeth frowned and set her glass down sharply. "I don't understand, Louisa. Who is Mrs. Hopkins?"

"Caroline Hopkins. Mrs. Caroline Hopkins. The widow Hopkins." She seemed ready to go off in laughter.

"Widow Hopkins? That doesn't sound very thrilling."

"Oh, my dear, La Caroline is criminally beautiful, though somewhat obvious, if you know what I mean. Her husband left her Hollandia with no executor, no restrictions, so she does what she pleases and doesn't care what anybody thinks. Half the women on the river would like to give her the cut direct, but somehow she appears at every ball. And the men all fall over their feet trying to dance with her."

Elizabeth's stomach churned. "And this widow

Hopkins—,'' she couldn't keep a touch of acid from the name, ''—is interested in Mr. Fallon?''

"Interested?" Louisa hooted. "I was there, a party at Oakview, the first time she saw him. It was like a dog catching sight of the fox. Though I must admit he didn't run very hard. In fact, it was almost the fox chasing the dog. They say he's got as much clothing at Hollandia as he does at Tir Alainn.'' Her eyes flickered to the door and her voice dropped. ''Henry and some friends, out riding near Hollandia, saw them down by one of the creeks, naked, swimming—and more.'' She nodded significantly and leaned back.

Elizabeth didn't feel the churning any more. In fact, she didn't feel anything. It couldn't end like this. "I, I suppose they must be very close to marriage.''

''Certainly not. Listen, Elizabeth, Fallon is the kind who won't stand for any nonsense.'' She smiled. ''Like my Henry. And Caroline will not marry someone who has a stronger will than hers. Not that there aren't a lot of women around here who'd love to see her made to toe the line. I'd even send him a bundle of switches myself.''

Louisa was beginning to look at her thoughtfully, Elizabeth realized. She'd better change the subject. ''Tell me about Henry. Does he really not stand for any nonsense, or do you just let him think he doesn't?''

That evening, exhausted by the journey, Elizabeth fell off to sleep without time to think. With the day came alertness, and more thought than she wanted.

In her mind she saw Michael. Michael and a woman. The woman had a thousand different faces, all of them, as Louisa had said, criminally beautiful. They were naked, always naked, in a hundred different places, writhing in an obscene tangle of limbs. God, why had Louisa ever brought it up?

Louisa. What was she thinking? Elizabeth watched her like a cat. She was shown the house, the gowns bought in London and Paris, the stables, the horse set aside for her to ride. Never once did Louisa mention Michael Fallon. Never once did that suspicious, thoughtful look come back. She'd be suspicious after tonight, for sure. But after tonight it would be too late.

"Elizabeth, I still think it's too late for you to go out riding. Oh, why isn't Henry here to dissuade you?" Louisa looked at the lowering sun, then turned worriedly back to the girl on horseback. "At least let me send a groom with you."

"No, Louisa." Elizabeth firmed the reins competently and shifted herself on the side-saddle. "In the city I always must have someone with me. It is such a pleasure to be alone." She smiled and appeared to relent a little. "If dusk comes before I get back, I'll stop at a plantation house along the river and send a message."

"But, Elizabeth—"

She whirled her horse and galloped off. Downriver. Toward Tir Alainn.

Darkness was just beginning to fall when she turned up Michael's drive. It hadn't looked so far when she'd sneaked a look at her father's map; she breathed a deep sigh of relief. As her feet touched the ground before the steps, Michael came out on the portico, shirtsleeves rolled up and long clay pipe clutched in his teeth. "Are you in need of assistance, madam?" She moved into the light, and he almost dropped the pipe. "Elizabeth? What are you doing out, alone, this time of night? What are you doing on the Santee? Where's your father? What's wrong, my darling?"

"I got lost," she said with a meekness she didn't have to fake. There'd been noises out there, and as it grew darker they'd grown louder, and closer. And the shadows moved strangely, as if they weren't shadows at all. "Michael, could I come inside? Please?"

"Of course! What am I thinking of!" He tossed the pipe away and ran down to put an arm around her. "Jubal! Jubal, get out here!"

The black butler appeared before the shout was finished. "Yes, Mr. Fallon?"

"Tell Sarah to prepare a room for Miss Carver. I'm afraid it's too late for you to leave tonight, Elizabeth. Then, Jubal, you get somebody from the stables for the lady's horse.''

"My saddlebags," she murmured.

"Have the saddlebags brought in and put in her room. Then go tell Esther to whip up something hot as quick as she can. Go on with you. You're shaking, lass. Are you sick? Is that it?''

The tenderness in his face almost took her breath away.

"I'm all right, Michael darling. Just a little frightened.''

"There's no need. I'm here to protect you." He resisted the urge to carry her, and merely tightened his arm around her till he could seat her safely in the drawing room. "Now then, darling, what on earth are you doing here?''

"I told you, I was lost. I was out riding, and I couldn't find my way back, and it got dark, and then I saw the lights, and, and—." Her lower lip quivered, and it was only partly an act. "I'm so glad I found you.''

"I'm glad too, love." He kissed her hand and smiled reassuringly. What a child she still was. "But I'm afraid you'll have to stay the night here. Lord! Spending the night in a bachelor's house! If that isn't a fine brew. Well, at least I can send a message you're safe. Who is it you're staying with?''

"There's no need for that," she said lightly. "I'm not afraid any more, with you here. And I feel perfectly—.''

"You let me be the judge of what's needed. They've likely sent search parties out already. Do they find you without you sending word I wouldn't blame them if they locked you in your room till they can ship you off to your father.''

Elizabeth suppressed a small sigh. She knew they needed to send a message, but it would've been nice not to. "I was visiting the Richardsons at Fairhope.''

"I'll send word you're safe, then." He pulled her to her feet, and she came up ready for a kiss that didn't come. "And now I'm afraid it's off to bed with you. Angel will bring you your dinner.''

"What? Michael, I won't be sent to bed like a naughty child! I'm a woman!'' She snuggled in closer and wet her lips.

Michael swallowed hard. "That convinced me, sweetling." Suddenly her wrist was swallowed up in his grasp, and she was pulled behind him out into the hall and up the stairs. "I'm putting you in chaperonage right away. Sarah!"

A neat black woman hurried out of one of the bedrooms. "Here I is, Mr. Fallon."

"Elizabeth, this is Sarah. Sarah, Miss Elizabeth Carver. I want you to sleep in the trundle bed in Miss Elizabeth's room tonight. No one shall think ill of her just because she had to spend the night under a bachelor's roof."

"Don't you worry, Mr. Fallon," Sarah smiled. "I take good care of this sweet child. You come along, Miss Elizabeth. I show you your room. It pretty. You like it fine."

As soon as they were gone Michael hastily poured a brandy and gulped it down. The thought of her under the same roof for the night brought a sweat. She was just a child in so many ways. It probably never occurred to her that her presence might bring thoughts to him, thoughts of her readying for bed, baring that pale, satin skin until—. God, he had to stop that, to blank his mind. And no more brandy, else he might lose what little control he had.

He hurried to his study. There was work there. He'd work until he was too tired to think of anything but sleep.

Upstairs, Elizabeth simmered with irritation. If she couldn't have time with him, the whole thing would be impossible. And this fool woman kept talking like a mauma to a ten-year-old. "Hush," she said, and brushed past Sarah into the room.

Sarah followed, blank faced. Several times as she helped Elizabeth undress she made a hesitant comment about how pretty the lace was, or how fine the silk, but Elizabeth met each with silence. Fretfully she ate the dinner Angel brought, and fretfully she threw herself on the bed in her shift, listening to the grunt and scrape as Sarah dragged the trundle bed out, the rasp of her shoes as she extinguished the candles, the rustle as she undressed in the dark.

"Good night, Miss Elizabeth."

Elizabeth stared at the bed's canopy in silence. She'd

planned on spending hours with him. Here there'd be no other woman. Only her.

She twisted painfully. She'd simply have to go to him cold, risk all on one turn of the cards. Well, it still might work. It must. It must. Tormenting images ran through her mind. Her, in Michael's arms, without the stifling cloth between, skin against skin. Her nipples were tight and hard against the cotton of her shift, and there was moisture on her that had nothing to do with the heat of the night. A dozen times she rose and peered out at the light spilling from the front of the house. Each time she sighed and padded back to bed. How long would Michael stay downstairs?

Sarah's bedclothes rustled as she stirred, coughed, stirred again. Wouldn't the fool woman ever go to sleep? She made her journey to the window again. Darkness. Michael was on his way to his bedchamber, or already there.

She turned her back on the window.

"I can't sleep with you in here."

The trundle bed creaked as Sarah sat up. "I sorry, miss. Maybe some warm milk—."

"It doesn't work for me. You'll have to go."

"But, ma'am, Mr. Fallon, he said—."

"I don't intend to spend the night awake, no matter what Mr. Fallon said." She tried to modify her tone. Damn it, she couldn't antagonize this slave woman, or make her suspicious. "We both know why you're here," she said smoothly. "We both also know there's no need for it. Mr. Fallon is a gentleman. I need no protection from him. You go on back to the quarters, so I can sleep. I said, go back to the quarters."

"Yes, ma'am. But Mr. Fallon, he said—." Elizabeth took one step toward her. Sarah got up. "I going."

Done. But there was no time to waste. Rummaging in the saddle bags, she took out a small package. And a thought struck her. What if Sarah had gone no further than the hall? What if she was out there now, asleep across the door, perhaps? She stalked to the door, tongue ready to flay, eyes ablaze, and flung the door open. The hall was empty. The way was clear. Hurriedly she discarded the shift, and hurriedly she sponged with cool water from the pitcher. Then there was the package. In seconds she was covered again, and moved to examine herself in the mirror by moonlight. Dim as it was she saw enough to be satisfied.

It was a gift, she'd told Madam Marie, for a friend who was marrying. And she'd described it in the terms an innocent girl would use. The worldly modiste had been amused at a blushing young lady ordering such a thing. She called it "a gown a man will tear off."

Two bows on the shoulders held it on. From there the sheerest silk fell to cling to her breasts, then touched nothing more till it touched the floor. It was more transparent than she'd remembered. She felt more naked than she'd ever felt before. Yes, he'd want to rip it off, all right. He wouldn't be able to help himself.

She entered the hall shaking with nervousness. She had to calm herself. There'd been a decanter at the head of the stairs when she came up. If only it was still there. It was, and glasses. The first glass, she slopped as much on the floor as she got in the glass. The second went better, though. The third better yet. Suddenly she didn't know how many she'd drunk. Only four glasses, she thought. Or five? The decanter had gone down considerably. She fitted the glass stopper back in place. However much it was, she didn't feel nervous any longer.

The door to Michael's room swung open without a sound, and there he was by his bed, naked, ready to blow out the last candle. Funny that she'd never realized a man's body could be beautiful before, all the tight roundnesses of it, the hard, flat planes. And that hardness that grew harder the closer to him she came.

Michael froze as an apparition floated in. It couldn't possibly be Elizabeth gliding toward him, round breasts caressed by silk, hips swaying gently, the dark triangle between her thighs alternately revealed and obscured by swinging, shimmering folds. Not until she put her arms around him did he move.

"God in heaven! What are you doing?" He tried to push

her away, but she clung tightly. "Go, go back to your room. You can't know—."

"I know I love you," she said. "I know I'm tired of waiting. Please." She went up on tiptoe to kiss him on the neck and under the chin.

His head spun, and his voice seemed foreign. "What are you, Elizabeth, child or witch?" His hands shook as they went slowly to the bows on her shoulders. "If you're playing a game, darling, then God help us both, for I'm playing games no longer."

She trembled as the silk fell to the floor. He swept her up in his arms then, and kissed her as he knelt to lay her on the bed.

"Darl—."

He put a finger to her lips. "Sssh. I'll be gentle, darling. My little innocent. Don't be afraid. I won't hurt you."

Elizabeth smiled at him and relaxed. He called her innocent. He was the innocent. He insisted on a gentleman's tenderness when she wanted a roughneck's forcefulness. But at least he held her. And then, his kisses set her breasts aflame.

His head moved, and she tensed in spite of herself. Was this it, the moment when she'd no longer be a virgin girl, but a woman? His kisses trailed down her ribs onto her stomach, and she almost moaned in disappointment. What on earth was he doing? His fingers were in her nether curls, parting, then his mouth followed.

She gasped and started to protest, when suddenly her lungs couldn't seem to get enough air. Oh, God, what was he doing? That feeling! Nothing ever like it, nothing even close. One hand went to his head, her fingers gripping his hair, unsure whether to push it away or pull it tighter.

Her free hand twisted blindly, one minute tangling in the sheets, the next groping in the air, for what she didn't know. She couldn't breathe except to pant. Every part of her felt tight, especially her belly. There was a knot there, growing tighter and tighter, closer and closer to pain, but never quite reaching it. She wanted to cry because it might end, and also for fear it might not. She was going to burst if it didn't. She was going to explode. She was—. She bit on a trembling hand to stifle her screams as the knot tore apart, and she with it.

She never knew how long she lay bathed in ecstasy. At long last she became aware of the sheet against her back, her sweat-slick body. Of Michael lying beside her, a tender smile on his face.

"I, I never dreamed—," she managed.

"Of course you didn't, love," he said, moving over her. "But there's more."

A momentary panic took her as the spear in his groin brushed her thigh. It was even bigger than it had been. It was too big. It'd never fit inside her. She tried to close her legs, but he was already between them. Then his mouth was on hers, his hand was parting, guiding. There was a slight stretching sensation, a filling. She tried to form a protest, tried to push him away. She could've been pushing at stone.

A sudden burst of pain flared. She groaned and fell back waiting to be split asunder. And she realized he was still kissing her, his tongue insistent at her lips. There was no more pain.

Then his hands were roving over her body, and he was moving in her, and the tightness was coming again. It was different this time, slower, not as rushed. She put arms and legs around him, writhing against him instinctively. Her mind was clouding again. She couldn't think, didn't want to. Her nails dug into the tensing muscles of his back as a bass rumble started in his throat. And then she was coming too, biting his chest to stifle her cries, spasming against his hard body.

After, she realized he'd moved off of her, and she was lying with her head on his chest. There was a strange taste in her mouth, salt and brassy. Her eyes touched the teeth marks among the silky hairs on his chest, and she knew what it was. His sweat and his blood. She smiled lazily. It was good she'd put her mark on him. Hers.

Michael reached down beside the bed and fingered the silk negligee. "Do you usually carry this in your saddlebags, poppet?"

She looked up at him. He looked strange. "You're not angry with me?"

"Angry? Lass, I've been gritting my teeth to keep from making a woman out of you, and here I find, virgin or no, you're a woman already." Suddenly he laughed and lifted her onto his chest, her head at a level with his. "Damn me, no, I'm not angry. There's not a man worth the name wouldn't give his soul to be loved by a woman like you. What worries me is the thought of stretching that silky belly of yours with a baby before we're wed."

A baby! She hadn't even thought of that. She didn't want to be all swollen with child. Still, if it was his baby, it might not be so bad. And now surely he would marry her quickly. "Yes, Michael. We should marry soon."

"Lord, that does present a problem."

She pushed up and knelt on the bed. "A problem? What kind of problem? Michael, you *are* in a position to ask Papa for my hand. This is one of the finest plantations in the province. Everybody says so."

"Elizabeth, I—."

"And this house," she pushed on as if he hadn't spoken. "I know what Turkey carpets cost, and furniture by Thomas Elfe, and, oh, a hundred things here. Michael, are you just trifling with me?" Her lip trembled uncontrollably. Suppose he was.

His answer was to sit up and pull her to him, cradling her in his arms and rocking gently back and forth. "No, no, no. Darling, you don't understand. This is your house. That's why I built it, and why I bought a tract in the city, on Queen Street. You didn't know that, now did you? Plans are being drawn for a house there." She kept silent.

"Elizabeth, the lot in town, these furnishings, making a place fit to bring you, it took a lot of money. I had to borrow. I paid that off with last year's crop, but it left me with barely enough to operate this year. If a hurricane hits, if the floods wash out my dikes, I could lose everything. Two more crops would give me a margin against disaster. I'd marry you then, was my plan. It *was* my plan."

She caught the emphasis and looked up hopefully. "And now?"

"Something I hadn't been planning on for a while yet. Something that means I'll have to borrow again, and I hate that. I'll buy a ship." He paused, frowning, and she waited for him to go on. "If I ship this crop myself, and put the money in what will fetch the highest return, I should make enough to pay off that loan and provide a cushion. Not as much as I'd like, and it'll take a touch of luck, but—."

"But how soon? How soon can we be married?"

He lay back, pulling her down in the crook of his arm. "Trivial things," he taunted, and laughed when she poked him in the ribs. "Well, first the crop must be harvested, manufactured, and barreled. I've yet to look at a ship or ask the best terms for a loan. Once done, I'll sail to Spain or Portugal, sell the rice and buy wine. Then to England to pay the duties and fill the rest of the hold, and back home to you." He didn't mention the biggest obstacle, the non-import. It'd already collapsed in Georgia and Rhode Island, and New York was at the point of rescinding. Others were moving that way as well, and for all the fiery talk, South Carolina wouldn't be able to stand alone for long. The question was, how long? He couldn't make enough on osnaburg, or cooper's tools, or any other exempted goods. And he couldn't risk returning with a cargo that'd be turned away. The non-import had to be repealed before he left.

He gave her a quick kiss. "Not knowing what sort of ship I can get, I'll have to expect the worst. A slow voyage, then." He paused, figuring. "June. You'll have a June wedding."

"June," she sighed. "Michael, that's a year off. Nearly a year to wait. Let's not. Please! I want to marry now."

He slid down beside her in the bed and kissed her tenderly. "Lord, but I love you. Too much to risk what you're asking. I'll set you up as a queen, not as a destitute."

She studied him, then. A sensuous smile curved her lips, and she stretched against him, catlike. "I love you, too. And," she looked away from him coyly, glancing back at him through the sweep of hair that fell across her face, "I want you to love me. Again.''

He groaned as she slid her leg across him, almost as if by accident. "A babe in the making—do you really want to chance it?''

"I love you enough to risk it,'' she murmured, throwing his words back at him. Then his lips fell on hers.

14

Once Michael saw the snow *Swift* at the Hobcaw shipyard, he knew he'd found his ship. As advertised in front of the Printing House, she was eighty-nine feet on the deck, seventy-five on the keel, of two hundred tons burden. But that didn't carry the feel of her. She seemed in motion even while tied to the pilings. She was made to knife through the sea.

Mr. Lempriere, one of the owners of the shipyard, showed him through. The wiry man was willing to tell him what he knew, good and bad, and what he'd heard, and, for a wonder, which was which. She'd been built on the Chesapeake of good Virginia oak. Her owner-captain had died two days out of Charlestown on her first voyage. His heirs were more interested in farmland than in ships. It was so she went under the hammer.

As Lempriere talked, Michael went over the ship rib by rib and spar by spar, even, to the yard owner's surprise, crawling down into the bilge to check its soundness.

Back on deck, under the raucous seagulls, Michael spoke.

"I'll want her name changed."

Lempriere grinned. "You buy her, you can do with her what you want."

"I'll buy her, all right. When I do I'll want you to put the name *Hussar* on her. And a new figurehead, a hussar in black and silver, with a lightning bolt on his shako, and his saber held out as if he's at the charge."

Catching his fervor, Lempriere eyed him curiously. "Done."

"Good, then. I'll be back. Daniel! Stir your stumps. Get me back to the city, and quickly."

"Do that be the one, Mr. Fallon?" Daniel asked.

"That it does," Michael grinned. "That it does."

Daniel grinned back, and called a faster stroke to the oarsmen than they'd ever heard before. The boat flew over the water back to Carver's Bridge. Michael hit the wharf running for his carriage. It was late in the morning; he must arrange his appointments at once. The ship might even be his by dark.

He left the first refusal from a banker surprised, but not downhearted. The second he left thoughtful. The man seemed to have no reason except that he didn't want to lend to Michael. There were still others, though.

The second day was the same as the first, only longer, and the third. He heard excuse after excuse. Money was tight, and there wasn't any to lend. The money market was so good they'd loaned too much and had no more available.

Michael left the last office scowling, deep in his own thoughts. He threw himself into his carriage, muttered orders to the driver. What in all the circles of hell was happening? And where was he going to get the money?

The carriage stopped, and he realized they were on Church Street in front of the Carver house.

Seth took his tricorn and walking stick, but after a look at his face bowed him in without speaking. Mr. Carver was coming down the stairs and he entered; he tried to put on a smile to greet the old man.

"It's good to see you, sir."

"And good to see you, Michael. Is something the matter?"

"I'm tired, sir. I came to see Elizabeth."

"Certainly. Seth, tell Miss Elizabeth that Mr. Fallon is here. Come in, Michael. A drink and a smoke while you await her."

Neither spoke again until they were ensconced, pipe and brandy in hand, in front of the fireplace in Carver's study. It had changed not at all from his first sight of it. The same large globe stood in the corner, and, as so often, a map was spread on the desk. Abruptly he realized Carver was watching him, waiting for him to speak. At random he chose a topic.

"I saw the statue of William Pitt the Assembly had put up. I wonder what the King thinks of that. Pitt so often opposes him over America. Or does he even know of it?"

"Since the Assembly voted public monies to pay John Wilkes' debts," Carver said drily, "I rather think His Majesty and his ministers are aware of almost everything that happens in South Carolina. At present, though, their attention is probably somewhat further north."

Michael nodded. "That massacre up in Boston back in March. I was surprised they were trying the soldiers in a civil court."

"Massacre," Carver snorted. "A mob of layabouts and dock idlers throwing rocks and ice at Customs House sentries till the soldiers were forced to fire in self defense."

"I've read an account of it, sir, by a Samuel Adams."

"Sam Adams, Michael? He's Massachusetts' answer to Gadsden, and he's as little regard for the truth if it'll advance his cause. He took a group of men, some of whom not even he would associate with, and turned them into heroes. All because it makes the British look bad, and he's in favor of anything that does that." He leaned forward intently, and his voice grew more impassioned. "Listen, Michael. Adams' own cousin, John, is one of the advocates for the soldiers, and he's a staunch man for American rights. It's as if John Rutledge was defending them. Massacre? Bah! It was a riot!" He sat back, and the color began to recede from his face. "I shouldn't get so worked up over something a thousand miles away. We've our own problems. How long do you give non-importation now that South Carolina stands alone?"

"Six months, perhaps." Had the answer to that seemed so important just a few hours ago? Now that there was no ship, it no longer mattered. "Not so long, I think. There have been fewer and fewer protests of late over the rest of the colonies breaking through except for tea. By the end of the year it'll end here as well."

A day ago he'd have been ecstatic to think it might end sooner, but now——. "Perhaps they just don't see the reason to keep the embargo on everything when all the duties have been repealed, excepting tea."

"Possibly. It's more likely that more and more are tired of watching our pious friends in the upper colonies pile up the shillings while shelves go bare in Charlestown. Michael, blast it, there's something wrong. Now what is it?" The old merchant hesitated a second. "I was on Queen Street yesterday, and I happened to see you coming out of Jacob Shuhl's offices. If you need a little assistance—. Tell me, Michael. Let me help."

Bit by bit the story came out, or at least the bare bones of it. He told Carver that he wanted to buy a ship, and his plans for it, but not his plans for Elizabeth. He told of the refusals he'd gotten at every turn. Carver regarded him sourly.

"Why didn't you come to me in the first place? I'll lend you the money right now. I know you'll stand good for it, and I trust you a deal more than some I've done business with."

"I can't do that," Michael said stiffly. "It's as a friend I think of you, sir, and a man can't be running to borrow from his friends."

"Damnation, man, if not your friends, then who? All right. I'll take a lien on your next year's rice crop, just as a banker would. I'll even charge the same interest. There. You can't say I'm giving special favors. Well? Will you take the loan and buy the ship, or will you let stubborn pride stand in your way?"

Michael hesitated. Borrowing from a friend was bad. If it must be done, then let it be done in the open. "I must tell you if I get this ship I'll be asking for your daughter's hand. I love Elizabeth, sir. I want her to be my wife. I'd meant to ask once I had the ship, but you can see that I can't borrow the money from you without you knowing."

Finally, Carver thought. He'd wondered how long it would take the young Irishman. In many ways he lived by a stiffer code than any aristocrat. "Michael, I'm delighted. Your answer must come from Elizabeth, but I doubt she'll disappoint you. Now, what is the name of that snow? *Swift?*"

On the veranda, where the day's briskness was giving way

to the cold of evening, Elizabeth stood watching the garden, unmindful of the chill. Sad, she thought, how it grew drabber the closer Christmas came. By rights that was when it should be in bloom. She tapped her foot suddenly. What *was* going on in there? How *could* Michael keep her waiting so long? When the door opened she whirled, a scold for Michael dying on her lips as she saw her father with him.

"Come in, child," Carver said. "You haven't even a shawl. You'll take a chill." As her father and Michael brought her indoors, the sudden warmth made her shiver. "You see, my dear. Now come into the drawing room. I've something important to say to you."

Michael smiled at her, relishing the primness of her proper attitude, hands folded in front of her. His memory held her in another posture, wanton, crying out—he pulled himself together.

"My dear, Mr. Fallon—Michael—has asked for your hand in marriage. I've given my blessing. But I've told him the answer must come from you."

A smile, half pleasure, half relief, spread on her face. "Yes, Papa. Of course." She rose on tiptoe to kiss Michael's cheek chastely, hoping he didn't smell the wine she'd drunk to steady her nerves.

Carver rubbed his hands together happily. "Yes. Well. I believe this calls for a toast. I'll ring for—"

Michael stopped him with a hand on his arm. "Sir, if I'm to get that ship, I'd better return to Hobcaw right away. Who knows who's there by now, trying to buy it out from under me. Elizabeth, you do understand?"

Elizabeth nodded. If he thought he needed that damned ship, let him get it over and done with.

"Very well," Carver said. "In that case, I'll leave you two to your goodbyes." He closed the door firmly as he left.

Michael waited no longer than the door's clicking shut to sweep Elizabeth up in his arms. She met his kiss with a half-sob. Her fingers cupped his head, pulling his lips against hers harder, till they felt swollen and bruised and burning.

"Oh, girl," he said hoarsely, "I don't know how I'm

going to wait till our wedding day.''

"Don't," she breathed. "Don't wait." She met his eye,
and hers were large and moist. "I, I've dreamed about—
what happened at Tir Alainn." And about what she'd do to
him when they were alone again, naked, and his hard body
belonged to her lips and fingers. "Michael, don't wait."

"God's name, and I want you. But the risk, to your name
and worse."

"Bother the risk." She showered kisses around his lips
and along his jaw. "Please, Michael. Please." She backed
away toward the door. "Seven o'clock, Michael darling. In
your old room. I'll wait till you come, no matter how late."
And she was gone.

Michael stared after her and took a shuddering breath.
Damn the woman, anyway. It was hard enough without this.
He'd have to be strong enough for both of them.

Hellfire and damnation! He must make haste to get to
Hobcaw and back by seven.

The *Hussar*, ex-*Swift*, was moved to Carver's Bridge for
the loading of her cargo. Lempriere had made a fine
figurehead, and at Michael's order had divided the stern
cabin into a captain's quarters and owner's quarters. Michael
had wanted Christopher for the command, but Byrne was in
England with the *Annalee*, or maybe on the way back. Either
way the *Hussar* would be gone long before he got back. In his
place was a dour Georgian named Barker, for whom four
words was a speech. Carver had recommended him. Michael
was expecting a safe but dreary voyage in his company.

Michael spent his days at the Bridge, overseeing the loading of his rice. Daniel drove his boatmen to barge it to
Charlestown, but the flow never seemed fast enough. The
nights Michael spent with Elizabeth, or a part of them at
least, hidden away in his old room over the stables with only
a few blankets and each other for warmth. They met now as if
by arrangement, with no words needing to be spoken, losing
themselves in their passion, talking of their life after marriage. She was surprised at his passion, wondering how a

man could be so innocent about so many things, yet so worldly in ways of the flesh.

Long before the formal announcement would have been made, an informal one appeared, almost by chance, in the *Gazette*. Appended to the sailing announcement for the *Hussar* was a brief line:

Also sailing with the vessel will be the owner, Mr. Michael Fallon, the Santee planter, who is engaged to marry Miss Elizabeth Carver, the daughter of Mr. Thomas Carver of this city.

Michael laughed over it, but Elizabeth was cross. It took away the fun of surprising her friends, she said, and with so long before the wedding, who could say what sort of bridal parties they'd give her. It was all Michael's fault. But the little spat was made up, and pleasurably, before sailing.

On a cold, mid-January morning in 1771, *Hussar* dropped down the harbor. With an offshore breeze she caught the tide at its peak and skipped over the bar, leaving the shore behind, and Elizabeth and her father, watching from the bridge.

The snow dipped her nose into the first gray-green swells of the Atlantic. Far ahead lay Lisbon.

15

Elizabeth peered into the bowl queasily, but the dry heaves were gone. Where was that fool Samantha? She lay down on her bed, a damp cloth covering her eyes. Suddenly the door burst open, and she snatched the cloth away.

"Well?"

Samantha's black face seemed tinged with gray. "Mamma Kamala, she say yes and no. You got a baby in you."

Elizabeth buried her head in her arms. She'd wanted it so badly that first time. If it'd come to her then, Michael wouldn't be off in the middle of the ocean. He'd be safely married. Then, when she'd stopped thinking of it even, it happened. She'd refused to believe it at first. She'd thought it was just some sort of female complaint. But if she'd really believed that, why hadn't she gone to Dr. Harker? She'd sent to Mamma Kamala.

"Samantha, what did the witch woman send?"

"Nothing, ma'am."

"Nothing!" She sat up, glaring at the trembling slave. "You go back there right now, Samantha, you hear me. I know she has potions to help women with, with difficulties. You go and get one."

"I don't go back. No, ma'am. She make me hold a rooster while she cut his throat and catch the blood in a cup. For later, she say, and the way she look at me like to shiver my bones. She cut that rooster open, read his insides. She say this baby got to be born."

"Nonsense. She's trying to drive the price up."

"No, Miss Elizabeth, it—."

"Oh, shut up, Samantha," Elizabeth said wearily. "She tried the same thing last year with, with a friend of mine. My

174

friend went back with a pistol and held it on this Mamma Kamala while her maid beat her with a stick, with a promise of worse if her powders didn't work. They worked, all right.''

''Miss Elizabeth!'' Samantha's eyes snapped shut and she shook from head to toe.

She'd certainly be no help, Elizabeth could see. She'd drop dead if that witch woman looked at her hard. Damn, damn, damn! It wasn't fair. Why should she be in this condition, with no one to help her? How could she face anyone, ever again? The Pinckney girls would cut her dead on the street. She'd never be allowed in the Manigault house again. And her father. Oh, God, she didn't even want to think of the horror and disgust on his face when he found out. Damn Michael for bringing this on her, for leaving her like this. It was all his fault.

She caught sight of herself in the mirror. No, that couldn't be her, with haggard eyes, mouth trembling on the edge of hysteria. She had to control herself.

She got up and soaked the cloth, then held it to her face. When she again looked in the mirror it was better. She *was* calm. She could think coolly. She must.

Michael was gone less than four weeks. He'd barely be at Lisbon yet. Then there was time there, time to sail to England, time in England. Lord, she didn't want to think of how many weeks it'd be before he returned. Not weeks. Months. Oh, God! Women went to the altar pregnant, but they were a month or two gone, or at most three. Not bulging as if they were ready to give birth in front of the minister. Not—she shuddered—with a nurse keeping the baby upstairs during the ceremony. No, Michael was gone. She pushed all thoughts of him aside. She had to make new plans.

''Samantha,'' she said abruptly. ''does Justin Fourrier still send flowers and invitations to go riding?''

''Every day since that piece in the *Gazette* 'bout you and Mr. Fallon. He always leave them with Seth. Don't never come in no more.''

Elizabeth hurriedly dug paper, pen, and ink from the

escritoire and began to write. "Take this to the Fourrier house. Give it to Mr. Justin Fourrier only. No one else." She misted the note with her best perfume and handed it to the serving woman. How to deal with Justin Fourrier?

Michael had a gentleman's instincts, if not the birth. Justin had the birth, but his instincts were all of a baser sort. There was no time for a slow falling in love, even if it would've worked. It had to be something fast, as fast as she could force it. The idea came to her.

When Samantha returned to say Justin was coming as soon as his carriage was hitched, she was searching through her dresses for just the right one. When Seth tapped at the door she was waiting calmly, a light shawl over her shoulders concealing the missing modesty piece.

The old butler bowed low. "Miss Elizabeth, Mr. Fourrier says he's here to take you riding, but your father's not to home."

She swept past as if he wasn't there, the slave woman behind her. Seth fell in, trying to think of something to say, but nothing came. Elizabeth set her smile for Justin as she turned to the last flight of stairs.

"Justin, darling. Your invitation came as a Godsend. I couldn't stand another moment indoors. How kind you are. She put up a cool cheek, and after a moment he kissed it. There was a strong odor of brandy about him. So much the better.

"I was surprised—," he began, but she took his arm, and he found himself escorting her out of the house.

Samantha was put up by the driver, much to her displeasure. She kept glancing back over her shoulder; her mistress was sitting much too close to the young gentleman. It looked wrong.

As the carriage moved off Elizabeth let her shawl slip, and he gasped as her breasts were bared almost to the nipples. He knew he'd drunk too much that morning. His father had laid into him about it. But every time he looked down at her, looked down at that pale satin skin, the fumes seemed to whirl even higher in his head.

"Elizabeth," he tried again, "about this Fallon—."

"Oh, I don't want to talk about him," she said, and clutched his arm tightly against her breast. "Can we ride up on the Neck? The river's pretty up there."

"The river?" He swallowed and wished she wouldn't look at him so often. Those eyes—that skin. God, he was burning. He thought of Fallon; his mouth twisted in a sneer.

Elizabeth ignored the sneer, as she ignored the continued worried glances from Samantha, but she noticed the way his gaze strayed to her bosom. She smiled to herself. Good. She kept up an inconsequential chatter about nothing in particular and waited to reach the real battle ground.

The carriage rolled rapidly northward. A few drab men labored at something around the Quaker Meeting House on King Street, and a ragged urchin or two ran playing in the street, but they were all who were to be seen. The sun in a clear, cloudless sky gave little warmth, and those who didn't have to venture out stayed in. Nothing impeded their way up the peninsula and out of the city gates, past the remnants of the old tabby-work wall.

Out of sight of the city on the Neck Road, Elizabeth suddenly asked Justin to stop the carriage, and pointed off toward a low, shrub-covered hill. "Look. There are wildflowers up there. And I'll wager the view of the river is beautiful."

Justin breathed heavily. His every effort to talk of anything but the damned flowers and the damned birds and the damned sky had been cut off short, or worse, ignored. "The carriage won't go up there," he explained with the last of his patience.

"We could walk," she laughed, and noted with pleasure the way his jaw tightened. Excellent. He had to be angry, almost angry enough to kill. Without warning she slipped out of the carriage and danced off toward the hill.

"Elizabeth! Elizabeth, come back here—. Damn it all to hell!" He leaped to the ground, freezing Samantha, who'd been on the point of following her mistress. The driver rolled his eyes once, then kept them straight ahead. "You two stay thcrc,'' Justin snarled. "Don't want to have to round up everybody." He stalked after Elizabeth.

She was on the far side of the hill, out of view of the carriage. "Look, Justin. I've never seen these blue ones before."

He grabbed her by the arms and began shaking her before he knew what he was doing. "What do you mean with all this? Betrothed to Fallon, riding with me, all these damned flowers. What do you mean?"

She managed to jerk free, and began to straighten her hair unconcernedly. "You're very domineering, Justin. One would almost think you were my husband."

He clenched his fists to keep from grabbing her again. "I want answers, Elizabeth. Why did you become engaged to that upstart Fallon?"

Elizabeth paused, as if for thought, then spoke coolly.

"Michael Fallon is the sort of man to sweep a woman off her feet, Justin. Gallant. Dashing. Impetuous. But he's gone now, and the longer he's gone the more I remember he's just an Irish serving man, for all his plantation." She gave a delicate shudder. He moved toward her, but she froze him with an upraised hand. "You?" she mocked. "Oh, no, Justin. You're all right for a carriage ride, but you're hardly a dashing, impetuous lover. Where Fallon doesn't have enough breeding, I'm afraid you have too much." And she laughed like chimes ringing.

Justin could feel the blood pounding in his head. Not dashing, like Fallon? Not impetuous, like Fallon? His face grew redder and redder, a vein throbbing visibly in his temple. Damn Fallon. He lunged forward and grabbed her.

She could barely bite back a scream. There was no reason at all behind his glittering eyes. He bore her to the ground, knocking the breath out of her as he fell on top. His hands were everywhere, turning her like a doll, pushing her skirts up, tearing at her clothes, at his. When he thrust into her she had to choke back another scream. Oh, God, it'd never hurt like that with Michael. Never. He pounded at her, bludgeoning her, grunting, across the ground, his red, sweating face staring down at her unseeing. She tried to grab at the ground, at bushes, at anything. Her hands caught air. God, help her. She was being split in two.

Suddenly he arched up from her, face straining, groaning, and she realized he was putting his seed in her. Triumph flared in her because the other was there first. He rolled off of her and muttered, "Damn Fallon." He panted and heaved like a spent horse.

She tried to shut the pain out of her mind, and almost succeeded. She needed to think of what was important. There. A first twinge of doubt on his face. He was beginning to realize what he'd done. It was all working out quite well. If not his gentleman's upbringing, then his fear of disaster would force a marriage proposal. No, it would not be too bad being Mrs. Justin Fourrier. That brutality of his. With proper schooling that might become something very, very interesting.

She turned to him and fell sobbing on his chest. "I'm ruined! Justin, you've ruined me!" Tears flooded his waistcoat.

What in God's name had he done? He patted her head with one hand and tried awkwardly to rearrange his breeches with the other. She saw from the corner of her eye and shuddered with distaste. He took it for more reaction to the rape. Damn. Rape. And this a girl of breeding, too. Not like catching some farm girl alone in the bushes. Well, his father had said to get the girl pregnant. Maybe he had. And he'd shown her impetuous. Hah!

He turned her face up. "I will, of course, marry you immediately."

"You will?" she sniffled, and carefully hid her triumph.

"Certainly. You are aware that I've always had great fondness, even love, for you. From that—."

His speech was made almost terrifying by the place and by his flat delivery. But when he helped her to her feet she smiled at him and matter-of-factly set to straightening her clothes.

Justin's self-satisfied expression faded when he saw the

condition of her dress. "Listen, my dear. I think we'd better
say you had a fall. To account for—." He finished with a
gesture.

"Whatever you say, Justin," she murmured with a secret
smile.

Justin took her arm and led her back to the carriage. He
could barely keep the conquering smirk from his face.
Wouldn't it be sport when Fallon returned. He'd certainly
clipped his comb this time.

The *Hussar* sailed into the Mar da Palha, the great inland
bay that served Lisbon, in early March. A speedy passage
had been ruined by more than three weeks of near calm,
where offal thrown over the side in the morning was not out
of sight at nightfall. Still, there was hope for a good market.
March was not too late.

Before the ship was well into the mouth of the Tagus a
small boat appeared off the bow, pitching up and down, its
occupants clinging hard. One risked letting go to cup his
hands to his mouth.

Captain Barker motioned the first mate, the man with the
best Portuguese, to the rail. He finally straightened with a
nod. "Says if we got rice he'll give half a moidore the
quintal, here and now."

"Good price," Barker said, and snapped his mouth shut as
though he'd said too much.

Michael shook his head slowly. It was a good price, just
about what he'd hoped to sell for. But—. "Why did he row
out here to offer it?"

"These buyers race each other, Mr. Fallon," the mate
said. "Why, half a dozen will likely be on board before the
anchor's touched bottom."

Michael waved the boat away. "We'll wait till quayside.
If they offer as much out here, it won't be less there."

The bay was packed with ships, and there was activity
around almost every one. No sooner was the *Hussar* seen
than a dozen boats broke for her, some from the shore, a few
from other ships. They raced like many-legged insects over

the foul-smelling, sewage-laden water, with much shouting and shaking of fists between them. But the first boat slid alongside far ahead of the others.

A swarthy little man whose clothes seemed cut too fine for him climbed over the rail and made a leg to the quarterdeck. "Your pardon," he said with an indeterminate accent, "this is an American ship, or an English ship?"

"There's no difference," the captain bristled.

"An American ship," Michael stepped in quickly, "from South Carolina. We have eight hundred tierces of rice on board. If you'd care to step below, we can talk over a glass of wine."

The little man waved his hands back and forth vigorously. "No, no. You misapprehend. I have no interest in rice. I may wish to ship a packet with you. Do you go to England from here?"

The other boats began arriving in knots, the buyers coming close to blows as they scrambled aboard. "Captain Barker, will you and Mr. Henning make those buyers comfortable? But don't agree to anything till I'm there. Now, if you'll come below we'll talk about your packet, Mr.—."

"Your pardon again. I am only a messenger. If you go next to England, I will take you to my master."

Michael frowned. It was a lot of to-do over what this man called a packet. Still, it might not be a bad idea to let the buyers stew awhile. "Captain Barker, I'll be going ashore for a time. Remember, no agreements till I get back."

Barker nodded briefly while he and the mate tried to keep the shouting, gesticulating buyers apart. Better him than me, Michael thought as he climbed down to the little man's boat.

The oarsmen were a dark-eyed, sullen lot, but they put their backs into it, and the boat fairly flew back to shore. The swarthy man kept silent all the way to the stone steps leading down from the quay, and then he leaped ashore and said, "Follow me, please." Michael had to hurry to keep up.

The way they took was alley and bypath, with stone and stuccoed buildings crowding in on every side, often even overhanging the street till only a narrow strip of sky showed.

Archways crossed the alleys at irregular intervals, and in spite of the laughing people Michael thought it had the feel of a prison.

The little man ducked through a doorway, and Michael followed, down a long, narrow hall, up a flight of stairs and down another hall. Suddenly they were in a space that was no part of an alley dwelling. The great floor was polished tile, and the sconces held candles that burned with the pure light of spermaceti. Portraits dotted here and there showed men and women in court dress of years past.

"Where in hell is this?" Michael asked.

"The embassy of His Most Christian Majesty," the swarthy man said, and hurried on.

The French embassy! He'd take a glass of wine maybe, and get the hell out of there. Without any packets that'd likely be getting him arrested as a spy.

The little man ushered him into a palatial room with a high, vaulted ceiling and bowed himself out. At first he thought he was alone. Two tall windows cast their light so that anyone behind the desk would be cloaked in shadow, anyone before it half blinded. Something moved in that shadow, and a man slender as a rapier moved into the light. "I am Charles Marie Giscard d'Empernay." He touched his lips lightly with a lace handkerchief. "Might I have the honor of your name?"

"I am Michael Shane Fallon," he said with matching dignity.

"Ah, most excellent. I told Belette to bring me an American ship captain, and he brings an Irishman as well. Most excellent."

It was trouble, all right. If he smashed one of those windows, how far would the drop be to the ground? "I'm the owner, not the captain. To what do I owe this honor, Monsieur d'Empernay?"

"I have the position most humble. A secretary, no more." He caught Michael's sardonic glance around the room and smiled. "Come, sir. Will you have a glass of Malmsey with me? A taste I acquired while serving in your England."

"As your man was so careful to discover, I'm not English. I'm an American." He took the proffered glass and raised it.

"Your health, sir."

"Um? Yes, and yours. American. Of course. A slip of the tongue," he said blandly. "Interesting people, you Americans. Two come to mind, Samuel Adams and Christopher Gadsden. Do you by any chance know of them?"

Michael felt a sudden chill. "I've met Mr. Gadsen," he said carefully. "We're both from Charlestown."

"Tell me, what do you think of their treasons?"

"Not treasons. They may demand too much at times, but they're loyal men. They commit no treasons. Nor do I."

D'Empernay looked amused. "Of course not. I would never suggest that you would." He seemed to make a decision." What I do wish is for you to take this to England." He took a foot-square bundle of heavily tarred sailcloth from his desk and held it out. "I will pay you one hundred pounds sterling."

Damn. "Just to be carrying a packet to England?"

"It is to a countryman of yours," d'Empernay went on. He considered Michael. "His name is Franklin. Dr. Benjamin Franklin."

Franklin? Benjamin Franklin had risen since being the deputy postmaster for the colonies. Inventor and publisher, founder of the American Philosophical Society and of the College and Academy of Philadelphia, he'd been honored by every university and society in Europe, including the Royal Society, itself. Men were already calling him the greatest man of the age. By God, what was he doing mixed up with the French?

D'Empernay sensed his hesitation. "I assure you, Mr. Fallon, you will commit no treason by the carrying of this packet. It contains only information that Dr. Franklin has requested, no more. This I will swear to you by whatever you wish. The Bible, my mother's grave, my honor. It is as I say."

Would Franklin be enmeshed in spying? He'd spoken often against the tyranny of Parliament and for American rights, but this? With the French? It couldn't be. "I'll take it," he said.

All the way back to the *Hussar* he had the feel of being

followed, watched. It wasn't true, he knew. Still, the feeling persisted. It was that packet. Normally he'd have taken the opportunity to see a little of the town. Now he couldn't wait to bury the packet in the bottom of his sea chest.

On the *Hussar* only two of the buyers were left. They stood on deck, sweating in spite of the cool breeze down the bay, eyeing each other suspiciously. The captain watched them impassively, but Henning, the mate, seemed excited. They must be getting close to a final price, Michael thought, and hurried below to hide the tarred bundle.

As he stepped back on deck one of the buyers said, "One moidore the quintal," in a slow, thick accent.

A moidore! God's name, that was nearly ten pounds currency. Before he could move the second buyer said, "Six moidores the barrel," and mopped the sweat on his thin face. The other exploded at him in a high-pitched tirade that even Henning couldn't follow. In seconds they were toe to toe, yelling in each other's face, waving their arms around so as to endanger anyone who came too close. The first man broke away and said, "Seven moidores."

Seven moidores! That was nearly seventy pounds a barrel. Over double the best Michael could have hoped for. He turned to Captain Barker. "Why, in God's name? Rice can't be in that short a supply."

"But it is," Henning broke in. "Rice and anything else you can eat. Didn't you hear it ashore? The crops failed in Germany. The whole Continent's running scared from a famine."

Michael began to laugh, and the captain and mate joined in. Lord, the irony of it. People were afraid of starving, and for that he'd get all he hoped for and more. He could pay the loan on this ship, and have his reserve. He could build that house in Charlestown for Elizabeth.

The fat buyer waddled up. "Other one go. I buy now, yes please."

"You buy now, yes indeed," Michael laughed. "Come below and we'll be signing the papers. Captain Barker, would you be good enough to go ashore and find some

Madeira at a reasonable price? I want to sail for London as soon as we can.''

''London! Plan was Bristol.''

''Well, it's London now.'' He grimaced. Franklin was in London. He could get rid of that packet quickly and safely. He hoped.

The Thames quayside was busy, as usual, and the river stank worse than the Tagus, but none of that had Michael's attention. The customs had come on board before the last hawser was around a bollard on the quay. They poked into every corner, certain that any vessel owned by those wretched colonials must be smuggling.

Finally they turned to settle the duties on the casks of Madeira cramming the hold. Then another argument arose. The duty on the wine was seven pounds sterling in the ton. Small enough, but the excisemen insisted that each cask must weigh two or three times what was listed on the manifest. Barker and Henning took turns trying to wear down the customs men's obstinacy while Michael watched impotently. Only the captain and mate had authority to deal.

''I say there, is this the *Hussar*, from Charlestown in South Carolina?''

The two young men picking their way up the gangplank made Michael stare. They wore suits of brocade, one in orange, the other a bright lavender, with matching tricorns trimmed in white fur, and each with enough lace for two men. Their faces were partially hidden behind their pomanders but they seemed familiar in some way.

They had reached the ladder to the quarterdeck and were waiting for him to speak. ''This is the *Hussar*. I'm her owner, Michael Fallon. What can I do for you?''

''Fallon?'' said the one in orange. ''Michael Fallon of Charlestown? You must be the man who had that set-to with Justin some years back. I'd have given a guinea to see that. Stab me, I would. I'm Louis Fourrier, and this is my brother, Henri. We want passage back to Charlestown.''

That was why they looked familiar. Justin at twenty,

perhaps, but smaller, and with the meanness gone, that was what they looked like. "I'm certain we can arrange something," he said slowly. "Perhaps you'd like to come below. Those excisemen may be reluctant to let you leave for fear you'd smuggle some dust off."

They turned as one to look at the captain and the still squabbling customs men, then at each other. "Capital suggestion, Mr. Fallon," Louis said. He flipped open an enameled snuffbox with a practiced twist of the wrist and extended it with a questioning look. Michael shook his head, and they occupied themselves as they followed him below with the ritual of sniffing a pinch up each nostril, then sneezing prodigiously into lace hankerchiefs.

As Michael set out wine glasses, Louis spoke again. "I fear we owe you an explanation, Mr. Fallon, for what may seem a disgraceful lack of family feeling." Henri nodded. "You see, there are a good ten years between Justin and ourselves, and there was never any brotherly interest on his part. The devil spit me if he ever noticed us except to cuff us aside if we got in his way. And when we got too big for that we were shipped off to the dungeons of Oxford."

"He never cuffed Brielle," Henri piped up. "That's Gabrielle, our younger sister."

Michael hurried away from more familial revelations. "Oxford, do you say? Going into the law?"

Henri and Louis glanced at each other and sighed. "We were to be admitted to the Inns of the Court later this year."

"The Middle Temple," Henri added.

"But Chaplin Ames never did get over finding a horse in his bed, falling down drunk on his best brandy."

"I think he minded the horse less than the brandy."

"Of course, he never did prove it was us."

"But he did have suspicions."

Michael stared at them in amazement. One took up the remark of the other so smoothly you could barely tell when one stopped and the other began. "Are you saying they gave you the boot?" he asked, and burst out laughing in spite of himself.

"Not for that," Louis said. "Not for pranks. No, it was the copies of David Hume in our digs, and worse, Rousseau and Voltaire. Might not have been so bad, but we'd had a bottle or so too many, and argued we had a right to read them. Hell, we said Voltaire and the rest were right. That's what did it."

"Might have been dunking the proctor in the rain barrel."

"Not at all, Henri. That was because he said it was a proven fact all colonials were bastards. Different thing altogether. Couldn't allow that, even if he was a proctor. You can see that, can't you, Mr. Fallon?"

"I can that." He was beginning to like these two. How could anyone have the Fourrier blood, yet be so unlike Justin?

Barker stuck his head in the door. "Excisemen are gone. We only paid half again as much as was due. Bah!" He withdrew with a grimace, and the three men found themselves all trying not to laugh.

"Listen," Michael said, "I intend sailing within the week. There's no reason for you to pay a landlord for that time, if you don't mind a little cramping. Move your things aboard the *Hussar*."

"Well, the gentleman we're staying with lets us stay gratis," Louis said, "but I doubt he'd object to our leaving."

"Yes, Dr. Franklin thinks we lack sensibilities."

It took an effort for Michael to finish rising smoothly. "Dr. Franklin?"

"Benjamin Franklin," Henri said. "Surely you know of him. He's the most famous man in England, some say in the whole world."

"Yes, I know of Dr. Franklin." He hesitated, then swiftly dug out the packet from Lisbon. "In fact, I'd like to walk with you, if you have no objections. I'd like to meet the great man in person."

The streets of London were unbelievably dirty. Grime. Offal. Filth. It was everywhere, in the streets, on the buildings, on the people. As they stepped over and around piles of garbage, Michael wished for one of the pomander balls that

the Fourriers kept tight to their noses. Once away from the
river, the garbage was gone, the smell less, but the dirt was
still there. It'd been in Lisbon, too, but that was different.
Lisbon was foreign. London was as much a part of him as
Dublin. Now it was foreign, too.

That came as a start. He'd changed in America, in Charlestown. There were ragged people there, too, and dirt in
plenty, but it was the dirt of a day, with the feel that a man
could wash it off and go where he would. These men had the
grime of centuries ground into their faces, inherited from
their fathers, to be passed on to their sons. The Old World,
with old ways, would go on forever, unchanging, with its
people trapped inside.

Glumness settled on him at the thought. Not even Henri
and Louis' high spirits made any impression, so that when
they reached the house they were glad to lead him to the study
and hurry away to their rooms. Michael tapped on the door,
and a murmured voice bade him enter.

Benjamin Franklin stood in the middle of the room with a
book under his arm, his finger marking the place. He was a
jowly man, with a large nose and an extra chin, in his middle
sixties. Michael had heard much of his plain dress, and
expected something on the order of Quaker or Puritan garb,
but Franklin's suit was of rust-colored velvet. He was plain,
it seemed, only in contrast to the rainbow around him.

Franklin looked at him questioningly. His eyes were clear
and keen. "Can I help you, young man? I don't believe I
know you."

"My name is Michael Fallon, Dr. Franklin." He held out
the packet. "I was asked to bring you this. From Lisbon."

Franklin turned the packet in his hand, then set both it and
the book on his desk. "Would you care for some wine, Mr.
Fallon, is it? Irish. Delightful place, Ireland. I was there for a
time last year, and I mean to go again."

"No, thank you, sir. I only came to deliver that thing. And
I'm American now. I'm sailing back to Charlestown within
the week. The two young Fourriers will be sailing with me."

"Yes, the Fourriers. Right-thinking lads, but with far too

much liking for the frivolous. Charlestown. As hot for American liberties as any in the colonies, but a bit inclined to let their passions sweep them along. I had an interest in a newspaper there, once. Perhaps you know the owner, Mr. Peter Timothy.''

"I've met him, sir.'' Damn it all, he should leave now. But he couldn't help glancing at the packet.

Franklin smiled. "You're wondering what's in there, aren't you? And yet you brought it to me unopened. What exactly do you think it is?''

"I don't know.'' He frowned and burst out with it. "Seeing as it's from the French, I'm beginning to fear it's to do with rebellion.''

"Rebellion? Lord, no, man. You certainly are Charlestown, aren't you? You've been listening to Christopher Gadsden is what you've been doing. He and Sam Adams are the only two I know of who'd risk such a fool thing.''

"But can the turmoil be settled short of it, sir? Perhaps if William Pitt is called to form another government. He has respect, here and in America, and he's a proper regard for our rights.''

"There are two reasons why Pitt will not return to power, Mr. Fallon. The first is that day by day he grows more infirm and more eccentric. He's aware of his diminished abilities. Witness that in the last administration he formed, he would only accept the position of lord privy seal, more ceremonial than anything else.''

"And the other, sir?''

Franklin smiled sadly. "George III does not share your respect for him. William Pitt is a man of integrity and courage, not afraid to say what he believes is right. He's opposed the King on other matters long before his opposition over America. The King hates him for that crime, and for the worse crime of being so often right in his opposition. He would as soon call the devil to form a government as call Pitt. I'm afraid a peaceful solution must be realized without his help. But what you brought may be of some aid.''

"What I brought,'' Michael said slowly. "I realize, sir, I

don't have any right to ask what's in that packet. But I can't help being curious."

"You deserve to know, Mr. Fallon. It contains opinions. The opinions of prominent men in Spain and Portugal on American events, and their opinions should this thing happen, or that thing. All sent courtesy of the French, who hope, of course, to make use of our troubles for their own gain. They try to use us; we try to use them. It is called diplomacy. If this letter were read in Parliament, there might be cries of shame, but that wouldn't make it treason. Only shameful diplomacy."

"This diplomacy, if you'll pardon me, is a little too sly to be comfortable."

"I don't mind at all," Franklin laughed. "It is sly. I hope we can rely on slyness, and not have to resort to direct action. Here are your two passengers now. Come in, Louis, Henri."

"Has he explained electricity to you yet?" Louis asked.

"Tried with us," Henri said. "Tried lots of times, but it never seemed to sink in."

"I fear your talents lie in other directions," Franklin said drily.

"He means he couldn't beat it into us with a stick," Louis laughed. "Goodbye, Dr. Franklin. It's been good of you to put up with us."

"I'm always ready to help a countryman, Louis. If there's time before you sail, come back to see me before you leave. You, too, Mr. Fallon. I'd like to hear first hand how things are going in the southern colonies."

Michael nodded. Yes, he'd make a point to return. "I'd like that, Dr. Franklin. Now can you be telling me, where would a man be buying a present for his bride?"

16

Hussar made the Charlestown Bar shortly after dawn on the eighteenth of May, 1771 and by nine, was snugly tied to Carver's Bridge. Saying goodbye to the Fourriers at the gangway, Michael never noticed the starts when the men on the wharf heard the name, nor did he see their intent eyes. One or two opened their mouths, as he hurried past, bundles under his arm. There was a Spanish shawl, and an ivory comb for her hair. He had a music box that played ten tunes of the sort that made her laugh, and in his pocket, a wedding ring by the finest jeweler in London.

Christopher Byrne was seated on a box near the street, the reins of his horse in his hand. As Michael approached he rose dolefully. "Michael, I—."

"Have you seen my carriage, Christopher? I thought *Hussar* would be spotted coming up the harbor, and they'd have word to come for me."

"I haven't seen them, Michael. Listen, I must tell you—."

"I've no time for it, lad. Sure and you don't mind if I borrow your horse." He snatched the reins from Byrne and vaulted one-handed into the saddle without spilling a package. "I'm on my way to see my bride," he shouted, and booted the horse in the ribs.

"No! Michael, wait! Michael!" Christopher watched the rider forcing his way through traffic and suddenly kicked at the box he'd sat on. "Damn all women! Damn them all to hell!"

Michael left the horse standing in Carver's carriage path and ran up the steps two at a time. When Seth opened the door he grabbed him.

"Run, man. Run. Tell her I'm here. Tell her I swam the

191

last ten miles towing the ship behind me to get here faster.
Well? Go! Go!''

Seth wet his lips and swallowed. "I, I'll tell Mr. Carver
you're here, sir."

Michael watched him disappear up the stairs. What ailed
the old butler? Ah, it didn't matter. In a minute he'd have
Elizabeth in his arms. Inside of a month they'd be man and
wife.

Mr. Carver came slowly down the stairs, silently took
Michael by the arm, and led him into the study. He looked far
older. Gray-faced, too.

"I came to see Elizabeth, sir. First thing from the ship."

Carver splashed a glass full of brandy to the brim. "Here,
drink this down."

Michael stared at the glass, the packages tumbling from
his grasp. "Oh, God! She's not hurt? Tell me she's not dead.
God, tell me she's not dead."

"She's not dead, Michael. She's alive and well." The old
man seemed close to tears. "Damn it all! There's no easy
way to tell you. She's married to Justin Fourrier."

"That's a hell of a joke." His voice sounded hollow in his
own ears.

"It's no joke. I wish it was. She's at Les Chenes right now.
She's—she's going to have his baby."

Michael didn't realize he was moving until his back hit the
door. Carver was following, saying something, but he didn't
hear. He just turned and ran. He vaulted over the veranda
railing, fell. He grabbed a branch, broken by his fall, leaped
to the saddle, and slashed it down like a whip. The horse
burst into the street scattering pedestrians like quail. Many
others fled as he headed north, peddlers jumping aside with a
curse and a raised fist, carriages lumbering to safety while
the passengers goggled. North, along the Ashley, to the
plantation there, to Les Chenes.

The sun was rising toward the vertical as he galloped up
the oak-lined carriage drive. A slave ran out to take his
panting horse, and stared in amazement as he began pounding on the door.

"Elizabeth! Where are you, Elizabeth?"

A butler opened the door, his black hands shaking. "I, I'm sorry, sir. The Fourrier gentlemen not to home."

Michael pushed past into the hall. "I want to see Eliza—." His jaw tightened. "I want to see Mrs. Fourrier."

"Sir, I have orders—."

Michael rounded on him. "You tell her, damn your hide. You tell her I'm here. Now! Go!"

The slave took one look at Michael's eyes, and ran up the stairs. Michael shook his head. Damn, but he needed a drink. Fourrier's study must be around there somewhere. The first door was the drawing room. At the second he smiled and went in.

He started for the decanters with a bitter grin. If Fourrier was going to steal his woman, he couldn't complain if Fallon stole his whiskey. Before he reached them his step faltered. On the wall, at the end of a line of miniatures of women, was Elizabeth. He took the ivory oval down as gently as if it were the woman herself. It fit neatly in the palm of his hand. But it didn't show half her beauty, he thought. Oh, damn. Why, Elizabeth?

Someone coughed behind him, and he slipped the miniature into his pocket and turned. Samantha stood warily in the door. When he stepped toward her she took two quick steps back.

"Where's your mistress?"

"She send me to say—." She checked to see that she had a clear path out the door. "She send me to say she don't want to see you, not now, not never. She won't talk to you, she won't even look at you. She don't even want you to mention her name."

"Samantha—."

"She say you don't exist no more. She tell me to say that. You don't exist no more. Are you all right, Mr. Fallon? You want some water or something?"

Michael forced his eyes open, but the pain was still there. He fumbled the small box out of his pocket and tossed it to the slave woman. "Here. Give her that. Tell her it's from the King of the Fools."

He stalked past her as she shrank against the door jamb,

out to where a slave walked his horse to cool it. Where now? Hell, maybe. It seemed as good a place as any.

Elizabeth watched him go from her chamber window. She'd thought he'd have more sensibility, than to come to Les Chenes. Papa must have told him she wished not to see or hear from him again. She knew he'd go there as soon as he arrived, and she'd left strict instructions. Ruthlessly she suppressed a glimmer of guilt. Papa deserved the burden for helping Michael go away. And Michael deserved the pain for not being there when she needed him.

She twisted awkwardly on the windowseat as Samantha came in: her body was clumsy with child.

"Well? What did he want? What did he say?"

"He leave this for you. He say, he say it from the King of the Fools."

Elizabeth slowly opened the box. What—? She flinched as the light caught the ring. Oh, damn him!

"He take it hard, real hard."

Samantha stumbled back, gasping, from Elizabeth's blazing glare. "Are you questioning my actions? Do you dare?"

"That Mr. Fallon a good man."

Elizabeth clutched the ring till it cut the skin. Damn him! Damn Samantha! "You go down to Job right this minute."

"Job?" Samantha's eyes blazed. "He whip the field hands. I a house—."

"You tell him twenty lashes, hard! You tell him that! I'll ask to see!"

The slave woman's face was stony. "He hangs them up without no clothes. You do that to me?"

"Go!" Elizabeth shrieked. Her eyes were shut tightly, and all her feeling seemed concentrated on the ring grinding into her palm. "Go!"

Eyes burning, Samantha left the room. Elizabeth's tears were beginning to fall. She threw the ring on the floor and stamped on it over and over. Damn him! Damn him! Damn him!

Christopher paid off the boatmen and scrambled up the

side of *Hussar*. The smell of fresh pitch was heavy on deck. As Michael climbed out of the hold, stripped to the waist and sweaty as any workman, Byrne greeted him cheerfully, though he was shocked to see how gaunt he'd become.

"Michael, lad. You're a rich man. You can hire your sweating done."

"Hello, Christopher," Michael answered bleakly.

Byrne grimaced. This wasn't going to be easy. "You ought to come down to Dillon's, man, or the Bacchus. It's been months you've been back, and they all miss you. Everybody asks after you, even—" he'd been going to say, even Fourrier's brothers. "Gadsden's asked for you, and Rutledge. Even Laurens."

Michael seemed to be listening. Then he spoke. "Would you like this command, Christopher? I need a good captain." Christopher's mouth fell open. Michael was picking a streak of pitch on his arm.

"Lord, man, six months ago I'd have jumped at it. But I managed to buy a half interest in the *Annalee* from, from—" Damn, he mustn't mention the Carver name, either. "Well, I managed to buy a half interest. You can see why I'm wanting to stay." He laughed suddenly. "In a year or two I'll be a full owner myself."

"Well, I'd hoped, but I wish you luck." He took a step away, shouting at some workmen. "No, not over there. It goes below."

Christopher sighed and decided to change tactics. "Ah, you're growing fast, lad. Refitting the *Hussar*, buying the two sloops. That must have been one damn profitable voyage."

"Profitable in some ways," Michael said. "In others not." Christopher grimaced, cursing his own mouth, and tried to speak, but Michael went on. "The sloops? I'd had some thought of building a house in town. I put the money to better use."

Christopher followed him as he picked up his shirt, coat, and hat. "Michael, I'm sorry. You know my brain never knows what my mouth's going to say."

"It's all right. I can think about it, now. Sometimes." He put on the shirt, tucked in, but open to the waist. "Mr. Corning, I'll have a boat here now."

"Michael, listen" Christopher said intently. "You need something of importance to be doing. Come back with me. Help the cause."

"I've set the sloops to smuggle tea and rum, Christopher, and that's as much fighting of the duties as I can do now."

"You have! That's wonderful. Man, you're already near in with us. Come on."

"It's almost time for harvest. If I'm not there they'll let the birds eat half the crop. I'm sorry." He patted Christopher awkwardly on the shoulder. How could he say that he needed the labor and the sweat to find forgetfulness? "Mr. Corning! Where the hell's that boat?"

A half-dozen house slaves were waiting anxiously at the corner of the house when Justin rode up to Les Chenes. He noted with surprise that his father was on the portico. Jean-Baptiste was a firm believer in letting sons come to him, never the other way round. He tossed the reins to a waiting groom and ran up the steps.

"What is it?"

Jean-Baptiste spoke stiffly. "Your wife has come to term before her time. The midwife is with her now." He frowned. "You should have been here."

"I've been about my politics, father. Remember?" He looked down at the waiting faces in the yard, turned up toward Elizabeth's chamber window. "Can't we go inside? Unless you want every damn black on the place to know our business."

Justin headed directly for the brandy, and poured a glass for himself. He turned away while his father poured his, a grimace twisting his face when he saw the blank space at the end of the line of miniatures. Damn. He'd personally supervised the whipping of every single housemaid, but they'd stubbornly denied any knowledge. He would simply have to have another painted.

"And what are these politics?" Jean-Baptiste asked abruptly.

Justin smiled complacently. He'd been expecting this. "The governor's expected back next month. From the moment His Excellency, Lord Charles Greville Montagu, sets foot in Charlestown, he'll be as much as one of our party. He'll be so closely surrounded by our people, whispering in his ear, that Rutledge and Gadsden and the rest will never get close to him."

His father grunted. "Excellent, so far as it goes. But what will your men whisper?"

A long scream drifted down from above, then another. Justin grimaced. Why did women make so much noise in birthing? He wished he were somewhere else, out of earshot.

"The Regulators," he said simply.

"Oh?"

"Montagu must deal with that backcountry rabble, daring to demand courts in their own lands, taking the law into their hands meanwhile. He must follow the example of Governor Tryon in North Carolina. They must be crushed by force, their leaders hanged. To this end we will see that men are sent among them to foment their grievances, get them to gather, as the North Carolina Regulators did at Alamance, and march on Charlestown. They'll be destroyed in one afternoon."

"Perhaps," the elder Fourrier said. "But there is much sympathy for them, among men who should know better. Give them their own courts, they say; why make them come all the way to Charlestown for a trial? Bah! They dilute their own power—and ours." He breathed heavily. "So. You must—"

A rap, and the door swinging open, brought them up short. The red-faced midwife, her gray hair pulled back under a mob cap, stood in the doorway with a bundle in her arms. "Your child, sir," she said.

The Fourriers nearly knocked over their chairs in their hurry. Justin snatched the child from the midwife's arms, and Jean-Baptiste threw open the blanket. Red and blotchy, the infant kicked at the air and squalled.

"A son," Justin breathed.

"A grandson," echoed his father.

"Your lady had a hard time of it," the midwife said, "but she's resting easy now."

"Um? What?" Justin looked at her blankly, then turned his attention back to the baby. "Oh, yes. He's healthy enough, it seems. I thought early babies were puny, spindly things."

The midwife sucked at her teeth and cast a cynical glance at him. If the quality wanted to play games, she'd play. "Aye, sir, that's generally the truth. But some men have the power, sir. They're just so virile the baby develops faster."

"I've never heard such," Justin replied, but she noticed he stood a little straighter. "You've done well. There'll be an extra five pounds for you."

"Thank you, sir." She ducked a curtsey. "Sirs."

Neither of them paid her any mind. "Robert Fourrier." Justin gave it the French pronunciation. "Born September 10, 1771."

Jean-Baptiste nodded, smiling. "He will grow to manhood as Fourrier power grows. He will be a power in this province and beyond."

"Yes, yes." Justin said impatiently. "I can't wait to tell the news. I'll wager I can still catch most of the meeting. They usually talk endlessly afterwards."

His father looked at him in surprise. "You will not go to your wife, congratulate her on giving you a son?"

Justin looked hesitantly at the stairs, then shook his head. "She probably wants to rest." A light of triumph appeared in his eyes. "Besides, I have to let them know I have a son." He dashed out the front door. "Moses! Get my horse, and hurry, damn your soul!"

Michael raised his glass as the young Fourrier brothers took their seats at his table. They were less flamboyant in their dress since returning to America. One wore plain blue silk, the other green. Still, they shone like peacocks in the dim light of Dillon's.

"Gentlemen. Can I be offering you a drink?"
Louis began. "You've been avoiding us."

"We're not to blame for Justin," Henri said.

"We never knew till after you did. Stab me if I think it's
fair."

"Louis is right. We, well, we admire you, and we want to
be your friends. Hell's bells, you can't hold Justin against
us."

Michael smiled in spite of himself. "No, lads, I don't hold
Justin against you. Perish the thought. Why, I hardly hold
him against him. Come now, how about that drink?"

They exchanged glances. "Why not come to our house?"
Louis said. "The wine's better, and we can talk without
being overheard."

Henri couldn't wait to ask what was on the mind of
everyone in the province. "Do you think the governor will
really pardon the Regulators?"

"Justin's furious about the talk. He calls them damned
Scovilites, and says they should all hang."

"Easy, lads, easy." Michael took a guarded look around.
The thin murmur of other conversations drifted through the
tobacco smoke. "That's near as touchy as the tea tax. We'd
better go where we can be alone. Not your place, though. I
doubt I'd be welcome under a Fourrier roof."

"Oh, Papa and Justin are upriver at Les Chenes with
Elizabeth and the baby," Louis said, missing the shadow that
passed across Michael's face. "There's no one there but
Henri and me. Oh, and Brielle, of course. And we've some
rum."

Michael let himself be convinced, and the brothers trooped
him out of the tavern and down Broad Street.

Gabrielle Fourrier was coming down the stairs, wondering
if the brown velvet had any more wear in it, when her
brothers entered the house, a darkly handsome man between
them. They were always bringing someone new home; who
was it this time?

"Michael," Louis said, "this is our baby sister, Gabrielle. Brielle, this is Michael Fallon."

She halted with a gasp, a hand flying to her mouth. "Then you're—."

"Oh, Brielle," Henri cried.

"The man who was to marry Elizabeth Carver?" Michael finished for her. "I was that man. Your servant, miss." He saw a slender, brown-haired girl, of medium height, with a tiny waist and large hazel eyes.

He made a leg to her as her brothers pulled him away, chattering about the governor to distract him. Louis shot her a frown over his shoulder as the three of them disappeared into the study.

Gabrielle sighed and stamped her foot. Oh, her tongue was always getting her into trouble. It wasn't as if she wanted to hurt him, but she knew she had. His eyes had gone blank and hard. Men! Instead of washing their hurts clean with tears, they walled them up inside and let them fester. She almost wanted to cry for him. Which was just being silly.

Still, she'd caused him hurt, and he was a guest. She wouldn't parcel her hospitality out. It must be the same for all under their roof, no matter what Papa and Justin thought. But what could she do to show him a true welcome? Thoughtful, she climbed slowly back up the stairs.

The rum was there as advertised, Michael discovered. They sat in front of the fireplace, hot toddies in hand, to proof them against the November chill, Henri said, since October hadn't been very cool so far, and bandied the new governor's plans about as if they'd have a say in the making of them. It was a satisfying, if brief, conversation, for all three agreed that the backcountry men deserved their own courts and sheriffs. And they all thought pardons were in order for those who'd acted without the courts.

As the logs crackled in the fire, and the talk ranged widely, Michael discovered that the younger Fourriers had indeed spent time with their John Locke and David Hume. They introduced Michael to the ideas of Adam Smith, and made him see why the Americas were potentially more wealthy than England ever could be.

Louis and Henri weren't deep thinkers, but they were

facile, and they accepted others' ideas as quickly as any in Gadsden's cabal. It was evident that Oxford had failed to cement their feelings as Englishmen.

"Well, we just aren't," Henri said, "and there's no use getting bluedeviled over it."

"And there's not an Englishman will pass the chance to let you know you're not," Louis added. "Why, most of them have more contempt for us than for a damned Spaniard. At least the Spaniard's got his own country. All we are is beastly damned colonials."

"Maybe we should have our own country," Henri said. Louis sipped his drink.

Michael looked at them and shook his head. "And just who've you been talking to to get an idea like that?"

"Just Mr. Gadsden," Henri answered.

His brother sighed. "I think you've drunk too much."

"But it's only Michael."

Louis cast a long-suffering look to heaven, but Michael only laughed. "It's all right. I'm maybe not a Gadsden man, but then maybe I'm not so far off. But think you on this. The hard part of getting your own country is, you must bleed for it." He looked at the bottom of his glass and set it down with a sigh. "And I must be going."

He took a deep breath on the steps. It was warm for an autumn afternoon. Perhaps the walk back to his rooms over Dillon's would do him good.

"Mr. Fallon, may I speak with you?" Gabrielle waited in the carriage path, clutching a book in front of her, until he joined her, a puzzled look on his face. "Some of my friends and I meet every week in a reading circle. Generally, we take turns reading aloud, but sometimes a gentleman will read to us. Would you please be one of them?"

He couldn't help frowning. Lord, but women were a deceitful lot. What did this one really want? "Why?" he asked sharply. "You've never seen me before today."

Her eyes went wide, and a blush mounted to her cheek. He'd been hurt. That was the reason for his rudeness. It didn't release her from her obligation. "You're a friend of my brothers, Mr. Fallon. And you're known as a gentleman of the best sort, no matter what Justin says." Another blush suffused her face, made worse by her anger at herself. "Oh, drat my tongue. Mr. Fallon, you've been shamefully treated by this house. Please let me make amends. Please?"

Her flaming cheeks and pleading eyes made him instantly contrite. She was a child. "It would pleasure me to read for your circle. But do you realize you've no idea how I read? For all you know every word must be dragged out bodily."

"Oh, I can't believe that," she smiled. Suddenly she remembered the book she carried, *Gulliver's Travels*. It had been the last book read by the circle, and seeing it had given her the idea. She thrust it into Michael's hands. "Here, Mr. Fallon. You will read to me, and I will see how well you do it. Come, now. You can't refuse. After all, it was you who raised the doubt."

He had to smile. "Very well, Miss Gabrielle. If you insist."

"Oh, I do." She led the way back to the garden, and sat on a stone bench beneath an old oak. "And please sound out all the parts, gruff voices for the villains and the like."

She seemed to find more ways to make him smile. He sat down and opened the book.

"Gulliver's Travels," he began, "by Jonathan Swift. Part One, A Voyage to Lilliput. Chapter One—"

She smiled, less interested in a story she'd heard a dozen times before than in the effect she'd achieved. He'd smiled, and the smile had almost reached his eyes. And he did read with expression, in a fine, deep voice. The circle would surely be delighted. In any case, it seemed she'd made up for her blunder.

When Michael finally closed the book on Gulliver's offer to go to war for the Emperor of Lilliput, Gabrielle realized to her surprise that she'd enjoyed herself. "Mr. Fallon, your voice is splendid. I promise the circle will take little of your time, and we do serve refreshments. Though not spiritous, I'm afraid."

"How could I refuse," Michael laughed, "even without spirits?"

On impulse, as she reached for the book, he swept his leg and kissed her hand. He laughed away her blushes and tucked the book into her hands. "Until your friends need reading to."

She'd certainly never met anyone like this Mr. Fallon. How could Elizabeth have possibly given him up for Justin? Gabrielle headed thoughtfully back to the house.

Jean-Baptiste studied the report with pursed lips, and consigned it to the fire with a muttered curse. Another meeting of that traitorous little cabal! Oh, it'd been disguised as a meeting of the Smoking Club at John Rutledge's house, but Gadsden had been there, and Timothy, and others whose names would one day figure in a state trial. And among those names: Fallon. And Henri and Louis.

Damn the boys. Damn them. They defied him. He thrust savagely at the burning logs with a fire iron. Why had they ever chosen to return on Fallon's ship last year. One thing was plain, though. During the voyage, in some way, Fallon had managed to gain their confidence and trust, and twist their minds toward this damned rebellious cant.

They were past the age when he could force them to obey, short of threatening to disown them. That he would not do, at least not now. They were Fourriers. If they could no longer be trusted to be a part of the grand dream, they could still be saved from themselves.

Mauma Rosa passed the door with year-old Robert, gurgling with laughter, in her plump arms. Distracted, Jean-Baptiste motioned for her to enter. It was good to be a grandfather. She held the boy up, and he reached to pat his cheek. An inch away his hand froze. His face was suddenly wooden. The boy's laughter died.

"Do you be all right, sir?"

"Hush." It was impossible. He simply had Fallon too much on his mind. And yet it was there to see. "Take him away."

He slammed the door behind her and her crying charge. How long since the child was old enough that he should have seen? Six months? But was it really there? The blue eyes could have come from Elizabeth. His coloring was easily Fourrier. But now, on that infant face, were the emerging cheekbones and the damning hook nose of Fallon blood.

God curse the name! He managed to calm himself. His heart pounded so hard that his chest and arm hurt. He sank panting into a chair and massaged away the pain. It must be kept from Justin. He'd go storming out to fight a duel, and no matter the outcome the Fourrier name would be stained forever. No, the boy would be raised as a Fourrier. If he must be watched, if he could not be allowed the highest seat, nevertheless, before Jean-Baptiste finished with him he would be a Fourrier.

Still, the snit must be dealt with, and now. He strode out of the study with a face like a thundercloud. The first servant to see him tried to duck out of view, but he stopped her with a gesture.

"Where is my son's wife?"

Relief shone on her face. "She be in the circular garden, sir. She—" but he was gone.

One look at his face, and Elizabeth stepped back, hands rising toward her face. He grabbed her wrists, crushing them together. With a scream she went to her knees on the gravel path.

"Tell me everything you know of Michael Fallon's past," he said. His eyes burned into hers.

"Oh, God, don't! It hurts!"

"Look at me, girl. Look at me. You talked often with Fallon. He seduces"—he paused craftily—"my sons into treason. I will know what I must to destroy him. Tell me."

She began to sob with relief, and to babble. "He was a soldier, a hussar. He lived near the River Shannon. He had a friend named Timothy Cavanaugh. He—."

Jean-Baptiste smiled thinly. Excellent. And the pain in his chest was completely gone, now, though when he thought of this woman in rut with Michael Fallon—. He tightened his grip. Most satisfying, the way her speech was punctuated by moans, and the way her fingers fluttered so helplessly. Most satisfying.

The man who sidled into Jean-Baptiste's study had common clothes, a common voice, a common face. There was a gleam of avarice in his eye as he appraised the rugs and furnishings, but it was gone in an instant. He stopped in front of the desk, hat in hand.

"You sent for me, sir?"

Jean-Baptiste fixed him with a silent, unblinking stare. Twice the fellow opened his mouth and closed it again. Fourrier watched the sweat pop out on his forehead. As he opened his mouth for the third time, Jean-Baptiste spoke. "You are a weasel," he said flatly. "A ferret. A slinker in back alleys."

The man started to protest, thought better of it. Fourrier smiled. "I am told you can find out anything, about any man, given the time and the money."

"Yes, sir," the man said nervously. "I—."

"Be silent! I have in my possession sworn affidavits. It seems there was a girl who claimed her child was yours. She was found in the river with her throat cut. A man in New York who owed you money was found with his skull split open and his strongbox rifled."

"It weren't me, sir." The man's voice held a vicious desperation. "I never—."

"I told you to be quiet. Now. If you betray me, if you fail me in the slightest, I will see that these affidavits are handed to the magistrate, along with your person.

The man twitched as if he was being prodded with hot irons. "God's love, sir, I'll do anything you want. Just, just don't—."

"At the moment I want quiet." He waited, watching the man sweat, letting the time weigh on nerves grown thin. "So. In this folder is information about one Michael Shane Fallon. He was a soldier. He is ambitious. He has a certain native intelligence. Yet he came here as a bound man. He was running from something. I want to know what. If it will hang him,—if you serve me well—one thousand pounds is yours."

"It'll hang him, I swear to you, sir. I'll find it to hang him."

Jean-Baptiste smiled, and the man shivered. "There are letters for you. One is to a man in England, where you will go first. He will dole out expense money to you, so long as it is properly accounted for. The others will do the same as you follow the trail. And you will follow it wherever it leads. But do not take too long. I might think you are running away from me. Now, I do not want to see you again until you have the information that will hang Michael Fallon." The man made it all the way to the door before Fourrier's voice reached out like venom. "And Toller, never think you can run so far I cannot reach out and snap you like a twig."

Toller closed the door tight. Then he began to run. God's bones, but he needed a drink. A viper of a man, that Fourrier. A viper.

On a cool October afternoon in 1772, Michael sat in Miss Pinckney's garden and read poetry. Around him in a rainbow of dresses were the Misses Manigault, Thibodeaux, Waring, Somers and Fourrier. And, of course, Miss Pinckney. He read from the proper poems of Milton and Donne, and the not-so-proper of Shakespeare, Marlowe, and Spenser. He was amused to see they liked the second better. When Christopher Gadsden appeared in the midst of "My Love is Like to Ice," they rose in a body against him.

"You shall not have him," Miss Waring said.

"It's ill of you, Mr. Gadsden, to break into a lady's garden unannounced," Miss Pinckney said.

"Please don't go with him, Mr. Fallon," Gabrielle said.

Gadsden looked around him in amazement. "Please, ladies, please. My need is of the utmost. It's urgent that I speak to Mr. Fallon."

The other girls began to depart, but Gabrielle lingered briefly. "You'll come back, won't you, Mr. Fallon?"

"If I can, child. Now go along with the others, or I'll tell your brothers who put the cat in their clothes press."

She laughed, stuck out her tongue, and hurried off after the rest.

Gadsden, already twitching at his sleeve, pulled him down the carriage path. "Hurry," he said.

"What is it? Drayton? I know. So he goes to England, gains an appointment to the Council, and ever since his return raises holy hell about placement—about appointing idiot younger sons to posts in Charlestown. As if it isn't exactly what he's made of himself. But it's not worth that time to trouble over it."

"I don't give a damn about Drayton," Gadsden burst out. "I don't give a damn about placement. I want you to shut up and listen." Michael stared. Gadsden sometimes got carried away on a point, but he never lost control completely. Now he grated out the words, "Governor Montagu's sneaked out of town, down the coast to Beaufort."

"A trip for his health, I take it. What the hell is *he* doing?" A slave Michael recognized as one of Gadsden's had knelt at his heels and was making a rough job of fastening spurs to Michael's buckled shoes.

"Montagu's called the Assembly into session, in Beaufort, tomorrow. If there's no quorum by the third call, he has legal grounds to prorogue. To end the session until it's his pleasure to call new elections. And God help us, the Assembly's scattered half-way to hell. He and the Council will be able to run the province like the King's private preserve. And you can wager he'll fend off a new election for months if not years."

"What do you want me to do?"

Gadsden motioned another slave forward with a saddled horse. "Ride! Take the Santee. Find any Assemblymen you can. Tell them there's no time. They're to ride like hell for Beaufort."

Michael mounted. Instead of leaving, he sat shaking his head. It had been building in his mind for a long time, at every discussion of political philosophy with Henri and

Louis, at every action of Parliament or the Royal Governor that struck at American freedoms. And now to have to scramble and scrabble just to keep they're own government. "It seems you are right, Mr. Gadsden."

"Right about what?"

"Independence, sir. Independence. We must take our country from the British, or they will surely take it from us." And he put spurs to the horse and rode.

17

Jean-Baptiste stared levelly at his daughter, standing in front of his desk so coolly, and drummed with the fingers of one hand. What was to be done? First, insolent disobedience from Henri and Louis, now this—this thing concerning Gabrielle. This summer of 1774 would be crucial; he could not be bothered by his children. She shifted, and he frowned at her, but she only smiled as though returning one of his.

How long had it been going on? And what was Fallon up to? Surely even Fallon wasn't foolish enough to involve women in politics. Still, it would be better to be certain. And he didn't want the man near her in any case.

"Papa," Gabrielle said, "it's obvious you're angry about something. But I don't know what."

Her father sighed. "It has come to my attention that you and a number of your friends often have a Michael Fallon at your poetry readings. I wish it to stop."

"Papa, Mr. Fallon isn't even in the city," she said sweetly. "He's been at sea for months."

"Are you being flip with me, child? I wish this thing to stop, and it will stop. He returns today. You will not see him again. This Michael Fallon is a dangerous radical, not at all the sort of man to consort with young ladies. In fact, I'm surprised the Manigaults, for one, allow him on their property."

"They find him most acceptable, Papa. His manners are perfect, and he is excellent company."

"That lies neither here nor there. He is not fit company. If necessary, you will simply stop visiting these daughters of foolish parents. If you must babble with another female, your sister Elizabeth is here."

Gabrielle stiffened. "Papa, I will not be separated from

my friends." She paused, then went on casually. "How would their parents take it if I were to be refused the company of their daughters?"

He looked up sharply. Was the girl hinting at blackmail? No, of course not. Still, the word could spread. And he couldn't afford losing those families' good will at the moment. Too many delicate undertakings were beginning. The local citizens might yet be incited to mimic the Bostonians' drowning of the tea; there was the public meeting to be manipulated. . . .

"I have said nothing of forbidding you your friends. I said 'if necessary.' But in my case, you will not see him. Now go, child. I have work."

"Yes, Papa." She dropped a curtsey, but he'd already picked up some papers and forgotten her.

In the hall, her hands shaking, she was amazed she'd managed to maintain her composure. When he'd summoned her, she'd been certain he'd found out. But then, how could he? No one knew but her. And how long had it taken her herself to realize? But it was true. She was in love with Michael Fallon.

In love. What a thing to happen to a girl who knew she was sensible and level-headed. It wasn't as if he'd encouraged anything, drat him. He most assuredly didn't have any such feelings for her, or any feelings at all. And that made it childish calfsickness. Not that it helped.

"Has Papa Fourrier straightened you out, my dear?"

With a start Gabrielle saw Elizabeth fussing with a bowl of July roses. A woman with that much bosom shouldn't show so much of it, she thought idly. "My father merely wished to speak to me."

Elizabeth smiled maddeningly, turning the bowl for a last look. "There. My child, I'm your sister. Your brother's wife. I know all about family discipline problems. And," she finished in a strangely greedy tone, "I know about your taste for low companions."

Gabrielle's face tightened. This, this woman had no right to talk to her that way, Justin's wife or no. "I see you're still as slim as ever, Elizabeth. Hasn't Justin been able to put another baby into you yet? Or has he stopped trying, now that he has that little French actress?''

Elizabeth whirled, white-faced and trembling. ''How dare you!'' She managed to control herself, and a malicious smile appeared. ''I had a suggestion for Papa Fourrier. Lock you in your room and feed you on gruel, with a dose of the switch before every meal. I shall have to suggest it again.'' Elizabeth seemed breathless as she finished, her eyes bright and moist.

Gabrielle sighed. Unless she put a rein to her tongue— ''Elizabeth, I'm sorry. But I don't understand. What was between you and him is long gone and done.''

''What was—Michael Fallon? Is it Michael Fallon you're seeing?'' Elizabeth's voice was calm, but her hands crushed the lace of her overdress.

''You didn't know?''

Elizabeth was churning. Justin had only said Gabrielle was seeing someone unsuitable. What could Michael possibly see in this child? Of course, that might be it. A girl on the blossoming side of twenty, with skin of childhood softness, childhood color in the cheeks. ''He truly is dangerous for you to see,'' she said suddenly. ''You mustn't see him again. You mustn't.''

The clock on the mantel striking the half-hour saved Gabrielle. ''I must go, Elizabeth.''

The other woman's voice stopped her at the door.

''He really isn't suitable. Justin isn't the only one with an actress in town. Michael Fallon has more than one.''

In spite of herself Gabrielle couldn't help one last retort before leaving. ''Why, Elizabeth, men must be men.''

Elizabeth unclenched her hands. Hell and damn. The girl might be serious about Michael. He'd run away when she needed him, but here he was sniffing around that simpering little wench. What could he possibly see in her? It wasn't that she was jealous. She had no more use for Michael Fallon. None at all. Justin was all she needed, now that he'd learned to control his brutality. Her breasts felt tight with the thought of what was going to happen that night. She'd gotten the idea watching the mares being bred, but it shouldn't be too hard to convince Justin he'd thought it up. And then——. What *did* Michael see in that girl?

In the hall the butler had stopped winding the tall clock. "Are you all right, Miss Gabrielle? Should I call Martha?"

Gabrielle took her hands from her face and opened her eyes. "No, that's all right, Asa. Is my carriage ready?"

"Yes, miss. And Martha too."

The carriage waited at the stairs, the four horses shifting impatiently, the big red wheels grating on the sand of the drive. Martha, her fat maid, herded her into her seat like an anxious mother hen, deploying her parasol, muttering about sunstroke and freckles.

Gabrielle could take the fussing no longer.

"Martha, sit down. Reuben, drive on. The Bay, please."

Thoughts crowded in on Gabrielle. Justin wasn't the only one with——. No, she wouldn't think about it. But how could she not? Everyone knew about Michael Fallon's lightskirts. All the gentlemen had stories about him. There was the actress who played boys' roles in tights and danced for Michael Fallon without them. And that awful Mrs. Selfridge was said to have lost her clothes to him on the turn of a card, paid without leaving the table, and wagered herself on the next deal. The young man who'd told her had refused to say the rest, but she could imagine. The Fallon luck was as much talked of as the Fallon women. Oh, damn it, he was a man who'd break her heart without ever knowing it!

Michael watched as the last of the crates swayed over *Hussar's* side and was lowered onto a handbarrow. It was good to be back in Charlestown, even in the July heat.

"Blind me," the wharfman swore as he took the weight with his back and shoulders, and the barrow barely moved. "What's in these here things? Iron?"

"Has to come from somewhere," Michael said. "Careful of those crates, now. Do you break one open, you'll carry every lump of it in your pockets." The wharfman swore again and managed to move the barrow off. Michael turned, and found Gabrielle smiling at him, parasol over her shoulder.

"Greetings from my brothers, Mr. Fallon, and from the reading circle."

"And none from you, little Brielle?" he laughed. He lifted her in a hug, and was startled at her softness. Damn, she wasn't a child any longer. He'd have to stop doing that, though he felt strangely reluctant. Hastily he set her back on her feet. God, she was his friends' sister. "The wharf is no place for a lady." From a barrelhead he took his hat and a package, and put her hand on his arm. "I'll take you to your carriage."

Gabrielle sighed. He embraced her only because she was a child. Idly at first, then with curiosity, she peeked around him at the package under his arm. "What's in the package?" she asked at last. "Is it a gift? For whom?"

"You're a nosy little minx, Brielle. I regret to say it's for you."

She laughed, and took it eagerly, tearing at the wrappings with a will. Inside she found an inlaid box, and within that a brush, a comb, and a hand mirror, all worked in delicate, filigreed silver. She touched each softly. "Oh, but this is a gift for someone important. I mean—."

"And you are. You're the sister of two of my best friends."

She closed the box with a sigh. He gave with one hand, took back with the other, and never realized it. "Thank you, Mr. Fallon. It's a lovely gift."

"I thought of you as soon as I saw it." He glimpsed Mr. Carver through a door of the warehouse and turned that way, then hesitated. "Brielle, will you wait here in the shade for me, just for a moment? I won't be long." He hardly waited for her assent before ducking into the warehouse.

"Mr. Carver?"

"Yes?" The old merchant looked up from his bills of lading and a smile lit his face. "Michael, my boy. Welcome home. A safe voyage, I trust?"

"Safe enough, sir, but passing long. I missed our chess games."

"And I. Were you able to make the purchases I requested?"

"Yes, sir. The packet of books is in my cabin. I intended bringing it by this evening." He paused. "In England word was the port of Boston has been closed. How does the city stand on it?"

"I fear it'll drive your friends to greater acts of desperation."

"Acts of desperation?"

Carver sighed. "There's a meeting under way at this moment, in the Exchange Building. More treason brewing. More trouble. The city is restless. I do not know what will come, now."

Carver was aging, Michael saw. It wasn't right to disturb him further. "Sir, I must go. I left a young lady standing outside.

"A woman's anger is indeed to be feared," Carver chuckled. "This evening will see you come for chess?"

"It will, sir. I promise."

Outside Michael bit back an oath when he found Gabrielle gone. Where was the girl? He walked out to the street, and there she was, in her carriage, with the driver and her maid up on the perch. He shook his head and started toward her, only to be stopped by Christopher Byrne, panting up to him before he'd gone five paces. "Where's the rest?" he breathed.

"The rest?"

Byrne took his arm and turned them away from the street's bustle. "Michael, fewer than fifty stands of muskets came to Gadsden's warehouse. You were sure you could get twice that."

"Well, I couldn't. Everywhere was suspicion. They hadn't heard of any Indian trouble. Hadn't there been a lot of rioting and such lately in the Americas? Man, as it was I was sure I'd be boarded before sailing. And Gadsden can forget about those eighteen-pounders, at least for a time."

Byrne ground his teeth in frustration. "Ah, Michael! We need cannon worse than muskets. Men have fowling pieces if they don't have muskets, but nobody has field guns hanging over the fireplace."

"There's a chance. A small one, but a chance. Franklin gave me a letter to a Frenchman. Reluctantly, I might add— but I think he's beginning to see it must come to a fight in any case. I crossed the Channel and talked to this Frenchie; but I don't know. He's a playwright, name of Beaumarchais, but he's some sort of tie to the French government. I couldn't pin him down. If the moon is high and the wind is right, there's a chance. And you couldn't get the word cannon out of him with a prybar. I take it you'd better luck?"

With a scowl Byrne shook his head. "Never a bit. Far from being willing to sell powder, our friends in the Caribbean wanted to buy it. I came back with not a pound more than I took."

"It's hell, so little trust in the world. Look you, I must go. I'm keeping a lady waiting."

"If you insist. But be at the Exchange early tomorrow morning. There's a meeting over the Boston to-do. Delegates from every parish in the province. You do know about the trouble, don't you?"

"I know about it. I know, but I'm not a delegate."

"Gadsden's taken care of that. Be there, Michael. Don't fail us." And he was off down the Bay.

Gabrielle swung open the carriage door for him. He shook his head. "I doubt your father'd approve."

"Papa specifically said it was all right for me to be at readings with you." Well, that was almost what he'd said. "If I may be with you in a secluded garden with only half a dozen girls for company, it must follow that a carriage on a public street is allowed."

"Sophistry, I think, but you dance it around as nimbly as a man." He didn't see her eyes blaze; he was climbing into the carriage.

"Like a man! And why can't a woman think? Not all of us spend all our time fretting over perfume and silk. The richest crop in the colonies, indigo, is due entirely to Eliza Lucas Pinckney. Why—"

"Easy, child, easy. If half the reason I read for your circle is that there's pleasure in being the focus of six or eight lovely girls, then the other half is that one of them has the wit to do more than blush and giggle at love poems. Now then, if I've not offended you too much, would you carry me across the peninsula? I've rented a house beyond yours.''

She gave the order in a happy fog, and the carriage threaded its way slowly out into traffic. He'd done it to her again, she thought. But then, how many girls would be flustered at a compliment to their intelligence? They wanted sonnets to the softness of their skin, or the curve of their breast. Lord, what a thought to have. If only he wouldn't smile at her so. She shook her head and took hold of herself.

''Mr. Fallon, may I offer some advice? If you don't mind taking it from a woman.''

''Lord, girl, am I not to be forgiven for a slip of the tongue? Yes, I'll listen, whatever it is.''

She took a deep breath and didn't look at him. ''If you're going to smuggle muskets disguised as iron, ship them to a blacksmith. Mr. Gadsden hasn't any need for iron, and someone might suspect.''

''God's wounds!'' With an effort he waited until Martha and the driver turned back to the front and several people in the street who'd turned to look had been left behind. He went on in a quieter voice. ''Is it such common knowledge, then, that schoolgirls talk of it?''

''I'm out of the schoolroom, Mr. Fallon. I heard you tell that wharfman those crates contained iron, but they were plainly marked for Mr. Gadsden. Iron would go to an iron worker. That said you were smuggling something heavy. My father calls you a dangerous radical. And, well, muskets were the first thing to come to mind.''

''God save us,'' Michael breathed. ''Do you intend telling anyone about this?''

''Mr. Fallon, I've no wish to see you hanged. I wish to see you take more care, or, or, someone else might—.''

''Tush, little Brielle! Childish worries!''

Her eyes snapped open. ''Childish! It's you acts the child! And I—'' she shuddered ''—I can't stand the fear. If you should—.'' She swallowed convulsively.

Michael stared at her in surprise. The child cared what happened to him. God's name, how long had it been since anyone cared what became of Michael Fallon, even Michael Fallon himself? Oh, if he died tomorrow Christopher would hoist a tankard in his memory, and Gadsden would regret the passing of a revolutionary, but who would care beyond the day? It seemed this girl would.

He touched her wrist. ''Look at me, Gabrielle. That's better. I promise you, Gabrielle, that I'll be as careful as I possibly can.''

She smiled wanly. ''I suppose it'll have to do.''

At nine the next morning he entered the Exchange. In the meeting, already under way in the Great Hall, a hundred or so delegates sat on benches in the center of the hall, with the walls around packed with mechanics and more than a few idlers. Some delegates cast wary glances at the spectators; others acknowledged friends among them. On the dais Judge George Powell presided.

Byrne appeared at his side as soon as he entered. ''It's good you made it, though I think we've enough votes as it stands.''

''I don't even know what I'm to vote on. And can I vote, just walking in off the street?''

''You can. Gadsden got the vote thrown open to every man present. Anyone can vote.''

Michael shook his head. That was like no voting he'd ever heard of. ''And what do we vote on?''

''Why, delegates, man. There's to be a congress in Philadelphia. Every colony will be represented. We'll present a united front to those English bastards.''

Suddenly Gadsden darted up. ''Come, Michael. I need you. Give them some fire. Tom Eadie's putting them all to sleep.''

It took a moment for Michael to realize Gadsden meant him to speak. Damn Gadsden! Even with his involvement he'd managed to avoid large public meetings, but to back down now was impossible. Gadsden was already on the dais, cutting into Eadie's steady drone.

"Gentlemen! Gentlemen! Your pardon, Mr. Eadie, but I believe it imperative that we hear immediately from one of our number who returned from England only yesterday. Mr. Michael Fallon."

Michael moved to the dais amid encouraging shouts. Even Eadie joined in.

"Tell us what it's like, Fallon!"

"What's Parliament going to do now?"

"Give them hell, Fallon!"

He turned to face them in a wide-legged stance, silent, with an eagle's glare. The shouts faded till there wasn't a sound. Even the idlers were silent. Every face was turned to him.

"I won't give anybody hell," he said grimly, "but England's going to give us hell. You want to know what it's like there? You want to know what they think? I'll tell you. They think we're unruly children who have to be chastised. Aren't colonies supposed to be managed for the good of the mother country? Can't they do any damned thing they want to us? You planters, you farmers with a slave to help with the harvest. They think of you in England as you think of your slaves." An angry muttering began, some contradicting Michael, others agreeing with him. "Yes, it's true. But which of you is mean enough to starve his slave to death? That's what they're doing to Boston."

The muttering grew to a rumble. One voice called out, "What about Wilkes?"

"There are a few. Wilkes, Fox, and Burke. But they're too few. They can't stem the tide; they can't even slow it. And that tide is sweeping down on Boston. If they can close Boston, why not here? Crawl or starve, Charlestown!" Dead quiet had fallen. "Save Boston, or we're next."

As Michael jumped down from the dais, men began shouting to be heard. The entire Hall exploded.

Michael shook his head ruefully at Gadsden. "Seems all I did was disrupt the meeting."

"No, no. You did fine. You put fire and life back in it."

"There was something I didn't say up there," Michael said. Gadsden waited. "In Bristol we received word of something called the Quartering Act. They'll billet troops in private residences, with or without permission. They're getting ready to send a horde of soldiers fast—no time to build proper barracks."

"Damn! It's moving too fast, Fallon. Too fast."

Michael looked at him in astonishment. "What are you talking about? You've been working for this for nearly ten years.

"Working for the time we're ready," the gaunt man said intently. "We're not ready yet. We should move like lightning, and the British like cold molasses, but I fear it's the other way around. Damn. Did you know your friend Carver and some other merchants have formed a Chamber of Commerce to oppose us?"

"No, I didn't. I suppose they feel like folk in England that Boston dumping the tea wasn't an act of revolution, but only theft."

"It wasn't only Boston destroyed tea. Do you realize we're the only colony allowed the tea to land? And don't tell me it's locked up safe below this very building. That's not the same. We should have burned the ship and the dock both."

"I always thought you were the one wrote those letters about burning," Michael said drily. "Have you considered this, though? Had we done it, when it was suggested, we'd have been first, ahead of Boston. We'd have caught Parliament's eye. It'd be the Charlestown Port Bill. And do you think those New Englanders would come to our aid?" Gadsden looked quickly around, and Michael laughed. "Don't worry. I'll not put that thought in any of their heads."

Words from the dais caught their attention.

"—Mr. Miles Brewton, Mr. John Rutledge, Mr. Henry Middleton, Mr. Rawlins Lowndes, and Mr. Charles Pinckney." Powell cleared his throat. "The other slate is: Mr. Christopher Gadsden, Mr. John Rutledge, Mr. Henry Middleton, Mr. Thomas Lynch, and Mr. Edward Rutledge.

The clerks will now pass among you with pen, paper, and ink. God guide your deliberations.''

How had Brewton been nominated, Michael wondered. He was respected, but well known for a King's man.

Young clerks hurried into the crowd, each carrying a tray with pen, inkpot, and sand shaker, and a stack of paper ballots. Following each was another with a closed box, a slot in the top. Men who couldn't read or write gathered up into knots, with one of their number showing the others how to trace out the letters. One of the clerks stopped in front of Michael and Christopher. Michael quickly wrote the names of Gadsden's slate, sanded the ink, and handed back the pen. He'd just folded his ballot and pushed it through the slot when something in the back of the hall caught his eye.

A large crowd stood around two men in the plain dress of clerks, who seemed to be showing them how to vote. Behind them, a rough-dressed man with a bulbous nose and tiny eyes moved around the group, clasping shoulders, speaking in ears. From time to time he'd talk to a man, then write his ballot for him. He seemed incongruous in the role.

The ballot boxes were stacking up on the dais.

The crowd shouted for those in the back to hurry.

As silence fell, Judge Powell and his assistants began counting out the ballots. Watching them pull out slips of paper, murmur to one another, and mark on sheets of foolscap soon palled on the crowd. A murmur rose as men began to converse, leaning over the backs of chairs, heads together along benches.

''Gentlemen,'' Powell announced at last, ''Mr. Rutledge and Mr. Middleton, being on both slates, have been named on almost every ballot. Some had names that weren't placed in nomination, which I tell you now is disallowed. Some were writ in hands too much like Arabic or Chinee to decipher. No one else has enough votes to be elected. Will this assemblage accept Rutledge and Middleton?''

A solid roar answered. ''Aye!''

''Gadsden may have made a mistake, throwing this meeting open,'' Michael said. Byrne only grunted.

"The clerks," Powell continued, "will dispense ballots once more. There are three more delegates to be selected. And please, gentlemen, only those names placed in nomination."

The clerks fanned out as before, waiting for ballots to be written and sanded, ballot boxes filling up, craftsmen's helpers and layabouts slowly scrawling names. Curious, Michael moved closer to the group at the back of the room. A horny-handed man in a cobbler's apron was talking to beady-eyes.

"Who do I want? Why, Gadsden, of course. You put it down there, Carey. Gadsden."

"Of course. I should've known. Gadsden." Michael was in a position to see the name Carey laboriously formed. Brewton.

With an oath he started forward, and stopped immediately. Carey looked up and nodded to the two clerks, and they nodded back. Damn it, he couldn't clear them all out himself. He hurried back to his place and bent to Christopher's ear. "There are some clerks and a man named Carey stealing men's votes." Byrne jerked to his feet.

"Easy. Easy, damn it. Don't scare them off. You see? Carey's the one with the round nose, whispering in everybody's ear."

Byrne studied him intently. "Anslow's around here somewhere. I'll have him gather a dozen of the boys and frogmarch Carey out. Those damned clerks, too!"

"God's blood, man, do you want riot? We'll have to do it ourselves. You get one of them aside. The one with the pinched face. Looks like he's costive; tell him you've got something to loosen his bowels. Keep him aside till after the next ballot. I'll take the other."

"What about Carey?"

"He's not brains enough to do anything by himself, I'm thinking—"

The second ballot had been counted, and Powell faced the gathering, hands on hips. "There is still no decision." A swell of sound rose and died away. "And there are still those writing names which are not in nomination. Now, is there a wish to reopen the nominations?'' A clamor broke out, and none could tell if it was for or against. Powell shouted vigorously for order.

Michael threaded his way back along the wall. No one noticed him, so caught up were they, some even standing on their chairs trying to catch Powell's eye. The stocky young clerk jumped when Michael's arm dropped around his shoulders. He was turned and walking for the door before he realized it.

"Let us talk in private a minute, lad. You seem a fine, upstanding young man. How are you called?"

"Ah, McDowell, sir. But, sir, I can't, I can't leave the hall at the moment."

Michael guided him smoothly through the door.

McDowell looked at Michael uncertainly and tried to back away. "I, ah, I am needed inside."

Michael caught him by the arm. The man tried to jerk away, and looked surprised when his arm didn't move. It had to. He was the bigger of the two. He jerked again. And again.

Michael moved off down the hall, pulling McDowell with him. The clerk didn't stop struggling until they were on the second story portico, looking down on Broad Street. Michael backed him to the railing. He looked at the street below, and back at Michael.

"Rest yourself," Michael said, "and tell me what you plan for your future."

"F—future, sir?"

"Aye, boyo, your future. Have you given a thought to it?"

"Sir, I'd better go inside. The vote—."

Michael smiled. McDowell tensed as if he'd snarled. "Ah, the vote, is it? That's thinking of today. Men who do too much of that can be misunderstood. And if a man's misunderstood, why he might be flogged, or tarred and feathered, by mistake, you understand. But a man who thinks to the future, and to what the future brings, well, a man like that does well."

McDowell licked his lips uncertainly. "I, ah—. I—. What is it exactly that you mean?"

''Well, lad, a man who thinks of the future would tell me who—.''

At that moment Byrne stuck his head out. ''The vote's done. Gadsden, Lynch, and Edward Rutledge are in. What do we do with this one? I turned his friend over for a ship sailing tomorrow for the Spice Islands and beyond. He'll spend the next two years learning to step lively at the end of a knotted rope.''

With a cry McDowell tore himself free and leaped for the rail. Michael grabbed for him, but the clerk landed a wild fist to the chest that felt as if every rib had been broken. He caught at the stone bannister to keep from falling. When he straightened, McDowell was rolling to his feet in front of a rearing team, dodging into the crowd with the driver's curses and the crack of his whip at his heels.

''Damn it, Christopher. We'll never catch him, now. We'll never find who sent him.''

''It's no matter, Michael. It's King's men who did it. King's men who weren't inside to twist the vote. That's enough.''

''Perhaps. But which King's men? You say Gadsden was selected? Good. But Lord, the things we do for the cause. What do you expect history will say about this?''

Byrne laughed. ''History will say we were all grand patriots and shining heroes, with right and justice on our side. Else it'll say we were traitors, and hung.''

''Well, let's get on back inside and see can we get an inkling which.''

18

The Continental Congress met in Philadelphia in September of 1774, with all colonies represented except Georgia. By October they had adopted the Continental Association, an agreement of non-importation, non-consumption, and non-exportation. They also sent a memorial to the British people, expressing hope for reconciliation, and another to the King giving assurance that the colonies would be loyal subjects if the offending laws were repealed.

In South Carolina a Provincial Congress was elected. It promptly appointed a Committee of Correspondence to keep touch with other Provincial Congresses, and a Council of Safety to see to the day to day affairs of running the province. William Henry Drayton was appointed head of the Council. By April of 1775, he was challenging the power of the Congress.

The air had the April feel of neither heat nor cold, and the water lapped mildly on the landing below the Exchange. In the small boat, a sailor swung in his oar and rose to toss a line ashore. Michael deftly caught it and tied it off. The boat's passenger, a ship's officer, stepped ashore and immediately stopped, gaping at the ring of men around the landing.

"Here, what's this? King's mail here. Royal Post Office." He seemed disgruntled that the magic phrases didn't act as a password.

"A committee from the Council of Safety," Michael lied. Christopher led five men toward the boat.

The officer puffed like a turkey cock. "We're not breaking your damned Association. We're not importing anything. This is the mail, I tell you. I'm from the Post Office packet *Swallow*."

"Of course," Michael said smoothly. "We'll escort you

to the State House." He gestured at Byrne and the others carrying the mailsacks up to toss them in a wagon. "That'll spare your men having to carry them. In fact, you might consider leaving them here. There's been considerable violence, lately, and some citizens can't tell packet seamen from Royal Navy."

The officer had swollen even further, face bright red, at the sight of Christopher's men handling the mail, but as Michael finished, he deflated. He was suddenly reminded of the riots in New York and Boston. And they'd burned a ship in Annapolis. "I'll go along to see it gets there."

"Certainly. Mr. Howe. Mr. Anslow. Would you gentlemen escort this officer? Perhaps you've some rum to help keep off the chill. The late cold comes on suddenly," he added to the officer, who'd made a noise and looked at the sunnny sky.

The caravan moved away smoothly, and melted into the flow of traffic on Broad Street. Michael led the way, followed by half a dozen men with an ill assortment of muskets and fowling pieces. Then came Anslow, Howe, and the packet officer, with the wagon close behind. The crowd split around them, instead of pushing closer to see what was happening, as Michael had hoped. Still, between the two men forcing rum on him, and the five men crowded across the seat of the wagon, the packet officer couldn't see into the wagonbox.

Christopher ran forward to join him. "What if he finds out we're from the Provincial Congress instead of the Council of Safety?"

"I doubt he knows the difference. Damn it, there shouldn't be a difference. Drayton is trying to run the Council of Safety like his private property."

"Aye. He's been as rabid as a reformed drunk since the placemen voted him off the Governor's Council. And then to have another placeman sent to take his judgeship, and him out on the circuit when it happened." Christopher winced as if he could feel it. "Lord, that'd turn any man."

"If he'd been turned to helping I wouldn't mind." A

crowd of boys ran up, jeering at the packet officer. He waited
till they started a game of tag and faded back into the flow
around them before speaking. "I loaded one of my coasters
for Boston. A hundred fifty barrels of rice and some money.
And a few hogsheads of tobacco to be sold in New York, the
proceeds to be carted on to Boston with the rest. Drayton
swells up like the whole damned Council of Safety and
allows as how the rice can go, because that's specifically
exempted from the Association. The money can go, because
that's not mentioned. But, says he, the tobacco is prohibited
goods. It must be off-loaded, or I'd risk the extreme displeasure and wrath of the Council of Safety. Right pompous,
Drayton."

"I've noticed. But did you then?"

"What? Unload? Hell, no. In the first place it's export to
Europe, that's prohibited, not to other colonies. In the second, even if it was, we must keep Boston going. It's likely
there the first blow will come, and if they've been weakened
enough to fall, then we'll go down like nine-pins, all down
the coast. Here we are."

"Mr. Anslow, Mr. Howe," Michael said, "escort the
officer inside. The rest of you get those bags unloaded.

The men on the wagon grabbed up the canvas sacks and
raced into the State House. The packet officer followed more
slowly for Anslow and Howe still pressing the rum bottle on
him. In a few minutes they were all back without the bags or
the officer.

Howe pulled a bundle of letters from his coat. "Here, Mr.
Fallon, sir. He didn't half raise hell about the seals being
broke without him there, but we danced him around about it
only being for ten seconds, and he'd enough rum in him not
to wonder how it could all be done so quick."

"All right, all you lads get out of here. Come, Christopher."

The two of them started down Meeting Street, away from
the bustle, Michael shuffling through the official despatches.
In no time they were around a quiet corner. Abruptly Michael
stopped, staring at the direction on one despatch. "To

Lieutenant Governor William Bull of His Majesty's colony in South Carolina, from Lord Dartmouth, Secretary of State for the American Colonies.'' He broke the seal and began reading.

God, it'd all broken loose. The English were sending ten thousand men to the colonies, just as he'd predicted last July. He turned and began to run toward the State House, phrases from the despatch whirling in his thoughts. Suppress the uprising. Enforce a blockade. Seize public arms and powder.

Christopher caught up to him. "What's the matter? What are you running off for?"

"No point telling it twice. Come on!"

Peter Timothy was in the hall outside the Assembly Room. He stared. "What's happened?"

"Get Pinckney out here for me, Peter." Timothy hesitated, and Michael plunged on. "It's important. Vital. Would I ask for the President of the Provincial Congress if it wasn't?"

After a moment Timothy nodded. "I'll try."

Michael and Christopher paced the hall, waiting. Michael checked his watch against the clock by the wall. What was keeping them?

Charles Pinckney stepped into the hall, shutting the door carefully behind him. He was a broad-nosed man, with a long upper lip and a second chin beginning to show. "I'll tell you, Fallon, sometimes we seem to forget we're a Congress and act as slothful as we did when we were the Colonial Assembly. What is it?"

Michael held out the letter, its official seal plain. Pinckney looked quickly around to see they were alone, and began reading. Suddenly he looked up and said, "God help us." At last he sighed and folded all the sheets together. "I'll take this in immediately. It will be a bombshell to those who are talking reconciliation."

"They deserve a bombshell."

"You don't have to deliver it."

Christopher barely waited for Pinckney to leave before bursting out. "Michael, lad, I've waited. Now, what the devil's happened?"

"The devil has happened. And hell's let loose," Michael said. "Ten thousand soldiers coming." And he explained the letter's contents.

When he was done, Christopher muttered a prayer and joined him in the pacing. The Congress must act, Michael thought for the hundredth time. What was delaying them?

More than once muffled shouting issued from inside the chamber, but no one came out. They paced through another hour.

Suddenly Pinckney was there again, mopping his forehead. "Something anyway. Copies of the despatch are being made. In ten days every colony will know of it. God knows what will happen then." He sweated, and kept dabbing at it with the handkerchief. "Captain Byrne, is the *Annalee* available?"

"At a moment's notice."

"And I've three coasters in harbor," Michael said. "They're at your service. But what of the rest? What of the powder? We must hide it!"

"Committees must be appointed. One will consider raising troops outside the militia, since we can't be sure militiamen won't obey Bull. The powder? The powder will be seized as soon as men are chosen." He stopped. "That sounds almost like a rebellion, doesn't it? Heaven help us." And he hurried back into the chambers, passing Thomas Lynch on his way out. Lynch, the stolid planter who had been a representative at the Continental Congress, gave Michael a jaundiced look. "You've certainly played hell, Fallon."

"Then it's hell they deserve. But why should you be upset? You're as much for independence as any man, now. And how did that question go in Philadelphia?"

Lynch looked hastily to the chamber door, and searchingly at Byrne, before he spoke. "Careful, Fallon, please. Not everyone is so willing to come into the open as you and Gadsden. Oh, very well. We felt out everyone we were able. I fear Gadsden went too far at times. Even the hottest New Englanders were taken aback. One of the Massachusetts lot said Gadsden was ready to shoulder a musket and march off to Boston on the instant."

"That sounds like him," Michael grinned.

"We could agree on little except that we must cooperate. But as to what end—." Lynch shook his head. "Those haddock-eaters are a mixed lot. Many abhor independence, a few say it's a last resort, and only a handful realize it's the only way. But they may wreck it all, those cold-faced bastards. They find you're from south of New York, and they begin preaching at you about slavery."

Michael was surprised. "Come now. Surely that's no news. How many long-faced New England slaver captains have you seen on the docks with Bibles in their fists, looking down their noses at those who own slaves while they count the pounds and shillings from their sale?"

"But what if they make it a condition for support of independence? Some of them said independence should mean independence for all men. An end to slavery is what they want."

"It's not so bad an idea, is it? I hold my own blacks as bound men, to be freed on eight years' service."

Lynch snorted. "Lord, you're beginning to sound like John Rutledge. Worse. Well, that's his business, and yours. Perhaps I wouldn't be so angry about it if it wasn't for their hypocrisy. I spoke to three of those fine merchants, owners of slavers, out of Salem and Boston. They claimed they traded molasses and rum, refused to admit to the third part of their trade. They claimed the *southern* colonies besmirched the American cause with slaves."

Lynch fell silent, and Michael didn't speak. Even Byrne seemed concerned. Did slavery become a bone of contention now, the colonies might forget about the British and start fighting one another.

The longboat slid through the dark harbor and the heat of August, a lantern above the sternpost marking its passage. Eight oarsmen bent and straightened in unison, water frothing and flashing round the oarblades in the faint moonlight. They were good, Daniel knew, for he'd trained them. He held steady for the lights of Charlestown, eyes probing ahead, but he spared a glance for Michael, seated in front of him and staring moodily at the water.

"That Mr. Ames," the boatman said suddenly, "I don't know as he can handle the harvest good as you, Mr. Fallon. Maybe you should've stayed."

"I was smothering in peace and quiet," Michael growled. He'd left for Tir Alainn as soon as the powder was seized, but the country had begun to wear. "As I told you halfway here, and at the mouth of the Santee, and at the boat landing, and when I said I was coming. If you want to worry so, I can always get you a job as a mauma."

"Ah, no, sir, Mr. Fallon." A sudden shriek rent the night air. "God almighty, what is that?"

"I don't know, Daniel. Douse the light, and steer for it. There, where the torches are."

The boat curved toward the closest wharves. Flickering torchlight on the shore partly illuminated a mass of men, throwing shifting shadows across their faces, so none could be picked out. Another ululating scream ripped from someone's throat. The oarsmen eyed each other nervously, shifting on the benches.

"They killing somebody, Mr. Fallon," Daniel said.

Something was carried through the crowd, which howled with mindless satisfaction. At the water's edge, to a great shout, it was thrown in. A feeble splashing started, carried further from shore every minute.

"Swing over a bit," Michael ordered. "He's floating right to us. Easy with him. Easy."

At a sign from Daniel two slaves shipped their oars and pulled the sobbing man aboard. His naked body was coated in sticky black tar; patches of feathers sprouted at random on him.

Michael bent over him grimly. "Who are you?"

One eye fluttered open. "Sergeant Walker," he breathed. "Gunner. Fort Johnson. Wouldn't—drink—to Drayton."

Tar-and-feathering and drowning, over a toast? It was an obscenity, and the Council of Safety was behind it.

"Daniel, drop me at the bridge, then take this man to the fort. Then take the boatmen straight to the house."

Daniel eyed the crowd dispersing on the dock. "Mr. Fallon, maybe I ought to come with you. And a couple of the rowers. They not much if it come to a fight, but they look mean enough."

Michael took his sword belt and a pair of pistols from the bottom of the boat. He checked the primings and slid an inch of razor steel out to gleam in the moonlight. "I'll be all right. Put me ashore, and take that man to help."

Michael found the Bay dark and empty, except for the lights from alehouses. Laughter and song drifted through tavern doors; a dog barked down the street.

Then torches rounded a corner toward him. It was a Council of Safety patrol. They slowed at the sound of his footsteps, peering for him in the darkness. There was always sport in lone pedestrians.

A hand on his sword hilt, he walked steadily toward them. One of their number took a swaggering step, but another stopped him with a hand. Michael was visible now. The sword was clear, and the pistol butts. His clothes were those of a gentleman, and his face had the look of a fighter. The patrol stood still, only their heads moving as a dozen unblinking eyes watched him pass.

Michael groaned in anger. It was worse than under the British. Men barely dared walk the streets alone at night, and no man could speak freely. The Council had much to answer for.

Outside the room in the State House where the Council met a young man stood sentry duty in a dove-gray civilian coat. "The Council is in session. You can't—."

Michael thrust him aside and flung open the doors. In the dim light the Council froze behind their long, polished table, every eye on him. Laurens suddenly looked worried. Pinckney gasped. Drayton smiled unpleasantly. Patricianly handsome Arthur Middleton seemed annoyed. The rest stared blankly.

There was a rush of feet, and the young guard ran in with half a dozen reinforcements. Frowning, Middleton waved them away. The doors closed. "You've interrupted a very important meeting, Fallon."

"I rescued a man tonight. Tarred, feathered, and thrown in the Cooper River to drown. His crime? Refusing to drink to Drayton. Have you thought how much of that is going on? And for what cause? Walker, Dealy, and Martin, tarred and feathered, for speaking disparagingly of the Council, for speaking disparagingly of Drayton. Mother of God."

Drayton's smile grew tight. "It should be clear to you: unity must and will be achieved at any cost. No dissent can be allowed."

A stunned silence fell on the table, some of the Council members looking furtively at the others.

"Is that the way of it now?" Michael asked softly. "I seem to remember not so many years ago a Mr. William Henry Drayton being listed among the returned cargo for refusing to agree to non-importation. You pled the right of dissent then, didn't you? You attacked Gadsden for stirring up, what was it you called them, the vulgar, illiterate masses. Now you loose your own mob on the city."

Laurens and Middleton surged to their feet.

"Easy, Michael."

"Come, Fallon."

White-faced, Drayton rose. "You interfere too often in things that don't concern you. Look to yourself, Fallon, before the Council must chastise you."

"If the Council wants me, if you want me, Drayton, then let it be now." He pulled open his coat and let his hands rest on the pistol butts.

The Council exploded. Drayton tried to force his way to Michael, but Rawlins Lowndes seized his arms. Laurens and Middleton hustled Michael out of the room.

"Go back, Arthur," Laurens said. "Soothe him. We can't afford a duel now. And you, Michael. Calm down. What do you mean drawing weapons on the Council?"

"I didn't draw them," Michael muttered. "Damn it, sir, the man believes in liberty only for himself."

"He's one of the most ardent for our cause in the colonies. There aren't so many we can afford to dispense with one.

And I'm not sure we could dispense with Drayton. He's gathered great power with that ardency.'' Laurens' eyes suddenly twinkled. "You're an ardent man yourself, Michael. Don't waste your passions; spend them on the British."

Michael drew a deep breath. "With no dissent allowed, we're worse than the British."

Their footsteps echoed in the empty hall, and the last sounds from the Council chamber faded as they emerged onto the broad front steps. The street was empty.

"There are more important matters than Drayton, Michael. Events move faster than I believe even Gadsden envisioned. Lexington, Concord. And every ship brings word of another skirmish. It's open war, now. We must think how to fight it."

"I intend fitting out *Hussar* as a privateer."

"I know we're going to issue letters of marque, but there are some who will see it as making a profit from the war."

Michael snorted. "You, Mr. Carver, and your friends won a battle for us once. You made the English merchants scream, and Parliament heard that if they never heard another thing from us. Think how they'll scream when American privateers start snapping up their ships, when they find insurance and freight cost more than the cargo. And of course, the English armies, in Boston or wherever else they send them, must be supplied by sea. It's long, lonely thousands of miles from Britain, and we'll be waiting like wolves behind every swell."

"An interesting image. Well, I'd better go see if Arthur's gotten Drayton quieted enough for us to finish. God be with you, Michael."

"And you, sir."

He kept a wary eye as he found his way to the street. Something moved in the shadows beside the steps. A foot scraped on the pavement. Six inches of his sword whispered from the scabbard.

"Hold on, lad. It's me, Christopher." Byrne moved slowly into the street.

"Lord, man, what are you doing here, and hiding?"

Byrne cleared his throat. "I was down below, you see, telling the lads the news of Boston, when this wild-eyed fellow burst in, yelling that Michael Fallon's gone mad and is killing the Council of Safety. They all of them go pouring out of the room, with me on their heels thinking to give you a hand with it. Only by the time I got there everybody was bowing and backing out, saying it was but a false alarm. So. Did you shoot them? Or did they shoot you?"

"Neither. Come stay to my house tonight. It's the same one I've rented before. What did happen in Boston? Another skirmish?"

They dodged across the street in front of a lumbering cart. A light, misting rain began to fall; they walked a bit faster.

"A big battle, Michael." Byrne's voice had an edge. "They say the British had over a thousand casualties."

"A thousand—." He stopped in the street, then started again, slowly. "That damn well is a battle. What happened?"

"Well, you have to remember I was in Salem, so I got it all second hand, or even third. And on top of that, the bible-thumpers weren't eager to talk about it. Seems they bungled it awful bad, for all the redcoats they killed."

"What happened?"

"In the middle of the night, the sixteenth of last month, a Friday it was, they sent themselves a party out to fortify a place above their Charlestown. Breed's Hill, or Bunker Hill. I heard both."

Michael nodded. "Go on."

"The next morning the redcoats crossed over, I don't know how many, and attacked. They were beat back two, three times before they finally broke in with the bayonet. The New Englanders had run out of powder."

"Why'd they invite the action if they didn't have the powder to fight it?"

"That's the part they're ashamed about. I had to dig it out piece by piece, and I don't know near the whole of it. It seems the men who fought the battle may have been no more than the working party. Most, or maybe all, of those who were supposed to fight refused to march, because it was daylight, and they'd be under fire from British ships before they reached the redoubts. For sure ten times the number who fought sat along the road and never stirred till the rout reached them. Then they ran like they'd bayonets up their backsides. I'm thinking those Massachusetts lads would just as soon forget it ever happened."

The light rain had grown heavier; sheet lightning flashed in the sky. They began to trot.

"Militia, Christopher. Militia can throw away a battle every time, even if it's handed to them." They fairly pounded up the steps of Michael's house. One bolt lit a covered carriage in the drive.

At a resounding crack of thunder, a tiny shriek issued from the shadow at the back of the veranda. Gabrielle ran out, smiling weakly. "I, I'm so sorry. Thunder doesn't usually frighten me, but that one caught me by surprise."

"I'd better be leaving you," Christopher murmured.

"No. Stay," Michael said quickly. He took her arm and led her a few paces down the porch. With an effort he managed to keep his voice low. "Brielle, what in God's name are you doing here? An unmarried man's house, in the middle of the night. And you don't even have Martha with you. Are you trying to ruin yourself?"

"That's why I sat outside instead of going in. I do hope Jem is all right. He's my driver. I told him to sit inside the carriage if it rained."

"Why?"

"One of the slaves told Martha you were in trouble with the Council of Safety, and then another said a man had been t-tarred and feathered, and I thought it was you, but I didn't know, or how to help you, so I came here, and——." She took a shuddering breath and closed her eyes. "When you walked in I felt so happy."

Michael smiled at her tenderly. Silly child. But so sweet. "Come along, Brielle. I'll put you in your carriage, and let you explain to your father where you've been."

"Oh, Papa and Justin are almost never in the city any

more. It's just Henri and Louis. Mi—Mr. Fallon—.'' She
paused to collect her wits. How could just his hand on her
arm have such an effect? "Mr. Fallon, I heard something else
tonight. Henri and Louis said a huge battle has been fought in
Boston.''

"Don't worry, child. It can't hurt you here.''

She rounded on him intently. "Don't cosset me. I'm not a
child. I know what it means. Those other things, Lexington
and the rest, they weren't the same. They were little things. I
know men died. But we could go back; it could all be as it was
before. But not now, not after this. It's all changed forever,
and I'm terrified.'' Suddenly she was shivering and couldn't
stop. His arms went round her, and for a minute he thought he
was going to kiss her.

Lightning flared again. Even in the harsh light her face was
alive and vibrant. "Jem,'' Michael called, "come for your
mistress.'' He watched her into the carriage, his thoughts
troubled. When he turned Christopher was looking at him
strangely. "And what is it you're seeing?''

"Nothing,'' Byrne said quickly. "Not a thing. Tell me,
now. Would you be having some good drinking whiskey
about the place?''

In the hall at Les Chenes, Justin flipped open the snuffbox
expertly and put a pinch up each nostril. A tremendous
sneeze followed quickly, but he stifled it in a silk hankerchief. It left him feeling clear-headed. God knew, he needed
it to face his father lately. The tirade flowed from the old man
at the slightest excuse. "I,'' he'd said, "worked for months
to ensure that the South Carolina delegation to this *soi disant*
Continental Congress would not only have no radicals, but
would have Miles Brewton, a complete King's man. The
chances of unity in Philadelphia with one delegation so
comprised would have been small. But no sooner does this
Fallon return to the city than he ruins it all. He appears
everywhere, meddling, disrupting, interferring. Damn him!
Damn him!''

He couldn't think of listening to it again without grinding

his teeth. Well, he had something to calm the old man. He straightened his lace in the mirror and entered the study.

Jean-Baptiste looked up from his desk. For once his gimlet eye carried no warning of a tirade to come. "Sit, Justin. You wish some wine?"

"Not just yet, no. I've some information." He paused for the old man to ask what, but Jean-Baptiste merely waited. He grimaced and went on. "Last night Governor Lord William Campbell departed." Still there was no reaction. "He sneaked down the back stairs of his house, rowed through the marsh, and is hiding on HMS Tamar in the harbor."

"You forgot that he took the seal of the colony with him," Jean-Baptiste said, and smiled inwardly at his son's chagrin. "At ten o'clock last Wednesday night a turncoat named Chaney introduced one Captain Adam McDonald of the rebels' 1st Regiment of Foot to Lord William as a loyal sergeant of Moses Kirkland's irregulars. He obtained the information that troops will be sent against South Carolina before next fall. Between Lord William's knowledge of this and the capture of Fort Johnson by the rebels, they were at the point of arresting him. That would have been most excellent." He busied himself with his quill. "I fear I did not foresee him rowing away in that fashion."

"Fallon was in that," Justin snapped. "Seizing Fort Johnson. As a gentleman-volunteer. Him, a gentleman. I begged Captain Thornborough of the Tamar to let us reinforce and hold the fort. He insisted on evacuating the garrison. Imagine, letting those damned dogs walk in without firing a shot. After they'd stumbled around in the swamp all night, we could've taken the lot with a corporal's guard."

"You leave that to Fletcher, Browne, and Cunningham. If they live, they will pay for their haste. The time is not yet."

Justin jerked to his feet and leaned against the mantel, peering into the fire, wishing there were rebels writhing in the flames. "The time is not yet, you say. Well, the time had better be soon. The damned rebels are winning, Father. Six months ago I had a hundred men meeting in the stables. I could've fielded as good a troop of light cavalry as any in the

British army. Today I've twenty. I don't even know where half of them are. A dozen have signed the Association and march in godforsaken Council of Safety patrols.''

"Listen to me, Justin. It all marches as I predicted, does it not? Everywhere the rebels run wild. They seize forts, yes. And Royal governors flee for their lives along the entire seaboard. But the rebels are so swelled with themselves they can see no chance of failure. Soon they may take the final, fatal step and declare themselves independent.''

"I see nothing to be happy about in that.''

"This unity of theirs is''—he held up two fingers less than an inch apart—''so deep. Everywhere, as with Drayton here, men build their own circles of power, with only the barest regard for anything else. A few hard blows, and all will shatter. And the blows come. So. Within the year, as I have said, the British will come. When they lay seige to Charlestown, you will ride forward with not a hundred men but a thousand.''

Justin was thinking. Something was not as it seemed. "Father, you're exuberant. You don't become emotional about anything in the future, however certain it is.''

Jean-Baptiste allowed himself a slight smile. The boy was right. It would be so sweet. "A man has arrived, a man who—.'' A half-hearted rap came at the door, and his smile broadened. "Enter.''

The man who called himself Toller closed the door behind him. "Your nigger said I was to come in when you said, but he made me come in the back way. Where's he get off ordering a white man—.''

"Silence!'' Jean-Baptiste's voice cracked like a whip, and he was pleased to see Toller jump. "Be thankful you are allowed in this house at all. I had thought to let Job peel your hide with his whip. A bad example, to have a white man flogged by a black, but considering the money you have stolen from me, it might be worth it.'' Toller began to stammer, the elder Fourrier's glare pushing him into incoherence. "What? Do you claim that you have not been a thief? That you are worth the thousand pounds?''

Somehow Toller managed to get control of his tongue. "No, sir. Yes, sir. I mean—. It weren't that way. I went straight to that Timothy Cavanaugh. Found him in no more than a month. Only he got suspicious. He were a strong bugger for an old one. I had to slip steel under his ribs to get his fingers off my throat. And then in Ireland, them damned Irish pigs wouldn't give spit to the likes of me."

"Ireland!" Justin's gaze jerked from Toller to his father. "What was he after in Ireland?"

Jean-Baptiste smile blossomed like an evil flower. It felt as good as taking a virgin. "The evidence to hang Michael Fallon."

"Hang Fallon?" For a moment a light flared in Justin's eyes; Toller backed away with a muttered curse. Then it faded. "The governor's gone. The only authority is the rebels. Fallon's one of them, for God's sake."

"There are ways." His voice hardened. "I would not like to think you have come here without what I need."

Toller hastily pulled a dirty, folded broadside from his coat pocket. "There you are, sir." He fumbled it open and laid it on the desk in front of the old man. "There you are."

Across the top it said:

WANTED
FOR THE MOST FOUL AND
HEINOUS CRIME OF MURDER
MICHAEL SHANE FALLON

Jean-Baptiste's smile broadened malignantly.

Elizabeth rose heavily from where she knelt by the study door and moved to the stairs. She climbed with one hand on the bannister and one on her swollen stomach.

Justin alternated between smug pride at getting her with child and disappointment that their love-making had had to cease. She missed it, too, with a sick-feeling hunger, the tangled variations, the sometimes pain. He didn't come to her bed now for those panting, sweat-slick nights. The thought came that he didn't really see her any differently from the women he now spent his nights with. Except that she could give him heirs, of course. The one in her, and little Robert, just turned four, asleep above.

When she opened the door Mauma Rosa stopped rocking and made as if to rise. She motioned the woman back to her chair and leaned against the bedpost to study her child as he slept, and to contrast his true father's firm gentleness with Justin's barely controlled violence.

The boy shifted on the coverlet with a murmured sigh. Was that how Michael had looked as a child? It was impossible to think he'd once been so angelic. But the child proved it could be. Robert had his father's face. She at least could see it clearly.

She sighed and sagged against the bedpost. Yes, she could see. How long before others could? How long before Justin saw? There had to be a way out. Unbidden, the secrets she'd heard below flooded her mind. The Cavanaugh man was dead, murdered by that common little creature. And he'd brought something that would hang Michael.

Bile rose in her throat, and she swayed. Michael, mounting the gallows. Michael, swinging on the end of a rope. Michael, his hands and mouth stilled forever. Her thoughts raced like a squirrel in a trap. If Michael were dead, Justin could not see him in the child. If Michael were dead, she'd be safe. If Michael were dead—. Pain ripped through her, and the room spun off into darkness.

19

The five schooners moved down the Cooper River, through the November chill of 1775, little faster than the tide could carry them. Even from the second floor veranda of this house on the Bay, Michael could see the first four were hulks. Could the British? He swung his spyglass to HMS *Tamar* and HMS *Cherokee*, anchored well out in the harbor, off Haddrell's Point.

No activity there. Wait. They were beginning to shift, both of them. But just at anchor. They must have anchored on a cable spring. Now they brought broadsides to bear. They weren't sailing up to engage.

A scrap of conversation drifted to him from the girls farther down the Warings' veranda, and he stiffened.

"Please, Gabrielle," one of the Waring girls was saying. "No one will tell us about Elizabeth's baby if you don't." A chorus of agreement echoed her.

"But why? It's been nearly a month," Gabrielle protested. "Oh, very well. But briefly. The baby came early, very early, and suddenly. Only the quickness of Robert's mauma kept both Elizabeth and the baby from dying." Murmurs of sympathy interrupted her, but she pressed on.

"When I arrived Elizabeth was pale, but mending, and the babe was crying. There was nothing for me to do but make posset for her and sing lullabies to young Master Gerard."

Michael touched the leather-cased miniature in his pocket and angrily jerked the spyglass back to his eye. The schooners were turning for the Hog Island Channel. Gabrielle touched him on the arm, and he jumped. "Oh, I'm sorry. I didn't mean to startle you."

"I thought you were in deep conversation with your friends."

241

''Deep conversation!'' She glanced fondly at the chattering young women clustered like silk flowers at the far end of the veranda. ''All they want to talk about are babies and gowns and parties. With a battle to be fought under our noses. It's preposterous.''

Michael smiled at her fondly. As always, the pleasure of her company cleared his mind of turmoil. ''Probably not a battle, though they'll try for one.''

''But if not a battle, then what are they doing?'' She frowned seriously. ''I don't understand.''

He pointed out to a large, low island of salt marsh and mud flats, and the mainland of Christ Church Parish beyond. ''On the other side of that island, Shute's Folly, is the Hog Island Channel, out of range of any of our guns. It's too shallow for most warships, but *Tamar* and *Cherokee,* and maybe *Scorpion,* could make it through, sail back around, and bombard Charlestown without us ever getting a shot at them.''

''Is that likely? That they'd bombard Charlestown, I mean?''

''Not at the moment, no. But it's not a good idea to gamble on cannon balls. Those first four schooners will be sunk in the channel. The last, the *Defence,* will bring off the crews.''

Gabrielle chewed at her pretty lip reflectively. ''You said they'd try for a battle. What'd you mean?''

He helped her adjust the spyglass to her eye, and directed her attention to the *Defence.* ''Drayton's on board her. He's trying to provoke an incident. Anything at all, so long as it happens under the eyes of Charlestown, will rouse the people like a tonic. Does he that, he'll make up for a lot.''

A blossom of smoke appeared alongside *Tamar,* then another. The first reverberating boom reached them just before the third cloud of smoke erupted from the ship. Short of the channel, far short. Silence fell. ''Six rounds only,'' he muttered. ''He knows he's too far off; he's giving it up as a bad job.''

''Are you Michael Shane Fallon?''

Michael turned in surprise at the male voice. A man clothed almost as a gentleman stood in the doorway. Three others who didn't come close crowded through.

"I am. What do you want?"

Suddenly pistols appeared in the men's hands. The others swung theirs wildly at the women and back again. The man who'd spoken kept his firmly on Michael. "You will come with us, please."

Gabrielle started to protest, but Michael took her by the shoulders and gently moved her out of the way. "I'll come quietly. There's no need to frighten the ladies."

The tall man moved aside and motioned him through the door. Four pistols, he thought. Too many to fight, especially around the women. But if he could take the stairs at one leap and dash out the door—. One of two men at the foot of the stairs raised his pistol toward Michael. The other held the servants cowering in a corner. What the hell was going on?

Once in the street, the men formed a semi-circle behind him, their guns openly held. To anyone who saw them, one thought came. Council of Safety business. They looked the other way. Nobody wanted to get involved in that.

More cannon fire sounded from the river, erupting into a steady fusillade. The escort looked at one another nervously. People streamed past, heading the same way they were, running to see the show, brushing right against Michael's guards. If he ducked into the crowd—.

The tall man seemed to read his mind. "If you run, we'll shoot you and take our chances."

Take their—. "You're not Council of Safety. Who are you?"

The tall man's jaw tightened; pressed his pistol harder into Michael's ribs and hurried him along. The rest of the guard trotted after them.

Down between the wharves a longboat waited. Half a dozen men in it, sailors dressed in grabbag fashion, kept a nervous watch on the nearby crowds who had eyes only for the harbor. One of the seamen turned as they approached.

"God blind me, Mr. Crisp, the captain's brought every rebel in the town down here."

Michael whirled. "You're Royal Navy." A pistol butt crashed against his head.

He woke to pain and a quivering, booming noise. It took

him a moment to realize that the latter was not in his head. He lay on a ship's deck, and her guns were firing. His hands went to his head, and he had to bite back an oath. Iron shackles were on his wrists, with three feet of chain between. With an effort he sat up. There were chains on his ankles, too.

A ship's gunner squatted beyond his feet, just putting his tools back into a chest. He looked at Michael's irons and sniffed. "Them'll hold you. Aye. Them'll hold."

Rough hands pulled him to his feet. On the quarterdeck he recognized Lord William Campbell. The red-faced officer trying not to shout must be the captain.

"And I tell you again," the captain said rigidly, "I first fired only as a diversion, to draw attention while Mr. Crisp closed in on this scoundrel. Who would have thought the impudent dogs had the nerve to fire back?" He sounded as if he still couldn't believe it.

Michael staggered forward, holding his chains up. "Lord William! What's the meaning of this?"

The former Royal governor glanced at him, and turned his back. The captain glared. "Mr. Crisp, get that man off my deck."

Below, two seamen dragged Michael aft, followed by Crisp, now in the blue coat and white facings of a Royal Navy lieutenant.

"Damn it, man, what's this all about?"

"The murder of Colonel Sir Anthony ffrench-Newton," Crisp replied coldly, "on the twelfth day of October, seventeen hundred and sixty-four. You'll be taken to England and hanged. After a trial, of course. I hope you enjoy the rope locker. We don't have a proper brig."

He was shoved forward to sprawl on heavy hemp cable, and the door slammed shut, leaving him in darkness.

He was stunned. How long since he'd even thought of the Englishman's death? And now they came to take him away in chains and hang him. He snarled in the dark. Well, he wasn't hung yet, and they'd play bloody hell getting it done.

Time passed; how much he did not know. Everything was

still in his coat pockets, even Elizabeth's miniature, but his watch was smashed. Eventually the guns fell silent. In the darkness there was only the smell of hemp and pitch, the rustle and squeak of rats among the cables, the creak of the ship's timbers.

The creak—. The ship was moving. Sailing for England? Already? He wanted to leap up and pound at the door, but he dug his fingers into the piled cables till the feeling passed. No, he must think rationally. The captain would not just sail away. On the heels of the exchange with the *Defence*, it'd be seen as flight. No, he must be simply changing anchorages. Michael lay back on the cables grimly.

The damp mustiness was oppressive. And then something ran over his hand, and something else brushed his thigh. He swore. The rats were losing their fear of him. Slowly he began to see, not their shapes, but scores of glittering eyes. Watching. He shouted, and they winked out. But pair by pair, they returned. The darkness was filled with their chittering, and the tiny, rapid padding of their runs, back and forth, and always closer.

Once the rats would not have seemed so horrible, but he'd changed in the years since the Englishman's death. He'd stood alone, then, as much as possible, and wanted it so. Now he enjoyed the company of others, and their friendship. Mr. Carver. Mr. Laurens. John Rutledge. Christopher. Henri and Louis. And Gabrielle.

It was strange how often Gabrielle was in his thoughts. She was just a child. No, at nineteen she was a woman, a caring woman, even a loving woman. Life with her would be more than most men could hope for. He touched the miniature. His heart was no longer his to give, but he realized in surprise that whatever else he had to give was already Gabrielle's. If he escaped—. No, when he escaped, he'd go to her. That thought became a light to him in the darkness.

Sharp pain stabbed his hand. With an oath he seized his attacker and hurled it against the bulkhead. At the thud and chattering death rattle the others disappeared. For the moment. He sucked at the gash on his hand. He'd heard of rats as big as cats, but he'd never believed, not till he held that one. His hand hadn't near gone around it, and it'd nearly squirmed free. The squeaking came again, and the eyes. He waited tensely. . . .

The crash of guns woke him. His first reaction was a cold shudder. He'd seen a man who'd been gnawed while he slept. It was a worse way to die than hanging. He must escape soon.

What was that firing now, he wondered. There wasn't any sound of hits against the ship. Wheels rumbled as cannon were run out, feet bounded across the deck, muffled shouts drifted down to him, and the smell of powder smoke, as one by one the cannon fired, again and again and again. After hours it stopped.

The door opened, and the seaman with the squint motioned Michael out.

"Why?" Michael said without moving. The Marine guard in the passage tensed at his musket.

"Come," said the sailor. "Mr. Crisp, he says take you to the jakes. He says you might knock over a slop bucket. He says he won't have his cable locker fouled. That's what he says." He laughed shrilly. "Me, I says let you wallow in it."

On deck dim moonlight was obscured by drifting clouds. In the paler moments he could see a single sentry, pacing the quarterdeck. They moved forward, toward the heads. One sentry with a musket, and the guard. Off the larboard side, perhaps two miles away, were the lights of Charlestown. The seaman was ahead with empty hands, the marine four paces behind. His hands came together, gripping the hanging chain.

Suddenly he stopped, pivoted, the chain whistling through the air. The Marine couldn't stop his forward motion. The heavy iron links smashed him to the deck. Michael launched into a shuffling run for the rail.

"Stop him," the sailor howled. "Shoot!"

A hand on the shrouds heaved him up; the sentry's musket cracked, and a rail splinter leaped beside his foot. He left the ship in a long dive. There was just time to remember the great shark two black fishermen had taken in the harbor before he hit the water.

The harbor closed over his head; the chains were pulling him down. Desperately he kicked for the surface, fighting till his head broke surface. No time to rest. With the chains, he couldn't float. He rolled on his side and began an awkward, two-handed stroke. Two miles. It began to seem like two thousand.

On the *Tamar* lanterns were appearing, orders shouted and countermanded. Irregular musket fire crackled, but they were shooting blind. So far as he could tell, no ball came close.

"Lower a boat," someone cried, and as if it was a signal he heard the creak of muffled oarlocks ahead.

God rot them. A boat between him and the city. He'd have to try for Haddrell's Point, or Sullivan's Island. If he wasn't swept out the harbor mouth to sea. He pushed that thought away and began swimming away from the city lights. The steady creaking followed, the light splash of oars worked to avoid noise. It came ever closer. Did the bastards think to sneak up on him? Well, he'd never outdistance them now. He turned and treaded water, waiting.

The boat loomed over him. Figures leaned and pulled him from the water. "It's him. Are you——."

"Sodomizing bastards!" he grated. His fist sent one man flying. "Mother-raping whores!" He slammed an elbow into a second man's mouth, kicked a third in the stomach.

Another reached for him yelling, "Wait——." Michael looped the chain around his throat and pulled him down.

"God's mercy! Somebody grab the man before he's murdered us all!"

At the brogue in that voice Michael froze. He pulled the man he was choking close. Even in the dark he could make out Henri. "God's name!" He loosed the chain and heaved a sigh when he heard the inrush of breath. "I heard you, Christopher, but who else?"

"You broke my nose, Mr. Fallon," Daniel said. "Damn it, you broke my nose."

"It can only make you look better," Christopher said. "He loosened every tooth in my head, and there's nothing uglier than a toothless Irishman. See can Louis straighten up yet, and get us out of here. They lowered that boat, and they'll likely have Marines in it." The boatman managed to get a gasping Louis to the oars, and they moved slowly toward the city as Christopher squatted down. He held a hammer and chisel. "We'll have you out in a minute."

Michael shook his head. "What in the name of God are you doing out here?"

Byrne wrapped the chisel head in a cloth and set the edge against one shackle. An experimental tap made a low clank. "Well, you see, it was like this. We were going to sneak in through the stern cabin windows, hold a gun to the captain's head, and maybe Lord William's, and make them let us all go." He hit the chisel again, harder.

Michael stared at them in astonishment. "You'd have all of you hung! A harebrained scheme if ever I heard one! What idiot made it up?" Henri winced and felt at his throat.

"Gabrielle."

"Gabrielle?" Warmth flooded him. He began to laugh, joyously.

"Aye." Christopher replied. "She said we had to rescue you, and she said—. Well, it doesn't matter what all she said. It was she got a pass from the Congress—and here we are." He swung the hammer again, and checked to see how the chisel was cutting. "What did they take you for, anyway?"

"Murder." Louis and Daniel stopped rowing and looked over their shoulders at him. Christopher hit his thumb with the hammer and bit back a curse. "Ten years ago I killed a man in a fight, an English colonel. He'd a sword in his hand, but him being who he was, and me being who I was, the charge was murder. Only they never caught up to me till now."

"Can't call it murder if the other man has a sword," Henri muttered. "Strike me blue if that's not a duel."

"Well, it's done with now," Christopher said. He split one shackle with a last blow and moved to the other wrist. "It puzzles me. How did those buckos get into the city? The Council of Safety patrols are supposed to prevent boats coming from the British ships most particular.''

Michael opened his mouth, then closed it again. How indeed? The cannon fire had been to draw attention while he was taken out. But coming in?

"Do you think Drayton hates you enough to arrange this?'' Louis asked.

"He hates the British worse than he hates me. No, he'd deal with the devil first. Maybe they bribed a Council patrol. Most of those lads are no more honest than they're forced to be.''

Christopher hooted. ''Those fine British officers bribing rabble to let them make an arrest? The notion's daft. No, if bribing was done, it was done by someone else. You've an enemy, lad. You'd best think who.''

The boat slid through the night toward Charlestown. Christopher worked on the chains, and Michael thought. Who?

Gabrielle sat quietly in the drawing room of the Fourrier's Broad Street house. A glass of wine was on the table beside her chair. If she picked it up, she knew, she'd start trembling. And if she started to tremble, she'd begin to cry. She sat with her hands in her lap.

The hands on the mantle clock seemed not to move at all. There'd been hours of indecision, hours of terror, when she thought there was nothing she could do. And then there had been the plan. It had seemed so simple, in spite of the men's objections. Now, perhaps she'd sent three men to their deaths. Four, counting poor Daniel. Four men to hang. And Michael most of all.

With a moan she closed her eyes. Michael most of all. That, she decided, was the only choice a woman could make. Men could divide their loyalties a hundred ways, but women kept theirs few, and gave each their whole heart. She prayed, the same simple phrase over and over again. God, let him come back. God, let him come back. When she opened her eyes he was standing in the doorway, dripping water on the rug.

His name hung in her throat. Half laughing, half crying, she ran to him, threw her arms around him. The wetness soaking through her dress didn't matter, only the feel of him, the feel of his arms going around her. "You're safe," she whispered against his chest. "You're safe. It worked."

"Actually, I jumped over the side before they could try it. But they picked me up and brought me back."

She backed away trying to smile, wiping tears away with trembling fingers. "Isn't this silly? You're safe, and here I'm crying as if—. Oh, your wrists! Your poor wrists." She caught his hands, staring at the raw, red bands where shackles had gouged away skin and flesh. "I'll get hot water, and bandages."

He reached for her as she turned to go, but it was his sapphire blue eyes that caught and held her. "Don't go, Brielle. Don't go. I've something to say." She caught her breath awkwardly, half-fearing what it was.

"Gabrielle, will you do me the honor of becoming my wife?"

She was trembling; she couldn't speak.

"You know I'm very fond of you, Brielle. You must know that. I can think of nothing I'd like more than spending the rest of my life with you as man and wife. I'll do my best to make you a good husband, and never make you sorry you said yes." He sighed and shook his head. "Damn, I'm no good at speeches. Not this sort, anyway. Will you marry me, lass?"

"Yes." She found her voice. "Yes, yes, a thousand times yes." He'd not mentioned love, and that caused a stab of pain. She'd accept it, though. In time he'd love her. She'd make him. Almost shyly she let him turn her mouth up for their first kiss, her lips trembling, his gentle and firm. With a contented sigh she sank against his chest.

"Have you thought about the banns?" Louis asked, and they both leaped guiltily.

Gabrielle swallowed heavily, one hand at her throat. "Louis, you took ten years off my life."

"Damn it, Louis, how long have you been hiding there?"

"I came in with you saying you're no good at speeches. I take it that means you made one. Bad form, speechifying to women. Sweep them off their feet." He gestured with his arms in demonstration. "Then kiss them without mercy and tell them what they're going to do. You will marry me."

"I haven't seen you sweeping Ann Lewis off her feet," Gabrielle giggled, and Louis turned bright red.

"That's of no object," he snapped. "And there's still the question of the banns. Posted at the church every week for three weeks before the wedding, remember. There's no way you'll keep that from Papa. You, Michael, will probably be shot. And you, Brielle—."

"Couldn't they be read in some country church?" she asked.

"You think Papa wouldn't find out?"

"We'll find a church to waive the banns," Michael declared. It seemed a small enough problem to him.

"I will not be married by a hedge-row preacher from some rag-tag church," Gabrielle said firmly. "How would you explain such a thing to the minister? You'll be taking instruction in the Anglican faith, of course."

"Ah, Michael," Louis laughed, "she has a whim of iron. Listen," he went on to forestall his sister. "There may be a solution. If there's any way round the banns, the Reverend Henry Cargill will know, and he's a staunch patriot, too."

"Who's a staunch patriot?" Christopher asked. Henri and Daniel entered on his heels. "We put the carriage up without waking any of the stableboys. Good evening, Miss Gabrielle. Would you have a mite of something about the place to warm a man after wet work?"

"Well, get the carriage back out. Then you and Daniel go help Michael pack. Henri and I will be Brielle's maids. They're running away to get married."

Daniel and Henri cracked broad grins, and Christopher

gave a joyous laugh. Louis herded them out the door.

Michael looked at her, smiling, and held out his hand. "Will you, Brielle? Will you run away with me?"

"But what if the Reverend Cargill can't find a way?"

"Then I'll hide you for three weeks while the banns are read. I defy your father to take you away from me."

He was so sure, so confident, she felt swept away. "I'll go with you anywhere, Michael."

Louis clapped his hands. "And that's settled. No, none of that kissing. You'll have time for that later. Come on, they're waiting for you." He hustled Michael out and hurried Gabrielle and Henri up to her room.

If she'd felt swept away before, now she felt caught in a whirlwind. The two brothers were everywhere, pulling out drawers, opening cabinets, making chaos, till she was forced to waken Martha. That required another round of explanation, and brought giggles from the stout black maid, but at least she managed to help more than hinder. Once everything was packed the brothers at last proved useful for carrying the heavy portmanteaus downstairs. Gabrielle followed more slowly. Martha tried to hurry her along, but Gabrielle was reluctant to leave. She didn't know why. Michael was waiting for her. Nothing else mattered. But when she closed the door behind her, she knew she'd never set foot in that house again.

The Fourrier coach was at the steps with Christopher at the reins. Daniel, in Michael's closed carriage, started off down the street. Christopher bundled her into the coach, and it lurched off through the night. With Martha jammed in beside her, and Louis grinning unromantically beside Michael, there was no talking. She could only look at the man she would marry. How many times had she looked at him, studied him when he didn't know? And each time what she saw was different. A man of will. A man who could be cruel. A man it would be wise not to anger too much or too often. A man with a gentle smile and eyes that softened when they looked at her. A man to love, and be loved. And he would be.

Suddenly she realized he was aware of her scrutiny. A

blush suffused her face. She tried to say something, but the carriage was jerking to a halt. He smiled softly, and handed her down.

Across the dusty road was a country church, a white, wood building with a short, open bell tower. And that small house to the rear, its lights warming the night, must be the parsonage. A raucous laugh from down the road drew her attention. With a gasp she pulled Michael back out of sight. There, only a few hundred paces away, was an inn, with men in front looking their way. In the moonlight, clouded as it was, they'd clearly see a man and a woman going into the parsonage. When Justin followed, and he would, they'd tell him. Michael led her slowly across the road. "I know what I'm doing, Brielle."

She studied him. Perhaps he did. Well, it was too late to hide now.

Christopher and Louis already had Reverend Cargill out of bed, with his nightshirt stuffed in his breeches, and were telling him the whole story. He was a white-haired man, balding, and he peered at them irascibly over his spectacles.

"Preposterous," he said, "is too mild a—You. You're Michael Fallon, aren't you? Thought I recognized you. And you, child. What's your name?"

"Gabrielle Fourrier, sir," she said.

Cargill pursed his mouth and looked down his nose at the floor. "There's a Justin Fourrier is a rockbound Tory. Believe his father leans that way as well, though I've no proof. Supposed to have two brothers who favor the other side." His eyes darted sharply to Henri and Louis. "You two?"

Louis nodded.

"I don't decide religious matters on political grounds," said Cargill. "Still, the banns aren't strictly religious. They're meant to stop snap judgments; they're to allow a change of mind. You two think you'll change in three weeks?"

"I want to marry her," Michael replied. "Now, or in three weeks, or in three years, it'll make no difference."

"I love him," Gabrielle said simply.

Cargill studied them both, and finally nodded. "All right. You can consider the banns were read in my church the past three Sundays. I have men who'll swear to that, so there's no worry about her father securing an annulment." He went to his desk for his prayer book. "If you've the ring, then, we can begin." He looked from one blank male face to the next and sighed. "One moment."

As he left, Louis flipped open the harpsichord sitting in the corner. "I can't play you any hymns, Brielle. Don't know any. But I can play something by that young German fellow, Mozart. Sounds as good as a hymn."

Christopher came forward shyly. "Miss Gabrielle, perhaps it isn't proper for me to give you these, but I expect a woman should have flowers on her wedding day." He handed her a bouquet of Cargill's cornflowers, blue, with the night's dew damp on the petals.

"They're lovely, Mr. Byrne. Christopher." She touched a petal softly with her finger. "I will treasure them always."

Reverend Cargill returned from the back of the house, a somber cast to his face. "My wife and I were childless until she died, five years ago. We were wed with my mother's ring." He opened his hand. A plain gold band lay on his palm. "I would be pleased if you would accept this from me, Mr. Fallon."

"Thank you," Michael said with equal solemnity. "I don't know how to repay you."

"Just smite the English hip and thigh." The minister stopped to clear his throat and rub at his nose with a handkerchief. The notes of a Mozart sonata drifted through the house. A log added to the banked fire brought warmth.

"Now, then. Let us begin. Dearly beloved——." Christopher soberly acted as best man, and a beaming Henri gave the bride away. Michael held her hand in his, repeating his vows solemnly.

She wanted to remember this, to cherish every word, but they all seemed to run together. Who giveth this woman? Wilt thou, Gabrielle Louise——. Love, honor, and obey. She was giving her life to this man. Panic washed over her. Did she even know him? One look at his face, lips repeating words she could barely hear, brought a measure of calm. Perhaps she didn't know him, but she loved him. And as he learned to love her, she would learn to know him.

He leaned toward her, and she realized the minister had given permission to kiss the bride. As his lips brushed hers she fought a wild urge to giggle. How many women married a man they'd only kissed twice? Then they were being bundled out to the carriage, Christopher and her brothers throwing rice they'd found somewhere. All three men crowded onto the driver's perch, leaving only Martha to watch her settle in her husband's embrace. Husband. It was done. She was Gabrielle Fallon, now. Mrs. Michael Fallon.

A mile past the inn, round a bend and out of sight, the coach slowly drew to a halt. Gabrielle looked up. Her brothers and Mr. Byrne were climbing down in the road, and there seemed to be other horses stamping and rattling harness in the night. "What—?"

Michael handed her out of the carriage. "We're changing conveyance, lass." He pointed down the road.

A short way ahead was a closed carriage, and with it Daniel. Michael's carriage. And Christopher and Daniel and her brothers were moving her trunks to it. She looked at Michael questioningly.

He smiled. "Whoever follows, and someone will, will see our names in the church register. They'll be getting confirmation from the folk at the inn, too. And they'll go burning along this road to catch that coach. Only you and I will be in my carriage taking a road that's little more than a track. While they chase off, we'll be at Tir Alainn." Suddenly he frowned. "I don't like hiding from your family, Brielle. But I want peace for our honeymoon."

Martha waddled up. "Miss Gabrielle, Mr. Louis and Mr. Henri say I got to go with them, so folks think there's a lady in the coach."

"It's all right, Martha," Gabrielle said softly. "Go. I'm with my husband now."

"Will you hurry?" Louis hissed as he ran back to the

Fourrier coach, the other two on his heels.

Christopher slowed long enough to say, "He won't catch us till we're past Camden. Now off with you."

Daniel cracked his whip over the horses as soon as they were in. The lurch threw her against him, and they kissed lightly. Gabrielle rested her cheek against his hard chest, listening to the steady beat of his heart, feeling the safety of his arm around her.

Michael wasn't certain exactly when he realized she'd fallen asleep. They were well down the half-cleared path, almost to a good road again, and dawn was beginning to show. She still had the bunch of cornflowers in her hand. He tried to put them aside, but even in her sleep she clung to them. He smiled, and contented himself with brushing rice from her hair.

When Gabrielle awakened it was full daylight, and oaks marched past the carriage at regular intervals.

"Where are we?" she asked sleepily.

"Home."

As the carriage halted before the house, liverymen came running in Fallon green and gold, laughing to see Daniel driving the carriage. They stopped in open-mouthed astonishment as Michael climbed down, and swung Gabrielle out in his arms.

"I can walk," she protested.

Michael smiled. "Not until I've carried you over the threshold, Mrs. Fallon."

She threw her arms around his neck and squealed in mock fright as he ran up the front steps, carrying her lightly as a feather. Mrs. Fallon. It sounded good, did Mrs. Fallon.

Lord, but she was lovely. Too lovely to be hurt. He must never let her know he didn't love her. How could he explain that affection was all he had to give? She had the right to more. He held her against a sudden turn from overgrown ruts to a well-marked road. He'd make certain she believed she had more.

Sarah, who seemed to broaden as her responsibilities increased, met them in the hall with her hands on her fat hips. "My Lord, Mr. Fallon. What you doing with that child? That ain't one of your Magdalenes. I knows a lady when I sees one. You send me to the fields if you want to, but I ain't staying in this house while you debauch that child."

"Brielle, this is Sarah, my housekeeper, and sometime protector of the innocent, Sarah, this is Mrs. Fallon."

Gabrielle slipped from his arms and stood with one hand on his wrist. "Thank you, Sarah. It is true. I am Mrs. Fallon." She smiled. "My Martha didn't want me to go off with him alone, either."

Sarah's mouth fell so far open she had a third chin. Then she whooped with laughter. "Bout time. Bout time this place has a mistress. Mmm-hmm." Gabrielle couldn't suppress a yawn, and the housekeeper threw a scowl at Michael. "He done had you out racketing around the countryside 'stead of letting you sleep in a proper bed, ain't he? You come with Sarah, child. Sarah take good care of you till your Martha come. Where am those boys with Mrs. Fallon's things?"

As the black woman began to guide her up the stairs, Gabrielle stopped suddenly. "Michael. Michael, you will come to me? I mean—." She blushed and couldn't go on.

Michael smiled. "I'll come, love."

Sarah gave a sudden high giggle, and set off with Gabrielle once more. Michael watched them. He'd go to her, but it had been so long since he'd been with an innocent girl—. He rubbed his chin and grimaced. He'd a three day growth of beard, only a hasty wash in that time just before setting out, and clothes that'd been in the harbor, and traveled in all night and part of a day. It must have been a close-run thing that she'd agreed to marry him.

"Lijah! Where are you man?" He strode off toward the back of the house. "A tub of hot water, and quick. And a basin and a razor. And a suit of clean clothes. Hurry man!"

It was an hour later that Michael found his way up the stairs. Sarah had finally come to tell him that Mrs. Fallon was ready, sir. He tapped on the bedroom door and entered to a soft reply.

She sat primly on the bench at the foot of the tall, canopy bed, in a heavy, brocade robe tied down the front with pink ribbons. Her brown hair, catching the light in auburn glints, was loose in soft waves around her shoulders, and her eyes were large and luminous.

A decanter sat on a table by the door, and he poured two glasses. "Would you like some wine, Brielle?"

She knew what he was doing. There had been giggling conversations, full of blushes, with Anne Thibodeaux, wed last year. Anne finally admitted she'd been terrified, though John had tried to soothe away her fears. That was what Michael was doing. Suddenly she loved him more than she ever had before. She would see that he never wanted any other woman.

She went to him, and pressed herself tightly against his back. He left the glasses and turned round in surprise. Her trembling fingers on his lips kept him from speaking. "I, I want you to kiss me, Michael. Not a child's kiss. A wife's kiss. A, a woman's kiss." And she closed her eyes, half-afraid she'd said too much.

He tipped up her face with a hand beneath her chin, and his lips came down on hers, tenderly at first, but growing more and more demanding. She broke away at last, breathing heavily. A tremulous hand went to her lips. They stung, and it was wonderful.

Her eyes fell to the floor. She knew what to do next, but she couldn't while looking at him. Misunderstanding, he started to go pull the curtains, and stopped as her hands went to the bow at her waist, the lowest ribbons that were tied. It slid slowly undone with a whisper of satin, and the next, and the next. With the last still tied beneath her chin she stopped. A wave of red swept over her cheeks. She couldn't. She'd thought she could, but she just couldn't.

A gasp broke from her lips as he took the ends of the last bow and pulled. The robe slid from her shoulders, and she stood blushingly, tremblingly naked, with a pool of brocade around her feet. Hesitantly she looked up at him, catching a strange look in his eyes. And then she knew what it was.

Desire. He desired her. With a laugh of joy she flung her arms around his neck and kissed him.

He held her there with one arm, bent to get the other under her knees and picked her up. He moved to the bed, gently laying her on the coverlet. His throat thickened till he was sure he couldn't speak. God, he'd known she was lovely, but this—. Those small, high set, pink-nippled breasts. That tiny waist and gently rounded belly. Those sweetly curved hips. God save him, he'd still half been thinking of her as a child. But this was no child. She made his blood burn.

Gabrielle trembled half in fear, half in anticipation. After this he would be hers, and she his, more certainly than even a minister's words could make them. His hard body felt strange to her, the firm muscle, the silky hairs on his chest. But it felt good just to have her arms around him, good inside.

He kissed her gently on lips and eyes and cheeks. His hands drifted at once lightly and firmly over her body. She trembled, and realized abruptly it wasn't from fear. She was icy cold. No, she was burning hot. No, she was both at the same time, and neither. She couldn't tell. She didn't know.

A sudden, sharp pain, flaring then fading, brought a groan to her lips. Instantly Michael was all contrition, caressing her face, whispering apologies for hurting her. She stopped him the only way she could, with her mouth against his.

Passions raged through her, feelings she'd never dreamed of. It felt strange; it almost seemed to hurt. It was like anticipating something, hanging on the edge of something. It did hurt. Oh, God, it hurt. Sweet pain. Sweet—. Suddenly the muscles of his back tensed and ridged beneath her fingers, and the breath was rushing out of him like a hoarse, heavy sigh. The world flew apart, and she screamed as she was hurled off into space.

After, he lay with his head propped up by pillows, and she with her chin on interlaced fingers on his chest. There was still a tinge of pink in her cheeks at the thought that she was lying there naked, in bed with a man, husband or no. She kept her eyes downcast, as if studying his chest.

"Michael," she breathed, "it was so wonderful."

His lips twitched. "Then perhaps we should do it again."

"Oh, could we?" At the sound of eagerness in her own voice the pink flared into red. "I mean—."

This time he couldn't keep back the deep-throated chuckle. "Yes, Brielle. As often as you wish. Or almost as often."

She smiled against his chest. "I love you."

There was just the barest pause in his reply. "I love you, too, Brielle."

She caught the pause. Caught it, and knew he lied. But he had said it, and if he said it today, it would be true tomorrow, or next month, or next year. But it would be true.

At Les Chenes Justin strode into his father's study, a black, frustrated scowl on his face. His father sat in front of the fireplace, staring into the flames. Justin splashed brandy into a glass and gulped it down.

"I followed the carriage into North Carolina," he said suddenly. "Henri and Louis were at McConnel's Tavern in Charlotte, drinking with that Byrne fellow. They claimed they didn't know where Gabrielle was, or her maid. I'll admit I couldn't find them. I'll even admit they weren't in Charlotte. But damn it, Henri and Louis know something." He glared darkly into his glass.

Jean-Baptiste spoke without taking his eyes off the flames. "She is no longer of the family. No longer of the blood. I disown her."

"What are you talking about?"

"At Dolbin's Inn they told you a carriage had passed, some men, a lady with her maid. You did not wait for more. You did not walk the hundred steps to the small church there, and so discover where your sister is. She is at Tir Alainn. She is Mrs. Michael Fallon."

He almost choked on the words. Fallon, who stole the first-born son of his first-born son. Fallon, who now reached once more into the Fourrier family. Gabrielle would have married well, perhaps an English nobleman. And she had been stolen.

He realized his son was speaking. "What, Justin?"

"But Fallon is in chains, on the *Tamar!* You arranged it. Word was sent he'd been taken."

"Yes. He was taken." Jean-Baptiste sighed and looked away from the fire for the first time. "Not until two days ago, with your sister already gone, did I learn that Fallon had escaped." Justin made a strangled noise, but his father continued. "He killed a guard and leaped over the side in the night. The captain assured me Fallon wore heavy chains. He assured me Fallon had drowned. He assured me—. Bah! The very night of his escape that Irish devil signed the register at that church you overlooked, and married Gabrielle. God rot his soul. Where are you going? Stop!"

The whipcrack word halted Justin with his hand on the door. "I'm going to kill Fallon," he grated. "We'll be done with him."

"No!" Jean-Baptiste's voice was steel. "What Fallon has done cannot be changed, only avenged. Vengeance will be sweet for waiting, very bitter for haste. If you kill him, this so-called Provincial Congress will hang you."

Justin sneered. "Their day is almost finished. Cunningham is beseiging Ninety-six with over two thousand men. Your agents among the North Carolina Scots tell us they'll march any day. And when the British come, we'll hand them the Carolinas neatly tied with a ribbon."

"Will we?" his father asked drily. "It will take months to bring those Scots to the point of fighting. And as for your brave Cunningham, he and Williamson, the rebel leader, agreed yesterday that neither could gain an advantage. Both of them, both, mind you, are marching away to claim a victory. There will be no ribbon."

"And Fallon? An arrogant clod of an Irish servant, who's had the effrontery to trick my sister, your daughter, into marriage. To smirch our name. To mix his mongrel blood with ours."

Jean-Baptiste bared his teeth. "An end will come. An end to this rebellion. An end to the herd ruling itself. An end to Michael Fallon."

20

March of 1776 was a busy month. The British evacuated
Boston, and Washington occupied the city. A British invasion of North Carolina under General Clinton was called off
when it was discovered that the Scots Highlanders, rallied to
the Royal Standard by Flora MacDonald, had been dispersed
in fierce fighting at Moore's Creek Bridge. With them dis-
solved the Tory support in the state. And in South Carolina a
republic was proclaimed. The Provincial Congress became
the General Assembly, with John Rutledge as President of
the new Republic, and Henry Laurens as Vice-President.

It amused Michael that they didn't seem to realize what
they'd done. They declared that neither King nor Parliament
any longer had authority, but denied that it meant they'd
declared independence. Everything for declaring independence except admit that's what they'd done.

Others knew what it meant, though. Clinton's invasion
force was diverted south. On the fourth of June thirty transports and a fleet of warships arrived off Dewees Island, north
of Charlestown.

Along the Bay warehouses were going down, being
leveled by gangs of slaves. Warehouse owners sweated
through their fine lawn shirts, laboring beside the black men
with prybar and pickax. No one seeing those Carolina gentlemen, faces dirty, swinging shovels with grim intensity,
doubted that the city's fate had been laid in the scales.

It was a Monday, this tenth day of June, 1776, the day the
Gazette normally published, but its printing presses had been
moved into the backcountry. Carriages, loaded with bundles
and portmanteaus, accompanied by wagons crammed with
furniture and slaves, trundled up the Bay in a steady stream.
Every man who could was shipping his household out of

town. Michael knew it was well Gabrielle had agreed to remain at Tir Alainn. The city was no place for a woman eight months with child.

He shook himself. He was due back at Fort Sullivan before nightfall, and even a gentleman-volunteer had to obey the rules. He dodged between a troop of backcountry militia, straggling along with their muskets at all angles, gawking at the buildings, and a party of slaves with ropes and axes, being trained as firefighters. Immediately he had to stop for a file of soldiers, each with a basket of sashweights in his arms.

"Every window in my house must be propped open." Christopher Gadsden, resplendent in his well-cut uniform as Colonel of the 1st Regiment of Foot, indicated the baskets and shook his head. "I doubt if I've a single pewter spoon left, either. Musket balls must come from somewhere, but I wish it wasn't my dining room."

"Are they sending colonels in from Fort Johnson now to pick up their lead?" Michael gestured at the sashweights.

"No," replied Gadsden with a laugh. "I came to town to confer with General Lee." There was a touch of something in his voice that brought Michael up short.

"You think well of Charles Lee?"

Gadsden frowned at the edge on Michael's words. "He's the third ranking general in the army, after Washington. He held a commission in the British Army, served in the Seven Years War. Some think we'd be better off if he was in command overall, instead of a surveyor who was never more than a militia colonel. You're a veteran of that war yourself. With your military experience, I'd think you could see how lucky we are to have him."

Michael hesitated. "Tearing our warehouses down to provide a field of fire for artillery is smart. I hate to think what would've happened if they'd run past the forts a few days back, instead of waiting so long to get over the bar. And Lee is right about Fort Sullivan. Colonel Moultrie should build a traverse at the rear of the fort, where the wall's only four feet high."

"But you still have reservations about Lee?"

"Yes. A general must understand two things. One is strategy; the other's tactics."

"I've read both Bland and Pickering," Gadsden said stiffly.

"Well, Lee says Moore's Creek Bridge wasn't important because it was all colonists, all Americans on both sides. But if those loyalist Scots had managed to fight their way across the river, they'd have grown from two thousand to twenty thousand. The British'd have a secure base for their operations on the North Carolina coast."

Gadsden hesitated. "That's opinion."

"Is it opinion that he took half the powder from the Fort Sullivan magazine, and little enough there to begin with? Is it opinion he wanted to build a mile-long bridge from Haddrell's Point to Sullivan's Island, with no mention of how to get labor or materials, or how to keep the British from knocking it down with one broadside when they wanted?"

"But—."

"And what of that attack he ordered last week against the British on Long Island? We'd have had to cross three to five miles of marsh in mud up to our armpits. What's the matter?"

Gadsden grimaced. "This morning, Lee ordered Moultrie to cross Breach Inlet and attack Long Island. But it was called off. The whole British army's ashore there, now, under a pair of generals named Clinton and Cornwallis. Lee wouldn't send one regiment and a few militia companies against an entire army."

They halted at the State House, now Lee's headquarters.

"The problem's still the same," Michael said.

"No," Gadsden said stubbornly. "Lee may make errors, but he's a brilliant officer. No, Michael, I'll not hear another word against him." At the top of the stairs, with the door open, he stopped. "Mark my words," he called down. "We'll win this battle because of Charles Lee."

"Or in spite of him," Michael shouted, but the door was already swinging to.

Michael started toward his own house wishing he'd kept

his peace. The worst thing Lee had done was divide Carolinians. And on the eve of battle.

He was half-way down his veranda before he saw the carriage at the stables. It was his, from Tir Alainn. He flung open the front door.

"Where the hell is everybody?" he shouted. "What's that carriage doing here? Is it Gabrielle? The baby? Jonas! Tam! Cleo! Damn it, where are you?"

As the butler pounded down the stairs, the door to his study opened. Gabrielle made an awkward curtsey in the doorway. "Does my lord and master shout for me, too?" she smiled.

With an oath he took her arm and guided her to a chair. "What are you doing here, you fool woman? Not an hour ago I was congratulating myself on your safety. Cleo, run fetch Mrs. Fallon a posset. The rest of you"—four maids had run to his shout—"go back to what you were doing."

Laughter burbled out of Gabrielle, and she held out a hand as though pleading. "Oh, please, Michael, not a posset. That's too great a punishment. You've no idea how many of them a pregnant woman must drink. Every woman who visits me has her own recipe, and I must try them all."

"This is no joke, Gabrielle."

She sighed, and the determination he was coming to know was clear in her face. "I want to have my baby, our baby, close to you," she said quietly. "I will not be brought to bed without you there."

Michael breathed heavily. "There are fifty ships out there, counting transports and all. They've an army on Long Island. Suppose a few frigates run past Fort Sullivan to bombard the city? The batteries along the Bay won't stop the city from being smashed and burned."

Her face had drained of color. He cursed inwardly. Damn it, he didn't mean to scare her. Well, yes, he did, but only enough to make her leave.

"Look you, Brielle, I need you safe at Tir Alainn." She remained firm, and he cast about desperately. Inspiration struck. Distracted, she'd be more easily convinced. He took the plans for the city house from the cabinet behind his desk.

"Darling, you've never even looked at these, to see what your new house will be like."

In a moment he had the plans unrolled on her lap, talking about dadoes and wainscotting. She touched the edge of the roll. It was dusty, old. And he'd had the lot on Queen Street for a long time, too. Why hadn't he built?

"Michael, when did you have these drawn up?"

"Um? Oh, back in '69. Now, I want to use a good bit of our own oak and cypress, but I've bought a shipload of mahogany from Jamaica, and—."

She let him go on. In '69 he'd been in love with Elizabeth; this house had been planned with Elizabeth in mind. It was hers. "I don't like it."

Surprise cut Michael short. "What's wrong with it?" he asked finally. "Whatever it is, I'll change it."

"Everything's wrong. I want a double-house. Oh, everything. Can't you just get new plans?"

She seemed so deadly serious, he thought; it must be the pregnancy. "All right, Brielle." He crumpled the plans into a ball. "New plans it is. Now—."

A furious knocking erupted at the door. By the time Michael had gotten to his feet, Charles Holt, another of the Sullivan's Island volunteers, had pushed by the butler. "We've been recalled. They've gotten the heavy warships over the bar."

Michael didn't waste a minute. "Have you a boat? Good. Cleo! You and Tam run pack me some clean shirts and smallclothes. No, just put the posset down and go. And soap, mind you. Lots of soap. Gabrielle." He stopped. She had both hands pressed to her mouth, and stared at him with wide eyes. He knelt beside her and took her hands. "Gabrielle, have the team put to the carriage. Whatever you want to take can follow after, but you must return to Tir Alainn."

She stopped him with a shake of her head. "No, Michael. And don't make it an order, because I won't obey, and you won't be here to make me. Please? Besides, the roads are very rough. I've already ridden them once. Will you make me do it again?"

She was right, damn it. With her time near, that lurching

journey could be as dangerous as the British attack. And he couldn't make her, in truth. "Brielle——. You're a crafty, devious woman, Brielle. I love you."

A light smile touched her lips. He'd said that almost as if he believed it. "I love you, Michael." And she kissed him as if they were alone.

Eighteen days later Michael sat in the camp behind the unfinished fort on Sullivan's Island, waiting for the sun to come up. He'd a pipe in his hand, but it'd gone out, and he hadn't noticed.

The warships moving had been a false alarm. They'd only joined the transports in the Five Fathom Hole, south of the harbor entrance. There'd been nothing but false alarms since, and few even of those.

The British army remained on Long Island. With miles of marsh on the mainland, across a narrow creek, they'd nowhere to go but across Breach Inlet, then down the narrow length of Sullivan's Island to attack the fort guarding the north side of the harbor mouth. But they waited.

They weren't the only ones waiting. The traverse across the back of the fort still wasn't up. In fact, it'd never been begun. Colonel Moultrie claimed they'd be done if the British got behind them, traverse or no, and he might well have been right. If any ship, however small, got into the creek behind the island, it'd be what Charles Lee had called it, a slaughter pen.

The fort was supposed to be a square, with a diamond-shaped bastion at each corner. Actually, only the front and right curtains were up, and only the front two bastions. To the left and the rear the wall was only four feet high in some places, no more than seven anywhere. The front did look impressive in the dark. In the dark.

In the light you could see the walls were made of palmetto logs, twenty to forty feet long, notched and laid like a log cabin. Two rows had been laid, twenty feet high, sixteen feet apart, with the space between filled with sand. To a civilian it'd seem impregnable, but when the fleet's guns began to splinter logs, and the sand poured out——.

He'd studied that fleet more than once. A deserter from the
British Navy, the old scars of floggings on his back, had
named them for him, and given their rates. *Bristol*, 50 guns.
Experiment, 50 guns. *Sphynx*, 28. *Acteon*, 28. Two hundred
and seventy guns, the British fleet could bring against Fort
Sullivan. And in the fort, on platforms held ten feet off the
ground by brick pillars, were only twenty-five. Even counting the six twelve-pounders in hastily built cavaliers to either
side, no more than twenty-five could be brought to bear at
any one time. It was ten guns to one, in a fort of kindling and
sand, and that floating bridge of Lee's, two planks wide on
empty rum kegs, wouldn't hold twenty men at a time. He
should write a letter to Gabrielle, just in case. He wondered
what Elizabeth would feel if he died there.

"You can't sleep either, Mr. Fallon?" Colonel William
Moultrie, the fort's commander, was a bluff, stocky man, but
he had a light step.

"No, sir," Michael replied. "Deer flies, sand fleas, and
mosquitos don't give much chance of it. The tobacco smoke
seems to keep them away, though, when I remember to keep
it burning."

"I find riding keeps them off. In fact, I'm riding down to
Colonel Thomson's position now."

"Would you mind if I joined you, colonel? The wind of
riding might be better than this smoke after all."

"I would appreciate the company, Mr. Fallon. My adjutant is suffering from bad water."

The island was low, with broad beaches of white sand
beginning to glimmer as dawn approached. The same sands
formed the dunes of the island, covered by palmettoes and
tangled thickets of myrtle, here and there a swamp oak or a
lone cedar poking above the rest. The horses' hooves sank
deep, and the impressions filled quickly. It'd be poor footing
for Thomson's men if they had to retreat from the Breach
back to the fort.

At Breach Inlet Colonel William Thomson was only a
spare shape in the early morning darkness, with the sound of
the backcountry about him. "Morning, Colonel Moultrie,

Mr. Fallon.'' He offered a twist of tobacco, and when they declined, cut off a chew for himself. ''What can I do for you gentlemen this morning?''

''Do you need anything?'' Moultrie asked. ''I'll try to get it for you, if you do.''

Thomson laughed quietly. ''Hell, colonel, these lads don't need much. I've known most of them since I was militia colonel up to Orangeburgh. Dan Horry's boys are fit, too, and even Clark's North Carolina bunch is ready.''

Moultrie nodded, studying the four hundred yards of water separating them from Long Island. The growing light revealed the gray mass of the far shore. ''Just keep them from crossing as long as you can. If they manage to make a landing, fall back to the quarterguard.''

''Activity out to the ships, colonel,'' one of the men shouted.

There was light enough to make out the ships, now. Moultrie and Thomson stared interestedly, but Michael swore. They were loosing their topsails. ''They're moving, colonel. The tide's at full flood, and they're moving.''

''Damnation! Thomson, hold them as long as you can. Come on, Fallon.''

They spurred away at full gallop, or as close to one as the shifting sand would allow. They didn't draw rein till they were into the fort.

''Sound the long roll,'' Moultrie ordered while dismounting, and the drums beat out the summons to the guns.

Michael shed his coat, tied a rag around his forehead to keep sweat out of his eyes, and ran to the gun platform. Powder-monkeys came running from the magazine with their leather buckets containing flannel cartridges. The gun crews—soldiers, sailors, deserters from the British—waited impatiently.

''Run in and load,'' Michael commanded, and the ten-foot length of his French twenty-six pounder rumbled back on its iron garrison wheels.

A mile and a half offshore the first British vessel, a squat, ungainly brig with its masts set too far to the rear, dropped

two anchors and swung bow on to the fort. Suddenly the
ship's bow sunk deeper, and a hollow, thumping crash
drifted toward the shore. Some crews in the fort looked up,
but Michael's men kept working. The iron shot was rammed
down to seat against the cartridge.

"Run out," Michael yelled, and his men took up the
carriage ropes, and pulled.

Something dropped with a thump in the soft sand in the
center of the fort. A moment later an explosion rained sand
over everyone.

A fresh wind out of the southwest brought *HMS Bristol*
and *HMS Experiment* in line, with frigates ahead and astern.
Another line of small frigates brought up the rear. The
right bastion began firing as soon as the British came in front
of their slewed-around guns, but the line came calmly on.

Michael thrust the priming iron down through the vent to
pierce the cartridge, then filled the vent with fine powder
from a horn. He picked up a slow match and breathed on the
glowing end.

The first ship-of-the-line let go its anchor not more than
four hundred yards off the beach. Almost immediately a
broadside lashed out at the log fort. The front wall seemed to
quiver under the impact. One ball struck hard by Michael's
embrasure, and he flinched in spite of himself. Then he
realized there'd been no whine of flying splinters. He leaned
out to take a closer look. The shot had hit squarely, but the
soft palmetto wood had been crushed by it. There was no
fracture, no splintering. As the second ship, *Bristol*, dropped
anchor and let go her broadside, Michael laughed. The whole
fort leaped and shook. The walls still stood. The damned
thing might stand up yet.

"Commence slow fire!" came the order.

Michael crouched behind the gun, motioning the men to
pull on the training tackle. He laid it squarely on the *Bristol*'s
quarterdeck. The slowmatch went to the vent, and the cannon
hurtled rearward with a roar. On the British ship a section of
rail rose and toppled into the sea. It could have been their
ball, or any one of the others erupting from the fort at the
same time.

The guncrew ran to reload, but the heat of their first battle was on them. He had to stop one from ramming a cartridge down the barrel, perhaps onto a spark and blowing his hands off. The man grinned nervously as the wet sheepskin sponged out the bore, but from then on the nerves were gone. The close call seemed to calm them. They worked as smoothly as any Royal Navy crew.

The fleet's guns fired in crushing broadsides, the sultry wind carrying the smoke of their firing down on the shore, so that even the crash of their guns seemed to smash at the fort. Inside, the men had grown used to the deafening thunder, but there was no getting used to the thick, acrid smoke. It blackened faces, burned eyes, and seared throats, turning the blazing morn into a foggy twilight. Only the blue flag on the left bastion—the Second Regiment's crest, a silver crescent, in the upper corner, and the word LIBERTY across the bottom—stuck up above the maelstrom.

How long had it been? An hour? Two? Michael blinked smoke-reddened eyes and checked his sighting again, then stepped back and touched it off. Before the gun had finished snapping back against the retaining cable he was peering through the haze, searching. Ships moving! Three frigates from the second British line were swinging wide into the harbor. Too few to be headed for the city—. Holy Mother of God, pray for them all. They were sailing around the island to enfilade the fort.

Gabrielle huddled at the attic window and kept the brass spyglass pressed hard to her eye. There was so little to see, and no details at all. The dull ache in the small of her back made her shift, but she refused to take her eye away.

Out in the harbor ships kept up a fire at the fort, and the fort was firing back. She could barely see through the haze of battle. The fort was shrouded with it. Something that seemed to wave through gaps in the smoke must be the flag. The fort still held. Michael still lived. He must. But what were those three ships moving out of the smoke?

A sudden, sharp pain made her fumble the spyglass. Astonished, she looked down at her swollen stomach. That wasn't the babe kicking her. It wasn't time, yet, not by more than two weeks, but the baby was coming.

Calmly she collapsed the spyglass and walked to the stair. Another pain sent her reeling to the bannister. The spyglass bounced its way down, step by step. "Martha! The baby! It's time!"

Martha and a swarm of housemaids appeared before her shout was finished. The pain was ebbing. She could stand, if they would let her. Another pang brought a moan to her lips before they reached her chamber.

As the women began undressing her, fear hit her. Oh, God, so much could go wrong. How many stories had she heard of women dying, of babies dying? She gritted her teeth. Nothing was going to happen, either to her or the babe. Michael would come home and find her with his child in her arms. "Martha, fetch the midwife. Right away."

The maid's cheeks wobbled as she shook her head. "Way them pains is coming, Miss Gabrielle, ain't no time. That young man's on his way now."

Gabrielle smiled as they slipped a clean white shift over her head, and helped her lie back on the bed. "So you think it's a boy, too?"

"Oh, yes ma'am. Cleo, Lilah, you runs to get that hot water right this minute. Yes, Miss Gabrielle. Ain't he acting just like a man? No sense of time, coming early."

Gabrielle tried to laugh, but half-way through it turned to a groan. "Oh, that hurt, Martha. Oh, Lord, that hurt."

Martha hurriedly tied a length of cord to one of the head-posts, and put knots in it. She guided Gabrielle's hands to it, and they gripped as if at a lifeline. "You gots to trust me now, Miss Gabrielle. I know what I's doing. I birthed babies in the quarters lots of times." She put the knife she'd kept ready under the bed to cut the pain.

"I trust you," Gabrielle panted. "I trust you."

"Then when you feels the pain coming, you pull on that cord just as hard as you can. Everything going to be all right." She patted the sweat on her mistress's face with a cloth. "Cleo! Where is you with that water?"

Sweat covered her from head to toe. The black women gently wiped it away, but it always came back. She wanted to pant, to breathe in short, sharp bursts, and Martha told her not to fight it. Rest easy, she said. Let it come. Rest easy? Oh, God, how?

Every muscle flexed, knotted, loosened, and began again. Her feet dug at the bed, cramping. Her jaws clamped shut till her cheeks hurt, and she could taste blood from a bitten lip. It came in waves that periodically washed through her, carrying her before them. She pulled at knots till she was sure the cord or the bedpost must one break. The greatest wave receded, and she dimly heard a cry that wasn't her own. "The baby," she gasped. "Let me see the baby."

"He a fine, healthy boy, Miss Gabrielle," Martha said. She motioned for the others to hurry. "Here he is. Just let me get this blanket round him."

And Martha laid the babe in her arms. She smiled down at him through her weariness. Such a red, hairless little thing to be so beautiful. She brushed the blanket aside, and he grabbed weakly at her finger. As if to see what he had hold of, his hazel eyes opened wide. Unless she missed her guess that little nose would turn out to be his father's.

He bleated a small cry, and she began to rock him soothingly. "Sssh, little one. You and I must both be pretty for your papa. Don't cry, my sweet." He fell silent, staring at her in fascination. She had to laugh. He looked so serious. "James Christopher Fallon. James, after Michael's father, and Christopher after his good friend. Michael will like that, won't he, Martha?"

"I expects he will." A broad grin split her face. "I expects he'll approve of most anything. Right now, though, you got to get you some rest, and I got to get a wetnurse. Young Master James coming early done bollixed up my plans. The woman I had planned, she ain't—."

"I'll nurse him myself," Gabrielle said quietly.

Martha bridled. "You ain't going to ruin your fine bosom nursing no baby. You ain't no up-country woman. You a lady."

"Martha, I will nurse the baby."

Martha began to swell like a frog. Gabrielle sighed. It would be a long battle.

At three o'clock Michael paused to wipe his face. That he was still alive he credited to Providence. As the frigates moved serenely through fountaining geysers, every man in the fort had known he was within minutes of death.

Then, as if Providence had put a hand to its wheel, the lead ship shuddered to a halt, spars and tophamper falling, wedged on the Middle Ground. The other two put their helms over hard. Too hard. Inexorably, they ran together, and drifted, tangled, to join the other on the shoal.

He'd little time to think about that now. Three men were gone from the guncrew. One was expected to live. He bent again to the gun. As he dropped the iron bar and checked the lay of the piece, his eye caught again the twenty-six pounder that had been next to his, lying upside down on the sand inside the fort. An arm stuck out from beneath it, a hapless corporal who'd been running past at the wrong instant. No one had time to shift two and a half tons of metal just to retrieve a body. There wasn't even time, or means, to put the gun back in action.

It was only one of those dismounted. The cavaliers to either side of the fort had had to be abandoned. The dead lay in a line along the low rear wall, faces covered by their coats. A steady stream of wounded limped, or was carried, to the camp behind the fort, where a handful or surgeons under Dr. Peter Fayssoux labored and sweated like fieldhands.

But the fleet had suffered, too. Two of the three frigates on the Middle Ground had been kedged off to limp away, but the third was stuck fast, hammered by the guns of the right curtain.

To the front, the bombship had withdrawn, though never a shot had gone near it. Shots had reached *Experiment* and *Bristol,* though. Half their spars were down, and their rigging hung in tatters. Gaping holes had appeared in their bulwarks, and *Bristol,* Admiral Sir Peter Parker's flagship,

had taken on a list. A flow of boats moved between the
transports and the warships on line, carrying fresh men one
way, dead and wounded the other.

Michael touched the slowmatch to the vent, and the gun
crashed back to the limit of the retaining cable. As if in
answer all four ships of the first line let loose broadsides. The
fort jumped and shook. A powdermonkey running toward
Michael suddenly took two steps without a head and toppled
from the gun platform. Between two guns men writhed in
agony and spreading pools of their own blood, cut down by
splinters of a ball that'd struck one of the guns square on the
muzzle. And with a crack that could be heard above the
screams and the shouting, the flagstaff parted in the middle,
and the blue flag fell to the beach outside the fort.

Instantly a uniformed man tore over the wall, dropping to
the sand and running to the flag. Some guns boomed
raggedly from the fleet, and grapeshot kicked up spurts of
sand all around him. Grabbing up the flag, he raced back to
the fort. In seconds he appeared again, on top of the bastion,
the flag tied to a rammer. Defiantly he waved it over his head,
yelling at the ships. Then he stuck the rammer upright in the
sand of the wall, shook his fist one last time at the British, and
dropped inside the fort.

Michael realized he'd been holding his breath. "And who
in God's name was that?"

"Jasper," one of his guncrew answered. "William
Jasper. Grenadier sergeant. That man'd pull the devil by the
tail for sport and bet on the outcome."

"Ware the commodore!" someone shouted. "The flagship! The flagship!"

Slowly, majestically, *HMS Bristol* was swinging away.
One of her anchor cables had been cut by cannon fire, and
now the tide swung her around the other, turning her guns
away from the fort, turning her stern to it.

Immediately Michael thrust the priming iron through the
vent, primed the gun, touched it off. Every other gun in the
fort did the same, every gun that could still fire. The stern
timbers weren't as thick and heavy as the sides. Every ball

that hit ripped through, and every ball that ripped through smashed the length of the gundeck, shattering into iron splinters against cannon, turning the deck into a hell where the few men left erect walked ankle deep in blood.

"Slow your firing. One gun every ten minutes by the glass." Moultrie himself strode down the gun platform, fury in his face. "Reduce the rate of firing. One gun every ten minutes."

Michael reached out and grabbed him by the arm as he passed.

"Colonel, another ten minutes and we'll have the flagship on the bottom! Another hour, and we'll sink the other, too. We must increase, not hold, our fire. They're already putting out boats to kedge the Bristol back into line."

"I can't. Don't argue, Fallon. Just hold your fire until it's your turn." Moultrie started to leave, then stopped. Visibly, he calmed himself. "We're running out of powder, Fallon. We're running out. Lee won't send more. We must make do with what we have, then it's spike the guns and retreat." He squared his shoulders and moved down the platform. "Slow your fire. One gun every ten minutes."

Michael turned back to his gun. *Bristol* was less than halfway to the British line again. He could put four more rounds into the stern, perhaps five. Bitterly he slumped beside the gun. Its still hot metal made cracking sounds.

Once the powder was gone, they were done. With the fleet's guns to support them, British Marines would land against the fort. It'd be a fine fight, and a short one.

In the overpowering quiet he could hear sporadic musket fire from the Breach Inlet end of the island, and now and again the heavy boom of one of their cannon. Retreat would leave Thomson and his men trapped. And staying meant sooner or later one position would give out, and they'd all be overrun. No powder? Charles Lee was an ass. A murdering ass.

In the long spaces between firing men stared toward Breach Inlet. They could see nothing but scrub myrtle, and there'd been no change in the sound of Thomson's guns, but rumors spread of a landing. Thomson was being pushed back. He was making a stand at the quarterguard. No, the British had landed between Thomson and the quarterguard. He was being pushed into the sea. The British were marching on the fort. Watch close and keep the bayonets handy. They're coming.

The slow stream of powder from the magazine sank to a trickle. At four o'clock Moultrie lengthened the time between firing again. Some began to look to the floating bridge, but none took to it. Every musket had its bayonet, and every man—laborer, doctor, powdermonkey—carried one. Michael was sure the rumors were false. Hell, if one redcoat had set foot on the island, Thomson'd have a messenger to them as fast as the man could ride. Still—. He sent a man to the tents for his pistols, and stuck a bayonet down his boot. It'd do for a dirk if the worst came.

He was crouched beside the embrasure, wishing they could fire massed cannon just one time in answer to the pounding they were taking. Suddenly he gave a start. Moultrie was ascending to the platform, with a tall man in the uniform of a major-general. Charles Lee had come to see for himself. Michael noted with a start that the general's bear-like Pomeranian, Pip, followed behind. Well, they said he took the dog everywhere.

The general bent behind one of the guns, directing the crew in shifting it. It wasn't the next due to fire, or even time for the next shot, but he curtly directed the slowmatch to be applied. Moultrie nodded, and the cannon roared. Lee started on down the platform without waiting to see the fall of his shot. Moultrie followed, speaking as quietly as the onslaught from the British ships would allow.

Two guns further on, Lee did the same thing, and Moultrie once more motioned for the cannon to be fired. And the general, again indifferent to his shot, resumed his casual stroll, Colonel Moultrie following, talking hard.

Was it just that the man liked to hear the guns fire, Michael wondered. They were going to stop at his next, it seemed. He got to his feet.

Up close it could be seen that Lee's coat had winestains and snuff down the front. He bent with a grunt, spraddle-legged, motioning for one man or another to haul on the tackle. He sniffed and rose, pointing a bony finger at Michael. "You, there. Touch it off, and be quick about it. Step lively, damn you." His voice was high and pinched.

Michael's scalp tightened; behind the general, Moultrie signaled him to fire the gun and keep silent. He brought the slow match down.

A splash rose at least six feet behind *Bristol,* and others came as the ball skipped uselessly over the water to sink somewhere beyond the second line. Michael resisted an urge to spit, but some of his guncrew weren't so constrained.

"Damn crews don't lay their guns very well," Lee said. He flipped open a snuff box, sniffed a small pile off his little finger nail, and put the box away without offering any. A large and dirty hankerchief muffled his sneeze. "Well, Moultrie, it seems you're doing quite well without me. I'd better be off, back to the mainland."

Moultrie strode worriedly in the general's wake. "General Lee, the powder!"

Michael could only shake his head. "Well, what are you standing around for? Load! Whatever happens, we'll get a few more off. Maybe we'll put one up Sir Peter's spout."

Less than an hour later a boat grated ashore on the mainland side of the island. Men began carting kegs up to the magazine. Powder kegs. Michael watched silently. More than one man cheered like a bedlamite, but the kegs were small, and there weren't that many of them.

Making his way down the platform came a man Michael knew from Rutledge's staff. "Hello, Mitchell," Michael said.

Mitchell stared at him coldly; then recognition dawned. "Fallon? Michael Fallon? Is that you? God, man, your face is black as a field hand's."

"Powder smoke does that," Michael said drily. "Look you, how much powder did Lee decide to send us?"

"I brought five hundred pounds." He jumped as massed broadsides struck the fort, setting it quivering. To cover he clapped his spyglass to his eye and peered out at the fleet. "They're damaged worse that I expected, I'll tell you that. Worse than anyone in the city thinks. What's that pouring out of the scupper on that big one? Good God! That's blood! I can see the color. It's blood, I tell you. Why aren't you firing more? That one must be ready to sink."

Michael pushed the spyglass down so Mitchell would look at him. "For one of those nine-pounders over there, it takes four and a half pounds of powder for the charge. For a twelve-pound gun it takes six pounds. And for a French twenty-six"—he slapped the gun beside him—"it takes eleven pounds. Tell me how many shots Lee sent us."

The other man was stunned. "I suppose I—. But listen, you've shot some of those ships to pieces."

"Aye, and we'll do more, if we get the powder. Lee's dribble won't do more than fire our one gun at a time a little faster. Get us more powder, and we'll sink some of those bastards out there. Beg for it. Steal it. Bribe somebody. I'll stand for the money myself."

Mitchell shook his head ruefully. "There isn't a prayer of it. Lee didn't send this powder. President Rutledge did. And you don't want to know how little he has left. The worthy general keeps most of it under his watchful eye. Lee! Lee's still saying the real thrust will come against the city in a few days." He added almost to himself. "But Rutledge's report can't wait for that."

"What report?"

Mitchell's mouth tightened, then he leaned closer. "President Rutledge feels this battle is a chance for us to push Congress in the right direction. He's already written two despatches. One will go to Philadelphia before nightfall, with orders for all speed in riding. If it looks like we're winning, the despatch will go saying we've won already. According to word just received, they've been debating independence these three weeks. Hold it! Don't draw attention. That's not to be noised about. I'll tell you this, though. If they haven't voted it yet, news of a victory should push them over the edge."

"For the love of God, man! Look out there! The British

fleet's hanging on by the skin of its teeth. With a ton or two more of powder, we'd put two or three on the bottom. Hell, the two biggest are nearly there now. Tell him that. Tell him these ships will take months in the shipyards to be useful for anything. Damn it, man, just tell him we're winning!''

Mitchell nodded, slowly at first, then with more resolution. "I will. Strike me dead, but I will. They look to have the hell beat out of them.''

Michael stopped him as he turned to go. "You said there were two messages. What was the other one?''

"It says we've lost, of course. But you'll like the ending. 'The fight continues. The torch of liberty still burns in the Carolinas. Damnation to the British.' But it's the other will be sent. Thanks, Fallon.'' And he hurried off the platform toward the creek.

Michael wondered. True, there was hellish damage to the fleet, especially *Bristol* and *Experiment*, but he hadn't mentioned the little matter of an army sitting on Long Island. He hoped Mitchell didn't think about that before he saw Rutledge.

If the right message was sent, if the rider felt the devil's breath on his neck, then in ten days the Continental Congress might well be voting for independence. By the eighth of July, with luck. If they hadn't voted already. Wouldn't that be a thing, now, to be fighting for an independent nation, and not even know it? The wall he leaned against quivered as a dozen cannon balls struck it. There'd be no turning back.

"Increase the rate of fire,'' came the order. "One gun every five minutes.''

The sun set at seven, but the firing—thunderous pounding on the part of the British, single guns from the Americans— continued until half past nine. When the guns fell silent, the chirping of crickets and mosquitoes' whines seemed overpoweringly loud. Weary men dropped beside their guns and slept. Those who prayed, prayed for a long, quiet night. And gunpowder.

A poke in the ribs woke Michael to humid, gray dawn. "What? What's happening?'' Michael asked, trying to fight off the fog of sleep. The crewman just grunted and looked out through the embrasure.

Michael looked, and yelled with triumph. Shouts rang through the fort as others saw what he saw. Between the fort and the first golden-red glimmers on the horizon was nothing but the sea; the British fleet was gone.

He leaped up on his cannon, shading his eyes. Yes, except for the lone frigate still stuck on the Middle Ground, the warships were back with the transports, the Admiral's pennant on the *Bristol* flying from a mainmast stump. Smoke rose from the grounded frigate; small boats were pulling away toward the fleet. She was being fired to keep her from the hands of the Americans. The *Prosper*, an armed vessel of the South Carolina Navy, closed to try to beat the flames. The cheers from the fort redoubled, and Michael shouted and howled with the rest. Damnation! The battle had ended while they slept, and they'd won. He had to find Moultrie.

"Colonel! Colonel Moultrie!"

"Fallon!" His broad tired face was beaming. "They're beaten. Whipped. Let Charles Lee talk of slaughter pens now." He threw back his head and laughed. Michael realized he was grinning broadly himself.

"Colonel, I've a wife in the city I haven't seen in near three weeks, and a baby that's due any day. I'm asking leave to go."

"Mr. Fallon, a corporal's guard with a six-pound gun could sink their flagship, now. They won't come back. Go, go. And I wish your wife and infant well."

"I thank you, colonel." And he ran for the creek. Was a boat there to take him? Well, if there wasn't, by God, he'd swim it.

Ten days after the battle, the British army began withdrawing to the transports. It took a month for the last of the warships to leave, limping over the Bar, running north for repairs before a hurricane caught them.

In the city was one long round of celebration. The garrison of Fort Sullivan was reviewed by General Lee, and the name changed to Fort Moultrie. And President Rutledge presented his own sword to Sergeant Jasper.

The story was growing, too, as soldiers made the tale better for their beery listeners. Men who'd never been close enough to hear the guns embellished it still more. Jasper came to say: 'Don't let us fight without our flag, boys.' And Sergeant McDaniel came to shout: 'Don't let Liberty die with me,' as he watched his life pour out through fingers that couldn't hold it in. Legends were in the making, and that was just as well. A nation aborning needed legends as much as it needed powder.

Michael snapped shut the spyglass and climbed back inside the window sill of Byrne's third-story apartments.

"They've gotten the *Experiment* over the Bar, finally. Seemed to be having a rough time of it."

Christopher, his feet up on the table, waved a tankard drunkenly. "May they all drown in their own blood and go to hell. No, that's no kind of toast. I've got it. We'll drink to Michael Shane Fallon, the man with the luck. I mind me the day I brought you ashore in a patched shirt and worn out cavalry boots. Now you've got a plantation, and ships, and a pretty wife, and a fine son. Let's drink to him. Let's drink to James Christopher Fallon. If he's half the luck his father has, he'll have ten times as much as other men."

"We've already drunk to him," Michael said patiently. He lifted his own tankard. "To the *Annalee.*"

Byrne laughed bitterly, then tipped up his mug. "Aye, to the *Annalee,* may she rest quiet on the ocean floor. Who'd have thought a bloody bastard of a frigate would be on the Florida coast? I barely managed to get the crew to the boats before she went down. But I've told you that. And to miss that grand party on Sullivan's besides." He shook his head, and gulped the rest of his wine.

Michael sighed. "It grieves me to come to you like this, but for your loss you can give me a hand."

"A hand?"

"I'm fitting *Hussar* out as a privateer, but there's a shortage of officers. I hate asking, after you've had your own

command, but will you ship with me as my first mate? I've
need of an experienced man I can trust."

Byrne shook his head. "Ah, Michael, Michael. Privateering. Have you commissions?"

"From both South Carolina and the Continental Congress.
Afraid you'd be hung as a pirate?"

"Might be. Might," Christopher said thoughtfully. "Still
and all, it'd be worth the risk to pay off a few markers."

"Man, you haven't taken to the gambling again?"

"Just a bit." Byrne took a deep breath and dropped his feet
to the floor. "Now. What weight of guns will you carry? I
know some are going out with six-pounders and lighter, but I
favor long nines, myself, or even twelves."

"Long eighteens," Michael said, and Byrne gasped.
"Sixteen of them."

"Mother of God, Michael, you're arming like a warship."

"If I can't outrun a British warship, I mean to outfight it.
Now are you with me?"

Byrne breathed heavily. "Aye, I'm with you. I'm daft,
mind you, but I'll do it. I need—." He couldn't tell Michael
what he needed. The wagers had been more than a few, and
none small. Had the lobsters not sunk the *Annalee*, he might
still have lost her. But here was a chance to recoup. "Oh,
hell, we've faced worse odds here in the streets of Charlestown. Remember the night the stamped paper arrived? But on
to business. Where will we operate?"

"The biggest concentration of trade is around the British
Isles, so we'll sail from French Channel ports, and in the Irish
Sea."

"That's where the biggest concentration of warships will
be, too, boyo."

"And we'll spend half our time disguised as one of them.
In another year there'll be fifty ships doing what we're doing,
but now there's none. We'll be a complete surprise." He
lifted his tankard. "Let the British look to their ships, for
they'll have a brace of Irish wolfhounds on the hunt."

On the fifth of August, the crowd packing the streets and

balconies around the State House was in a festive mood.
Even as the last British ship had limped out of sight a packet
had hove anchor in the harbor with news from the north, and
Congress. For these two things the crowd celebrated, though
some had worried eyes.

A squad from the 2nd Regiment performed the manual of
arms under the barked commands of a corporal, the envious
gaze of a hundred small boys, and the approving glances of a
score of ladies. A guncrew with a shining six-pound field
piece performed the steps of loading and firing, with enough
flourishes and spins of rammer and sponge to do credit to a
Turkish band.

There were bands, a dozen of them, though none could
march in the press. Each, surrounded by clapping, cheering
crowd, was playing French tunes, German songs, Scottish
airs, and Irish ditties, anything and everything that wasn't
English. A number of singers attempted the newest and most
popular air in the city:

> Sir Peter Parker, foolish man,
>   came to Charlestown harbor;
> the twenty-eighth attacked the fort
>   and wounded Young the barber.

Michael pushed past jugglers, orange girls, and fiddlers,
drawing Gabrielle behind him: She, in turn, made certain that
Martha, with the baby in her arms, kept close.

"Michael, we should not have brought James out in this
crowd. Keep the parasol over him, Martha."

"Nonsense. Here we are." He cleared a space at the foot
of the State House steps, ignoring the frowns of those he
crowded aside. "One day, Brielle, the lad'll say he was one
of the first in South Carolina to hear the words. Even if he
doesn't remember much of it." He smiled down at the child.
"My son," he said, "would insist on being here, and he
could."

Gabrielle exchanged amused glances with her maid.
"Michael, sometimes I think you believe you brought that
baby into the world by yourself."

"Look you, lass. He's got a nose like mine. If you'd had any part of him, he'd not have such a beak. You've better taste."

"I think it's a beautiful nose," she said, leaving some doubt which nose she meant.

While he was trying to decide, Henry Laurens came down the steps with a handsome young man who resembled him. "Michael, I'd like to present my son, John. He's some fool notion of going north to join Washington. Talk him out of it. John, this is Michael Fallon, one of the heroes of Sullivan's Island."

"Please to meet you, John. I'll not try to talk anyone out of fighting. And my exploits at Sullivan's consisted entirely of being erect when it was over, with no false modesty in it."

"I'm told that's the most any man can expect from a battle, sir. A great day, today." He gestured to the head of the stairs, where the speaker would appear.

"I've been waiting for it for years, though I'll admit the first time the idea crossed my path, nearly eleven years ago, I wasn't so eager as I am today. What's the matter, Mr. Laurens?"

The elder Laurens shook his head glumly. "I've done more than a little to help its coming. But now that it's here, I feel cut off from all the years and generations behind me. I feel like a faithful son who's asked redress of grievances, and been thrown out of the house for his troubles."

Deafeningly the crowd exploded into cheers. The State House doors were opening. John Rutledge, President of South Carolina, came out first, a roll of foolscap in his hand. Behind him, taking places across the top of the stairs, came William Henry Drayton, Chairman of the General Assembly, and the members of the Legislative Council. Henry Laurens climbed the stairs to take his place at Rutledge's shoulder as Vice President.

The cheering flooded on, men, women, and children all screaming themselves hoarse, artisan, planter, and merchant all as one. Rutledge waited calmly until complete silence fell. In the quiet he surveyed the crowd before he spoke.

"Citizens of South Carolina. Little more than a month ago, in full view of the people of this town, a desperate battle was fought. On the day of that battle, as for many days before, my brother, Edward, and the other delegates to the Continental Congress were locked in debate. Four days later, the Congress voted, and two days after, signed—this." He thrust the rolled foolscap out in his fist as if offering it to them. A low murmur ran through the assemblage. He unrolled the paper and began to read. "When in the course of human events, it becomes necessary for one people to dissolve the political bands which have connected them with another, and to assume among the powers of the earth, the separate and equal station to which the Laws of Nature and of Nature's God entitle them, a decent respect to the opinions of mankind requires that they should declare the causes which impel them to the separation. We hold these truths to be self evident—."

As he read, a wave of exultation swept over the listeners. Michael could feel it, could see it in their faces. They had a nation, by God. They had a nation. He held James up to see the nation of the Fallons read into being.

21

The first long swell of the Atlantic dipped under *Hussar* beyond the Charlestown Bar, and the first spray flipped over the quarterdeck rail. Michael stood at the stern as they turned north, his thoughts in Charlestown still.

He'd been in Gabrielle's sitting room, dangling his watch over James' cradle for the lad to catch at, with Gabrielle sitting in the corner, working her embroidery.

"You're really going, aren't you, Michael," she said quietly.

"Going where? That's it, lad. Catch it." He tugged at the chain, careful not to pull it out of the chubby little hands that grasped it. "He's got a grip on him like a blacksmith, Brielle."

"This privateering venture." She dropped the embroidery hoop in her lap with a sigh. "You're actually going."

He frowned at her tone. "What would you have me do? I'm not old enough to hide behind the counter of a counting house yet."

It was her turn to catch something in his voice. He was ready to be a man at his most male, and that meant at his least sensible. She'd have to be careful. "You haven't even told me how long you'll be gone. It depends, you say. On the weather. On how many prizes there are. On a thousand things. Why, I've no idea if you'll be gone one year or ten."

He went to her and pulled her up out of her chair, took her in his arms. "You're a darling little peagoose, Brielle. I'll wager I know what's bothering you. You're thinking I'll be taking up with some buxom French girl."

"I'd cut her heart out," she said softly, but he realized with a start she meant it. "Don't you realize that I could bear it if only I knew when you were coming back?"

Gently he stroked her hair. He could see she was truly worried. "All right. I sail in October. One year from the day I sail, thirteen months at the most, I'll step back on the dock in Charlestown. November, '77."

She bit her lip to keep it from trembling again. "No tears, Michael. I love you too much for that. Come back, and come back whole." And with that she'd broken her word and run sobbing from the room. It had taken a long and pleasurable night to restore her smile.

The deck of the *Hussar* came back to him with a rush. The harbor mouth was out of sight. He cast an eye aloft; there was a moderate spread of canvas on.

"Mr. Byrne," he shouted, "lay on as much canvas as she'll hold. Remember, we've a schedule for getting back to keep."

Gabrielle sighed as she turned away from the cog-machine. All she really knew about it was that oxen marched in a circle, to power it, and in some fashion the chaff was taken from the rice. She would learn more; now she must pretend she knew.

The coopering shed was her next stop. Outside, however, Lijah was waiting. "Mr. Ames up to the big house, ma'am. He say for you come directly."

"Oh, he does, does he? Come with me, Lijah. The overseer can wait."

She took her time. She saw the coopering; she went to the sawpit and watched logs cut into timbers and boards. She walked down by the river to see the warehouse framework going up. She watched the sheep cropping the lawn between the house and the river.

"Now," she said at last, "for Mr. Ames."

Ames was waiting in Michael's study, a dour-faced man growing dourer by the minute. "Running this plantation is quite time consuming, Mrs. Fallon," he said as soon as she entered the room. "I really don't have time for—."

"Please rise when a lady enters the room," she broke in. Stiffly he got to his feet and moved out from behind the desk to make a leg. She quickly moved behind it and sat down, picking up one of his papers as if to study it.

Ame's mouth tightened. "Mrs. Fallon—."

"Mrs. Fallon," she said suddenly. "You say that quite often, but you don't seem to understand it."

"Mrs. Fallon, I assure you, if I've shown any disrespect—."

"Not open disrespect, no. But you have acted as if I'm a schoolroom miss who's keeping you from your work." Ames opened his mouth; she went on. "Whereas I'm not that at all. I am Mrs. Michael Fallon. And I not only intend to take an interest in Tir Alainn, I intend to run it."

Ames closed his eyes. "Let me speak, please, Mrs. Fallon. I need only remind you of your latest interference. You're having that damned great warehouse built—."

"You'll please not to swear in my presence. I don't propose to explain every decision I make to you, nor to obtain your approval for them. This time, however—. The price of rice is high. But it is high in inflated money, in paper money that grows more worthless by the day. So Tir Alainn won't sell. It's rice will be stored."

"But—" he began insistently.

"But? Sooner or later the market will come back for rice. Sooner or later the price will be paid in gold. And when the gold market returns, one plantation will have as much rice to sell as anyone wants to buy. Tir Alainn. Because I mean to plant as much as I can clear land for, sell only what I have to, and store the rest. If you will help me, then stay. If you will do as I say. If you cannot, then you must leave." She eyed him sternly, but her heart was pounding fiercely. He was off balance, completely surprised. She only hoped he was too surprised to realize how much she needed him. He knew all about rice; she knew nothing. Without him her plans would grind to a halt. But he had to accept her terms. He had to recognize her authority.

"Very well," he said slowly. "Tir Alainn is yours, and you may do with it as you wish. I'll help as I'm able."

It took an effort for her not to sigh with relief. "Good.

That's settled, then. Now, before I forget. I want you to buy as much osnaburg as you can. Use all the Continentals before you touch gold.''

"I'd intended putting off new clothes for the slaves." She frowned at him, and he sighed. "Yes, Mr. Ames, cloth *is* priced far too high. But I fear it'll go much higher before it comes down. If it doesn't, you've my permission to put this down to a woman's whim and gammon, but I'll not have my people in rags because cloth has become too expensive to buy."

"Yes, ma'am. I'll order the cloth. And on the slaves, I've sent you the manumission papers on the first dozen hands Mr. Fallon purchased. They've served their eight years. Only, you've not given them back yet. I can't release them without signed papers. They'll have trouble otherwise."

"Have you spoken to them about this?" she asked casually.

The overseer's voice stiffened. "No, ma'am, I haven't. I hope you'll pardon me, Mrs. Fallon, but with your well-known soft treatment for your blacks, I'd have thought you'd have signed long since."

"Did my husband leave specific instructions with you concerning manumission?"

"No, ma'am."

For the second time she had to suppress a sigh of relief. It was bad enough going against Michael's wishes, but she could not have disobeyed his orders. She'd gone over the plantation's books again and again, and one thing was clear. The price of everything was rising. Already it cost more to run Tir Alainn than could be realized from the sale of its rice. If new slaves had to be bought, then Tir Alainn was doomed.

"There'll be no slaves freed, Mr. Ames, not those or others, until I decide differently."

"But Mr. Fallon—."

"My husband isn't here. I intend to make the decisions I feel are best for Tir Alainn as long as he's gone. And I'll apologize to him if I go against his wishes, not to you. Is that understood?"

"Perfectly, ma'am," he said, and there was a new note of respect in his voice.

She'd done it, she realized. She'd openly countered Michael's expressed wishes. She'd been sure she would be swept by guilt and remorse, but all she felt was a little excitement. She took a deep breath and smiled. "Next, Mr. Ames, I'd like to consider building another cog-machine. With new fields producing rice—."

The curtains across *Hussar*'s sterncabin windows kept out night fog, but they couldn't keep out the dank cold. Michael rubbed his knuckles briskly before picking up the pen and opening the capture log.

30 December 1776. The Irish Sea. *Mary B*. Three hundred fifty tons. Four three-pounders. Bound for Liverpool from New York. Surrendered after short chase and one shot across bow. Cargo: Turpentine, pitch, cordage, and oak ship timbers. Sent into Morlaix.

And now today's:

5 January 1777. South of Land's End. *Green Dolphin*. One hundred sixty tons. Six four-pounders. Bound for London from Oporto. Cargo: oranges, lemons, and olives. Took off ten casks of lemons and sent into Brest.

There was a rap at the door, followed by Byrne's head. "Masthead lookout claims a sighting, captain, though how he can see anything in this—."

"Where away, Christopher?" The book flipped shut.

"Dead ahead, he says. Ship rigged. Even says he can hear her rigging creak. Another man I sent up says it's the wind, but you wanted to be advised of anything."

"I did. Let's see if there's someone thinks the fog and the night will make him safe."

The fog pressed in over the bulwarks, and the bow was completely obscured by dingy gray billows. Only the steersman and a few seamen were on deck, grumpily frowning at the fog, but they perked up when Michael came on deck.

"Where's the lookout, Mr. Byrne?" They maintained

formality in front of the crew.

"As high as we could get him, captain. The mainmast royal yards. With a messenger, in case he spots something."

"And maybe he has. I'd better be taking a look myself." Without waiting for a reply he mounted the rail and disappeared up the shrouds. The lower mast top wasn't a stopping place. He mounted to the small top, then, though the deck had long since disappeared below, through dark and mist up the topgallant shrouds, and so to the royal yard.

Below the yard he stopped and tapped one of the men on the foot. "Climb down, lad, and let me up for a look." He and the messenger worked their way past each other, and he took a seat on the opposite side of the mast from the lookout. "All right, now. Where?"

The seaman shifted his cud of tobacco. "Dead ahead, sir. You can't see her but when the fog shifts a mite, and not hardly then. Just keep an eye peeled forward, sir."

Michael nodded and kept a silent watch. Ahead was nothing but fog. It might be like this, he imagined, if a man could get in amongst the clouds. Everywhere he looked would be mist. Was it possible the lookout really had seen something? What were the odds that on a particular night, on a particular part of a foggy ocean, two ships would be on the same course, and close enough to each other to be seen? Add to that the fog—. The shifting billows rolled, parted, and closed again, but there it was. Three masts, square-rigged, jutting momentarily above the amorphous gray into moonlight.

"You've just earned an extra fifty pounds," he told the lookout, "no matter what that turns out to be."

Down the shrouds he scrambled, with thought neither for height nor darkness, wringing a startled oath from the messenger waiting on the small top, flinging himself without a word into the topmast shrouds. He didn't slow until his boots thumped on the quarterdeck. Byrne and the helmsman jumped.

"It's there," Michael said. "Don't use the drums, but get the men to quarters. Put on staysails. Move, man."

Bare feet padded on the deck as the crew rolled out of their hammocks to whispered instructions. Lashings were cast off, and guncarriage wheels rumbled as the guns were loaded and run out. Blocks and rigging creaked and groaned as the triangular staysails were hoisted between the masts.

Too much noise, he thought. If the other ship heard and shifted course, or worse, heard and simply ran out its guns for a quick broadside into the rigging—. He took his pistols and a cutlass from a seaman. There might be need of them.

Slowly something became visible ahead, a shape in the mist, an outline. Michael signaled to the helmsman for a slight change of course. The stern of the ship ahead could be dimly seen now. That tubby shape spelled merchantman.

Slowly they glided up beside the other vessel. Still no sign that they'd been seen. Michael motioned, the helm went over, and *Hussar* crashed against the side of the other ship. He snatched up a speaking trumpet. "This is the forty-gun American frigate *Eagle*. Surrender or suffer a broadside." With a shout he leaped to the other deck, and half his crew followed, howling like the fiends of hell.

"Don't fire!" someone on the merchantman screamed. "The powder! For God's sake, don't fire."

A frantic shape in a nightshirt came bumping up the companionway onto the quarterdeck. "I surrender! In God's name, don't fire! You'll blow us all to hell! I'm the captain! I surrender." Barefoot and wide-eyed, he stumbled to the rail. When he made out the *Hussar*, his mouth fell open. "That's no frigate."

"Would you care to change your mind, then?" Michael asked.

The captain eyed the privateersmen swarming over his deck and shook his head. "No. I'm Captain Peter Phillipson, and I formally surrender the *Brent* to you, whoever you are. Rebel privateer, I take it?"

"You take it correctly, captain. Michael Shane Fallon, captain of the American privateer *Hussar*, at your service. I suggest we retire to your cabin. Mr. Byrne, come with me. Let's see if we can find a manifest."

Phillipson sat in a corner, disgruntled, drinking a glass of his own wine, while they opened every drawer, chest and cabinet in his quarters.

"I've found it, sir," Christopher announced. "In with a stack of letters from his wife."

Michael straightened with a small chest in his hands. "Read it while I open this."

"Merciful God!" Byrne barked. "No wonder they were screaming we'd all blow up. They've twenty tons of gunpowder on board."

Michael looked up sharply. "Storeship?"

"God's wounds, yes. Two thousand muskets. Two thousand bayonets. One thousand uniform coats. One thouand pairs of breeches. Five—. Damn, but this is a prize. Eight six-pound field pieces with carriages and full equipage, plus one thousand six-pound shot. Michael, you could outfit a small army from this ship."

"Well, it'll be our army, this time." He'd forced the lock with his cutlass; now he opened the chest. The first things out were two large bricks of lead.

"I was supposed to throw that overboard if there was any danger of capture," Phillipson said with a resigned shrug. "If I was navy instead of contract, I suppose they'd courtmartial me."

"Not for these," Michael said, ripping open the despatches one by one. New regulations concerning enlisting Tory troops around New York. A complaint about expenditures for medical supplies. A report that a general named Burgoyne would take command of British troops in Canada.

Michael picked a last letter and broke the seal. It was a personal letter, not a despatch.

Michael scanned it quickly. He was about to throw it back in the chest when something leaped out at him. He checked the address. To a Lieutenant Colonel Francis Holbein, attached to General Howe's headquarters in New York, from someone who signed himself Tom and could get his personal mail in with military despatches. Hurriedly he searched back for one of the despatches, folded the two together, and stuck them in his pocket. "Captain Phillipson, if you'll give your parole, you can stay in your cabin."

"Certainly, so long as I may have my wine."

"Of course. Christopher, come on." Michael hurried back topside with Byrne following. The fog showed no sign of lifting. "Get a prize crew on board and send her off to Charlestown. This cargo will do more good there than in France. We're sailing for Brest, immediately."

"But the fog—."

"If it doesn't clear, we'll wait offshore. Immediately, Christopher. Immediately."

"Aye, aye, sir."

Michael frowned and touched the papers in his pocket. Once in Paris, he hoped he'd find he was on a fool's errand.

The antechamber of the American Commission in Paris was crowded, as it'd been crowded for each of the four days Michael had been fuming in it. The first, after a three-hundred-and-fifty mile ride across mid-winter France, stopping only long enough to change horse, he'd sat in the mud and sweat of his journey, expecting to be called at any moment.

Thomas Martin, the Commission's secretary, entered the antechamber and was immediately beseiged by a mob of waiting petitioners, privateer captains, military men offering to sell their swords, and inventors with weapons which would sweep the British from America in a week.

Martin seated himself at his desk and fussed with papers, all the while ignoring those who fought for his attention. Or seeming to. Suddenly he flashed an unctuous smile. "You'll all have to sit down. The Commissioners are very busy. Please, gentlemen, sit down. No. No, we're not interested in muskets powered by air. Please, gentlemen. Please." He watched the men back to their seats, basking in their disappointment as he had in their attention. His eye fell on Michael. "You again? What's your name? Fallon? I've told you, the Commissioners are very busy men. They can't give personal interviews to privateer captains come to wallow in the fleshpots of Paris."

Michael gritted his teeth and pushed his fists into his coat pockets. "Martin, I've told you fifty times why I'm here, and it's nothing to do with fleshpots or wallowing." Though he had considered wallowing his fist in Martin's face a time or two. "But be that as it may, I've something important here to show to Dr. Franklin. Dr. Benjamin Franklin. And don't try telling me again he's not in France. He's been in Paris since December."

The secretary carefully measured the distance across the desk between him and Michael. "It's true Dr. Franklin is in the city, but he cannot be disturbed. If you'll leave whatever it is with me, I'll see that Commissioner Deane looks at it." The oily smile was back. He held out his hand for whatever it was, the picture of reasonableness.

"Deane!" Michael exploded. "I've had dealings with Silas Deane before. There's been more than one time I've questioned whose side he's on." A murmur of agreement from the other privateers in the room backed him up. "I'll deal with Benjamin Franklin, and with no other."

"In that case," said Silas Deane, ghosting up to the desk, "you may very well deal with no one."

Michael eyed Deane distastefully. There was nothing precisely rodent-like in the man's looks, but his creeping, handwashing, nose-twitching, darting-eyed furtiveness was a perfect imitation of a wharf rat. "Dealing with you, Deane, is like dealing with a wall. No matter what you say or do, nothing ever comes of it."

There was only silence in the room this time. No one there wanted to antagonize Deane. A Commissioner could cause untold trouble for an American in France.

Deane's nose twitched, and his mouth drew up.

Michael suddenly pounded on the desk. Martin jumped in his seat. "God's wounds, man. What game are you playing at keeping me from Franklin? Send my name in to him. I met him once. Perhaps he'll recognize it and consent to see me."

Deane's face was white with anger, and his teeth were bared in a half snarl. "Your name has already been mentioned to Franklin. He doesn't remember you, and he doesn't want to see you. Now will you leave, or must I have you ejected?''

''I don't believe that will be necessary.'' The entire antechamber surged to its feet as Franklin entered. He waved them away with a shake of his head and a sympathetic gesture, and, for him, they sank back with a few protesting murmurs. ''You were shouting so loudly, I could hear you in the other room. You, sir. Don't I know you? Yes, of course. Michael Fallon, Christopher Gadsden's Irish firebrand from Charlestown. Come in, sir. Come in.''

Michael followed him into the next room, Silas Deane's eyes boring into his back. Franklin was almost unchanged. Except for being in black velvet this time, he could have just stepped from his chambers on the morning Michael had first met him in London. He realized with a start that Franklin had spoken and was waiting for a reply.

''I'm sorry, sir. It's just that you've not changed a hair since I saw you last. I realize you're busy with important matters, but it was also important I see you, I believe.''

Franklin laughed. ''I may not have changed a hair, Mr. Fallon, but I've lost any number of them. And as for my onerous duties. Women, sir. Women. I'm not complaining, mind you. My taste in clothing piques the ladies' interest, and when they discover I'm the man who gives talks on electricity, though most aren't certain whether electricity is a fish or a plant, they seek me out. It seems that having me for a lover confers a certain status. From there it's but a short step to meeting their husbands and—amis. And those, my dear Fallon, are the men who run France, and provide guns and money, and perhaps, one day, more for the American cause. In such ways do we serve our country. Wine, sir, or brandy against the cold?''

''Brandy, thank you. I can see, Mr. Franklin, that women would take even more of a man's time than academicians and philosophers. I don't wonder you didn't remember my name when it was mentioned. I'm only glad you recognized me.''

Franklin's face grew somber as he handed Michael a glass. ''Your name was never spoken in my presence, Mr. Fallon.

We have, in the cant, a rum lot here. I play the part of a randy goat, if it is playing, for the cause. Arthur Lee works to feather his own nest, and for little else. I've suspicions as to what Silas Deane works for, but even if I could prove them, he's well padded by his friends in Congress.''

''We've more than a few whose only good is friends in Congress,'' Michael said, thinking of Charles Lee. ''I sometimes wonder if we'll ever get what we were after.''

''It's the way of all nations, and has been for all time, though here and there it's disguised a bit. Very likely it will be in the future as well, even in our nation.''

''Do you wish for an end to it, sir, a reconciliation? I recall at one time you hoped for a peaceful solution.''

''We are committed, and have been since the day your Edward Rutledge, John Adams, and I left our talks with General Howe on discovering that he was empowered to talk, but not to negotiate.'' He sighed sadly and gulped the last of his brandy. ''I grow maudlin with the years. You said it was important to see me. What is it?''

Michael quickly put the letter and the despatch on the table by Franklin. ''These, sir. Neither means much by itself, nor maybe even together, but if you dig out the right parts—.''

Franklin scrutinized the despatch. ''Burgoyne, hmm? I've heard that name before. Why don't you summarize for me, since you've already done the digging out.''

''The despatch says a General John Burgoyne is being sent to take command of British Army forces in Canada. No surprise. I hear Benedict Arnold came within an eyelash of taking the province from the present command. But put it with what's in the letter. The writer tells his friend at Howe's headquarters that he should be operating up the Hudson River Valley toward Canada before the year is out because Sackville has all but approved Gentlemanly Johnny's plan. I recognize Sackville's name. I was at Minden when he refused to attack with the British cavalry, and was cashiered for cowardice for it. He's Lord George Germain, Secretary of State for the American Department. He'd not be approving plans of anyone but a general. If this Gentlemanly Johnny is

General John Burgoyne, then all hell's about to break loose in New York.''

Franklin nodded vigorously. "Yes. Gentlemanly Johnny. That's what I was trying to remember. It must be the same man. Mr. Fallon, you've hit on something vital, I believe. If those two armies move as this suggests, they could slice New York in two, perhaps pull it out of the cause altogether. That would cut off New England from the rest of America. And I'll tell you, for your ears, in this room only, there's been entirely too much disaffection up there since the fighting's moved into the Jersies. I'm not entirely sanguine about what might happen then."

"Then you'll send this to Congress?"

"Better still, direct to General Washington." Franklin folded the papers and stuck them in his pocket. "I'll have my personal secretary make copies tonight. It's better if Deane and Martin don't know of this. Or Lee, for that matter. Now tell me, Mr. Fallon, will you come to a small soiree tonight? Small for Paris, that is. Two or three hundred people."

"I'd best leave for Brest, sir. My crew's likely swimming in brandy by now. It's time for *Hussar* to be back to sea."

"*Hussar!* Is that your vessel? Lord, man, there's a ditty just over from England about you and your ship that's all the rage among those favoring our cause." Franklin began to make a rumbling noise; after a moment Michael realized he was singing. 'The terror of the Irish Sea, the tiger of the Channel.' You'll help the cause immensely. Good, then. It's settled. I'll meet you at your lodgings at eight."

Michael had to laugh. In such ways did they serve their country.

22

Gabrielle felt cold in spite of the light spring warmth in the air. As her carriage rolled toward the river, down to the warehouse and the loading dock, she kept her eyes turned from the empty fields. They should have been full of slaves, making ready for planting, but their emptiness reminded her of what she had to witness, what the slaves had been confined to the quarters so they wouldn't witness. Martha, sitting across from her, kept eyeing her worriedly, and Ames had tried to talk her out of it, but if she could order a thing, then she could watch it done.

The carriage drew to a halt in front of the warehouse, and Ames joined her, doffing his tricorn. "Mrs. Fallon, we're ready to proceed." He hesitated. "I wish you'd go back to the house. I can see no need for you to witness this."

"And despite letting you convince me to let it happen, I'm still not certain I can see the need for it. Mr. Ames, in the years since ground was first broken on Tir Alainn, there hasn't been a single flogging—." She felt a quaver coming into her voice and snapped her mouth shut. She refused to show him weakness.

"Mrs. Fallon, perhaps you're forgetting just what this Tib did. He hacked another man with an axe, half killed him, so he could take the other man's wife."

"But he's being sold off the plantation, Mr. Ames. Isn't that enough?"

Ames stared at the ground and sighed. "I hadn't meant to tell you this, ma'am. Still. I've reason to believe this Tib has raped three of the women. They're too scared to talk, but there's evidence, a little. One of them is pregnant, and the last is only thirteen."

She felt bile rising in her throat.

"It be the truth, ma'am," Martha said suddenly. "Them girls, they afraid to say nothing, afraid he come after them."

"You knew," Gabrielle gasped. "You knew? And you didn't tell me?"

Martha shifted uncomfortably. "I couldn't tell you about no rape, Miss Gabrielle. I couldn't tell you about nothing like that. But you got to whip him, now. Your people in the quarters, but they watching at the windows and round the corners, and listening, too. They ain't meaning to disobey, Mr. Ames. Miss Gabrielle, it's just that you justice. You punish Tib for what he done, then there is justice. You don't, and there ain't. Tib cut a man to get his woman, and all he get is sent away? The mens get to thinking maybe that ain't so bad. And maybe worse could happen."

"Your Abigail's right," Ames said.

Gabrielle drew a long, deep breath. "Very well. It has to be done. I will stay, Mr. Ames."

Hesitating for just a moment, Ames nodded. He turned to wave at the four field hands waiting by the doors, the biggest men he could find on Tir Alainn. They disappeared into the warehouse, emerging with the struggling Tib in their grasp. Quickly they lifted his bound hands over a hook on the wall, and tore his shirt away. There was a moment's pause then, until Ames indicated which one should take up the broad, leather strap. Some plantations had a regular ritual for it, and a regular man to carry it out. Tir Alainn wasn't one of them.

Gabrielle kept her eyes open while the big field hand brought the strap back, but as it started forward they snapped shut. The crack of that first blow ripped through her as if she'd been struck herself.

Gabrielle concentrated on not flinching as each flat crack and its following scream knifed into the darkness she'd surrounded herself with. She tried to pretend the sounds were something else, to disguise them, but they were only what they were. A man was being beaten at her order. A dozen times she wanted to scream for it to stop. Let someone else be—justice. She clenched her jaws. She wouldn't be weak. She wouldn't.

"It over, Miss Gabrielle," Martha whispered.

Behind the overseer Gabrielle saw the fieldhands taking Tib down, and quickly jerked her eyes away.

"Mrs. Fallon," Ames said, "I want to tell you how much I respect you. Both for doing what had to be done, and for your obvious reluctance to do it."

"Thank you, Mr. Ames. I—. Drive me back to the house, Aesop." She closed her eyes again until they halted at the steps. The sound of a horse trotting up the drive brought her head up.

"Justin," she gasped. A scurry of thoughts flooded her head. She knew her father had disowned her. And Justin was rumored to have ridden with Tory raiders in Georgia and East Florida. And he had no love for Michael in any case. And—.

He eyed her sardonically without dismounting. "I witnessed that little exhibition of yours. I always take Elizabeth to witness floggings at Les Chenes, but I didn't know you took a proper interest in such things."

Half a dozen other horsemen waited down the drive, motionless except for the occasional pawing of a mount, watching. A stab of fear went through her. "What do you want here, Justin?"

"Is that any way to greet me? I'm your brother, after all. What's this?" he added, glancing at the ends of the house. "You having some work done?"

She followed his gaze. At each end of the house stood a dozen fieldhands, with Daniel at the head of one group, and every man had an axe or a bushhook in his hands. "Yes. Yes, I'm having some work done, just as soon as you're gone. And don't cry the question of blood with me. You and Papa forgot I existed on the day of my marriage."

His mouth twisted; he made it into a smile.

"Justin, you've never had any but ill feelings for anyone of this house. My house, now. I've hinted for you to leave. Now I'm telling you. Leave Tir Alainn, and don't come back so long as you harbor ill will toward any member of the Fallon family." He jerked his horse around cruelly; she couldn't resist one last thing. "Justin, be careful."

His surprise was clear, but he covered it quickly. "First you tell me to get off your land, and now it's be careful."

"You are my brother, Justin. You're still that." Her eyes flickered to the men down the drive and away.

"I'll take care of myself," he snapped. With crude emphasis he added, "You've chosen your bed. Now lie in it. As long as you have it." And wheeling his horse, he galloped down the drive. The horsemen split to let him past, and fell in behind by twos.

Daniel hurried to her, hat in hand, a worried look on his creased face. "Miss Gabrielle? Are you all right, ma'am?"

"Of course she ain't all right," Martha snapped. "What you expect with all this commotion today?"

"That's enough, Martha." Gabrielle summoned up a smile. "Thank you, Daniel. I'll admit I was afraid until I saw you with those men. Whatever made you think to do it, I thank you."

"It wasn't me, Miss Gabrielle. Some of the fieldhands come down to me at the boats. They say there be some rough men near the house, and they afraid for you, but they don't know what to do. Mr. Ames, he already left in a boat with Tib, so I give them axes and such and brought them up to do what we could. You got no call to be afraid, ma'am. They ain't going to let nothing happen to you."

"Thank you, Daniel. And thank them. And get their names for me. I must show my gratitude."

She began to tremble uncontrollably. Martha helped her into the house, crooning in her ear, but she barely heard. What a way to learn of the fieldhands' loyalty. And what a way to earn it. Being justice. The year had to end soon. Michael had to come home.

The Bristol Channel narrowed down by the time it reached the port, but it was still short of becoming the River Severn. Ships swung on every side of *Hussar* as the anchor let go, the quay only a short row away. Prizes were easier to find in port than at sea, Michael had decided, so they would cut out a vessel from under British noses.

Michael took a last tug at his uniform coat before turning to inspect the crew. The sailmaker had done a fair job of altering it to fit. The buttons on the lapels, to denote seniority, had been changed to six rows of two, to indicate less than three years. It was still a worry, though. If any of those he met started thinking about it, they'd realize a ship of that size wouldn't be captained by anyone higher than a lieutenant. But there'd been no way of making Christopher's lieutenant's uniform large enough to fit, and it was the only other officer's garb they had.

The crew had presented a different problem. The Royal Navy had no true uniform for its seamen, but he'd managed to achieve some uniformity out of the slop chest. Each man wore wide canvas pants, a striped shirt, an open coat, a scarf around his neck, and a tarred hat. They'd do, unless they had to speak in their Carolina drawls and Georgia twangs.

Byrne waited on the quarterdeck with Mr. Petrie, the second mate, in a master's uniform, and young Mr. Oliver, in midshipman's gear. He met Michael by the wheel, and spoke in a low voice. "Have you happened to think that the *Glenarch'* s passengers might have reported having their uniforms stolen? Making them strip down like that on the deck. And only the Royal Navy men. I mean, we took a full complement of uniforms, and they might wonder why. Damn it, Michael, they might be waiting for us."

"One, they likely thought we were just getting back for some of the things the Royal Navy's done to privateers. Two, were they waiting, they'd have opened fire by now. And three, they'd never think of it, because none but a madman would try it."

Byrne's mouth was still hanging open when Petrie walked up. "Jollyboat's in the water, sir. The men are going in now."

"All right, then. Mr. Byrne, remember to keep your eye on me; and don't make a move till I signal." Michael headed for the jollyboat. Ten men waited for him, holding their oars erect in the best Navy tradition. He smiled and checked the priming on his pistols. "Pull for that one, there. The fat brig lying low in the water.'' His attention went to his quarry. Setting low, but with what? They swung in toward the side, and one of the oarsmen stood, ready to heave a line. *"Hussar,"* he sang out in Navy fashion.

Michael swarmed up the side of the ship and glared around him at the officers gathering to greet him. "Captain Fallon. HMS *Hussar*. Bring out your manifest, and be quick about it."

The stout little captain puffed up like a pigeon. "What's the meaning of this?"

"Royal Navy business," Michael snapped. "Either trot your manifest out, or spend the next six months in quarantine on this spot while the teredos worms eat your hull out. And it strikes me you've got some likely looking lads in your crew here. Damn me if I don't press the lot. Except for the old one-eyed man with the arm and the leg gone. You can keep him."

The captain trundled hurriedly below. By the time he got back on deck with the manifest, he was running.

Michael read the manifest and smiled. Flemish lace and French brandy. Brussels velvet and Dutch gin. The owner ought to send him a letter of thanks for the customs duties he was saving him. He read it through, slowly, three times, frowning as if his worst suspicions were confirmed. That, he was sure, would keep the captain's attention on him while his men left the boat. But when he looked up the captain was staring at them. The question was plain on his face. What were they doing all coming on board? And only half were on deck. He needed another minute. "Tell me, captain. What news have you?" The round little man looked at him, surprised by the sudden friendliness. "I've been at sea for weeks, and I've heard nothing of what's been happening."

"They got Jack Dalby to Tyburn Hill at last."

"Jack Dalby?"

"Yes. The highwayman who killed six men on Hounslow Health. They saw five thousand came to see him hang." His words had been slowing as he spoke, and now he stared at Michael suspiciously. "How do you not know of Jack Dalby? The papers have been full of him this year and more." He seemed to gather strength. "What's this quarantine you've talked so much about? I haven't heard about any quarantine, not until you mentioned it."

"Black plague," Michael said, and counted on the terror of the very name to shut him up for another minute. The last man scrambled over the rail. Michael dropped the manifest and pulled his pistols, "If everyone does as he's told, you'll all come out of this with a whole skin."

The captain goggled at Michael's guns, and whirled when the boatmen pulled theirs. "What—? What—?"

"It'll come to you. Jacobs, put the brig's crew on the windlass and get the anchor up. Thomas, get some men aloft and put some sail on her. Jackson, take the helm." Temporarily sticking one pistol back through his belt, he stepped to the rail long enough to wave his hat in the air. On the *Hussar* sails began billowing out. His prize took a strain on the anchor cable and moved as soon as it was clear of the bottom. The windlass clicked and clattered still as they moved out toward the Bristol Channel.

They passed Cardiff and Barry, with the sea still a way before them, but Michael couldn't wait. "Jacobs, break out the colors."

— The Grand Union whipped aloft, thirteen red and white stripes with the British Union Jack for a canton. In seconds the same flag appeared on the other ship. The captain made a strangled noise when he saw it, and whirled on Michael. "You're rebel pirates. Fallon! *Hussar!* I thought they sounded familiar. You're the one sank HMS *Charon* in the Saint George's Channel."

"I said it'd come to you," Michael laughed. He leaped to the rail and balanced there with a hand on a shroud line. Ahead he was looking out into the open Atlantic. No Britisher could catch them now. It'd be clear sailing to Brest.

Gabrielle settled back in her carriage, smiled a goodbye at Lucy Mainwaring, and motioned for Aesop to drive on down the Bay. Almost immediately she called for him to stop. That man waving to her. Surely that was——. Yes, it was Mr. Carver, Michael's friend. Lord. He looked as if he belonged in a sickbed. His years were on him heavily.

"Why, Mr. Carver, how nice to see you. And how well you're looking."

"I'll take that for the polite fiction it is," Carver laughed.

"Not at all, sir. Have you heard the latest news? Ralph Izard has been appointed Commissioner to the Grand Duke of Tuscany."

"Just this morning. But surely that wasn't what held you and Miss Mainwaring in such heated talk."

She shook her head in exasperation. "Prices. Imagine, seven shillings sixpence the pound for beef. Ten shillings for butter. Six pounds the pair for turkeys, four for geese. And it's worse in dollars since no one's sure what they're worth from week to week. Do you know there are people in Charlestown on the edge of starving? That's never happened before. I've organized some of the ladies to help provide food, but we have to work almost entirely through the women. Most of the men are too stiffnecked to admit being paupers."

"With those prices I'd think you'd bring your rice down to sell instead of storing all of it in that warehouse." He frowned suddenly. "Or almost all of it."

"Nearly all rice is paid for with Continental paper," she said carefully. "I'll sell only for gold."

"Do you hear from Michael often?"

"Of course." The sudden change of subject caught her by surprise and wrenched at her till she could hardly keep her face calm. One letter since October, on that shipload of guns and powder he'd captured. There couldn't be more. They couldn't all have been captured. And she wrote to him at Brest every week, and posted them on the first available ship. She'd tried stopping for two weeks, and felt so guilty she'd written three letters on one day to get them all on a ship leaving for France. Damn him. She smiled as if her thoughts were the most pleasant in the world. "Often."

"But I don't suppose you write about what you're doing,"

he mused. He eyed her narrowly. "Michael has been like a son to me, and I had a daughter not much older than you, though she's lost to me, now." The pain in his voice drove all thoughts of letters from her head. "For these reasons, I take it on myself to speak to you. I know what you're doing with the coasting schooners."

"What—? What do you mean?" His words chilled her.

"You've been barging rice down to the mouth of the Santee and loading Michael's coasters there. Then they work their way down the coast to trade in the French and Dutch West Indies. I know the profits are large. Two ships coming in can completely pay for the loss and cargo of a third. But it's dangerous."

"Nonsense," she said, but looked around quickly to see they weren't overheard. "Scores of people are doing it. Strict non-import and non-export would kill Charlestown, and I don't mean the loss of trade. Where's everything from salt to coals going to come from without trade? It's not as if I'm trading with the British, after all."

"You're right, child, right in every word you say. But so am I. There are still men in this city, Drayton's friends, who'd like nothing better than to proscribe Michael Fallon's wife for breaking the Association. I must go now, but I tell you again, be careful. What I hear, others can hear. Be very careful."

At home, she closeted herself in Michael's study. That was where he always went to think. Maybe it'd help her, too.

Three times, now, she'd sent a coaster out, and all three had returned safely with valuable cargos and hard money. At that moment one was waiting near the mouth of the Santee, keeping out of sight of Americans and British alike, waiting for a load of rice to be brought down from the warehouse.

Despite the fact that many of the most prominent men in the state were doing the same thing, she'd been careful. Or thought she had. One by one she'd picked the captains for their loyalty to Michael. They'd picked their own crews, and done so as if discovery would mean disaster. The rub was that it might. She'd worried about a return to strict enforcement, about moves against those who were known to have broken the Association. Why hadn't she thought of those who'd move against her just because she was Michael Fallon's wife?

They were there. Satellites of the Council of Safety, condemning Michael for being fainthearted in the American cause, though their strength seemed to be demanding proofs of loyalty from others. Disgruntled Liberty Boys, angry at seeing their power fade, feeling betrayed by Michael because he'd risen in the world while they still worked with their hands or spent their days swilling rum. They were the ones who'd cry for an example to be made. They were the ones who'd peek, and poke, and pry, until they discovered what was going on.

Maybe they already had. Mr. Carver knew. And as his influence waned, was it likely he'd still be among the first to hear things? Perhaps they already knew. Perhaps they were already preparing to move against her. Perhaps—.

With an effort she got hold of herself. Better to have done with it. She took up pen and paper, and began to write.

She tugged at the bell-pull, and the butler entered silently. "Have a liveryboy take this to Daniel. He's with Tir Alainn's cutter at Motte's Wharf. It's for the captain of the *Santee Flyer*. Daniel knows where to find him. And tell him it's urgent."

The letter going out the door took her worries with it. Captain Rogers would go right ahead with loading, but he'd bring the rice to Charlestown to sell. The danger was gone. The worry was gone. She felt almost like dancing. When the butler announced an old friend's arrival, she rushed to meet her with a light heart.

"Sally, how good to see you."

"And you, my dear. You look wonderful, though how you keep that smooth skin at Tir Alainn is beyond me." Sally Howe was a diminutive blonde who ruled her husband with an iron rod. She smiled at Gabrielle and nodded. "And I must say you look ready for a soiree. Now don't say a word. I know you say you won't go to so much as an at-home until your husband comes home, but this one's special."

"You're going too fast for me," Gabrielle laughed.
"What party? And what's special about it?"

"Why, Antonia Waring's levee. Haven't you heard? She
sent me especially to bring you. There'll be nobility there. A
German, Baron de Kalb, and a real French Marquis, the
Marquis de La Fayette. They landed at Georgetown, and
Benjamin Huger brought them to town. It's going to be the
grandest assembly of the year, my dear. Three orchestras.
Dancing in the garden. You must come."

It was the mention of dancing that decided her. Damn
Michael and his silence. "I'll come, Sally. It's ages since
I've danced. Oh, but what will I wear? I haven't had any new
gowns made for I don't know how long. You'll have to help
me choose. Martha? Martha!"

The levee was everything that Sally promised. Musicians
played in the downstairs drawing room, and more on the
veranda. A third assemblage was in the garden for dancing
under the trees. In fact, there was dancing everywhere. She
was swept into a country dance as soon as she was through
the door, and two more before she caught her breath.

All the talk was of the noblemen. Rainbow clusters of
women, carefully coiffured, put bejeweled heads together.
This Baron de Kalb is a positive giant, my dear. The young
marquis is so handsome he's almost beautiful. And the way
he talks—lovely. In spite of the talk she didn't see those rare
and wonderful noblemen anywhere. But in the garden she did
come on Elizabeth, in a green velvet dress that made her pale
skin almost luminous.

"You may go, Solange," Elizabeth said to the black
woman at her shoulder. She regarded Gabrielle with a vulpine smile. "So you've finally come out of hiding. I thought
all that pining for a far-off husband would wear thin eventually."

Gabrielle's face tightened, but she was determined not to
let anything spoil her evening. "Is that a new maid,
Elizabeth? What happened to Samantha?"

"Yes, Solange is new. Samantha could never remember her proper place. I had to sell her."

Gabrielle gasped. "You sold her?" Selling a house slave would be bad enough, but Samantha had been with Elizabeth since childhood. "How could you?"

"Don't lecture me. I won't be lectured by any woman who ran off in the middle of the night to get married." She almost choked on the last word. What had Michael seen in the girl, anyway? She was pretty enough, Elizabeth decided grudgingly, but even after a child she was a girl. Michael had always had an eye for real women.

Gabrielle refused to be drawn. Well, perhaps just a little. "And Justin? Is he here this evening?"

"To be arrested?" Elizabeth smirked. "That's not likely, is it?" With a throaty laugh she left Gabrielle. She'd just seen what she was after.

Baron de Kalb didn't see her coming, and she had a leisurely chance to examine him. God, but he was nearly the giant they named him, a broad, towering, muscular man. She eyed him from head to toe, and bit at her lip as a shiver ran through her. When she looked up, he was smiling at her.

"Oh. I beg pardon, baron. You, you do speak English, don't you? English?"

"I speak little bit English." His voice was a bass rumble.

"You speak wonderful English." She laughed and spoke with naughty emphasis. "But all the ladies want to do something other than talk with you. I mean dance, of course."

He stared into her decollatage openly and appreciatively, and his smile became knowing. "You one Gott verdamnt good looking woman." He seized her wrist.

"Why, why, baron. That's, that's quite a compliment." She was flustered. His crudity was more than she'd bargained for. And yet, there was something—appealing— about it.

"Endless weeks on boat I have been, with no company but horses and a Frenchman. Now to some gottverlassen place, this Philadelphia, I must ride. Bei Gott, I want to ride a woman. Zum Teufel, woman! You think we dance? We dance laying down. So! You want to yell help, I let you go, and go find a woman for me. Otherwise, we go find corner in stable. Now answer me."

Elizabeth's mouth trembled as she tried to form an answer. It was what she'd been after, but not like this. They'd dance. They'd go in to supper together. And after, there'd be more wine, and a gentle seduction. But he was treating her like any common blowze, like a tavern wench who could be bought for a few shillings. He didn't care who or what she was. To him she was just a woman he wanted to take. A queer thrill shot through her. She wet her lips. "I won't yell help."

Gabrielle watched, stunned, as Elizabeth and the huge Bavarian walked back toward the stables. When he grabbed Elizabeth she'd started to scream. Then she realized Elizabeth didn't want help. It froze to her the spot.

"He is crude, even for a German," came a pleasantly accented voice over her shoulder, "and very rough on women. If you wish it, I will rescue your friend."

"She—. I—." Blushing furiously, Gabrielle whirled. He was a slender young man, richly dressed even among the planters, and boyishly handsome to a striking degree. "What I meant to say was, my, my friend doesn't need to be rescued. And if, by chance, she does at some later time, I'm certain she's capable of calling for help." She wished he'd stop smiling at her like that. She was a married woman, now. She had to remember that.

"I think it is just as well that I do not have to antagonize him," the young man said. "He will be very, very useful, that one. He knows infantry, for all he does not know the difference between a lady and a—. Forgive me. I am so long in his company, I begin to speak as he does. And I forget myself. I am Marie Joseph Paul Ives Roch Gilbert de Motier, Marquis de La Fayette."

She wasn't certain what she said, but in some fashion they were inside, dancing, and he was calling her Gabrielle, and she was calling him Gilbert. It came as a shock to her that, for all his accomplished air, he was but twenty, a year younger than she herself. He really *was* just a boy. Not a man, like

Michael. The thought of him, and of the letters he hadn't written, roused her anger. She threw herself whole-heartedly into enjoying the charming young marquis.

It amused him that her name was French and yet she had only a few words of the language. He taught her more, and they laughed over her pronunciation. So much seemed to amuse him, and for some reason it all amused her, too. She laughed at his stories of the court, and danced with him time and time again, with wine between. At supper he claimed the right to carry her plate to the buffet, and to sit by her. She fed him cold shrimps with her fingers, and he kissed her finger-tips after each one. After, there was more music, more wine, more dancing. And then they were dancing in the garden, with only the crickets and the stars for company.

He tilted up her chin and kissed her, and for a moment she kissed him back. Suddenly she pulled free of him, gasping, heart pounding. "Gilbert, no. I'm married."

He drew her back to him so gently she barely realized how she'd gotten back in his arms. "Ah. One of those stout merchants, perhaps?"

"He's a privateer captain. Please, Gilbert."

His fingers ran gently along her cheek, turning her face once more up to his in the moonlight. "A brave man, then. I apologize, to you and to him, for thinking any other kind of man could have won you. No, Gabrielle, do not tremble. There is no need to fear me. I take only a few kisses. We are a lonely man and a lonely woman, seeking solace. There can be so sin nor harm in that."

As his lips came down on hers she thought, damn Michael. This would teach him to write her.

23

The fireplace of the new house on Queen Street was large. It took the chill from the January air, but Gabrielle still felt the cold. A copy of the *Gazette* lay on the table beside her, but she didn't bother to read it. The news would be bad. 1778 looked to be as bleak as 1777. Word of Saratoga had been a bright spot in a year filled with disaster. Defeat piled on defeat. Brandywine. Germantown. Philadelphia abandoned. The Congress fled to York, in western Pennsylvania. And the rumors. Washington's army was disintegrating at a place called Valley Forge. Washington was being given dictatorial powers—made a new King George. Michael was off, God alone knew where, and his cause was falling apart.

She winced. Be damned to the cause. It was Michael that mattered. Two months past the time he'd set as the latest for getting home. Suppose he was dead. Suppose he'd died while she was kissing Gilbert.

That brought a bitter laugh. There was no possible way for Michael to be away so long and remain faithful. She loved him, but she knew him. Then damn it, why did she feel so guilty about kissing Gilbert a few times under the moonlight?

Martha scurried in like a ruffled hen. "Miss Gabrielle. Miss Gabrielle, it time we leave."

"Leave? What are you talking about, Martha?"

"The fire, Miss Gabrielle. The fire. It done got worse. It spreading."

"Nonsense. The Fire Company will soon have—." For the first time she became aware of a flickering, red glow through the windows.

"They say the Fire Company can't stop it no more. They say the Library Society done burn up with all the books. They say the whole city going to burn. Miss Gabrielle, don't go near that window.''

Gabrielle threw open the window and stared out at a scene from hell. The night sky was swept by flames billowing into the air. They seemed to go on for blocks and blocks. Nearly everything between Church Street and the Bay must be burning. And the edge of it was no more than a block away.

"We're not leaving, Martha."

"Miss Gabrielle, this ain't no time for being brave. This a time for running."

"Michael had this house built for me. I can't lose it." She'd move into it before it was even finished, so he'd come to her there. Sooner or later, he'd come. "Get all the livery-men up, Martha. Boys too. And all the stablehands. Get buckets. I want a steady stream of water over this house. And over those on either side, too. Well, what are you waiting for?''

The slaves, rousted from their beds, looked fearfully to the red-splashed night sky, but Gabrielle soothed them, calmed them, bullied them, anything to save the house. She was everywhere. She climbed into the attic, up the ladder to stick her head through the trapdoor onto the tile roof. Ash and even burning sticks and shingles rained down continuously, but two stablemen hoisted buckets of water from the garden on a rope and doused everything. Slaves on the side balconies, hanging out the windows, on the front verandas, splashed bucket after bucket of water against the house. It dripped and glistened as if after a heavy rain, lurid in the firelight. The roar and crack of the flames could be heard now, the crash as a building fell in.

A rider reined in beside her as she stood in front of the house. "You'll have to leave immediately. There's only a prayer of stopping it short of—." He gasped as he got a good look at her, in the light from a collapsing house.

"Ma'am, are you all right?"

"I'm fine." Angrily she wiped at a smoke-smudged cheek; her hand was even dirtier. "And I'm not leaving." A half dozen slaves with shovels ran up, and she turned to them. "Begin digging in the garden. Fill buckets for the men on the roof. We can't spare any more water from the sides of the house."

"Ma'am, you must go. You can't save your house like this. If the fire gets this far—." She kept right on directing the work. He tried another tack. "Ma'am, listen to me, please. It's said the British started this fire, and may still be in the city—." He shied back as she rounded on him fiercely.

"Damn you! Damn you! Why aren't you doing something instead of trying to frighten a woman? Anything that happens in this city those same few poor sailors get the blame. Now get out of here, and leave me to save my house. Jubilo! Hercules! Go up and help on the roof."

She stalked away to make her rounds again. All the men were working. All the housemaids and the liveryboys too. Then she saw it. Cleo fell out of line, tumbling to the ground in a faint of exhaustion.

She took the slave woman's place in the line of slaves passing water-laden buckets to the house. The man gasped, goggle-eyed, at her; the next man seemed almost afraid to take the bucket from her. She didn't see their surprise. She took the heavy buckets and swung them with a small grunt of effort on down the line.

The flow of water went on. And Gabrielle worked until she worked in a fog. Pivot, take the bucket, pivot, give the bucket, and never see the man it was taken from or the man it was given to, never see anything but the endless buckets. A hundred. A thousand. On and on.

It was Martha's scream that brought her back from semiconsciousness. "Miss Gabrielle! What you doing?"

Startled, Gabrielle lost her grip, and the bucket dropped, splashing its water over the ground and her dress. She bent to pick it up and was suddenly aware of pain shooting through her back and up her thighs. Her legs quivered. "Fighting the fire," she said dully. "Got to fight the—."

Martha caught her as she nearly fell. "You come with Martha, Miss Gabrielle. Oh, your hands! Your poor hands! What you want to do your hands like that for?"

Gabrielle held her hands up in front of her face and stared at them. Ridged blisters criss-crossed the soft palms. But she didn't feel a thing. How odd. The sky was turning gray. Almost dawn. If they could only hold out till dawn. "The fire, Martha. Get in line."

"The fire finished, Miss Gabrielle. They done got it penned up; it done for. You come with Martha now. I fix you a nice bath, and some ointment for your poor hands."

She let Martha lead her away, stumbling down the drive. The smell of burned buildings was heavy in the air, and suddenly she was aware of every pain. Her legs screamed, and her hands were on fire. The night, the pain, everything, was suddenly more than she could bear. Sobs wracked her, and tears coursed down her cheeks. But the house was safe. That was the important thing. The house was safe, and Michael would come home to it.

Byrne, Petrie, and young Oliver sat around Michael's table in the sterncabin of *Hussar*, frowning at the chips of wood he was laying out, three columns of them.

"There," he said, setting the last one down. "That's the way the convoys are running now. If there are two escorts, one is ahead, and one astern. With three, it's one ahead and two astern, outboard of the columns."

Byrne nodded glumly. "Aye. And they won't chase you out of sight of the convoy. They just won't be drawn off any more. We've done too good a job—scaring the bloodybacks till they shepherd the merchantmen like sheep."

Mr. Oliver, the baby-faced young officer, shifted nervously and cleared his throat. "Ah, I—. Well, sir, I was wondering why we don't stick to picking up stragglers. There are always a few."

"Which of you wants to answer him. Mr. Byrne?"

"All right, captain. I'll explain it to the boy. Have you happened to notice, boyo, that nine out of ten of those stragglers are the worst sailors in the worst condition, with the most worthless captains and the most worthless cargos? So we take a brace or so, and divide them up. One third to the owner, the rest to the crew. Half a share to ship's boys, powder monkeys and the cook. A share each to the seamen. A share and a half to the carpenter and the sailmaker. Two to the chief gunner. Three to junior lieutenants, five to senior, and ten to the captain. Then there's an extra half share to anyone who loses an eye or a limb, and an extra whole share to the family of any man killed. Add it all up, and your share of a pair of stragglers would come to, oh, say three days with that Consuelo of yours in Ferrol."

The table exploded in laughter as Oliver's face went red. He was still young enough to be in love with every girl he had in every port they visited, and the sultry Consuelo was the latest. The mirth was cut short by a knock at the cabin door. A seaman stuck his head in. "Masthead reports a sail, sir. A point on the port beam."

"Tell the steersman to alter course toward it," Michael said. "Well, gentlemen. Shall we be seeing what it is we've found?"

From the first it was clear their quarry was a massive ship. Even from a distance two stern galleries could be seen. Bluff-bowed and tall, she plowed through the sea under heavy sail, the Union Jack at the stern and the Red Ensign at the masthead.

Byrne snapped his glass shut after a short look and shook his head. "A sixty-gun ship-of-the-line. Maybe larger. It's as well we're no closer."

"Then why hasn't she turned toward us?" Michael kept his spyglass to his eye, studying the ship from heavily gilded stern galleries to ornately carved lion-and-unicorn figurehead. "If that's a ship-of-the-line, or any sort of warship, why hasn't it turned toward us?"

"Because they've no interest in us, thank God." Byrne looked at Michael suspiciously. "If it's a warship? God's blood, look at it. The size. The flags. That's a sixty-gun ship of the Red Squadron."

"That flag could be the Merchant Ensign as easily as the Red Squadron flag. And what sort of merchant vessel that size would be passing through these waters? An Indiaman.

Built to fight off Lascars and Malay pirates, and weather storms around the Cape of Good Hope. And in waters known to be frequented by American privateers, her captain'd not be wanting to get too close to a strange vessel. A warship would come closer, just to be sure of us." He shut the spyglass with a decisive click. "But we'll make certain. Hoist the American flag."

One of the seamen opened the flag locker and hunted through the colors they used to close on unsuspecting merchantmen. French. Spanish. Portuguese. Danish. Venetian. Every country that ever had a ship, and some that didn't. In minutes the Stars and Stripes ran aloft and broke at the masthead.

On the huge ship ahead the reaction was instantaneous. Two dozen gunports swung open along her side. Aloft more sails broke out until she carried every scrap of canvas she'd hold. And she altered course two points away from *Hussar*.

Michael looked at Byrne and the mate shook his head. "All right, she's an Indiaman. But you yourself said they're built to fight off pirates, and I've seen a dozen Malay dhows swarming together, each with as many guns as we have."

"We've bearded the British Navy time and again, Christopher. Would you turn from a fat merchantman, no matter his weight of guns? Make all sail, and beat to quarters."

Hussar picked up speed. It was a strong wind, not quite over the stern. The sea was calm, with long, low swells. A heavy sea would have favored the bluff-bowed Indiaman. In that sea *Hussar* flew, and the huge merchantman wallowed ahead.

Every gun on deck was manned and primed, but every man hoped they wouldn't be used. Shot-up prizes had a way of sinking before they could be brought to port. Cutlasses and boarding pikes were being handed out. It was on them they'd depend, cold steel and the rush of over a hundred men.

The distance grew shorter. The time until they'd be boarding could be measured in minutes. A low, anticipatory murmur ran across the deck.

On the Indiaman, it looked to Michael as if they were

swinging yards. What—? They were going to swing broadside to *Hussar* and fire! Their head was already falling off to starboard. "Starboard your helm," he ordered. "Fire as they bear."

As the Indiaman swung away to starboard, *Hussar* heeled to port, across her stern. Eight eighteen-pounders thundered and leaped back, solid shot smashing through the stern cabins. And then they were upon her. Hand-mortars fired grappling hooks to pull them tight against the bigger ship. Men aloft swung grapples into the Indiaman's rigging to make them faster, and lit and dropped grenades on her deck. With a roar like the fiends of the pit a hundred privateers and more swarmed up the side of the ship looming over them.

A man leaned over the rail above Michael to aim a musket, and he ran him through and boarded over his body. He slashed away a bayonet thrusting for him, pistoled the wielder, and hacked at another man. Already the deck was covered with milling, desperately fighting men, and the air was filled with the screams of the wounded and dying.

An officer in a coat covered with gold braid rushed at Michael. The captain. "You pirate bastard," he screamed.

Michael beat aside his clumsy thrust and, in one move, dropped his sword, pulled the man to him, and presented his second pistol to his head. "Surrender, man." He jerked the captain around where he could see the fighting on deck. "Surrender before your whole crew is killed. Shout it loud."

The captain looked at his crew being cut down and shouted. "I surrender! Lay down your arms! The ship is surrendered!" He breathed heavily as his orders were obeyed, and the privateers roughly shoved survivors to the center of the deck. "Damn you," he rasped.

"Perhaps I will be. In good time. I'm Michael Fallon, captain of the American privateer *Hussar*. Who are you, and what ship is this? Bound for where, from where?"

"Charles Thomas Forsythe," the captain choked. The *Empress of India,* bound for London from Calcutta, in the Bay of Bengal. You'll hang for this, you realize. You're pirates, and you'll hang."

"But before that happens, Captain Forsythe, suppose we go below and fetch the manifest. Mr. Byrne, come with me. Mr. Petrie, get a damage report on our prize. Mr. Oliver, a report on casualties. And now, captain, if you please."

The captain's cabin showed the effects of the battle. Three large holes gaped in the stern windows. The furnishings were overturned or smashed, but they'd have done credit to any house in Charlestown. Instead of a ship's bed, there was an ornately carved four-poster, and a crystal chandelier hung over the demolished table.

While Byrne stood gaping, Michael went to investigate a large, square bulk, sitting in the corner with a rug over it. The rug whisked away to reveal an iron-bound chest with a heavy lock and hasp on the front. It took three blows of the cutlass to break the lock. He swung open the lid and felt his breath go. The chest was filled to the top with gold coins. There were coins with six-armed demons, and coins with dragons, and coins with strange markings he thought might be some sort of writing. He didn't know a one of them, but he knew gold, and this was a fortune in it.

"Michael, I've the manifest. It's—. Holy Mother of God! I never saw that much gold in my entire life."

"Well, you've seen it now." He closed the lid and fit the broken lock back on the hasp. "Better than a straggler, aye? Young Oliver'll be able to afford more than three nights with Consuelo on his share of this."

"And that's not all. It may not be half. Look at this manifest. Spices. Silk. Ivory. Pearls. Casks of pearls. Can you believe such a thing?"

Michael waved away the manifest and laughed. "I believe it. After this chest, I'll believe anything. Ah, Mr. Petrie. Mr. Oliver. It seems we've taken a treasure ship."

"I know, sir," Petrie replied. "The men are already toting up their shares."

"Time enough for that when we get it to port. For now, what's it cost us? Casualties, Mr. Oliver?"

"Light, sir, considering. Four dead, about twenty wounded. The Indiaman's worse off. A dozen dead, and every man of the rest has a wound of some kind.''

Forsythe, who'd been staring dejectedly at the ruins of his cabin, and possibly his career, stirred. ''My crew. You will take care of them? Or at least allow us to use our own medical supplies?''

''Your men will be cared for along with ours, captain. Damage, Mr. Petrie.''

''Bad enough. The steering's shot away, tiller, wheel, and all. Thank God the rudder's sound, or we'd be here for hours. I've started them jury-rigging. Carpenter says another forty minutes.''

''She'll steer like a bullock. We'll head for the nearest port, and repairs. That's La Morelle. Captain Forsythe, if you'll join your men below, I think you'll see they're being cared for. Mr. Petrie, have some men move this chest to the *Hussar*. Mr. Byrne, let's work her clear. I'd be afraid of a cutter with a swivel gun hung up as we are.''

As Michael had predicted, the *Empress of India* steered like a bullock, slowly and ponderously. Men below heaved at block and tackle to force the rudder round against the weight and momentum of the ship. Even a gentle turn left them spent and gasping. They made for the port that was nearest as the wind took them, where they could run free instead of tacking. And *Hussar* ranged around her, watching, always watching, for sign of an enemy sail.

The French coast was in sight ahead when the masthead sang out. A flung arm sent Michael's gaze astern. On the horizon a topsail slowly climbed into view, and inch by inch, a mast, and a ship. A frigate. Normally *Hussar* would dance away, leaving another English captain, if he recognized her, to curse that damned pirate Fallon. But now she was tied to the prize.

Michael measured the distances ahead and behind. The frigate was coming up fast, and the wind seemed to be faltering around *Hussar*. It'd be close.

With infinite slowness the arms of the bay at La Morelle opened ahead and enfolded them. Behind, he could make out the frigate's figurehead, an angel holding a sword aloft.

Well, that angel'd get no chance to try his sword against a
Hussar's saber. As the thought came, the wind died.

Hussar and the prize floated just inside the bay, surrounded by cliffs, becalmed. Outside, the frigate still came,
slowing, but still slicing toward the mouth of the harbor.

"Damn! Mr. Byrne, lower the boats. We're towing *Hussar.*" Some of the crew stared at Michael as if he was a
madman, but Christopher raced to get the boats out. "There,
two hundred yards ahead and to the starboard, where the
white streak is, down the face of the cliff. From there he'll
come head on at our guns down the channel, or run on the
shoals. We'll see if he fancies that."

He ignored the hubbub as the boats were swung out.
Empress of India's anchor was down. To get to it the frigate
would have to pass *Hussar*. He gave orders to anchor on a
cable spring. The cable was passed through a stern port and
brought forward to be bent on the anchor before it was
dropped. By taking up or letting out the cable the ship could
be swung through a wide arc, and the broadside directed
almost anywhere. Let the lobster come on in.

Beyond the headlands the frigate's sails suddenly emptied,
and hung loose. The captain dropped an anchor, riding
squarely across the channel out. There was no activity. It
might have been a ship of dead men.

Michael quickly drew Byrne aside. "I took this position
when I was sure we'd have to fight. But he'd be much less
likely to try cutting out our prize if we were where any trouble
would mean damage to a French town. I'm talking about tied
up to the quay. It's deep enough to take us, for all this is a
fishing village."

"You mean to tow us in?"

"I do. But not with our boats alone. You saw how the wind
failed in here before it failed for the Britisher. Suppose he got
enough breeze to bring him in gun range while we're being
towed along?"

Christopher looked sick. "He'd blow us out of the water."

"So I intend giving him as little time to do it as possible. If
we had two or three dozen of the fishing boats out here—.

You see it? They could move us as fast as a medium breeze. Until then, we stay right here. Now ready the jollyboat. I'm going to see the mayor.''

The mayor received Michael at the townhall with his council, six long-nosed men who looked alike enough to be brothers. The mayor himself was short and round, and he spoke effusively. ''Ah, Capitaine Fallon, mon brave. It is an honor to welcome you. You are most well known as a gallant among gallants. And now you come to our village with another prize from the goddamns.''

Michael bowed formally. ''I thank Your Excellency for the kind words. It is I who am honored.''

''No, no, Monsieur le Capitaine. Perhaps it is that we are both honored. And perhaps you will tell us the reason for our part of the honor.''

''You're all aware, of course, that my ship and my prize are becalmed in your harbor. If you could lend me your assistance in gathering the fishermen, so they could tow us to the quay with their boats, I'd be forever grateful. And of course I'd pay them well.''

The effusive smiles disappeared as he spoke, and now they broke into a torrent of rapid French, every man seeming to speak at the same time. Michael had a sinking feeling. The mayor turned back to him, blandfaced.

''I regret, capitaine, but it is impossible. There is the small matter of a frigate of the goddamns, yes? If your so famous vessel is at our quay, this frigate may fire at you, and many of the shot will hit not your ship, but our village. You understand, of course.''

''Excellency, he'll not fire on your village, nor anywhere near it. Why, it'd start a war.''

''That this other capitaine's feelings are so peaceful toward France is a chance we are not willing to take. *Non! Impossible!*'' He pursed his lips, and rolled his eyes toward the others. ''It is much to be regretted, *certainement*, that this prize may be returned to the goddamns. Some, shall we say, small amount of assistance might be given in running it aground. Just to keep it from the goddamns, of course.''

Michael had difficulty in not laughing. They'd swarm over it like ants the minute the keel touched bottom, claiming right of salvage. "I don't think that'll be necessary," he said. "Do you think I could borrow or rent a horse to ride up to that fort on the headland?"

"But of course, Captaine Fallon. I myself rent the horses. But I must tell you, the commandant can help you no more than we."

The commandant was a dark-eyed colonel with a thin mustache and the star of an order on his tunic. "I have watched your ship in the harbor below, capitaine. And the other outside. It is a good name, *Hussar*. I myself was of the chasseurs before this." He tapped his leg, and limped to his desk. "You would care for a brandy? Or perhaps wine?"

"The brandy, colonel. I was one myself, once. A hussar, that is. That other ship, colonel. He's likely to try coming in, to try taking my prize out of a French port. It'd be nice if you were to inform him, sort of casual like, that you've no intention of letting French territorial waters be violated."

The commandant smiled and swirled the brandy in his glass. "It was a long time ago for me, the chasseurs. And for you, too, I think, the hussars. No more the gallant charge, the dashing sortie, with no more to think of than horse and saber and lance, and the next woman. Now, there is politics."

"Colonel—."

"*Non*, Captaine Fallon. Let me finish. If I let this frigate come into the harbor and fight you, let them take this ship you have captured, it would be dishonorable. But if I fire on it, the guns of this fortress may well sink this frigate. That, monsieur, will mean war. And it is the business of a soldier to fight his country's wars, not to start them."

"Colonel, it's no secret that there've been moves toward an agreement between the American Congress and His Most Catholic Majesty. Soon we'll be allies. We may be allies at this moment and not know it. From that time you'll be at war with the English, and it won't matter what you do to one frigate here."

"Moves. Soon. May be. But not yet, capitaine. War with the milords is not something I have a fear of, but neither is it something I rush toward." He touched the decoration on his chest absently. "I have marched against them before, and I have no doubt I will again, someday. But that day is for others than me to decide. Non, capitaine, I will not sound the charge for my nation just to save your ship."

Michael nodded sadly. "I understand, colonel. If you don't mind, I'll be getting back to my ship."

"A moment, capitaine. I am perhaps not so neutral as I should be. Before you arrived the milords sent me a message by a Lieutenant Lord Carrington. Most arrogantly he informs me that if I should fire at his vessel, it will be regarded as an act of war. I, of course, replied that I had no wish for war, but any shot fired by his captain at any portion of the shore would be regarded by me in the same fashion. From the words he sent I deduce this. This Captain Harris will not wait for wind to come against you. Nor will he send his boats in the night to, how you say, cut out your prize. Within the hour he will use them to tow his vessel into place to engage you. I thought that would interest you. God speed, capitaine, and may your lance strike true."

Michael flogged his horse all the way from the fort to the quay, rousing his oarsmen from their sleep as he scrambled straight from the saddle into the boat. "Row, damn you. Row for your lives. Pull, God blast your eyes."

Out by the frigate, its boats gathered. At least they hadn't started towing yet. He climbed to the *Hussar*'s deck and pushed his way through a crowd of clamoring seamen to the quarterdeck.

"I'll answer your questions later, damn it. Can't you see there's no time now? Where in hell are the boarding nets? God's wounds, there's not a gunport open, or a gun run out. What the hell's going on here, Christopher? Don't you realize that's a damned great frigate out there?"

Byrne's foot nudged back the corner of a cloak on the quarterdeck to reveal a duckfoot, a pistol with five barrels like spread fingers. It was for use in a riot. Or a mutiny. And there were other bulges under the cloak.

"A little trouble, Michael. There's been some talk of surrender."

Michael's face darkened like a thunderhead. "There has, has there? Back me up. But don't show those things unless there's no other way." He strode to the rail and stared down at the milling mass of seamen until they quietened and stood staring back at him. "I hear there are some cowards among you. How they got there I don't know. There were none when we fought HMS *Charon*, gun to gun, and sank her."

A wave of whispering and shoving ran through the men. No one wanted to be the first to speak. Finally a bulbous-nosed old sailor was pushed forward. He snatched off his cap and ducked his head.

"Begging your pardon, captain, sir, but that *Charon* had only eighteen guns against our sixteen. And we fought because, well, hell, you made it sound easier to fight than to run, though a stiffer fight I've never been in. But that ain't the *Charon* out there. That's HMS *Apollyon*, thirty-eight guns. I was on her just two years ago, till I—." He sniffed and rubbed his nose. "Well, that's as may be. Anyway, Captain Sir Henry Harris had her then, and he's likely got her now. He'd work the gun crews till they'd drop, but they can load and fire faster than the devil's children. That's a crack frigate, captain, not a sloop-of-war."

"All right," Michael grated. "You've had your say. Now I'll have mine. Surrender's been mentioned. No, you didn't say it just now, but the word's been said by you before I did. And just what do you think to get by that? Oh, they've not hanged any privateers as pirates, yet, though they've threatened it often enough. They'll just lock you up in Mill Prison. You have a man among you who's one of the few ever escaped from Mill. You, Philpott, tell them what it's like."

Everyone turned to look, and a space formed around a gaunt, almost skeletal, man with the sallow skin of sickness on him. He wet his lips. "Its a hell made out of stone. I'll not go back. I'll die first."

"A hell made out of stone, he says. Well, maybe you'll come to think better of it after you've been there a time. After all, what do you have to fight for? Just a shipload of ivory and gold and pearls. Just your dreams you're holding in your hands, that's all. The meanest powder monkey of you will be able to buy his own farm. You can spend ten years swimming in rum and women. Or you can rot the rest of the war in Mill. It's time to make a decision. But not between fight or surrender. Between fight or get the hell off my ship. Because I'll fight if I have to load and lay and fire the guns myself. Now's the time. Cowards over the side and swim for shore. The rest of you to the guns. Move, damn you!''

He turned his back and went to the rail to stare out at the *Apollyon*. The boats were out in front, now, cables stretching back tautly. The frigate was moving into the channel. Behind him guncarriage wheels rumbled, and ports creaked open.

"Christopher," he said without turning around, "how many left us?"

"Not a one," Byrne replied in amazement. "If you asked for a boarding party, I think they'd all volunteer."

"Let's hope we don't need it." He wheeled back to the men in the waist. "Listen to me, now. With the best rowing in the world it'll take an hour for that lobster to get in to where he can turn and fire, an hour for you to show how good you are shooting at targets. And that's all she'll be. They won't be able to fire a musket at us till they clear the channel. You there, captain of the number one gun—Henriks. Every second shot you fire, fire at the boats. The rest, do like the other guns. Hull the bastard. Hit him hard. Make him pay the price for coming to us. We'll see how crack they are after an hour, with their ears beat down around their ankles.''

"Three cheers for the captain!" Henriks yelled, and Michael had to stand while they howled them out at the top of their lungs. As the last one faded they bent to their guns, and Michael returned to watching the frigate draw closer. The angel was painted black, his sword as well. What sort of angel was it supposed to be?

The first shot from *Hussar* made all the frigate's boat crews duck as if they could hide in the bottoms of their boats, but it had no other effect that he could see. The second, though, opened a gap above the bowsprit, and the third brought down a spar. From then on *Hussar*'s gunners had the range, and they hammered the frigate repeatedly. Like the barrel they often tossed over the side to practice on, it only bobbed closer and closer, but it was ten thousand times larger and ten thousand times easier to hit. And hit it they did.

For an hour and a half *Apollyon* ran the gauntlet. The angel's sword disappeared, and then the angel was splinters. The foretop came down, and half her spars. Torn rigging littered the deck, and sails hung in ruins. The bowsprit was chopped off short. The port side of the forecastle had a hole a dozen feet long. And the frigate came on.

The boatmen had learned quickly that the shots weren't aimed for them. They stuck to their rowing and ignored the firing. Then Henriks' second ball raised a geyser in their midst. The panic was such that one boat overturned. From then on they gave full attention to every shot. And if they began to forget, Henriks' shots reminded them. Once a cable snapped, whipping into the boat, snapping arms and legs, and twice more boats overturned, one disintegrating under a direct hit from an eighteen pound ball.

Michael watched the coming in an almost detached fashion. It was the target practice he'd named it. But battle was coming. *Apollyon* began to swing, under the action of rowers and rudder. Gunports came into view, already open, red squares above black ones. Before the frigate's anchor dropped, smoke blossomed at nineteen gunports with a roar.

Hussar seemed to jump in the water under the impact. Splinters whistled through the air, and a line of wetness stung across Michael's cheek. His own eight-gun broadside answered back raggedly. He turned to call to the gunners, and another hammer struck from the frigate. He fell, and a spar smashed to the deck where he'd been standing. God, he thought, they were a crack crew to get their second shots off so soon. He crawled over the spar and pulled himself up on the splintered quarterdeck rail.

"The decks and the gunports! Aim for the decks and the gunports! Langrage against the deck!"

Powdermonkeys ran to get the canvas bags of nails, old bolts, rusty scrap iron, and anything else that could be found to put in them. When that bag hit the enemy it'd rip apart and shower iron in all directions.

Time slowed, or else it ran on quicker than before. The broadsides came all at once, or they came after interminable waits. A haze of powder smoke obscured both ships, reddening eyes and blackening faces. More spars were down on *Hussar*, falling silently amid the din of the guns. Rigging hung in tatters. A dead man lay in front of the wheel, a splinter as big as his forearm sticking from his throat. No one had the time to cover or move him. Once Michael saw a cannon, nine feet and two tons of black metal, rise into the air, spinning, to fall into the water on the far side of the ship. Those of its crew who were still alive lay screaming on the deck.

How long had it gone on? Michael fumbled out his pocket watch and was stunned to see they'd been at it for five minutes short of an hour. It didn't seem possible to survive so long under that pounding. There seemed to be something wrong with *Apollyon*. But what? He rubbed his eyes, and his hand came away red. Gingerly he felt his forehead, and the wicked gash that ran across it. He hadn't even felt it, he realized wonderingly. But the frigate?

Through the smoke from both ships' guns he could barely make the enemy out. The foremast was gone. That was it. They'd shot away the bastard's foremast. No. There was something else. The frigate seemed shorter, the masts too close together. What in the—. A wisp of breeze curled the haze in front of him, and he knew.

"The misbegotten bastard's running! That whoreson got a breath of wind, and he's running!"

He turned from the beautiful sight of the frigate making its way down the channel to sea, and stopped. The wind had freshened and carried away enough smoke to make the rest of the ship clearly visible. Two guns lay on their sides, and there were three and four foot gaps in the waist bulwark. The deck was littered with blocks and cut ropes and pieces of rigging.

It was littered with men, too. Dead men, dying men, wounded men. Not a man or a boy was without a rag for a bandage, and blood seeping through it. His throat tightened.

He looked for Christopher, and found him braced against the rail, strangely bright-eyed. "We whipped them, Michael. Damn—. Damn British can't beat the Irish." And he fell forward on the deck, the back of his coat shredded and blood soaked.

Stunned, Michael went to his knees. Before he even touched his friend he knew it was too late. The familiar sardonic grin was still on Christopher's lips, but his eyes were already dull with death.

Young Oliver, his face haggard, stopped by Michael's side. "Sir. Sir, I believe the men are expecting a word from you. Sir?"

Michael rose slowly and made his way to the quarterdeck rail.

"Men of the *Hussar!* You've done something no privateer has ever done before, nor any other American ship. You've stood toe to toe with a frigate of the Royal Navy, one of their finest, and made the frigate turn and run. It is a thing to be proud of, a think to tell your children about, and your grand-children. It's a thing to be remembered." His voice sank; it was difficult keeping his eyes from Christopher. "I only regret the price that was paid." To his embarrassment they cheered him again.

Oliver touched his shoulder and held out a spyglass. "Maybe you'd better hold off on talk of victory, captain. Look."

Michael looked, and muttering curses under his breath he watched *Apollyon*, the wreckage of its foremast cut away, sail across the harbor mouth. It followed a regular pattern. Sail across the opening at an angle to the wind coming straight out of the harbor, then tack back in toward shore to sail across the other way. Captain Harris of the *Apollyon* wasn't about to let a damned rebel privateer escape. He was staying put.

A cutter with a pair of lugsails rigged darted away from the frigate and headed out to sea. Michael ran off a string of curses aloud. "What'll you wager he doesn't know right where to find more British ships?"

"Not a clipped farthing, sir." Oliver replied.

Michael looked toward the *Empress of India*. She'd laid dead in the water, stern to the action, but now Broadman had managed to get her turned to present a broadside to the channel. It wouldn't be much help. Petrie couldn't spare more than two or three slim gun crews from guarding prisoners.

"We're not waiting. If we can run out past him, we're faster than he is. Even the Indiaman might keep ahead with that mast gone. Send a boat over there. Tell Petrie to follow us out, but once he's clear of the shoals he's to head north for Brest immediately. If he gets so much as a sniff of a sail, he's to put in at St. Nazaire of Lorient. Then you start repairing enough rigging to shove us out of here." He stopped as his gaze fell on Christopher, a piece of sailcloth over his head and shoulders.

"The rest of your orders, sir?"

Michael sighed. No time. "Put as many guns back in action as you can. Double-shot everything with bar-shot and chainshot. We'll try for the rigging, to slow her as much as possible. Take the carpenter's report, but don't bother me with it. If there are any holes too close to the waterline, fother a sail over them. That'll hold us till Brest. And bring all the scrap you can back here to the quarterdeck, all the spars and rigging that're down. Bring some spars from storage, too, and a spare sail, and one of the extra anchors. And the sailmaker."

As *Hussar* slid down the channel, a huge, ungainly bundle wrapped in sailcloth and fastened to a cable lay across the stern. Michael went over everything one more time, to make certain the party of seamen gathered there understood what they were to do.

"All right, then. When I shout 'heave,' you six push that overgrown sea-anchor over. When I shout 'cut,' you with the ax, you cut the cable. With one blow, mind you." He whirled on the helmsman. "And when I shout 'helm,' you starboard your helm like the devil's at you. Do you all understand?"

They nodded and muttered ayes. It'd have to do, he decided. Everything had to be done on the split second, but if they didn't have it now, they wouldn't get it at all.

Behind, the Indiaman followed, and ahead, just coming into view beyond the headland, *Apollyon* tacked back toward land. With luck they might be clear and running free before the frigate could reach them.

"Hoist the colors, Mr. Oliver."

The Stars and Stripes broke at the masthead. From the fortress came the boom of a cannon.

"My God," Oliver gasped. "The Frenchies have fired on us."

It couldn't be. Another single gun fired, and another. And then Michael understood. He looked up at the flag, standing out from the masthead. Before it'd been just another of the endless stream of flags American ships flew, from the Congress, from the states. Suddenly it was different. He wanted to stand up a little straighter. As *Hussar* sailed from the harbor the fortress of La Morelle was firing eleven guns, salute to the flag of a friendly foreign power. If only Christopher could've seen.

"Captain," said Oliver. The British frigate had begun its run across the harbor from further out, not waiting to get close to shore. It would cross at a shallower angle, and *Hussar* would be running directly toward its broadside. Yet it could all work to their advantage. If Captain Sir Henry Harris had enough hate built up in him for the American. If he wanted to get close enough to destroy them with the first broadside. Michael nodded to himself and waited. If.

The three ships moved as if they were all aiming for the same spot in the ocean, the British frigate, the American privateer, and the lumbering Indiaman. If they kept on, they'd all collide. The Indiaman curved away toward the north, and only the two kept on. The distance was growing shorter. *Apollyon*'s broadside could rake *Hussar* then.

Every moment simply brought them closer to sure hits, to a rain of death, and to boarding. How long would the frigate's captain wait? How long?

"Heave!" Michael shouted, and the bundle went over the stern. The weight of the spars took it deep, the canvas ballooned, and *Hussar* shuddered to a halt as suddenly as if she'd run into a wall. Men staggered, and everything loose went flying. In that instant *Apollyon*'s guns roared, and the sea ahead was whipped into a froth.

"Cut! Helm!" The axe sliced through the cable, and the *Hussar* leaped ahead. The helm went over, and the ship raced to port, behind the frigate. "Fire as they bear!"

One by one the cannon answered him, hurling balls connected by bars and balls connected by chains into the enemy's rigging. Slowly, like a collapsing house of cards, the frigate's remaining masts crumpled. A huzza went up from the *Hussar*'s waist. The frigate drifted backwards with the tide, until finally someone managed to drop an anchor, and she swung there beneath the guns of the fortress.

"I'd never have believed it, sir," Oliver said. "I'm not sure I do even now. Where away, captain? Brest?"

Michael looked from the shattered frigate to his own deck. *Apollyon* couldn't be much worse off than his own crew. "Brest? Yes, for the moment. And then Charlestown, Mr. Oliver. I think it's time we went home."

24

The hired carriage wheeled briskly up the drive at Tir Alainn and deposited Michael at the foot of the double stairs. He tossed a coin to the driver and got out with his arms full of packages.

Daniel, standing by the stairs, stared at him as if seeing a ghost. "Lord, Mr. Fallon! We all just about give you up for dead! How are you, sir?"

"Alive and fine, Daniel, as you can see. And yourself?"

"Married, sir," the boatman said morosely.

Michael burst out laughing. "Married? Aren't you the same man told me he'd buy a nice girl and keep her, but he'd not get married?"

"Yes, sir. And I did, for a while, that is. Only, Callie, that's my wife, she started in to working on me, about how she loved me, and didn't I love her, and how nice it be for us to have children. Then Mrs. Fallon, she say I immoral and repre-, repre-, something or other. She say I got to marry Callie, and I got to free her first and then ask her if she will." He shook his head at the unfairness of it all, but a grin crept in. "Course, it ain't too bad all the time."

"That's the secret, lad." And Michael sprinted up the steps.

Caesar, the butler, opened the door and froze, staring at him goggle-eyed. He turned toward the drawing room door, but he was still opening his mouth when Michael entered the drawing room and spilled his packages into a chair.

"I'm home, Brielle."

Gabrielle looked up from her embroidery hoop. With a small cry she was in his arms, kissing him.

He managed to get the door closed with his foot, then crushed her to him and kissed her as thoroughly as possible.

She'd matured while he was away. The pretty child's face had become a beautiful woman's. Her figure, though still slim, had filled and rounded. And her ardor!

Why had he ever left this, he wondered. They broke the kiss, both gasping and swallowing. "If this is the kind of welcome I get," he said, "I'll have to go away more often."

She had been smiling at him tenderly, her fingers gently tracing the half-healed slash across his forehead. At his words her face blackened. She beat at his chest, pushed herself out of the circle of his arms. "You! You utterly despicable animal. You've no feelings at all, have you?"

He stared at her, completely bewildered. "What are you saying? Have you gone daft?"

"November! You said you'd be back by November. At the latest, you said. You'd be here for Christmas, you said. Six months! It's nearly six months since you were due. And in all that time not one word to say you were still alive. Only one letter in all the time you were gone." Tears streamed down her face. Sobs rose, choking off her words.

He shifted uncomfortably. "I wrote more," he lied. "The ships must have been taken.' He put his arms around her in spite of her efforts to fend him off. Her tears soaked into his waistcoat. "Brielle, you must believe I'd never hurt you, not on purpose. And for whatever sins I've committed against you, I apologize as humbly as I'm able. Come here, girl. Come, see what I've brought you. Maybe that'll bring a smile back to your face."

Quickly he seated her, his handkerchief in her hand, and spread out the packages before her. Fans, and gloves, and shawls, and carved ivory figurines. A broad, flat box he opened with a flourish. Diamonds flashed within, bracelets, earrings, necklace, and tiara.

"I thought of you when I saw them," he said. "Fit for a queen, they are, and a queen they'll grace."

She touched them hesitantly.

"Of course, this isn't all, Brielle. The rest is following behind. A huge bundle of plumes and feathers. Silks, satins, velvets, laces. Everything I ever heard of a dress being made of or decorated with, in every color I could find."

She snatched back her fingers as if they were burned. "They say sailors have a woman in every port. How many ports were you in? Ten? A dozen? More? Like the Grand Turk with his harem, I imagine."

"God's breath, woman! What brought this on?"

"Go ahead, strike me. I can see you want to. If you beat me I've no doubt I'll apologize for being in the right, and say you're right to be in the wrong. But I won't mean it."

Michael took a deep breath and made an effort to hold on to his temper. "Brielle, I've apologized to you. I don't know how else to do it, except getting down on my knees to beg, and I'm not made to do that. I've come home, I thought, to you and our child—."

"Our child. I was beginning to wonder if you remembered. Would you care to see him?"

Michael nodded stiffly, and she swept grandly out of the room ahead of him. At the nursery door she stepped aside.

The child lying there asleep, under a mauma's watchful eye, surprised him by his size. But of course, James was close on to two years now. And the mark of the Fallons certainly hadn't passed him by, with his high cheekbones and his small eagle nose. Two years old, and he hadn't been with the boy for a birthday or a Christmas.

Gabrielle watched quietly from the door, and slowly the tension went out of her. A tightness came in her throat in its place. He was just the same, indestructible, with that crooked smile on his face. And yet the year past had put its mark on him. The tiny lines at the corners of his eyes didn't belong on a man of 36. Now, gently, he took a tiny hand in his big, strong one.

"It's sorry I am, lad," he said softly. "I shouldn't have been gone so long. I'm sorry."

Her heart went out to him. She reached out her hand. "Husband." The joy that swept over his face made her want to sing and cry, all at the same time. And then he swept her into his arms, and he was kissing her. It was all right again.

He was home, and nothing else mattered. He was home.

Michael's pen scratched as he wrote on his lap desk, piling
sheets on the floor beside his chair as he finished. From time
to time he looked at Gabrielle. She had her easel set up
across the room and was sketching the river view below Tir
Alainn. They'd driven to Charlestown so she could show him
the finished house on Queen Street, and toured the new fields
at Tir Alainn, and the warehouse. They'd also spent a considerable amount of time in bed. When he joked that she'd
built up some decidedly unladylike hungers while he was
away, she hotly and blushingly denied it, but her ardor hadn't
cooled.

That wasn't all he found different about her. Those fields,
for instance, and the warehouse. He'd told her to care for the
plantation more to give her something to do than from any
thought she might really take charge. And now Ames de-
ferred more to her than he did to Michael.

And her reaction to the letters he was writing. For all he
wanted to spend his time with her and little James, he had to
see to getting *Hussar* ready for sea again. He'd expected a
display of temper when she found out, perhaps a fit of
sulking. She'd patted his cheek and said she was sure it was
interesting, dismissing him like a schoolboy who rattled on
about the games he played.

"Another letter to Mr. Petrie," he said. "It seems they'll
be putting the guns back on board this week, and I want him
to arrange for a pair of stern chasers. In another month we'll
be ready to sail."

"Mmm," she said vaguely, and stared vexedly at a tree
badly smudged when her hand jerked.

He frowned. Something didn't seem right. She didn't
seem interested. "You know, Brielle, you've done wonders
with Tir Alainn. Everything I expected, and maybe more."

Her face lit up. "Oh, and I enjoy it so much. I didn't think I
would, but I do. And I've so many more plans."

That was the way he wanted to see her, bright-eyed and

sparkling. "I see you hired the house servants to stay on. How've you gone about replacing the field hands as they're freed?"

She tried to conceal a guilty start. Oh, God. She had to tell him. She'd been dreading that question since their first walk by the new fields, and now there was no way to get around it. Just as she opened her mouth the door opened, and Henri and Louis sauntered in.

" 'Lo, Brielle," Henri said. " 'Lo, Michael."

"Sarah said you were in here," Louis said, "and since we're family—. Hope we're not disturbing anything. No? It's good to see you, Michael."

Full of relief, Gabrielle hugged them as if she hadn't seen them for years. Michael, who very nearly hadn't, shook their hands warmly. They still hadn't changed from the first day he'd seen them. Except their clothes. They were as somber as Franklin now.

"What are you lads doing in civilian clothes? I'm told you're a lieutenant in the First Regiment, Henri. And you a captain, Louis."

"Stab me if we're not mustered out," Henri chortled. He rubbed his hands together as if at a pleasing prospect. "We've come to join this regiment of hussars you're raising."

Michael stared at him. Gabrielle started for the door.

"Brielle," Michael said ominously. "Come back here."

"I'm needed in the kitchens. I hear Sarah calling." And she was gone.

He rounded on the other two. "All right, then. Out with it. Talk."

Henri shifted under his brother's glare. "Well, I'm no bloody good at working round to things. Stab me, I'm not."

Louis sighed. "We confess. Doesn't seem much point not to, now that—. At any rate, we were supposed to work you round to raising a regiment. No, let me finish. You're the only shipowner I ever heard of sailing with his own ship. What's the point? It'll do as well if you're there or here. If

you've been in Charlestown, you've seen what passes for
cavalry around here. We need that regiment, and we need
you."

"I've seen them," Michael growled. "Pretty boys, cutting a fine figure for the ladies. They won't last through the
first campaign. And it'd be no regiment, either. You'll not
find six or seven hundred men to meet the standards I'd set."

"Does that mean you'll do it?" Henri asked.

Michael sighed and looked down at his letter. Gabrielle
wasn't over her fear; that she'd taken all this trouble was
proof of that. It would be good to spend a Christmas with her
and James. And *Hussar* no doubt would do as well without
him. And Petrie was ripe for command. And—. "All right,
I'll do it."

Henri grinned broadly and called for a drink, but Louis
had been watching him thoughtfully. "Why do you say you
couldn't find six hundred men? Once word gets out you're
raising horse, they'll flock to ride with you. You could have a
thousand men who were born in the saddle."

"That's the trouble. They're game young fighting cock-
erels, but they were put in a saddle the day they were born,
and shot their first gun the next morning. Because of that,
they think there's nothing they need to learn and nobody they
can't fight. You mark my words, somebody with a quarter
their number of dragoons who are twice their age will cut
them to ribbons."

Even Henri was sobered by the image. Louis nodded.
"Then what do we do?"

Michael brushed aside the letter to Petrie and began writing again. "First, we need a commission from the General
Assembly. You, Louis, take this letter to my banker. You'll
buy horses. Two hundred head, though we'll be lucky to find
that many men. You look for mounts with endurance, about
fifteen hands high, perhaps twelve or thirteen hundred
pounds. Yes, I know the lads in the city favor bigger, but
we're light cavalry, not bloody great dragoons. Now, you,
Henri, see Bicaise in Charlestown. He may have some
French carbines and—."

In the hall Gabrielle leaned against the wall weakly.
"Thank you, God," she whispered under her breath.
"Thank you."

Gabrielle paced the drawing room at Tir Alainn. She'd
been waiting for this day—November 25, 1778—till it stood
red in her mind. For months Michael had trained his soldiers,
and not until today was she to be allowed a look at them.

Michael entered, and she had to clap her hands. It was the
first time she'd seen him in uniform; it was beautiful. His
dark green coat with black facings made his broad shoulders
broader; the snug white breeches with high cavalry boots
made his long legs longer. There was a saber at his waist, and
on his head a brass helmet with a bearskin roach across the
top and horsehair plumes hanging down the back. She ran to
kiss him.

"Enough of that now," he said finally.

She blushed, and remembered the presents she had for
him. "All the ladies tell me that when your husband is given
command, you must sew him a sash, so he'll stand out, and
his men can see him. So." Laughing she unfolded a long sash
of scarlet silk. He took off his saber, and she wrapped the
sash around his waist herself, taking great care that the ends
hung down his right leg just so. He reached for his saber, and
she stopped him. "I've one more gift. A sword."

He made an effort to keep a smile on his face. He knew the
sort of sword women bought, fancy dress swords, useless in
the field. She handed him her gift, and he grunted when he
felt the weight. It had a handle of staghorn and a guard in the
shape of a dragon, but the blade was heavy steel.

"I told him I wanted a sword to bring my husband back to
me," she said quietly.

Gently he lifted her face with a finger beneath her chin.
"I'll always come back to you, Brielle. No matter what. I
promise you, I'll come back."

She turned her head quickly and kissed his fingers, then
blushed. "Come along, Michael. I want to see this famous
Legion."

Mauma Jana had young James on the veranda already. His eyes were bright with excitement. The young bugler stood stiffly on the steps, waiting. Michael nodded, and the boy whipped up his horn to sound attack.

From out of the trees along the river burst a small knot of horsemen. They wheeled; men dismounted, and took their horses to the rear, revealing two grasshoppers pointed at the house. In an instant they loaded, and the guns roared and leaped back. Martha screamed and ducked, Gabrielle covered her face with her hands, and James howled with glee.

At the cannon's roar a line of cavalry burst from the trees, bent low over the saddle, sabers extended, and then a second line. Perfectly formed, Michael thought with satisfaction. Ranks in a slight chevron, and two hundred paces between.

Wheeling, the lines charged back to the guns. There most dismounted, every sixth man leading five horses to the rear, and formed three ranks on either side of the guns. The carbines and cannon all fired together, and as the smoke cloud rose, James clapped his hands together and crowed with pleasure. He seemed to think it was better than a raree-show. And Gabrielle clapped and squealed and jumped up and down like a child herself.

The horses were brought forward, the men mounted, and the guns withdrawn to the side. Then, to thunderous applause, the Legion went through maneuvers, galloping by twos, wheeling into line to trot toward the house, then breaking by squadrons and wheeling into ranks. And when it was all finished, they drew up in front of the house in four ranks, guns to the side and officers in front. Louis moved forward, followed by the Legion banner, a gold harp on a green field, and whipped his saber up in a perfect salute.

"Fallon's Irish Legion is assembled, sir. Major Louis Fourrier temporarily commanding. One hundred sixty-two men, six officers, all present and accounted for." Michael gravely returned the salute. Then Louis surprised him. He turned to Gabrielle, saber coming up once more in salute. "Madam, the Legion wishes to request a favor of its commander's lady." The flagbearer leaned forward to raise his staff toward the portico.

Gabrielle felt flustered. A favor. What—? Suddenly she knew. Taking the long, green ribbon from her hair she bent and tied it around the tip of the flagstaff. The bearer raised it high, and the Legion burst out cheering.

"Well done, lass," Michael murmured. "You did that very well indeed."

Thank you, Michael." She frowned suddenly as a carriage, approaching unseen during the display, drew up at the steps. "Are you expecting anyone? I don't recognize it."

"No one," he replied, but made his way to greet the man limping up the stairs.

He was a dessicated man, not far above middle years, but bald enough for seventy. He bowed stiffly. "Colonel Fallon. Mrs. Fallon. You don't know me, though I recognize both of you. I am here on a matter of grave importance."

Michael ushered him into the drawing room, and Gabrielle rang for a servant. "You'll have some wine, Mr—?"

"Forgive me, please. Stonewell. Oliver Stonewell. I represent the affairs of the late Mr. Thomas Carver."

It took a second for the word to get through to Michael. Late. The old man was dead. He sank into a chair. "I saw him not a fortnight gone."

"It was sudden, sir, but painless, I am told. In his sleep. I have not come to tell you of that, however. In fact, I find the purpose of my visit most irregular." His face pinched momentarily as if irregularity were the greatest sin he knew. "However, I have come to carry out Mr. Carver's instructions. I am to read you a portion of his last will and testament."

Gabrielle stirred uneasily. Michael looked bewildered. "His will?" he said. "I don't understand."

Stonewell drew some papers from his pocket and fastened spectacles on his nose. "Here it is. I read. 'The wharf known as Carver's Bridge, on the Cooper River, together with the attached warehouse, the property on which wharf and warehouse stand, and the contents of said wharf and warehouse, the company known as Thomas Carver and Company, together with all ships owned by that company, all accounts in that company's name, and all property owned or contracted for by that company, I herewith and hereby leave to Michael Shane Fallon, whom I regard as I would a son, and whom I hold in the deepest affection, regard and respect.'" He fussily returned the paper to his pocket.

Gabrielle couldn't take her eyes off Michael. For all the words about love and respect, why had Carver left so much to him? Whom he regarded as a son. And his daughter was Elizabeth, whose picture Michael still carried in his pocket. No.

"It's not right," Michael said suddenly. "He'd a daughter who should inherit. What about her? What about Elizabeth?" Gabrielle's face went white. She rushed from the room. He jumped from his chair. "Brielle? Brielle, what's the matter?" From the door he could see Martha following her up the stairs. What the devil was it? "I apologize, Mr. Stonewell. My wife must have been taken suddenly ill."

"It does happen to women, sir, especially in the face of death. Now, as to how Mrs. Elizabeth Fourrier has been cared for under the will of her father, I can, you understand, give no details. Considering the effects of the war on trade and shipping, though, I should think she has been left, certainly, the bulk of the estate."

Justin spat into the drawing-room fire. "I can't believe it. To my wife, his own daughter, he leaves half a dozen plantations that haven't made a crop since the war began. The source of his wealth he leaves to Fallon, may his soul rot in hell."

Jean-Baptiste glanced at his son with distaste. Justin's habits had become gross; even his once trim form had thickened. "This is unseemly. Calm yourself."

"Calm myself?" Justin snapped. "How can I calm myself? Fifteen ships that I had every right to expect would be mine—stolen from me!"

"Come, Justin," Elizabeth said irritably. "Even I know half of those ships have been taken by the British; many of the rest are shut up in New York." She shifted uncomfortably as both men stared at her unblinkingly. "Well, they can't be worth very much."

"This is an affair of importance," Justin said. "You'd better retire."

She rose angrily. "The ships were, after all, to be mine."

"I said retire. Absent yourself."

For a moment their eyes locked, then hers slid away. Not a week gone, as they lay tangled nakedly, he'd put his hands around her throat and squeezed. She hadn't been sure he'd stop. His eyes looked now as they had then. She hurried from the room, slamming the door behind her.

"Woman or not," Jean-Baptiste said, "she is correct. And we may make use of that. With proper representation the ships in New York, and at least some of those taken as prizes, will be transferred to the proper heir, your wife, and so to you."

"But—"

"Enough, Justin. Remember that you are a Fourrier. When a civilized form of government rules this land, merchants will bow to you and to all of your blood." He thought of the bastard upstairs and grimaced. "Of your blood. Yes. And men such as Fallon may be disposed of without difficulty or question. Now, are you prepared to bring your mind to matters of importance?"

"Certainly," Justin replied with a bitter laugh. "Though when I have to enter my own home by night for fear of arrest by mechanics and shopkeepers—. Well, as you say, to important things. The courier met us where you said he would. The British should have left New York by now, though he couldn't or wouldn't say how many or who commands."

"Lieutenant Colonel Archibald Campbell with the 71st Regiment, two battalions of Hessians—. No matter, I will tell you later." He noted his son's look. "I find it well to have eyes among my friends as well as among my enemies. But go on."

"I've scouted the best landing sites, and I'll take my men south before dawn to act as scouts and guides. Have those fishermen of yours take this map out to Campbell when his

ships come down the coast. The best site is marked. The
Girardeau plantation.''

In the first frosty December light on the Savannah River,
Justin watched from concealment with half a dozen of his
men. The first boats had grounded. British soldiers were
leaping out to wade ashore. He stepped out with his arms held
clear to show he was unarmed. Instantly a dozen cocked
muskets were aimed at him.

"I'm Justin Fourrier. Your commanding officer should be
expecting me."

A redcoated captain pushed through the soldiers. "Four-
rier, do you say?" He spoke with a heavy Highland brogue.
"I'm Cameron, 71st Regiment of Foot. The cross of St.
George.''

"The torch of King George," Justin replied, as agreed.
"Carolina to the Royal Standard. Now Captain Cameron, at
the head of that causeway over there to the high ground,
you'll find some sentries. I haven't taken them; I wouldn't
risk an early alarm."

"You did right, Mr. Fourrier. We ken how to take care of
sentries. If you wait here, the colonel will be ashore soon. No
doubt he'll want to talk to you. All right, Highlanders, follow
me." He disappeared up the causeway followed by his men
in their flat Scottish bonnets. Musket fire racketed as Justin
joined his men and mounted.

After a time some soldiers returned with Cameron's body
and put it on a boat. Later still some horses were swum
ashore. And all this time no one paid any attention to Justin
and his men. He sat his horse and fumed. The rebels were
getting time to prepare. He'd mapped every path and trail
around Savannah with the full expectation of leading the
British army to a surprise attack. Now the bastards would be
ready and waiting. Finally more officers arrived, among
them a lieutenant colonel. He rode to meet them.

"Colonel Campbell? I'm Justin Fourrier. I've half a dozen
of my scouts here, and another thirty toward the city—"

"Very good," said Campbell as he swung into the saddle.

"You and your men may prove invaluable. I intend to attack before sunset. Major Heath, get the Hessians and the Loyalists ashore and move them up to join the 71st. Mr. Fourrier, shall we take a look at what this American General Howe has to offer?"

Justin followed, gritting his teeth. "Colonel, there's no time to waste. We should be attacking now." Campbell acted as if he hadn't heard. Several of the other officers stared at him rudely, clearly surprised that he'd spoken without being addressed.

At the edge of a copse looking toward the city they drew to a halt. Campbell and his brother officers put their heads together, excluding him. They were waiting, all right. He could see their lines plainly, one end fastened on the town and the river, the other on the swamp. The only way at them was straight ahead. Damn it, if the British hadn't delayed so in—. Wait. The only way. No it wasn't.

"Colonel, I think I know a way to outflank them."

Campbell snapped his spyglass shut. "If you do, I'd appreciate your telling me. I don't enjoy the idea of sending my men into this frontally. Look at that. The stream, and those mud flats. We'll have to cross both. What is this way of yours?"

"There's a path through that swamp. I've used it more than once going to and from the city. It's not much, but I can lead troops over it. And they'll come out behind the rebel lines."

"Excellent. Excellent. I said you'd be invaluable. But not you, Mr. Fourrier. You're too valuable to risk in something of this nature. Tell off one of your men for it."

"The only one who's traveled it with me is my manservant. Pompey! Get up here. Him, colonel. He can take them, and he'll do it right because he knows I'll have his hide if he doesn't."

"Very well," Campbell said. "Sir James? Where's Baird? Oh, there you are. Sir James, you're to take the light infantry and the New York Loyalists and follow this black fellow. He'll lead you through the swamps to a place behind the rebel rear. I shall use the 71st and the North and South Carolina Loyalists to hold their attention to the front. When you strike their rear, I shall attack. Good then. Off with you, and God speed.''

Hold their attention? How did he intend doing that, unless he was going to make that frontal attack? Justin shook his head.

Moments laters Campbell gave him his answer. He formed the 71st, marched them out into the open, and then back again. The effect on the rebels was galvanic. Shouting ran from one end of the American line to the other. Their artillery opened fire, spraying shot indiscriminately. Even muskets were let off, though there was no chance of the ball traveling that far. When the rebel fire began to slacken, Campbell repeated his performance, and the rebels repeated theirs.

Then, suddenly, there was a tumult from the rebel flank, shouting and the din of musketry. Baird was out of the swamp. Campbell moved the 71st forward, and the Loyalists. This time they advanced on the rebel lines.

''Forward,'' Justin barked, and put spur to his horse. His men followed him toward the collapsing American army.

They pursued, sabering men whose only thought was to flee, until a message from the colonel brought them back.

An hour later they marched behind Campbell into Savannah.

25

Michael rolled over in his cot. Drums were rattling furiously in the night. Sentries around the encampment bellowed, and Charlestown Neck began to stir with men answering the summons. What was it this time, he wondered. Another riot in the city, or a farm burned by Tory partisans? He sat up with a sigh and started pulling on his uniform. A soldier trotted past the flap of his tent.

"You there! Soldier! What's the alarm this time?"

The man shifted his wad of tobacco from one cheek to the other and spat. "Don't know, colonel. Don't think anybody knows. One thing. They do say the officer what brung the word from headquarters was white as a sheet." He disappeared at a run.

As Michael hunted up Louis, the Legion readied their horses with the creak and jingle of leather and harness. "Everyone present, Louis?"

"All present, colonel. We can ride in ten minutes, perhaps less." He looked eager. The feeling was contagious. Surely this was more than the usual night alarm.

"Not until I've discovered where we ride to," Michael said drily. "In the meantime, put a hot meal into everyone. If this is what it seems to be, it may be a while before their next one. Distribute double issues of rations and ammunition. And no one mounts until we move. I want those horses fresh."

At Moultrie's headquarters everything was confusion. Everyone ran, even to cross the guardroom. Michael tried to stop one of the officers, to find out what was happening, but they all pulled away with shouts of "Urgent!" or "No time!" He couldn't even gain the same room with Moultrie.

A mud-splattered man in the blue of a Lieutenant Colonel

of Continentals strode in shouting over his shoulder "Get that saddle on another horse. I ride back within the hour."

"Johnny!" Michael said. "Johnny Laurens! What the hell's going on?"

"No time! I—. Oh, it's you, Michael." Laurens looked as if he hadn't slept in a week. "'All hell's broke loose. The British have Savannah."

"That's impossible! We'd a rider from there two days ago."

"Their ships appeared in the river one day, they landed the next, and by nightfall they had the city. Don't ask me how. Three quarters of the American army are dead, wounded, captured, or missing. General Lincoln arrived in Purrysburg expecting a retreating army and found a starving pack of refugees with muskets for only half of them."

"Lincoln? Who's Lincoln?"

Laurens laughed tiredly. "Seems as if it's all happening at once, doesn't it? The Congress, finally, are replacing Robert Howe. They sent us General Benjamin Lincoln. Looks like your old family doctor, round nose, round chins, round belly. But he's a good man. Methodical."

"Methodical? Not exactly a prime quality for a field general."

"Don't worry. I said he's a good man. He was second in command to Gates at Saratoga. Look, I must go in to General Moultrie, now. When I come out—"

"I'd better be getting back to camp. But try to pry some orders out of them in there."

A few minutes after Laurens went in, a captain panted out with a folded paper, a few lines scribbled on it over Moultrie's signature. The Legion would stand ready to ride on a moment's notice, but would not move until further instructions. What they were already doing.

Something that had been buzzing in the back of his head finally came to the front. Lincoln had been second to Gates at Saratoga. That was where the battle was won by Arnold and Morgan, but the credit was taken by Gates. If this Lincoln was anything like his former commander it would be a bad time for the Carolinas.

The three months following Lincoln's arrival were frantic, and usually futile. At first they marched and countermarched along the border as if Lincoln couldn't make up his mind what to do. Then General Augustine Prevost moved up from Florida to take command of the British. Suddenly the redcoats took Sunbury, and then Augusta. And just as suddenly Lincoln decided to strike into Georgia with the bulk of the army, leaving Moultrie with twelve hundred men to defend the state.

On the third of May in 1779 Michael sat his horse on Tulfinny Hill, studying the Coosahatchie River some fifty miles south of Charlestown, no more than forty above Savannah. Where there should have been three or four good fords were now two dozen places to cross after the dry April. Only the alligator holes were deep.

Time to report. He snapped his spyglass shut with a sigh and turned his horse.

In Moultrie's tent the general was bent over a map, measuring distances with a pair of dividers. "It doesn't look good, Fallon. Another message from Lincoln insisting this is a feint."

Michael traced a line north from Purrysburg. "One hell of a feint, general. Prevost and the whole damned army." The Legion had been blooded along that line. Ebenezer. Dupont's plantation. Bee Creek Bridge. "He'll come around. He always does. I just wish he didn't take so damned long to make up his mind."

Moultrie snorted. "You know better than to talk of your superior officers that way. But I will agree, privately, that he could be a touch quicker. With luck, however, we may hang on here long enough for him to be convinced and turn back. Your last report of Prevost put him just this side of Bee Creek, correct?"

"Yes, sir."

"We can't stop him from crossing the Coosahatchie. It's impossible to cover every possible ford. Once he crosses, however, he cannot afford to pass us by. This site is perfect for defense. With luck, we can bloody him severely. I just hope Colonel Laurens returns quickly."

"Johnny, sir?"

"He still thinks he's with General Washington," Moultrie laughed. "They must use large numbers of troops for everything up there. I sent him to bring in the sentries from the river, and he requested three hundred and fifty men for it."

Michael had to smile. "A quarter of our force to bring in sentries? I hope you didn't—."

A rattle of musketry came from down the river, and again, fiercer. Moultrie looked suddenly ill. "As a matter of fact, I did." Michael whirled for his horse, but the general flung out a hand to stop him. "No, colonel! I'll not risk my entire cavalry at this juncture. You'll send out one squadron only, with orders to help if they can and retreat if they can't. In any case, I want a rider back here immediately with a report."

Michael watched thirty Legionnaires disappear into the trees, heading downriver with Louis at their head. Drums were beating assembly in the camp behind the hill. Soldiers had already begun to march to their places on the slope. To a civilian they'd have looked impressive, but he knew if things had been bad before, they were worse now. Those men were militia for the most part, with a thin cadre of Continentals. Many of them had been planting crops a month before. How well would they stand up to three or four times their number of British regulars?

An hour later the squadron was back, surrounded by limping, dispirited infantry. Many hobbled along, musket for a crutch, or were supported by friends. There were dozens of litters, including some hung between horses, but he saw with relief that none seemed to bear Legion men. The ranks on the hill stirred at the sight, and a murmur ran through them. Some officers had to force men back into line.

An officer with a torn coat and no hat, a rag tied around his forehead, stopped at the foot of the hill as if nerving himself. Finally he climbed to General Moultrie's tent and saluted, swaying.

"Well, Captain Shubrick," Moultrie said, "where's Colonel Laurens?"

"Johnny is wounded, sir," the captain replied. Suddenly he stiffened, staring straight ahead, and made a formal report in a flat monotone. "Pursuant to Colonel Laurens' orders on reaching the river, we crossed over to engage what were believed to be foraging parties of the enemy. It developed that they were instead advance elements of the enemy main body. We found ourselves engaged against approximately four times our number. After sustaining numerous casualties, including Colonel Laurens, I assumed command and retreated back across the river, where I fell in with elements of Fallon's Irish Legion. Sir."

"Damn, blast, and hell!" Moultrie made a gesture that took in the men returning from the river and those in ranks on the hill. "It'll take a sennight to convince those men they could face a corporal's guard of ragpickers after this. If we fight today, they'll run at the first shot. What in the hell was Johnny—. Hell, that doesn't matter, now. Colonel Fallon. Put the Legion out as a screen between the British and us. Keep them off us if you can. We'll fall back to Salkehatchie Chapel. Baker! Send dispatches off to General Lincoln and Governor Rutledge. Say what's happened, and tell them to come fast, before the British snaffle us all."

The Legion skirmished and fell back, skirmished and fell back, screening what was left of Moultrie's force all the way to Charlestown. In less than a week they were back in the city, waiting once again.

On May 10, returning from patrol, Michael led his men through gaps in the unfinished abatis, the tangle of uprooted trees with sharpened limbs pointed toward the enemy. At the old city gates he swung out of the saddle. Moultrie was waiting.

"Colonel Fallon," Moultrie said patiently, "I am not aware of any army in which a lieutenant colonel personally leads scouting patrols."

"Even a colonel needs exercise, general." He fell in beside Moultrie, leading his horse, as the general started back into the city. "There's more than dragoons on the Neck, sir. Prevost has most of his army across the Ashley River Ferry. If we'd made a stand, we could've stopped him there."

"Yes. If that were all there were to it."

A party of backcountry militia passed, their only uniforms sashes worn over homespun coats, and a group of black workmen, shovels on their shoulders, headed for the entrenchments. "This militia would have disappeared out on the Neck. Even now, with water on three sides and entrenchments to the front, we lose twenty every time Prevost goes burning and looting. I find it hard to blame them. They want to take their families to safety. Speaking of families, what of yours? Mrs. Fallon has left the city, hasn't she?"

"Yes, thank God." Michael laughed. "She announced that she'd better see to the planting." For a moment they walked on. "General, you say that there is more to it than I know. Can you tell me what it is?"

Moultrie hesitated. "Colonel, you'll be the fourth man besides myself, Governor Rutledge, and General Lincoln to know. I trust that gives you some idea of the confidence in which you have to keep it."

"It does that."

The general paused again, then spoke quickly "Lincoln is coming, finally. I've had several letters from him. If we can hold Prevost here until the thirteenth, just three days, we'll have him between us." He clapped his hands together as if the British general was between them. "Burgoyned!"

That night Michael ghosted out through the lines again, with a dozen men. Moultrie could say what he wanted to about colonels and patrols, but information was needed. And from someone with experience enough to know what was important.

A fog had drifted in with evening, and the night was gray and cottony. At the scrape of a horse's hoof against rock ahead Michael halted. A mounted shape appeared, then another, as a column emerged from the mist. Michael could make out unfamiliar coats with rows of braid across the front, hussar jackets slung on one shoulder, shakos with a burst of white feathers. They obviously weren't British. Motioning to the rest to be still, he rode toward the strangers, whistling.

Almost at the first note the column wheeled toward him, drawing sabers. Two of them rode a few paces forward, and stopped. The night air carried their words to him, but he didn't recognize the language. He fell silent.

They were swarthy men, drops of mist clinging to their curled and pointed mustaches. The one slightly to the rear, fierce-eyed and with a great hooked nose, looked a vigorous fifty. The other, about Michael's age, had a high forehead and fine features. "Tell me, Irisher," the younger said, "do you whistle for King or Congress?"

Michael started, then realized he's been whistling *Siúbhail a Ghrádh*, sung by Irish mercenaries around half the campfires in Europe. "The question, gentlemen, is who are you, and for whom do you declare? Do you recognize that song from a British camp up the Neck?"

The younger man nodded. "Very well, then. I am Count Casimir Pulaski, commanding these fine fellows, Pulaski's Legion, by name." He nodded toward the fierce-looking man. "My second in command, Colonel Kovats, recognized your song, having served often with Irish troops. And,"— his voice rose to a challenging shout—"we declare for America and Liberty."

"If you please, count, lower your voice! I'm Colonel Michael Fallon, Irish Legion, and I ride for the cause myself. But if you don't take a care, we'll all end being taken by those redcoats up the Neck."

"You mean the British are already here?" He seemed astonished, and so did Kovats, who seemed to swear under his breath. "But I crossed the river, the Cooper, I believe it is called, only an hour ago. And we have ridden the length of the peninsula to here."

"Then you rode right through the British army," Michael said drily. "May I escort you into the city?"

"Yes, of course." Pulaski frowned. "If the British are so lax, then we must consider an attack. Yes, we must."

Michael's smile was hidden by the fog as he turned back toward the city. What was Moultrie going to think of this firebrand?

There was no moon on the night of the twelfth. Even with a spyglass Michael could make out nothing. No movement.

Not a candle flicker.

Behind him every horse of the Legion was saddled. The men slept with saber and carbine by their sides, and with their boots on. The same thing was repeated all down the entrenchments. Men slept by their guns, in the trenches. There wasn't a man under arms in the city who wasn't at the lines.

The rattle of harness made him turn. Moultrie dismounted on the city side of the entrenchment and walked across. "Good evening, colonel. Still quiet, I see."

"It is that. Not so much as a cough."

"Let's hope it stays that way a little longer. I hope the first we know of Lincoln's arrival, and the first Prevost knows, is when his guns open up."

Michael nodded. Yes, if Lincoln waited until he was about six miles out, and dug in his guns there, Prevost would have an army to front and rear, and enough marsh on either side to prevent him getting so much as a platoon away by boat.

"I'm glad it's over, general. I know all the negotiations have been simply to hold them here, but they're making the men nervous. Some of the rumors are outrageous. I heard this afternoon we'd offered to make the state neutral, put everyone on parole as it were. You can imagine how that affects morale."

"If I find out who let that out," Moultrie snapped, "I'll have his hide."

"God's teeth! You mean it was really offered? What if they'd accepted?"

"Then we'd have had to delay, find fault with the arrangements, anything." He breathed heavily. "I'll tell you now, Fallon, this cannot be affecting the men any more than it's affecting the Privy Council. Some of them are beginning to take the negotiations seriously. Prevost's refusal of that last offer came with a demand for immediate and unconditional surrender, and some of those fools want to consider it."

"General," Michael said slowly, "I'll not be bound by any such thing. If those bastards surrender the city—"

"You won't have to," Moultrie cut in. "I told them they

could consider it if they wanted, but I wouldn't. It didn't take them long to realize they can't surrender the city if the army that's in it refuses."

"Then God send Lincoln quickly, general. I've heard civilians explaining to the soldiers that they're to obey orders from the Privy Council as well as their officers."

The night stretched on interminably. Men ignorant of what the night should bring were infected by tension. Infantry moved up, waiting restlessly; artillerymen checked their pieces, and rechecked them. Mutters rose to growls, subsiding only at an officer's command. The Irish Legion no longer slept. Each man sat by his horse, ready to ride. And Moultrie did ride.

All through the night he rode up and down the line, stopping here to confer with officers, there to quiet nervous volunteers. But every time he came near, Michael could see he was feeling the tension himself. His glances at the sky became more frequent. When light came, he seemed to expect what he saw. There was the Neck, empty of Lincoln. And empty of Prevost. The British army was gone.

His orders to Michael and Pulaski to pursue were almost perfunctory, but they pushed their Legions unmercifully. They crossed the river at the Ashley Ferry, riding hard, but the enemy had already reached the Stono and were digging in with their backs to the river. Dejectedly the Legions returned to the city, to find a message from Lincoln. He was on the Edisto, sixty-five miles from the city and, he said, still pressing on.

"I don't understand," John Laurens said. "From what General Moultrie says, he's only three miles closer than he was the day Prevost crossed to the Neck. We could have had a great victory here, if only he'd acted as he did at Saratoga."

"I think he did," Michael replied. "I think he did."

26

All the windows were open in the study of Michael's Queen Street house, and it was certainly cooler inside than out in the September sun, but he still fanned himself with a palmetto frond as he wrote. It wasn't the place of the commanding officer to keep a legion history, but he'd begun his jottings in Purrysburgh and it had grown. Now he was trying to catch up, adding details to skirmish reports while he could still remember them. A lot had happened in the four months since Prevost escaped at Charlestown. In South Carolina the Legion had skirmished the length of the state, harrying the redcoats back into Georgia. From elsewhere the news was not so good. Spain had declared war on England in June, but what that meant to America was yet to be determined. The British had raided and destroyed Norfolk, Virginia, and burned three coastal towns in Connecticut. The New Englanders had sent an overwhelming force to take a fort on the Penobscot River in Maine. They'd been defeated, lost nearly five hundred men, and had to burn forty-nine of their own ships. The British lost thirteen men.

He threw down the pen. As if it had been a signal Henri and Louis burst into the room.

"Strike me blue," Henri said, "if I've ever seen anything like that French fleet off the Bar. It ought to make short work of the redcoats once it reaches Savannah." He dropped into a chair and swung his leg over the arm. "What's that admiral's name, Louis? Papa always did get mad because I couldn't get my tongue around the French."

"He is," Louis intoned, "Jean-Baptiste Charles Henri Hector Théodat, Comte d'Estaing."

"The admiral who abandoned General Sullivan in Rhode Island last year," Michael said.

"Damnation, Michael," Louis said. "He had to cut his anchor cables to run ahead of a storm."

"And by the time he could return," Henri added, "It was all over."

"I heard he never tried to go back. I heard he sailed straight to Boston." Michael sighed. "I suppose the rest of the army shares your good opinion of d'Estaing?"

"From General Lincoln on down," Louis said. "The militia think we're going down there and march right into Savannah."

"I'd better not hear any of the Legion saying that," Michael snapped. "They know better than to expect an easy fight. Ever."

Louis raised his right hand. "None of them has, or will in my hearing. It's just that everybody's so eager to retake Savannah, especially after all this useless skirmishing."

Henri brandished an imaginary saber. "It'll be a beautiful fight."

"God help us," Michael murmured. "Look you, Louis, if you can keep your brother from attacking before the rest of us leave Charlestown, the two of you might meet with Count Pulaski's adjutant. Pulaski, MacIntosh, and myself are being sent down ahead to make first contact with the French when they land. Just don't go down there thinking we'll take the town in one day because the British did."

"We won't." Louis looked questioningly at his brother, who immediately began studying his boots.

Michael eyed them both suspiciously. "What is it?"

"Nothing." Louis sighed. "Oh, hell, we've heard Justin is in Savannah with about a hundred irregulars. He's supposed to have been burning and looting while Prevost was in Carolina, and worse things in Georgia."

"We thought you ought to be the one to tell Brielle, since we haven't seen her, out at Tir Alainn as she is," Henri piped in, and immediately went back to his boots.

"If you think I'm going to tell my wife that I'm marching off to shoot at her brother, you'd better think again. And neither of you will be babbling it to her, either. Do you understand me? As far as she's concerned, Justin is in New York or London or anywhere but Savannah.''

"I understand," Louis said, and Henri said, "I understand, but—'' before his brother punched him on the arm.

None of them wanted much talk after that. Michael tersely gave them their last instructions, and they replied in monosyllables. Even after they'd gone, though, and he'd turned back to the battle-history, he couldn't get Justin out of his mind. Michael had also heard the tales, some of them horrible. Justin couldn't expect gentle treatment if captured. How did a man tell his wife he'd killed her brother in battle? Or hung him?

Thoughts of Justin brought, almost inevitably, thoughts of Elizabeth. With a sense of shock he realized he hadn't thought of her in—how long? It was impossible. A man didn't simply stop thinking about a woman he loved. Why, he could visualize her. Five years had passed since he'd as much as seen her in the street, but it was almost as if she was standing right there, in the door.

"I thought they'd never leave," she said.

Starting, he jerked to his feet. She was lusher, riper, and still gut-wrenchingly beautiful. "How did you get here?''

Elizabeth laughed throatily. "I came by carriage, of course. No, I know you didn't mean that. Papa Fourrier has simply dozens of those French officers up at Les Chenes. They drink wine, and the officers tell him how unfortunate it is that Huguenots of noble blood were forced to leave France. I took the chance to get away. You aren't going to be stuffy, are you?''

"No, I—'' He stopped and made an effort to regain his composure. He had to stop babbling. "I'm afraid I'm not being much of a host. Most of the servants are with my wife." He turned away and missed the ugly look that flashed across her face. "Would you care for some wine? I still have some good Madeira.''

"Could I have some brandy, instead? I've developed a—a taste for it.''

When he turned back with the glasses, he nearly spilled them. She was smiling at him, hands clasped behind her, childishly demure. Only, for her, it wasn't demure, and she was no longer a child. Her soft breasts were pushed into even greater prominence. Her violet eyes smouldered.

Damn it, he had to get hold of himself. "I've never had the chance to tell you how deeply I regret your father's death. I had great affection for him."

She reached for the proffered glass with both hands, and left one on his wrist. "Thank you, Michael. But surely, there's something else you regret."

Somehow she'd drawn closer. She was almost in his arms, and her perfume made his head spin. No, not the perfume, damn it. Her. Her violet eyes held his, hypnotically. "I don't understand," he lied.

"So many years, and you've never once tried to see me. I've never stopped loving you, Michael. Never stopped wanting you." Their lips were almost touching.

Suddenly he jerked back. "Elizabeth, we're both married."

For a moment she seemed off-balance with surprise, but she quickly regained her equilibrium. Her voice was low, a whisper more compelling than a shout. "Gabrielle can't give you what I can. She can't give you what we had. Remember, Michael? The nights above the stable? And before? You were the first, Michael. You should have been the only one."

Again she brushed her lips against his, but after a ravenous second he tore free again. "Elizabeth, it'd be adultery for both of us."

He couldn't believe his ears. What was happening to him? So long as a woman was pretty and said yes, he'd never before concerned himself with whether she had a husband. And now to start talking about adultery with the one woman he should want more than any other. Should want? Did want. He did want her more than any other.

Elizabeth dropped her hands to her hips and stared at him in exasperation. "Good God. I'd think you'd want to cuckold Justin. You should want to put as big a set of horns on him as you can."

"That was all long ago between Justin and me."

"Long ago? Haven't you ever wondered how, after all those years, you were seized for murder? Oh, you needn't look so surprised. Rutledge and Laurens made a good job of hiding the truth. But I know." She drew breath; now for a partial lie. "It was Justin and his father sent a man to England to gather evidence against you, a greasy little gray man who killed another friend of yours, a man named Cavanaugh. That's another thing for you to hold against them, isn't it? God, Michael, if you never had any love for me at all, you ought to take me just for being Justin's wife."

Michael was barely listening. How did they ever think to send a man looking? And Timothy. Oh, God. "How did this man find Timothy? There'd be no one to put us together, except a few hussars."

"Oh, dearest, that's not important—"

"I never mentioned his name to a soul. Not a—. Wait. I did once. To your father, in his study, the day he told me—." He looked at her, and it was if he saw her clearly for the first time. "You always did like listening at doors, didn't you?"

His hands caught her around the throat, a firm grip that lifted her off her heels. She gasped, but the realization she could breathe didn't lessen her panic. His hands were like iron bands. She couldn't budge them. And his eyes. They were on fire. His eyes looked murder.

"No, Michael, please. You don't want to hurt me. You don't want to kill me. I love you. I swear it. If you want to punish me, then beat me. Beat me, and we'll make love. But don't kill me." For the love of God, wouldn't he stop staring at her?

"I know more now than I did then. It wouldn't be just you making love to me. I'll be the one to kiss you all over, this time. Wouldn't you like that? God's mercy, Michael. Don't kill me. I didn't mean to tell them. I swear I didn't. Oh, God, I swear it."

He pushed her away, and she fell, her dress flying up and twisting under her. From the waist down she wore only shoes, stockings, and garters with red rosettes. She made no effort to cover herself.

"I'm not going to hurt you," he said. He felt tired. "I'm not even angry with you. Not for Timothy, and not for acting so much like a Winchester goose I near thought to ask your pimp the price. But it's changed. I'm not talking about husbands and wives. You're different. I'm different. It's no good any more." He gave a puzzled laugh. "I thought it would be, as much as you, but it isn't."

She laughed, too. Disbelievingly. "You can't just walk away from me. Not you, Michael. Do you remember the last time you saw me like this? Shall I tell you what came of that little encounter?"

"Will you tell your doxy to cover herself?" Gabrielle closed the door behind her. "I mind my house being used as a bordello." She went about the business of removing hat and gloves, ignoring their consternation.

Michael stood staring curiously at Gabrielle, but Elizabeth scrambled angrily to her feet, hastily adjusting her clothes. "Why, you little bitch, what would you know of doxies, or of what a man wants in bed, either? There's not enough life in you to rumple the sheets."

Gabrielle's face paled, but she gave no other sign that she'd heard a word. "I suppose I really should tell Justin about this. Or perhaps my father. I'm certain he would see, Elizabeth, that your, shall we say, appetites are curbed."

"Papa Fourrier would have you shown the door before you opened your mouth," Elizabeth said with an ugly laugh. "He considers you little better than a trull, yourself, for marrying Michael Fallon, and he'd never listen to a whore. I'll visit my darling Michael when and where I wish, and you can—."

"Elizabeth!" Both women jumped at Michael's roar, but Gabrielle quickly turned away. "You've said a lot of things, and I don't know if there's a word of truth in the lot, but you'll stop right now. You won't visit me. You won't come to this house again. And you'd better leave it, now, before I put you out."

Elizabeth flung a look at him, halfway between fear and anger, and stormed out of the house. He watched her go without regret, he realized, without a one.

"Very impressive, darling Michael," Gabrielle said flatly. She clapped three times as if applauding, and left the room.

Hurriedly he followed. "Brielle, Brielle, wait."

"Martha awaits me in my chamber; I must go up and freshen. Will you permit me, or shall I spread myself upon the floor? I fear I'm a trifle more encumbered than your blowze."

"God's teeth, woman! Will you listen? Why must you see things the worst way?"

"And what other way is there? Your trollop was on the floor with her skirts up and her legs spread. If I'd come in a minute later, you'd have had your breeches off. And a minute after that? I don't even want to think of it."

"Damn it, Brielle, you will listen to me! I didn't bring her here. She came, and I didn't know she was coming. And she was on the floor because I pushed her away and she fell. That's all there was to it. Don't you realize, Brielle, I love you." The truth of it hit him, and all he could do was echo his own words. "I love you."

Her face crumpled, and she sagged. "Don't you say that! Damn you, don't you say that! For years I've waited to hear those words, wanted them, hoped for them, while you carried her miniature next to you. I won't take them like this, with you fresh from her arms." Weeping, she ran up the stairs.

For a second he stared after her, then followed, running up the curving stair to get ahead of her at the landing. "I do love you, Brielle."

"Let me by." She darted to his right.

Later, he could never remember exactly what happened. He reached for her, and she stepped back out of his grasp. Suddenly her foot slipped and she tottered, eyes wide, mouth opening. He reached; his fingertips brushed hers, and she was gone. A long scream, abruptly cut off, ripped through his mind. He stood frozen, hand still outstretched, watching her tumbling, falling like a broken-doll to the entry hall below.

"Gabrielle!" He raced downstairs, not hearing Martha's piercing shriek from the landing rail, not seeing the butler drop his salver with a yell. He knelt beside her, hands trembling. No! He mustn't move her. Damn it, he had to control himself. She was barely breathing. "Martha! Caesar! Send for the doctor! Hurry, damn you. Hurry!"

The pendulum of the clock in Michael's study swung once to the left and once to the right every second, one hundred and twenty swings a minute. Twenty-five thousand three hundred forty swings were three hours, thirty-one minutes, ten seconds. Eleven seconds. Twelve seconds.

The doctor had flung back an old-fashioned black cape, taken a grave look at Brielle, and told Michael he'd been right not to move her. Then he'd had the serving women pick her up, and they'd all disappeared upstairs. He hadn't seen the doctor since, just maids running for more hot water, or for something from the apothecary. But he knew one thing. Those women were frightened. And so was he. Fifty-eight seconds. Fifty-nine seconds. Thirty-two minutes.

He pulled himself away from gazing at the clock. He wasn't frightened. He was terrified. If he hadn't argued with her. If he hadn't chased her up the stairs. If he hadn't reached for her. A thousand ifs, and then she'd be all right. She'd be alive. She'd hate him, but she'd be alive. God, let her hate him, but let her live.

What a strange thing to discover, that he was in love with the woman he'd married four years ago. Four years of her laughter and her smiles. Four years of the surprises of her. Watching her with young James. Watching her alone. Watching her change from a girl to a regal woman. A woman of appetites and life. Sometimes enough for two women. And surprises there, too. But she made him feel tender. Lying upstairs, maybe dying, she made him feel empty, and afraid.

When the butler announced General Moultrie, he only stared.

"Good God, Fallon. You look like dea—. I mean, I heard

what happened, that your lady'd had a fall. She isn't—."

"Dead, general?" His voice almost broke. "No. No, they'd have told me if—. She's still alive."

Moultrie walked to the lowboy and came back with a decanter of brandy. "Here, man. You need this. Drink it. Drink all of it."

Michael shook his head as if dazed. "Haven't time to get drunk. I'm supposed to, supposed to—. Wagons. That's it. Wagons, to carry forage and supplies for the Legion. It'll be pretty uncertain at Savannah."

"You won't be going to Savannah. I've transferred you to my command here in Charlestown. Mrs. Fallon needs you."

"It's no good," Michael said dully. "The Legion will be needed. Pulaski hasn't enough by himself. I have to go."

"The Legion is going. Under the temporary command of Major Fourrier. I'm assigning you to this house until further notice."

Michael's eyes stung, and he looked away angrily. "I should be saying something about duty, shouldn't I? About my place being with the Legion? Thank you, General."

Moultrie pushed the decanter across the desk. "Do as I say and drink that. When it has Moll Thompson's mark on it, it'll soak up some of the pain. I must go, now."

"General," Michael called, and Moultrie stopped at the door. "If we fail there, they'll be coming here next."

"Then we won't fail. Now drink. It's an order."

He stared at the decanter for a time after Moultrie had gone. He poured a glass and stared at that. Just obey orders. Pick up the glass and drink. And then another, and another, and—. Oblivion wouldn't be far off, then. Oblivion. An hour later, when the doctor entered, he was still staring at that glass.

"A difficult day, Mr. Fallon," he said. He finished putting on his coat. "Ah. Brandy. Just what I need."

Michael leaped to his feet, reaching across the desk to grab the doctor's lapels. Glass and decanter both toppled to the floor. "How's my wife? Damn you. How is she?"

"For the love of God, sir! She's all right. Your wife lives, sir."

A sigh ran out of him, and the anger with it. He sank back into his chair, leaving the doctor to straighten his rumpled clothes. "Thank God," he whispered.

The doctor eyed him warily and took two careful paces back from the desk. "There were, I must inform you, some complications." He put another pace between them as Michael looked up. "I was unable to save the baby." Stunned, Michael mouthed the word. "It was, sir, you see, no more than two months along. There was no way to—. Well, you understand." He cleared his throat, and his voice became firmer. "There is, of course, no reason why Mrs. Fallon should not recover fully, in time. I've left laudanum with instructions for its use. Sleep is the thing, and of course all the windows must be kept shut and the curtains tightly closed. Putrid airs—. Mr. Fallon? Mr. Fallon?"

Michael got up and left without speaking. He'd heard only a word here and there after hearing about the baby. Mother of God, pray for him. If he hadn't killed her, he'd still killed their baby. But she lived, and she'd recover. He'd heard that much. It was enough.

He opened her bedroom door gently. He didn't see Martha or the maids, and never noticed them leaving as he sat beside the bed. She looked so fragile, there against the pillows. Her breathing was shallow. The bedclothes, pulled up to her chin, didn't stir with it. Almost reverently he turned back a corner to take her hand. It lay on his with only the barest hint of warmth to say there was life in it. He clung to it desperately. However long it took, he'd be there.

Gabrielle swallowed the thin broth Martha spoonfed her and grimaced. "How many times must I tell you I'm not an invalid?"

"Yes, Miss Gabrielle," Martha said. "Now why don't you take a little more of this broth? You finish it all up, and maybe Mr. Fallon come up to sit with you awhile."

Gabrielle turned her head away. "No!"

"Miss Gabrielle, this ain't right, the way you treat that man. Three days now you been awake, and you won't let him in the room. The whole two months you lay there not waking up except to scream and cry, he sat right here and held your hand. When we couldn't get nothing into you but caudle, he spoonfed you most nearly every drop with his own hands. And now you won't even let him come in."

"I don't want to talk about it any more, Martha. I don't want to see anyone but you and the doctor. Please." How could she face Michael? How could she listen to his lies? He *hadn't* been faithful! Oh, he'd been discreet, never flaunting, and she'd ignored it for the sake of keeping him. But this! In her house, with that woman. That unclean whore! She couldn't ignore it. She wouldn't.

And the baby. Oh God, the baby. Death on top of all. It was his fault. And she knew he'd blame her for it. That precious Fallon blood!

Martha was muttering to herself, eying Gabrielle craftily. "Yes, ma'am. I won't let nobody bother you none. I'll send your brothers away."

"My brothers? Here? Now?"

"Yes, ma'am. Down with Mr. Fallon in the—Miss Gabrielle, you get back in that bed. Miss Gabrielle, you don't get back in that bed, I going to put you there."

Gabrielle sat on the edge of the bed, head spinning. "Be quiet, Martha. Get my robe." A grip on the bedpost pulled her to her feet through a swarm of black and silver flecks.

Martha gave in. As she helped Gabrielle into the robe, she kept up a worried tirade against this foolishness; but she supported her out of the room and down the stairs. Gabrielle started to open the study door but stopped with an inch-wide crack. Louis was speaking.

"—and the 2nd Regiment lost worse than two out of three. The Legion—. The Legion lost twenty-one dead and forty wounded."

Michael handed each a glass of brandy and sat across from them. They hadn't changed in the ten years, almost, he'd known them, but now they looked their ages, and ten years more. Their faces were drawn, and fine lines webbed the corners of their eyes.

"I've heard a dozen stories the past two days, and no two alike."

Louis looked at his brother, but Henri was silent, gazing into his brandy. "I remember you saying we mustn't expect to take Savannah in one day. What was that? Two months ago? Seems like two years. We could have. Taken it in one day, I mean, if that day had been the first day the French landed."

"Ten guns," Henri said quietly. "On that day they had ten guns mounted in Savannah."

"And when we finally attacked, they had over a hundred. Well over a hundred, Michael."

"What was Lincoln doing? He may not think particularly fast, but he must have seen."

Louis laughed bitterly. "He saw what he wanted to see. Or rather, what d'Estaing told him to see. We tried to tell him what was going on. Johnny Laurens and Francis Marion raised such hell, I thought they'd both be courtmartialed for insubordination. The trouble was, as soon as Lincoln realized they were contradicting d'Estaing, he'd start telling them how the Frenchie captured Grenada with only nine hundred men."

Henri broke in. "He acted like he was a bloody demi-god. Stab me if he didn't."

"Yes, that's close enough, Michael. D'Estaing could do no wrong. But the battle. It took d'Estaing a week after landing to call for the city to surrender. And then he demanded it in the name of the King of France! I ask you! The men were suspicious enough of the French to begin with."

"Well, stab me, what was the use of taking the place for a French colony?"

"A week after he demanded surrender, a week, mind, we started trenches. Then—. Oh, hell, it doesn't take long to tell. We were there for over a month, and the British sortied against us twice, before we fired our first cannon at their emplacements."

"Don't forget the reinforcements, Louis." Henri gulped his brandy and poured more. "The British got in perhaps a regiment of reinforcements by water."

Louis took it up. "We fired the first cannon on the fifth of October, and kept it up from then on. One of the Frenchies, a

Major L'Enfant, tried to fire the abatis, but the wood was too green. Took courage. I could almost forgive them d'Estaing for L'Enfant. Almost. Prevost asked to send out the women and children, but d'Estaing refused. Lincoln went along, but I think he was beginning to doubt for the first time. And then, after all the delays he'd caused, that whoreson Frog bastard said the Americans had been too slow. He'd been away from the French Indies too long. The British might be down there at that moment. We must raise the seige, or attack at once, because he intended sailing within the fortnight.''

"The trenches," Michael said. "How close were the trenches? Fifty yards? A hundred?"

"The closest were four hundred yards from the British lines," Louis replied, and laughed at Michael's gasp. "Oh, there's worse. That's not where we attacked from. Most had to cross over half a mile of ground, and some had to wade through rice paddies.''

"That's insane," Michael said.

"Insane," Henri laughed bitterly. "That's the word for it.''

"Huger's men bogged down crossing the rice fields, and were cut up without ever making it to the British lines. Dillon lost his way in the swamp, finally extracted his men and tried to form them in daylight, under the British guns, and never managed to launch an attack at all. But the rest of us—the Frenchies, Marion, Laurens, Pulaski, MacIntosh and us— made our attack on the Spring Hill Redoubt as planned.''

Henri lifted his glass. "To the Spring Hill Redoubt." His face was grim.

Louis didn't notice the interruption. "The Irish Legion was supposed to follow close behind, to dash through and exploit any breakthrough. I saw soon enough that we'd never get the horses through the abatis, so we dismounted and went in on the flank of Marion's 2nd Regiment of Foot. They went in like they were on a parade ground; you could hear their officers calling, push on, push on. Through the abatis, across the ditch, and up the slope into the redoubt, all you could hear was cannon balls striking the ground, musket balls smacking into flesh, and those men calling, push on. They had a battalion of dismounted dragoons in the redoubt, with Tories from the Carolinas. The French never made it past the rim of the redoubt, but we and the 2nd fought our way inside. We almost had it clear when they hit us in the flank.''

''60th Grenadiers and Royal Marines,'' Henri said.

''They pushed us back, then. Pulaski saw what was happening and tried to break through; the artillery slashed them to pieces. We were pushed back into the ditch. We'd got our colors out of the redoubt, Sergeant Jasper died trying to rescue the 2nd's, and the last I saw was when Bush fell into the ditch with them.''

''Jasper's dead? And Bush?''

''And Motte,'' Henri said, ''and Wise, and Beraud, and Shepherd, and Hudson, and Pulaski, and—hell, think of everyone you knew and take every other name.''

''I should've been there,'' Michael said.

''You couldn't have changed anything,'' Louis said wearily.

''They'll be coming here soon enough,'' Henri added.

''I still should've been there.''

The bitterness in his voice hit Gabrielle like a blow. First that woman. Then the baby. And now this. It was too much. She couldn't face it all. She had to get away.

''Martha, have Caesar make the carriage ready. Now. Then go bundle James against the chill, and bring me a dress. Hurry. A word to Mr. Fallon, and I'll—I'll sell you. Hurry.''

She managed to make Martha go, leaving her tottering in the entry hall. Unsteadily she made her way back to a writing desk. The first note began My Dearest Michael. After staring at the three words she tore it up and began again.

November 10, 1779

Dear Husband,

I am leaving for reasons that we both know too well. What stands between us now can never be eradicated. What I had hoped we would have is irretrievably gone.

There should be no need for me to say that I have little wish to see or hear from you. If you wish to come to Tir Alainn, please write to me beforehand so that I may remove to the house in Charlestown until you are gone.

Gabrielle

Twenty minutes later the carriage rolled out of the drive and headed out of the city.

27

The British transports in the North Edisto Inlet were quiet. They'd had most of General Clinton's soldiers ashore for a month, now, since the middle of February, and they were living off the countryside. It still seemed strange to Michael that he could stand twenty miles from Charlestown and be in enemy territory.

Even there he couldn't keep his mind from Gabrielle at Tir Alainn. Daniel had carried letter after letter, but always returned empty-handed. But then, he'd said it, hadn't he? Let her hate him, but let her live. He should be satisfied. God, how could he be?

He slid back into the brush, where ten Legionnaires waited with the horses.

"See anything, colonel?"

"Nothing, Sergeant Bakeman." He stowed the glass in his saddlebags and mounted. "Looks as if the army that's ashore now is all we have to face."

"That's enough for me, colonel," somebody laughed.

"The colonel ain't interested in your opinions, Collins," Bakeman said. "Where to now, colonel?"

"Back to the city, sergeant. We've spent a week discovering nothing we didn't already know."

They picked their way through the pine woods, keeping the marsh along the Stono always in sight to their left. Wadmalaw Island was firmly in British hands, along with Johns Island and James Island. The usual crossings all had sentries, and fifty men or more encamped there. Along this side of Wadmalaw, though, where the marsh thinned away to nothing, horses could be swum across. The British need never know they'd been there.

Campaigning had changed the Legionnaires from the

rigidly erect horsemen who'd paraded at Tir Alainn. They rode slouched, saving their energies for battle. Anything that could clink was wrapped with cloth; each man's head swiveled constantly, on lookout for ambush.

The patrol swam from the island to the mainland, fighting a current that threatened to sweep them down to Wadmalaw Sound, and crossed the Rantowle Bridge over an arm of the Stono, then swung north, away from the British controlled side of the harbor. They crossed the Ashley well above the ferry, using a leaky bateau to cross a few men at a time, swimming their horses alongside. It wasn't a normal crossing point, or even a good one. But the usual crossings to the south were in British hands, and those to the north were too far off. The boat was one of a dozen kept hidden in the Neck marshes for quick crossings into British territory.

On the ride down to the city Michael kept a close eye on the far bank of the river, several times stopping to look through his glass. At several points boats were gathering, the same launches and cutters, it seemed, that he'd reported being moved through the inland waterways earlier. And there wasn't a sign of anything being done to impede them.

He galloped across the bridge over the wetditch before the city and through the embankments and abatis with a frown on his face. There was plenty of activity there, at any rate. Parties of slaves worked feverishly increasing the network of fortifications. The remnants of the old hornwork city wall around the gate on King Street had been enclosed to make a strongpoint. He glared around at the work going on and motioned Bakeman to him.

"Take the men to the encampment, sergeant. I'll be at General Lincoln's headquarters if you need me."

From a distance the swirling traffic in the streets might have seemed normal. It was certainly as heavy as ever. But the men jostling their way through the streets were militia, identified by the muskets they carried and white patches sewn to their hats, and uniformed Continentals. The Continentals—there were just enough of those regulars to convince most people the city was impregnable. Some men had counted the soldiers, and looked at the enemy, though. The few carriages to be seen were all headed out of the city, piled high with baggage and filled with women being sent to safety. At least he didn't have that to worry about.

When he saw Petrie trudging down the street, he could hardly believe his eyes. "Petrie, what are you doing here? How's *Hussar*, and the crew?"

Petrie dropped his luggage and offered a hand as Michael dismounted. "Fine, Captain Fallon. Everything's fine with us. I suppose I should say colonel, now. It was a good cruise, sir. No fat Indiaman, but good enough. It was my decision to come back to Charlestown, sir; bad judgment, it seems."

"Well, yes, Petrie. You'd better make to sea immediately. We may have to abandon the city, and—." Petrie was shaking his head. "Why not?"

"Not with seven ships-of-the-line and a swarm of frigates already inside the Bar."

"What! But how? I've heard not a whisper of a naval fight."

"There wasn't one," Petrie said acidly. "It was our Commodore Whipple." At mention of the name both men involuntarily looked toward St. Michael's towering steeple, painted black by Whipple's order so the enemy couldn't use it for a landmark. Now it stood out against the sky like a beacon. It was told often in Charlestown, and generally to great laughter, but neither man was smiling now.

"When I arrived," Petrie went on, "I put *Hussar* with the American frigates just inside the Bar. If the British tried to cross, we could've played bloody hell with them. But Whipple claimed we'd be in danger of running aground during the fight—I ask you! He pulled us back. The British took the guns off their ships, crossed the Bar, and rearmed without hindrance. This Abraham Whipple may be a hero in New England, but he's a fool in South Carolina. And Lincoln isn't any better, if you ask me."

"Then the harbor's theirs!"

"Yes, Mr. Fallon. It is theirs, any time they run past Fort Moultrie. The American Navy," Petrie spat, "is sitting behind a barrier of sunken hulks in the Cooper River, along with such privateers as are in port. The Royal Navy can't get at us, but we can't go anywhere at all until the channel's cleared. They've already begun taking some of the guns ashore. I let them have *Hussar*'s. They were doing no good where they were."

Michael nodded "Aye. I suppose. It's a hell of a way for —. Listen, Petrie. Are any of the crew left?"

"About ten." He was clearly puzzled. "The rest either deserted or joined the militia."

"Then strip *Hussar* of everything. Store it at Carver's Bridge. There you'll find twenty hogsheads of turpentine and some barrels of pitch. Load them on *Hussar*, and if the city—. If she's going to fall into British hands, fire her."

Petrie nodded, slowly at first, then more firmly. "I'll see to it. I promise."

"Then it's settled," Michael sighed. "I'm due at headquarters. In case we don't meet again, good luck to you, and God favor you."

Lincoln's headquarters, in a house on Tradd Street, was almost deserted. A pair of sentries at the door saluted as he came in; a single officer scribbled at a desk in the hall. All else was still.

"I have to see General Lincoln," Michael said.

"He can't see anyone," the writer said without looking up.

Michael slammed a fist down on the desk, and the man jerked erect, frowning when he saw Michael's rank. "I've urgent reports on the enemy's movements and intentions. Now do we understand one another, lieutenant?"

"I'm sorry, sir, but I've orders—Sir? Sir! You can't go up there."

Seeing a group of officers coming down the stairs, Michael had darted up to meet them. Rotund Benjamin Lincoln led the group, William Moultrie among them.

"Ah," Lincoln said. "It's good to see you, Colonel Fallon. Gentlemen, one of our finest cavalry officers. What information today, colonel? No more troops landed, I hope.''

"No, general, but they're massing. It's my estimation they'll be crossing the river at the Ashley Ferry and Drayton Hall within twenty-four hours. I believe they're moving for the Neck." He added, "And with the British Navy in the harbor, we must evacuate before we're completely surrounded.''

Lincoln's chins wobbled. "They don't have the harbor yet," he snapped. Some of the officers behind the general shifted uncomfortably. His mouth worked, and he made an obvious effort to moderate his voice. "Colonel Fallon, you're simply not aware of our higher strategy. The British Navy will be severely mauled if they attempt the run past Fort Moultrie. And if General Clinton lands his army above the city, he'll discover he has cornered a bear. We've a strong force here, and it will get stronger. General Scott is expected any day with troops from Virginia. I have Thomas Jefferson's word on that. We will get troops from Virginia. And if worst does come to worst, we shall still have our way out of the city across the Cooper River, to Lempriere's Point. But it will not come to that, Colonel Fallon. Now, we all have duties. I suggest you be about yours and stop spreading defeatist talk about evacuation. Good day to you.''

Lincoln waddled down the stairs and out of the house, followed by most of the officers, who avoided Michael's eyes. Only Moultrie remained, tattered maps under his arm, shaking his head. He glanced over the bannister at the lieutenant writing below, and nodded toward a door. Not until they were inside, with the door closed, did he speak.

"That was a fool thing to do, Fallon. The rest of the city doesn't know it, and you may not, but evacuation is the main topic of every council of war, lately.''

Michael threw up his hands. "God's teeth! Then why did he blow up? We must get out. General, if we get field pieces up the Neck, we can delay Clinton's crossing a week or more. We can expect no help from Scott. Jefferson promised troops before, when Prevost came, and never sent them. Even so, in the countryside, we'd have enough to make a fight of it, instead of waiting here for the axe.''

''He blew up because he's straddling the fence, dreading coming down on either side. Most field officers want evacuation but the civilians—. The civilians, damn their souls, want a seige. Gadsden carries on like the firebrand he's always been, as if this were a clash between his Liberty Boys and a few King's men. His brother-in-law, Ferguson, is even worse. He says he'll rouse the citizens to fire at us if we try to run away, as he puts it. And Rutledge refuses to discuss it. But then, what governor could easily countenance leaving his capital to the enemy?''

Michael listened in disbelief. ''God's wounds, general, you're talking politics. The Council has no place deciding when or where a battle's fought.''

''Civilians always decide, unless you've a Washington to stare them in the eye and tell them to leave him to the fighting. All we have, God help us, is Benjamin Lincoln. Here.'' He suddenly spread a map on the table. ''This is the battle ground they've chosen. The harbor and peninsula of Charlestown. With the British fleet in the harbor and the British Army on the Neck, they have two thirds of a circle around the city. But as long as we hold Lempriere's Point across the Cooper, we still have a gate to the outside. God send we have the chance to use it.''

''God send Lincoln remembers he's a general, not a politician.''

''Generals have to be politicians, Colonel Fallon. Even Washington, I understand, has to spend as much time dealing with the Congress as with the British. I constantly pour oil on the waters between the Privy Council and the backcountry militiamen. And the British are as bad off. Half their generals have refused to serve in America for political reasons, and half those here are here for politics.'' A sour expression came on his face. ''Not the way we thought it'd be when we all started, is it? All we can do is our duty. What did you discover toward the Edisto?''

"Nothing to help," Michael said. "Not a thing."

The next morning Clinton's army began crossing the Ashley River. After an afternoon-long skirmish between Johnny Laurens' light infantry and Hessian jaegers, the army started digging their first gun emplacements. Charlestown was cut off by land.

The dirt sifting from the cellar roof onto his face woke Michael; another mortar bomb had exploded in the yard. He spat and rolled over, but another exploded only a little further away, and more dirt fell. The bombardment was intensifying; there'd be no more sleep. He threw off the blanket and rose.

Outside, young Tom Jarvis, the bugler-boy, slept curled beside the steps of the ruined house. Michael frowned. No matter where he ordered the twelve-year-old to sleep, he always ended up in the same spot.

A British mortar gave a deep-throated cough, and Michael paused to listen. At the first whine he relaxed. It wouldn't fall near. Not a good morning, Michael thought, as the bomb tore open a building three blocks away. Every time he saw the British flag above the battery at Lempriere's Point, which in falling had snapped the city shut, he wished to throttle Lincoln. Now, after seven weeks of siege, Lincoln was surrendering. God's teeth! They were down to six ounces of meal a day for each man, and the third British parallel wasn't more than twenty-five yards away. But the real defeat was in the spirit. The congress had written them off, saving men for fighting in the north. And firebrands for liberty were howling that Clinton's force was huge—and could no longer be resisted. No, they'd gone soft.

Gently he woke young Tom.

"Tom! Up, lad. I know you're awake. We may find barley soup at headquarters."

The boy jumped to his feet and wobbled to attention. "I don't need nothing extra, sir. I can eat meal with the rest of the men."

"Just like you ate horse, lad?" Tom studied a scuff mark

in the mud. He'd cried when they'd had to start killing the horses. "It's no matter, boy. I could never take it for beef, either. Look you, now. What it is, I need that soup myself. But I can't go asking for it alone, now can I? So come along, then. It's an order."

Plumes of smoke rose from burning houses along the way, and geysers of debris were kicked up by cannon balls or mortar-bombs. Down the street a party of men clambered up mounded dirt, thrown up against most houses for protection, to pour water on a blazing roof. All of them dropped as a cannon ball smashed into the roof of the house next door, sending tiles and timbers flying.

At headquarters the first man Michael saw was Moultrie, hurrying down the steps. It seemed deserted.

"General, is there anyone in there?"

"Only Lieutenant Bascombe." Moultrie's face was haggard. "He's packing."

"Today? They've come to terms?"

"Almost. If Clinton refuses his last offer, Lincoln will accept what he can get."

"God's wounds. It's soft we've gone. No, no, not you, sir—"

Moultrie shook his head. "Fallon, Fallon. Clinton's is the second largest army ever sent into battle in the Americas, maybe the largest. Do you really think we could bloody him enough to pay for what would follow? Burning. Looting. Rapine. You've been in cities taken by storm. I'm sorry, Fallon. I'm sorry."

Michael watched him walk away. He felt a tug at his coat; it was the bugler, looking frightened. God, but he was young!

"Mr. Fallon? Mr. Fallon! Sir!"

Michael looked up, and his jaw dropped. "Daniel! Man, what are you doing here? How did you get into the city?"

The boatman's eyes darted at a distant explosion. "Mr. Fallon, you know I know every blade of marsh grass round this city. Ain't no sentries going to keep me out. One thing, Mr. Fallon. That ship of yours, that *Hussar*, I seen it in the

Cooper, and it burning like I never see nothing burn before."

"Good man, Petrie," Michael said half to himself. "Daniel, you have to get out of here. I don't know why you came, but whatever the reason, you must go back."

"Mrs. Fallon send me." Daniel took a note from under his coat. "She send you this. She know the city's done, sir. She tell me to bring you out."

Michael held the paper a minute before opening it.

Dear Husband,
I beseech you for the sake of your son to leave Charles-town before it is too late. Daniel will bring you out safely in his boat. You will aid nothing, and only bring hurt to those who love you, by remaining.
                                        Gabrielle

Refolding the note, he took out a leather case. It held the last letter Gabrielle had written, smudged from handling, tearing along the creases despite his care. The note joined it.

He pocketed the case. 'For the sake of his son.' "My wi—." He cleared his throat. "Mrs. Fallon is well?"

"Yes, sir. She well." A mortar shell blew the roof off of a house in the next block. "Come on, Mr. Fallon. Let's go. Please. Mrs. Fallon, she have my hide if I don't get you to her in one piece."

"You exaggerate like an Irishman, Daniel. Now, you tell Mrs. Fallon her brother Henri is safe and unhurt. Her brother Louis broke his leg, but we evacuated him three weeks ago. He's hidden, so she'll have to wait for him to reach her. But let her know they're both alive."

"Do that mean you ain't coming, Mr. Fallon?"

"Even if I could walk away from the rest of the garrison, I couldn't leave my own men. There are still ninety-seven Legionnaires." Suddenly Michael grabbed Tom's skinny arm and pulled him forward. "But here's a passenger for you. His people have a farm up the Ashley. Take him there before you go back to Tir Alainn."

The boy squirmed in Michael's grasp. "No, sir. No! I put

my name on the papers! I'm a Legionnaire!''

"Hold still, lad. That's an order. What's this bundle up in your shirt?''

The boy froze as Michael took out the Legion's colors. It wasn't quite the same flag they'd flown that morning at Tir Alainn, showing off for Gabrielle. There was a patch over the rip made at the siege of Savannah, and, lower down, two more for Ebenezer Heights and Dupont's Plantation. Across the bottom was a row of gold stars, embroidered when there had been time, a star for every action from Purrysburg to Dorchester. There were no stars for John's Island, or the Wappoo Creek Bridge. There'd never be a star for Charlestown.

Tom drew himself up. "The enemy must never take your colors. I know that, sir. And I figured, well, I'd hide it under my shirt when they, when they—.'' He swallowed. "The redcoats won't get our colors, sir. You can trust me.''

God send the Legion never learned their colors left Charlestown like a stolen pullet! Briskly Michael folded the flag. "I expect that I can, Private Jarvis. I'm entrusting the colors to you. But, of course, this means your leaving is twice as important as it was. No, lad. You listen to me, now. Private Jarvis, I order you to take the colors out of the city, and hide them at your father's farm. To keep them safe, you'll act the part of a farmboy, and no more, till I send word the Legion is ready to ride again. Now, both of you go.''

The boy replaced the flag inside his shirt. Michael pushed him toward Daniel. "Mr. Fallon,'' the boatman said, "everybody know you snuck the governor out. Why you got to stay if he don't?''

"Go, Daniel,'' Michael said. "Tell Mrs. Fallon—.'' He stopped abruptly and turned away up the street.

Daniel started slowly for the waterfront, holding the boy's hand. The whistling whine didn't sound any different to him than any other he'd heard since getting to the city, but in the same instant he heard Michael shouting something, and looked back. Michael was running toward them waving violently. Down. Down. Daniel fell, pulling Tom with him. Before they hit the ground the world blew up.

Groggily, Daniel pushed a board away and sat up. Tom was looking around, wide-eyed. But Mr. Fallon—the street was empty except for rubble. Tom started to scramble past him, back the way they'd come. He grabbed his arm. "No, boy. There ain't nothing we can do to help him, now. We just got to do what he told us. Come on, boy. Come on."

Hand in hand they ran for the docks.

28

Elizabeth kept the curtains open to the sunlight as her carriage approached Charlestown. Some people said God was smiling on the king's victory; Elizabeth thought the sun would still be shining had the Congress won.

Les Chenes had been full of politics during the siege, a constant stream of British officers wined and feted. General Clinton. Admiral Arbuthnot. General Lord Cornwallis. General Leslie. And, of course, there'd been the favored few among the young officers.

They and Papa Fourrier had seemed to get on very well, full of smiles and private talks. Toward Justin, however, they'd been quite cool. Oh, he'd been commissioned a major, and his unit taken on the list as the King's South Carolina Horse, but his being at Thompsonville had told against him, even though they didn't mention it. When the rebels surrendered at Thompsonville, Justin maintained, he'd gotten the Indians under control as soon as he could, but the fact remained that all forty-seven prisoners had been killed and scalped. Almost worse than that were the nine women who had been there. They simply disappeared. Some of the junior officers whispered that they'd been given to the Indians as payment, but none said it to Justin's face, or in his hearing. They'd all heard of his prowess with a pistol, and seen his saber practice with Colonel Tarletan.

Banastre Tarletan was the only one of the British officers who seemed to like Justin, talking and drinking late into the night together with Captain Houck, one of Tarletan's men.

In the Jersies, Tarletan had made a reputation as a cavalry leader. It was said the rebels there called him Benny. But he didn't seem like a Benny in South Carolina. He struck hard, and with complete ruthlessness, inflicting fearful casualties.

And, except for William Washington, his opponents always lost. His name was hated among the rebels, and feared.

He'd wanted Elizabeth to call him Ban, making his approach in the garden while Justin slept off their drinking. She almost fell into his trap. He was boyishly handsome, with a polished grace when he cared to use it. But she'd looked into his eyes when he tried to kiss her, and seen the tiny spark deep inside that told her why he wasn't repelled by Thompsonville. He revelled in pain and fear.

She'd torn away from him, but he'd been persistent. Oh, so persistent. And then she'd seen two of the farm girls Tarletan had used for his entertainment. No matter how decent they were before, after they acted like whipped curs. That was why she was on her way to the house in the city.

For some time she'd been passing large groups of men under guard on both sides of the road. Some were obviously soldiers, in the blue of the Continental Line or the motley of militia units, but many were civilians, or dressed as such. There were boys barely into their teens, and old men who couldn't stand without their walking sticks. The carriage stopped; a redcoated sentry tapped on the door.

"Ma'am? I must know who you are, and what you want in the city." His tone was half-way between impatience and respect for the equipage.

"Those men," she said. "The boys and the old men. What are they doing out here?"

"Part of the rebel militia, ma'am, brought out to have their names took—"

"What is this?" a voice cracked, and the sentry snapped to rigidity.

"Sir," he said. "This lady wishes to enter the city, sir, and I was just making inquiry as to her purpose there, being as I was instructed to take the utmost care against the entry of rebels into the city. Sir."

"Didn't sound like inquiry. And I seriously doubt this carriage conceals a rebel column." A young officer, trying to appear both bored and authoritative, appeared at the window. "Why, Mrs. Fourrier," he said eagerly, and stopped in confusion. "Your pardon, ma'am. No reason why you should know me, of course, but I've often admired you from afar, if I may be so bold. Jerome Dudley, cornet in the light infantry of the 23rd Foot."

Elizabeth gave him a slight smile. He reminded her very much of a puppy she'd once had. "Why, Mr. Dudley, I do hope you won't remain a distant admirer. You must leave your card on Broad Street. That is, if I'm to be allowed into the city? Please say you won't turn me away." She wet her lips, carefully leaving them ever so slightly open.

The young cornet stared at her for a full minute before managing to reply. "Turn—. Oh, no, ma'am. I should say not. Clear a way there. You men, clear a way for this lady's carriage. Clear a way, I say." He was still shouting when the carriage rolled away.

Elizabeth fell back against the cushions. Oh, most certainly a puppy. If he'd had a tail, he'd have wagged it. It might be amusing to watch his innocence disappear. Unbidden, Michael came into her mind. His innocence had been of a different kind. Damn him. Any real man would have welcomed her with open arms. Justin now—her mind flinched away.

The carriage moved slowly through clogged roads, parties under guard going one way, troops and wagonloads of baggage going the other. At every intersection the flow snarled into a knot, and the carriage jolted to a halt.

Elizabeth fanned desultorily during one such wait, her eyes falling on a long line of wounded men, lying motionless in the side street.

And there was Michael. He lay on a pallet, the nearest to her. His face was covered with dirt and a week's growth of beard, a soiled, bloody bandage wrapped around his forehead. Another showed at his waist, and a third banded his thigh. He looked dead. At the far end of the line a man checked bandages, and there was as a British soldier standing with musket and bayonet, watching. Neither doctors nor guards would be set on dead men. He must be alive.

She felt a flood of relief, and then it disappeared as she was back at Les Chenes, while Tarletan tossed a paper to Justin. "That should be what you want," he had said. "It authorizes his arrest when you find him, and calls on any officers present to sit for a court. Signed by Clinton, Cornwallis, and Arbuthnot."

Justin had laughed mirthlessly. "A prompt arrest, a quick court, and a speedy execution."

It came to her now, that there was only one man Justin would be that happy to see dead. Suddenly she was in his arms again, in memory, in the cool dark above her father's stable. It had been so clean, almost innocent. There had been no fear, then. He'd been so tender, so gentle. And he was lying there unconscious, waiting for Justin to come and—.

The carriage started forward, and she quickly halted it with a tap on the roof. The driver's black face appeared in the trap.

"Sampson. That gentleman at the end of the row of wounded? I want you to get him into the carriage without anyone seeing. The carriage will screen you from the street."

The driver swallowed convulsively. "That guard, ma'am, he got a musket."

"I'll distract him, and the doctor, too. You just do as you're told. And, Sampson. No one is to know about this. No one."

As she stepped to the ground, the sentry's face turned in surprise, and the doctor froze with his ear six inches from a patient's chest. She walked down the row slowly, looking at each face, but never stopping. For the soldier she had a pleasant, but not inviting, smile. His head turned after her, and when she reached the end of the row and turned around, he was facing her, his back to the carriage.

The doctor bounded to his feet and hurried to her, trying not to ogle as fine a figure as he could remember seeing. "If I may say so, this is hardly the place for a lady. Are you searching for someone among the wounded?"

Elizabeth moved a little to one side, so the sentry would still be able to see her. "No one in particular, sir. I had friends who remained in the city, and I simply wondered whether any of them were among the wounded."

"Almost I wish you had recognized a few, if you'll forgive me. At present most of them are listed as 'unknown rebel found among ruins.' Why, we could have John Rutledge himself here, and not know it."

"Then you're not—. You must forgive me this time, I'm afraid. I thought you were one of the rebel doctors."

"No, no. I'm Dr. Lynus Allen, of New York, and a good King's man."

"How interesting." She glanced toward the end of the row. Michael was gone, and his pallet with him. "However, Dr. Allen, since you don't have anyone I know, I expect I'd better be going."

His fatuous grin faded. "But I don't even know your name, Miss—

"Doctor Allen," she said over her shoulder, "so very nice to have met you." With an enigmatic smile, she left him standing there.

Sampson's face was covered with sweat despite the spring coolness, but Elizabeth didn't notice. She had eyes only for what would be inside the carriage. Michael.

He half sat, half lay on the floor, still unconscious, his pallet wadded up beside him. Lord, but he was dirty. But the dirt could be washed away. And with the help of Sampson, and Solange, whom she'd sent ahead to open the house, she could keep him hidden. Once he was healed—she smiled, and touched his face in spite of the dirt. Once he was healed, and knew who'd cared for him, she'd have her Michael back. It'd be as it had been, innocent and clean again.

Gabrielle's carriage rolled to a halt at the old city gate. The sentry spoke, casting a curious glance at Daniel, who, in livery, was following on a horse. "Can I see your pass, ma'am, please?" As in England, it was best to be very polite to people with carriages and footmen.

"I'm afraid I don't have a pass, sergeant," Gabrielle said. "Perhaps I could speak to your officer."

The sentry blinked. No pass, and wanting to see an officer. Lieutenant Fortnum didn't like things that weren't routine. "Yes, ma'am. I'll see, ma'am. And I'm a private, ma'am."

Gabrielle waited until the officer appeared, then put on her prettiest smile and began to chatter. "I know I should've asked my brother for a pass, captain, but I quite forgot until it was too late. I was ready to visit dear Elizabeth, that's my brother's wife, whom I've not seen in I don't know how long, but he was off being a soldier. I don't really think it's fair of General Clinton to order him off somewhere just when I need him, do you, captain? I mean, whatever am I to do? I do so want to see Elizabeth." She finished up breathless, and fluttered her eyelashes at him shamelessly.

The lieutenant found himself caught between confusion at her words and admiration for her eyes. His chest puffed out. She really ought to be under the protection of an officer. Perhaps—. He saw the sentry out of the corner of his eye, looking at him in astonishment. He tried to make his voice gruff. "I'm a lieutenant, miss, not a captain. Lieutenant Thomas Fortnum, 33rd Foot. Now, miss, who are you, and who is this brother of yours who could've given you a pass?"

"Well, you should be a captain. You certainly look like a captain. My brother? Why, Justin Fourrier, of course. Major Justin Fourrier. I'm Gabrielle Fourrier. Surely he's mentioned me."

"I'm afraid I've never had the pleasure of meeting Major Fourrier. I have heard of him, of course."

A sigh of relief escaped her. Quickly she covered. "Then you will help me? Oh, thank you, captain. I mean, lieutenant. How sweet you are to let me in."

"But I didn't say—I can't—" He took a deep breath. "Wait just one moment, please, Miss Fourrier." Gabrielle smiled as he disappeared inside the guardhouse, and darted out again. "A pass, Miss Fourrier. I can't let you into the city, or out of it, for that matter, without one. Therefore—" He smiled and made a leg.

"Why, I just don't know how I'll ever thank you. Really, I don't." She fluttered her lashes again, and tapped on the carriage roof. The vehicle rolled into the city.

Fanning herself with the pass, she fell back against the cushions. Thank God, that was over. She'd had no idea how she was going to enter the city. She'd only known she had to.

When Daniel had returned to Tir Alainn and told her Michael was dead, it'd been more than she could bear. She'd taken to her bed for two days, crying constantly, refusing to eat, refusing to see anyone. Something had happened, though. When she woke up on the third day, she found she'd cried away all the belief that he was dead. Another thing she'd cried away. It didn't matter any more that he'd been Elizabeth's lover. At least, not as much as it had. She loved him more than she hated what he'd done. He couldn't be dead, or she'd know it. And that meant she'd wasted two days she could've spent helping him.

Immediately she set out to discover everything she could about the prisoners taken at Charlestown. She read every list of them put out. And the lists of the dead, as well. She had Daniel deliver letters to everyone she knew and devoured the replies he brought her. She bribed boatmen going into Charlestown, and questioned them closely when they left.

She found Mr. Petrie, confined in the Provost below the Exchange. He'd burned *Hussar*—destruction of captured property, the British called it—though she couldn't imagine why. She'd found Henri, on parole, but confined to Charlestown and sharing rooms with four other officers on parole. She'd even discovered Louis, being cared for on a farm and forgetting his leg with the widow who owned it. But there was not a whisper of Michael.

It had taken a lot of agonizing before she could admit that there was one person she hadn't tried who might know where he was. Know where he was? He might well have gone running to her, if he could. Elizabeth. She could still hardly bear to think the name. Every time she thought of the woman, she saw her naked, her arms and legs wrapped around Michael. The trollop! Damn her! She had to grit her teeth to keep from screaming, or snarling. She wasn't sure which.

She alighted before the house on Broad Street and calmly started for the door. Before she'd taken two steps she saw Elizabeth, back in the garden, and had to master her emotions again.

Elizabeth laid a last flower in the basket and motioned the maid to take it away. "Why, dear Gabrielle," she said in a velvety voice. "Crawling back to Papa Fourrier, are you, now that the city's lost? A hint. Be very humble, very contrite. Perhaps then he won't be too hard on you. Of course, you must realize you'll have to be cloistered at Les Chenes for a time, until the scandal of your having been married to a rebel dies down."

"Where's Michael?" Gabrielle asked bluntly. The look that came on the other woman's face jumbled her emotions. Elizabeth knew. He was alive. Thank God. But he *had* gone to her. Damn him! Damn Elizabeth! Damn the slut!

Elizabeth tried to cover. "God knows where he is, but I rather doubt he wants you there."

Gabrielle's palm exploded against Elizabeth's cheek. Before the stunned woman could move, all the pent-up fury in her let go. Again and again she struck, as fast as she could, ignoring Elizabeth's attempts to fend her off.

It wasn't enough, Gabrielle thought savagely, just beating her. She had to show Elizabeth for what she was. She'd strip her naked, like the common tart she was. That was it! She grabbed the shoulders of Elizabeth's dress.

Elizabeth struggled to get loose. Then she was free, and only the side of the stable kept her from falling.

"Now, you bitch," she hissed, and cut off with a strangled gasp. Her dress, pulled off her shoulders, had rolled and twisted in the struggle, until it held her arms pinned tightly to her sides. She was naked almost to the waist and couldn't even defend herself. She took a deep breath to scream.

"Be quiet," Gabrielle snapped. "Do you want the servants to see you like that?"

Elizabeth was silent. She wet her lips and tried to slide along the side of the stable, but Gabrielle followed. "Leave me alone!"

Gabrielle smiled coldly. "Your hair is disarrayed. I'll fix it." She fastened two hands in the raven locks.

"I don't—" Elizabeth begam as Gabrielle pulled her away from the wall. Then she saw the rainbarrel. "No!" was all she had time for before she went into it head first.

Gabrielle forced her head as deep as she could and held her there. Elizabeth's feet kicked wildly in the air. Did she never wear drawers, Gabrielle wondered. If only she had a stick and a free hand. She'd beat a tattoo on that pale rump to rouse every redcoat in Charlestown. Suddenly she pulled the other woman up. "Where?" she asked simply.

Elizabeth gasped and gulped for air. "You—! You bitch! I'll kill—. Don't!"

Gabrielle shoved her down again. This time she tried to ignore the widely kicking legs, the body writhing vainly on the barrel rim. She had to hold her down until she broke. She had to make her talk if she half-drowned her. She had—. Elizabeth's struggles had faded to weak jerks. Hastily she pulled her into the air. Before she could ask, Elizabeth was gasping out the answer.

"The attic. Please. Don't. The attic. Swear it." She began to sob softly. Gabrielle released her, and she fell to the ground.

Gabrielle's mouth twisted as she looked down at Elizabeth. In the attic, she said. They'd see. In the mean time, though, she didn't want to touch the woman again. She found a stick and prodded her. "Get up. Get up, I say."

Elizabeth's sobs diminished. "It's no use, you know. You can't get him out of the city without the army finding him, and Justin has an order for his arrest and trial. If the British take him, they'll hang him. If you don't leave, I've a good mind to call them. Just one shout in the street would do it." Half-soaked and half-naked, she began trying to wriggle her dress straight.

Gabrielle flicked her knuckles with the stick. "Stop that. Call them, Elizabeth. Call them and explain why you have a rebel colonel hidden in your attic. Oh, you don't want to? Then maybe I should. Michael Fallon is mine. He belongs to me. I may not be able to keep him out of other women's beds, but before I'll let *you* have him, I'll march him to the gallows myself. Now get up and take me to him.''

Elizabeth believed every word. It was just what she'd do herself. "I—. I have to straighten my clothes. The servants.''

"Leave your clothes as they are. Get up. Now.''

Elizabeth opened her mouth, and closed it again. Gabrielle's eyes left no hope of argument. She had a tiger's-eye ring that had that same look when the light hit it right. Awkwardly she rolled to her knees and got to her feet. Gabrielle prodded her toward the house.

Just as they started down the third-floor hall, toward the ladder that led to the attic, Solange, Elizabeth's maid, came into the hall.

"My God, Miss Elizabeth! Oh, my God, what happened, ma'am? Oh, my God!''

"Hush,'' Gabrielle said, "or you'll get this.'' And she brought the stick down hard across Elizabeth's shoulders.

With a startled cry Elizabeth staggered forward into Solange's arms, and they both fell to the floor. Gabrielle stared at the stick in her hand as if she'd never seen it before. The depth of her own rage frightened her. She'd enjoyed hitting Elizabeth. She didn't want to kill her, not quite, but if she'd had a whip, she'd have used it. She wished she'd had one.

The maid helped Elizabeth rearrange her dress, and Gabrielle made no move to stop them. She had no time for that now. She must think cooly, calmly, and clearly. "Both of you, up the ladder. And remember, if the soldiers come, if anyone comes, you're in much worse trouble than I am.''

Once she entered the attic, she forgot them altogether. Michael lay on a cot near the dormer, the blanket pulled up to his neck, chest rising and falling only slightly with his breathing. Tears started in her eyes as she knelt beside him. For the first time in a long time, he needed her, even if he didn't know it.

"I've had Solange bathe him,'' Elizabeth said, "and I've

shaved him every day. Be careful touching him. He's delirious most of the time, and sometimes he's violent. He half killed Sampson the first night.''

"Then you haven't—,'' Gabrielle murmured, smoothing his brow.

Elizabeth's face tightened. God, how she wanted to tell the chit they were in each other's arms every hour. She turned away and strode to the window.

"He's got a fever," Gabrielle said. "I'll need some Peruvian bark, and—.'' Suddenly he moaned and lashed out, striking her arm. She stared at him, horrified. Little James had hit her harder in play. He stirred again, dislodging the blanket. His side, from the ribs to below his waist, was a puffy mass of inflamed red, and in the middle of it a black shard of metal. She turned her blazing eyes on Elizabeth. "You left this in him?"

"I couldn't get it out of him. Or the piece in his leg. Don't look at me like that. I tried. The first time was when he attacked Sampson. Then later, he moaned so, and there was so much blood. I said, don't look at me like that. Men can live with such things. William Darby has fought three duels, and he has a pistol ball in him from each of them. Michael is certainly hardy enough—.'' She stepped closer and, for the first time, got a better look. Her face went pale. "It, it didn't look that bad the last time I—. He's going to die, isn't he? God help me! He can't die up here. He can't—.''

Gabrielle surged to her feet and took brief pleasure in slapping Elizabeth's face. "Get hold of yourself. He isn't going to die. Not if you help me. Do you have any medicine at all? Any Peruvian bark, or laudanum, or—?"

"This isn't a doctor's house," Elizabeth snapped. She was still on the edge of hysteria.

Gabrielle considered another slap and regretfully decided not. It might send her over the edge instead of pulling her back. "Then I need a small pair of tongs, or large tweezers, or even a pair of scissors. And lots and lots of boiling hot water. And mouldy bread. Is there any mouldy bread in the kitchens, Solange?"

The maid tore bulging eyes away from Michael's wound.
"Yes, ma'am, there be some. It always happen when the
weather wet. Ain't no way for to stop it."

"Good." Gabrielle turned the black woman toward the
ladder. "You get me all the mouldy bread you can."

"Mouldy bread!" Elizabeth exploded. "What in God's
name are you doing?"

"Our head groom used to make poultices out of it. He
cured hurts where other men would have shot the horse."

"Grooms. Horses. This is a man you're talking about."

"Yes, it is. My man. And he's not going to die. If that
means horse cures, witch doctors, or sacrificing you to Jupi-
ter, so be it. And you'll help. You and Solange will hold him
down while I, while I take out the metal."

"You're crazy! He's strong as a bull. The three of us
together couldn't—"

"He's dying!" Gabrielle squeezed her eyes shut and
opened them again. She had to keep control. "He's dying,
and he doesn't have a baby's strength left in him. With the
fragments in him, he hasn't a chance. So you'll help me,
damn you. You and Solange will help me."

Solange brought the things Gabrielle had asked for in three
trips up the ladder. The bag of mouldy bread had a pair of
scissors in the bottom, and two basins. Since she assumed the
water was to wash something, she brought soap and towels.
Her last trip was for a pile of freshly laundered sheets, for
bandages.

The last shook Gabrielle. She'd forgotten something as
important as bandages. What was she doing? She didn't
know anything about doctoring. She should get a real doctor
for him, a doctor who—. A doctor who might very well turn
him in to the British. No, she had to do it herself. She'd just
have to use common sense. Pray God her common sense
didn't kill him.

Because there was soap, she washed her hands, though the
other two looked at her oddly. For good measure she washed
all around the wound, as well. Then it was time to put a basin
tight against his side beneath the dark metal and begin.

Solange lay across his feet, and Elizabeth held his hands in place against his chest. Muttering a prayer, she used both hands to grip the metal splinter with the scissors.

He moaned, but he couldn't move against them. It made her want to weep. Normally he could've picked all three of them up in his arms, and now they handled him as they would a child. But she couldn't weep. There wasn't time for it. She took a deep breath and pulled. He groaned, but the fragment didn't move. She pulled again. Harder. Harder. A strangled breath whistled out of his throat. Suddenly the splinter came out, followed by a stream of blood and corruption.

Elizabeth and the maid gagged and turned their heads away, but Gabrielle forced herself to put trembling hands against the inflamed flesh and knead. Bloody pus flowed into the basin. She made herself continue until all that came out was blood. With a sigh of relief, she reached for a bandage. And stopped.

Suppose that wasn't the only piece of metal. Suppose there was another. Would it do any good to remove one, and leave a second? There was only one way to find out. Whitefaced, she hesitantly put two fingers into the wound. Was there anything hard, anything that might be—? There. She gripped it precariously, pulled slowly. Slowly. A second piece of metal joined the first. Smaller than her fingernail.

She swayed and caught herself. It didn't matter. All that mattered was Michael. She made the poultice of the mouldy bread—horse medicine, her conscience shrieked—her hands shaking so she could barely put it in place. Then she went on to his leg. It had to be done, and she did it. She tied the last knot in the bandage around his thigh, and began washing her hands again. She felt so tired, but there was no time to rest.

"I'm taking him back to Tir Alainn with me, Elizabeth. And you're coming, too, for insurance. Have Solange pack for you, and have your carriage brought round. Then—."

The small caravan, two coaches, one piled high with luggage, and a liveried Negro riding in front, halted at the Meeting Street guardhouse. Ahead lay Tir Alainn.

"May I see your pass, ma'am? I beg your pardon—ladies."

"Of course, lieutenant."

The officer read the pass, and read it again. "I'm terribly sorry, ladies, but this pass is only for one, a Miss Fourrier."

"I am Miss Fourrier," Gabrielle said. "This is Mrs. Fourrier, my sister-in-law. She's quite ill, I'm taking her to the country."

Elizabeth was so pale with fear that their skirts, or the lap-robe she clutched, would shift and reveal Michael hidden under the seat, that she did indeed look ill.

"I quite see that," the lieutenant said. "And I do sympathize. Stab me if I don't. But, you see, I just can't—."

"Can't?" Gabrielle snapped. "Can't, lieutenant? My brother, this lady's husband, is Major Justin Fourrier. Perhaps you've met him, or his friend, Colonel Tarletan. Or seen him accompanying General Clinton? I am to tell them that you made Mrs. Fourrier languish here, expiring? Because you *can't* let us by with a signed pass?"

He swallowed suddenly. "Perhaps if I get someone senior to myself. If you'll just wait a moment?"

"I've had quite enough of waiting." Gabrielle tapped on the roof. "Drive on."

The carriage lurched forward, and then both had passed the guardhouse. Gabrielle held her breath. If that young lieutenant wasn't sufficiently overawed by the names she'd flung around, then dragoons would be sent to bring them back in minutes. Five minutes passed. Ten. At twenty minutes she fell back on the cushions.

"We're clear," she whispered. Immediately she turned to Michael, making him a more comfortable place on the other seat. Elizabeth, whimpering with self-pity, was staring dully straight ahead. Daniel was hurrying on before them; a doctor would be waiting at Tir Alainn. Michael would be safe. And she'd see he was never touched by the war again.

When Justin dismounted at British headquarters on King Street, the sentries on the gate snapped to attention, took a second, startled, look at his scarlet coat, and slowly went back to rigidity. That he was a major was clear enough, but the color wasn't quite right, and the cut was definitely wrong, for an officer of regulars. And provincials just didn't wear the red.

Justin hurried through. He knew what had engrossed the sentries; he had no time to correct their impudence. Before this campaign was over, though, he'd get the recognition he d_served. And damn fool sentries would bloody well know his uniform.

He grabbed two captains in the entry hall. "Where's Ban?"

"Tarletan?" said one. "Think he's trying to avoid old Pratt, here. Ay, Pratt?"

"Owes me twenty guineas," Pratt said. "He bet I wouldn't ride my horse up to the third floor veranda the other night, then, me being bosky, slipped away without paying. Ain't right, that. Ay, Fourrier? Ain't right, taking advantage of a man being in his cups."

"If you can't hold your liquor," Justin said with a thin smile, "then don't drink, or don't gamble."

"Major Fourrier?" a lieutenant said above the laughter of Pratt's companion. "Major Justin Fourrier?"

"I am," Justin said shortly.

"Thomas Fortnum, sir. 33rd Foot. I had the pleasure of signing a pass for your sister to enter the city this morning."

"Gabrielle? You signed a pass for Gabrielle?"

"Yes, I did. Seemed she'd forgotten to ask you. It was my privilege, of course. But since she's visiting you, I wonder if I might call on her. I say, she isn't engaged, is she?"

"No, she isn't engaged," Justin said slowly. "Are you certain it was my sister? Slender, hazel eyes, brown hair?"

Another officer piped up before Fortnum could answer. "Afraid you're out of the money, Fortnum. Lady ain't in the city any more."

Pratt laughed. "And how would you know, Gorman?"

"I know because she went through my post about two o'clock, her and the major's wife. Said they were going out to the country because Mrs. Fourrier was ill."

"I say, I hope there isn't anything off about this. Lady gets a pass to come into the city for a visit, and three hours later she's gone."

Why? It kept pounding in Justin's head. Why would Gabrielle come to Charlestown? Why would she and Elizabeth leave the city? Why would Elizabeth go with her? Pratt's last remark caught his ear. "Off? Certainly not. My wife has been feeling badly for the last few days. No doubt she and my sister have gone up to Les Chenes."

As the chance of trouble dispersed, so did the officers, and so they missed the look on Justin's face when the answer came to him. Michael Fallon. He couldn't reason how, for Gabrielle and Elizabeth fought like stray cats, but Fallon was at the root of this. By God, he'd find out how.

He strode out of the house, a scowl fixed on his face, and met Tarleton coming up the walk. "So there you are, Justin. Get your men mounted. The fox is afoot; we must move fast if we're to run him to the ground."

"What? What fox?"

"Continental foxes, that's what I'm talking about. Those Virginia reinforcements have finally reached the province, or so a deserter tells me. Four hundred men under one Buford. Only, now they've discovered the true situation in South Carolina, they're trying to escape back to Virginia as fast as they can. It'll be saber practice. Come on!"

"I must stop off on the Santee. My wife—"

"Hell's teeth, man, we have to ride our bums off now to catch them before they're in North Carolina. We can't go to the Santee just because your cods are hot. Man shouldn't waste that on his wife, anyway. When this is done, you'll find some little rebel wench and split her up the middle. It's fighting now. Come along, then. Let's go."

Justin followed slowly. Damn Buford. Damn all Virginians. Well, if it had to be done, they'd ride the bastards into the ground. And then he'd find some answers, if he had to flay the hide of every man, woman, and child at Tir Alainn.

29

Daniel carried Michael up from the drive laid him on his bed. The doctor turned to Gabrielle and Elizabeth, rolling up his sleeves.

"If you ladies will leave now, I can begin."

"I'll remain," Gabrielle said.

"And I," Elizabeth added with a defiant look.

He smiled and took an avuncular tone. "I'm afraid you don't quite understand. This isn't going to be pleasant, even for me. For delicate persons such as yourselves—"

"I intend to stay with my husband, doctor," Gabrielle said sharply. She looked contemptuously at Elizabeth. If she tried to put her out, Elizabeth would likely cause a fuss. "And this—lady might as well stay also."

"Very well," the doctor sighed. He removed the poultice, snorted, and threw it on the bedtable. Palpating the wound area he spoke without looking at the women. "You really shouldn't have removed the metal fragments. Not knowing what you were doing, you might have done great harm. It should have been left to a trained physician."

"Had I left it," Gabrielle replied levelly, "you'd have a mortician's part to play. And now?"

"First he must be physicked. Peruvian bark for his fever, and it's a grave one. Jalap and tartar emetic to purge his system. Cantharides for a blistering plaster to stir the production of good blood. And, of course, I'll draw off some of the bad blood that has his wounds so inflamed." He chose a medium blade on his fleam and wiped it on his sleeve.

Gabrielle took a step toward him. "If you—. If you touch him with that, I'll order my slaves to whip you off of this plantation."

"He's a doctor," Elizabeth gasped. "He must—" She

faded into silence as the other two ignored her, the doctor
startled, Gabrielle fiercely determined.

"My dear Mrs. Fallon, I assure you there's nothing to
worry about. The blood drawn off is replaced in an hour or
two. Why, venesection is as close to a sovereign cure as
exists. It's an ancient science, and believe me, it—."

"No!" Gabrielle bit her lip. Suppose he was right. He was
a doctor, after all, and—. No. She still had to rely on
common sense. God help her, she had to. "Doctor, I'm
sorry, but if bleeding would cure Michael, the British have
already made him immortal."

"Mrs. Fallon—."

"I'm sure you know what you're about. Really, I am. But
this time is different. I'm sure of that, too. So I'm going to
ask you to leave me as much of your Peruvian bark and
landanum as you can, and go. Please."

At last she managed to soothe his bluster and bundle him
into his carriage. She hoped he'd calm down enough to
remember not to talk about Michael Fallon. Just in case,
though, she'd better set men watching.

When Gabrielle reentered the bedroom, Elizabeth jerked
back from stroking Michael's forehead. They glared at each
other and Elizabeth defiantly stretched out her hand, but
stopped short of touching him. Gabrielle was staring at her,
eyes blazing. After a frozen moment Elizabeth made an
angry sound and moved away. Michael stirred, murmuring
in his sleep. Gabrielle put a hand to his cheek. The fever was
worse. She quickly began grinding the Peruvian bark. An
infusion would help. It had to.

"You shouldn't have sent the doctor away," Elizabeth
said. Gabrielle kept silent. "You can't know more than the
doctor does." Gabrielle ground more vigorously. "If he
dies, it's your fault."

"Shut up."

"I said—."

"And I said shut up." Gabrielle pounded the pestle vici-
ously.

Elizabeth's cheeks went red with rage. She opened her

mouth, and Michael sat up. Gabrielle gasped and ran toward him. She stopped as he stared with unseeing eyes straight ahead and stretched out a hand to Elizabeth.

"Don't leave me," he pleaded, and his chest heaved with the effort. "Please. I need you. I love you. Please don't leave me." Elizabeth flashed a triumphant look and started around the bed to him. His gaze never wavered. "Brielle. Love you. Swear it. Please. Brielle." Gabrielle brushed past a stunned Elizabeth. As soon as her hand touched his he sank back with a sigh. "Love you, Brielle. Must believe. Love you."

She clutched his hand. "I believe, Michael. I believe, my darling. And I love you."

His breathing seemed to ease, and he relaxed against the pillows. "Love you," he murmured again, desperation gone.

Elizabeth's eyes glittered, and her teeth were bared in a snarl. He was gone. It was all gone, all the hopes and dreams. She wanted to scream that it was a lie. But the old saying kept repeating in her mind. In wine and sleep, men never lie. Damn him. Damn her. Damn everything.

It was time to go. Gabrielle, crooning softly in Michael's ear, never noticed as she slipped from the room.

Her carriage still waited outside, luggage piled on top. Barring instructions the stablemen had watered the horses, and no more. Sampson moved along the team, checking harness. He opened the door for her, but she leaned her head against the carriage instead of getting in.

For the first time in hours, though it seemed like days, she remembered that she would have to face Justin and explain leaving Charlestown in Gabrielle's company. Before, she'd put off thinking about it. Something would occur to her, a way to wriggle out or shift the blame. It always did. But this time it hadn't. Her brain had been full of Michael, and nothing had come.

Michael. God snatch him to hell! Betraying her. Giving his love to that little bitch. And why should she care? Had she really ever thought of going back to when she had little idea of what he was doing and none of what she could do? That could never compare to what she had with Justin, the constant search for greater thrills that left her panting raggedly just from thinking of what they'd done, of what they would do. Like when Justin—.

Justin. She had to keep her mind on Justin, on explaining what had happened, on protecting herself. If it could be a way that gave Michael to Justin. How sweet that would be. Justin was always especially randy after killing. How would he be after killing Michael Fallon? And for her there'd be the added fillip of knowing she'd given him to Justin. It would be better, more exciting, than it had ever been before.

She stepped up into the carriage without looking back at the house. "Charlestown, Sampson. And quickly. Quickly."

Gabrielle and Martha held Michael while Sarah pushed the sheet under him, then turned him for her to tug it smooth and tuck it on the far side. He seldom woke, and though he recognized her when he did, he was always fearful for her, believing he was at the defense of Charlestown, or on the quarterdeck of the *Hussar*. That one terrified her, with him crying out that she had to run before the black angel. But at least he knew her. And his wounds seemed to be mending. She sat beside the bed and fanned him.

Daniel burst into the room, panting. "Mrs. Fallon, it's your brother, Mr. Justin. He's coming, with a lot of men." A crowd of murmuring servants gathered in the hall.

Gabrielle calmly laid down the fan. "How long before he gets here?"

"Hour, ma'am, maybe little bit more. They ain't pushing hard, but they done crossed the Black River."

"Then we'll have to leave. Quickly." A collective sigh went up from the listening servants. Gabrielle shook her head. "Elizabeth!"

"She didn't set them on us, ma'am. Somebody seen her take the Clements Ferry Road. She gone to Charlestown. These coming from the north." He stopped awkwardly, his black face creased with worry. "Ma'am—. Ah, ma'am, they say Mr. Justin, he mixed in some killing up to the Waxhaws, with that Colonel Tarletan. I hear they kill a whole bunch of soldiers after they surrender."

Gabrielle sighed. It sounded like Tarletan, and like Justin. She'd given up long ago trying to disbelieve the tales. "Well, he won't kill anyone here because he won't find anyone. Daniel, you hitch the best team of horses to the carriage. Martha, you get James and his clothes together. I'll pack for my husband and myself. Sarah, set some men to burying the plate. And send runners to the quarters. Tell the people they're to hide in the woods, and drive all the stock with them. Horses, cattle, pigs, sheep, chickens, everything. And they can use what they need until we come back. Now move."

Justin studied Tir Alainn from the tree line. A flash of light came from the far side of the house, and another from the trees behind it. He smiled and spurred forward, the squadron bursting out of the trees behind him.

They'd done it before, and each man knew his task. Some peeled away toward the slave quarters, and others toward the stables. Justin leaped from his horse and ran up the front stairs, pistol in one hand, saber in the other. A half dozen men followed at his heels. He kicked open the door and plunged through with a cry of, "Come out, Elizabeth! Gabrielle! Come out!" The words rang emptily in the hall. Everywhere were signs of hasty flight, half-open drawers with clothes and linens hanging out, cabinet doors standing wide, light patches on the walls where pictures had been removed.

He pushed open the study doors. Fallon's private place. He put up his weapons. It was just an empty room, but it had the feel of Fallon in it, as if some part of the man was imbedded in the walls. It was almost as if he had Fallon in his grasp. He trembled with the thought of it. That Irish guttersnipe, daring to touch a daughter of the Fourriers, daring to mix his bastard blood with theirs. And he'd dared to touch Elizabeth, once? What else had he done with her? Everything came to Fallon. Money, ships, plantations. Everything that

Justin wanted went to him. Jean-Baptiste seemed to take—. No, not Papa. It was Fallon who would burn. He pushed over a cabinet in a crash of breaking glass, and it felt like hitting at Fallon himself.

A man looked in the door, and quickly moved on. Justin was busy. He tipped over the desk next, then smashed chairs against it. He ripped down curtains until there was a mound of broken wood and stiff cloth in the middle of the floor.

Next to the fireplace, among the fire tools, was a turkey-wing fan. He used it to brush away ashes, and then to slowly fan the coals he uncovered. Bit by bit he added kindling, and then larger pieces of wood, fanning all the while. The knots that gripped his brain always went away when something was burning. A lean, long-nosed officer strode in, raising his eyebrows at the blaze in the fireplace. "We found four marsh tackies in a pen by the river, and we've rounded up nine blacks. That's all. I know for a fact this plantation has over three hundred slaves and one of the finest stables in the colony."

"Did you expect them to leave it all for us when they went, Captain Gordon?" Justin was transferring a burning knot from the fireplace to the pile of demolished furniture, and then another. "Get everyone clear of the house. I'll question those blacks outside." Runnels of fire ran quickly along the heaped curtains as he followed the captain outside.

The captured slaves, seven men and two women in rough, field-hand's clothing, lined up in the drive. Justin took a pistol in each hand and motioned to the first man in line.

"You there, fellow. Yes, you. There were ladies here. Two ladies. I'll put an ounce of lead between your eyes, unless you tell me where they went."

The slave burst out volubly. "I works the rice, sir. I don't know nothing about the house." He jumped as Justin thumbed back the hammer with a loud snap. "I swears to you, sir. I don't know nothing about no ladies. Please, sir. I don't know nothing." Suddenly he darted between two horses, running down the drive.

Justin pivoted smoothly. The gun in his hand barked. The

man fell, jerked once, and was still. Justin sighed raggedly. It felt good, almost as good as taking a woman.

"One of us could've ridden him down, major," Captain Gordon said. "That was four hundred pounds on the Charlestown dock."

Justin pointed to the woman who was next in line. "Where did they go?"

The woman threw her hands up to her face. "Lord have mercy, sir, I don't know. I just knows they gone." Justin cocked his second pistol, and she screamed.

"Major," Gordon said. "Major, there's a rider coming. A rider, major." He heaved a sigh of relief when Justin eased the hammer back down. They always lost money when Fourrier got carried away.

Two of Justin's men escorted the rider—one of Tarletan's green-coated troopers. Before he could speak a shattering of glass brought everyone's head around. Flames roared out of the study windows.

"Well?" Justin said, turning back.

"A message, sir." The trooper leaned forward to hand a sealed note to Justin. "From your wife, sir."

"My wife?"

"Yes, sir, so Colonel Tarletan said. It came from Charlestown, with orders for the colonel to search this plantation for some rebel officer. The colonel said you'd be taking care of that, sir."

Justin turned the note over in his hands, staring at it with hooded eyes. "And this, ah, rebel officer's name?" he asked softly.

"Fallon, sir. Colonel Michael Fallon."

Justin ripped open the letter.

Darling Justin,

I have a wonderful surprise for you. I was starting to leave the city for Les Chenes when I encountered Gabrielle. It didn't occur to me then to wonder what she was doing there, but mindful that it would please you and Papa for her to return to the family, I managed to extract an invitation to Tir Alainn. Despite her reluctance I hoped to persuade her to come to Les Chenes. Imagine my surprise at discovering on arrival why she had been reluctant, and why she had been in Charlestown. Michael Fallon is there, wounded, and she had gone to buy medicines. Of course, I immediately returned to Charlestown and informed the authorities.

Despite her hysterial threats against me, I plead your understanding and forgiveness for Gabrielle. I fear her mind may have been unhinged by all that has happened, and she may not be entirely responsible for what she says.

When you have taken Fallon, my dearest, come to me. I will await you in our special place, in the way you like me best.

With all my love,
Elizabeth

He read it a second time and shook his head. An explanation for everything. Or was it, a tiny voice whispered.

"Burn everything," Justin said. "Burn it all to the ground."

"Sir, there's a warehouse down by the river bulging with rice, a fortune in it. And there are barges, too."

"Are eight blacks sufficient to row a warehouseful of rice to Charlestown, Captain?" Justin swung into his saddle. A smile came on his face. Flames shot up from half the house, now. "Burn it," he said. "Burn it all."

Michael lay in the farmhouse and took the broth Gabrielle spooned at him. He'd been demanding something solid for three days now. She'd only smile at him infuriatingly and push more broth into his mouth, or worse, mush.

By the fireplace Mrs. Johnson, the farmer's wife, watched Martha intently as she minded the pots, stirring this one, seasoning that one. Several times her hand twitched as if she wanted to take the spoon herself. Finally she turned away with a small laugh. "I do declare, Mrs. Fallon, I'm just not used to having somebody do for me."

Gabrielle cast a sidelong glance at the farmwoman, still

pretty, but fading from years of harsh work. "Every woman should be able to sit back and let someone else do for her once in a while. Mrs. Johnson, we owe you our lives. Accept our assistance, since you will not accept our money."

"The colonel's shed blood for the cause," Mrs. Johnson said. "Least we can do is give him and his lady a place to rest and some food." She whirled as the door burst open and her daughters ran in, swinging James between them. "Mary! Alice! How many times do I have to tell you not to burst in here like that? And put that child down before you hurt him."

They obeyed, but Mary, just sixteen, kept a hand on him. "Ma, can I play with him? Just in the corner, with that old top? I like playing with babies. I hope my first is a boy." A blush covered the freckles that bridged her nose.

"Best wait till you're married," her mother said drily. "Mrs. Fallon?" She looked for Gabrielle's nod. "All right. You can take him over in the corner, then."

Mary beamed, but Alice, a year younger, sulked. "I don't want to play with no baby. They're messy."

"In that case," Mrs. Johnson said, "you can help with dinner. No. I won't force you to play when you don't want to. You just take up a spoon and help watch those pots."

Alice glared at her sister, spinning a top for James in the corner, and they stuck out their tongues at each other, but she did as her mother bid.

By the time Daniel and Mr. Johnson got back to the house for dinner, Michael had finished the broth. He looked wistfully at the roast as it was set on the table, but said nothing. It was no use asking just to be told no.

"Where's Ben?" Mr. Johnson asked as he put his hat on a peg.

"Over to the Corbin's to trade some eggs for butter and cheese," Mrs. Johnson said. "I told him to be back before dinner, but you know the boy."

"Like as not he and Patrick Corbin are off fishing." He sniffed at the roast. "That boy ain't here, he don't eat." He looked up in surprise as his fifteen-year-old son pushed open the door and ran in.

"Pa," Ben panted, "Pa, there's redcoat horsemen to the Tyrell's. A whole lot of them."

"At Tyrell's?" Mrs. Johnson asked. "That's out of your way by—."

"Hush, Ma," her husband cut in. "Tyrell leans to the crown." His voice shook. "Maybe they're just watering horses."

"Yes, sir, they were. I watched from the bushes. But I heard them talking, too." He swallowed and looked at his father. "They're looking for a lady and a wounded man, a rebel officer."

In the silence that fell the sound of Michael's feet striking the floor was loud. Sweat broke out on his face from the effort of sitting up on the edge of the cot. Gabrielle and Martha rushed to him, but he shrugged off their efforts to make him lay back down. "We must leave. Now. Not just for ourselves, Brielle, but for the Johnsons. If the redcoats find me here, they'll likely put Mr. Johnson, and maybe even Ben, in the same cell with me."

"Colonel," Johnson said. "You ain't in no condition to travel."

"Colonel Fallon is right," his wife said quietly. Everyone turned to look at her. "They have to hide until the soldiers are out of the area. The horses and the carriage are safe in the woods, and if they aren't at the house when the soldiers come, there's nothing to connect us to them."

"You're right," Gabrielle said. "Come, Daniel, help me get him to his feet."

"No need for that," Johnson said. "Just pull that cot out from the wall." He climbed up to the loft and returned with two long poles. "I made that cot when my wife was ailing one time, so we could get her out in the sunshine. See?" He fumbled under the edge and pulled out four leather loops, through which he ran one of the poles. Daniel quickly did the same on the other side.

Hastily everything that might tell of their presence was gathered up. Mary stuffed the top in James' pocket and reluctantly gave him to Martha. The procession left the house, first Johnson and Daniel with the cot, then Martha and James, and finally Gabrielle and Ben with the bundles of clothing. Johnson led them into a small hollow surrounded by a tight growth of myrtle. No stranger would ever suspect its presence, or theirs.

Gabrielle caught Johnson's arm as he was leaving. "God be with you, Mr. Johnson."

"And with all of you, Mrs. Fallon." He took one last, worried look at them, and hurried off after his son.

Michael moaned suddenly, and Gabrielle hurried to him. "Damn, the jouncing has opened his wound. Quickly, Martha, the laudanum."

She made it a large dose. When his breathing slipped into the deep, regular pattern of sleep, Daniel looked at her curiously. "Ma'am, you think you should of give him so much? He going to sleep for hours, now."

"It'll be best. We're going to move him."

"Miss Gabrielle, we safe here," Martha protested.

"Now listen to me, both of you. That woman doesn't want to hurt us, but her family must come first. Her husband might not betray us, but if they threaten him or her son, or worse, her daughters, she'll tell those soldiers where we are in an instant. I'd do the same for my family. And it's my family I have to protect. Now let me see. From what I remember, the Tyrell farm is that way. So we'll go just a little to the south of that."

"Ma'am," Daniel said, "that be toward the soldiers. And it straight away from the carriage and the horses."

"That means it'll be the last direction they'll think we'd go." She fastened the last bundle onto the cot. "And I know someone in that direction who might be able to help us. Come. We don't have much time."

30

Justin watched the man and his family being herded out of the farmhouse by his troopers. The woman didn't look bad, although a bit long in the tooth for his taste, but the daughters were a juicy pair. Perhaps there might be time for a little sport.

"Henry Johnson," he said slowly, and watched the man jump. "I've heard it said you're a damned traitor and a rebel, Henry Johnson. And that boy of yours. What is he, sixteen, seventeen? Prime age for the rebel militia."

Johnson followed Justin's gaze, and a low moan escaped him. Two ropes had been hung over a tree limb in front of the house. "Please, sir. You've made a mistake. We've never been on either side. The boy's just fifteen, sir, too young to be in the militia if he wanted to."

"On neither side, man? On neither side? You're either for the King, or against him. You're branding yourself a traitor."

Mrs. Johnson left her daughters for the first time, looking nervously at the mounted men. "We're King's people. Before God, sir. All he meant was, it takes him and the boy both to work the land, and that's why they never went forward to join the militia, the Loyalist militia. They'd never have truck with the other kind."

She'd spoken levelly, but wringing her hands all the while, and darting quick glances at the nooses waiting for her husband and son. She was ready to talk, Justin thought. She'd tell everything she knew.

411

"Then prove your loyalty," he said. "I'm looking for a man named Fallon. He's wounded and traveling with his wife. His carriage was seen heading this way six days ago. They may have a few blacks with them. Now, what have you heard or seen of these people? Quickly, now, and the truth."

"Nothing," Johnson said before his wife could speak. "We ain't heard nothing, seen nothing. I swear it."

Justin kept his eyes on the woman. She shook her head tightly and said simply, "Nothing."

The woman was terrified. The frustrated rage that'd been building in him for days was near boiling. She'd tell, damn her, or—

A gaunt trooper pushed his way past the prisoners. "Sir, I found this in the midden."

"God's teeth, man, I can smell where you found it. No, don't hand it to me. What is it?."

"Bandages, sir. From the look of them, whoever wore them was bad hurt."

"Hang them," Justin snapped.

All three women began screaming at once as the man and boy were dragged struggling to the tree. The boy leaped and bucked, fighting in silence except for ragged panting, but his father roared.

"You can't do this! We've got a right to a trial! You can't hang us without a trial! God's mercy! At least take the boy in! Take the rope off him! Ben! Give him a trial!"

Mrs. Johnson clawed at Justin's coat, sobbing, until he deigned to look at her. "I can tell you where they are. Please. We didn't know who they were. Oh, God, please don't hang them. Please."

"Where?" Justin growled.

Wild-eyed, she stared at her husband and son, nooses snug around their necks. The men at the ropes paused. "Not more than two hundred yards straight west from the house. It looks like a big clump of myrtle, but there's a hollow inside. We put them there just an hour ago."

"Hamilton! Reilly! Take twenty men. If they're not there, track them. They'll head west. With luck you'll find Fallon by dark. If you're not back here by daybreak, I'll follow with thre rest of the men. And remember, if anyone touches either of them, especially the woman, I'll kill him. Now go." He rounded on the men under the tree. "What are you waiting for? Get on with it, damn you."

Mrs. Johnson's scream ripped the air. "God, no!" She pulled her daughter's heads to her chest and put her face down. None of them saw Henry Johnson, or Ben, pulled kicking into the air.

"You people," Justin said when it was done. "You want to be on both sides. Every third farmhouse has a rebel dog hidden in the loft. But when the King's forces come around you're all Loyalist to the bone. Well, you'll learn better. We'll see how many of your neighbors still have trouble choosing a side after this."

"The women, sir," Captain Gordon said. "What do we do with them?"

"Let them show their new-found loyalty by entertaining His Majesty's troops. But save the youngest one there for me."

Shrieking, Mrs. Johnson tried to claw a way out for herself and her daughters. Laughing, the men grabbed her and Mary, dragging them to the barn, strewing torn bits of their dresses along the way.

Justin dismounted and pulled a dumbstruck Alice into the cabin. He threw her down on her parents' bed, slapped away her will to fight, and tore off her dress. It was all coming to a fitting end, he thought. By tomorrow Fallon would be in his hands. Alice's scream as he thrust into her seemed to be Fallon's scream. He began to laugh.

Gabrielle stumbled once again. Pain ran up her arms and legs, but she wouldn't let go of the stretcher pole. In truth, she was afraid that if she set it down, she wouldn't be able to pick it up again. Martha was laboring as hard as she, sweat rolling down her face, and even Daniel was panting. Only Michael, in his laudanum-deepened sleep, and James, sleeping beside his father, had made the night's journey easily.

Just after dawn she'd looked back. A pillar of smoke rose far behind them. The Johnson farm. She said a silent prayer and kept walking. She didn't mention it to Martha or Daniel. There was no need to frighten them.

As the sun gathered strength, the terrain became familiar. "Once we're over this rise," she panted, "we're safe. It's Tribando, the Hudson plantation."

She fell silent as they staggered to the top of the rise. Defeat washed over her, and she sank to the ground. The other eased the cot down and dropped beside it.

"Maybe—," Daniel said, but he didn't finish.

Below them a wide marble stair swept up to a pile of blackened timbers. Not even a tendril of smoke rose. Yet it had to have happened within the past few days. That much they could tell from the animals. Pigs, sheep, even a few cattle, perhaps two dozen in all, lay scattered haphazardly, clouds of flies buzzing over each one.

"What happened?" Martha asked, her voice hanging on the edge of tears.

Gabrielle shook her head. "I don't know. I just don't—. I wonder if this is what they did to Tir Alainn?" She took a deep breath and tried to catch hold of herself. Sally Hudson—her friend, widowed at Savannah—owned Tribando. Was she dead?

Something crackled in the brush, and a woman sidled out, watching them with feral eyes. Her hair was matted and her dress was torn. She held a brushknife in front of her with both hands.

Daniel moved between her and the cot, but Gabrielle motioned him back. Slowly, so as not to frighten the woman, she rose. "Don't be afraid. We won't hurt you. My husband is injured, and I need help for him."

"Fourrier," the woman barked. "Gabrielle Fourrier."

"Sally? Oh, my God, Sally. I'm not Fourrier any longer. I'm Gabrielle Fallon. Remember, I married the man who came to the reading circle? Michael Fallon."

Sally's knuckles whitened on the knife hilt. "Your brother

was here. Two days ago? No. Three. Sometimes the hours seem to go so fast, and then they hardly pass at all. I can't seem to keep it straight.''

"Sally, I—''

"He had men with him," she went on as if Gabrielle hadn't spoken. "Some had green coats, and some had red. Green coats and red coats. Tarletan and Fourrier." She made a horrible sound; it took Gabrielle a moment to realize it was laughter. "I couldn't chase them away, so I sent servants out with water. They forced their way in, and Fourrier knocked me down when I tried to get in their way. Tarletan made me serve them. Jack's brandy in Jack's study." Tears rolled down her cheeks, but she cried silently.

Gabrielle felt a desperate need to stop her. No more of what her brother had done there. She couldn't bear to hear more. "Sally, we can't carry Michael much further, but we have to keep going. Is there a cart left?"

"Why should I help a Fourrier?"

"Michael's not a Fourrier. Don't you remember him? He put a sprig of dogwood in your hair, and read you the poem about the shepherdess."

Sally peered at him blankly. "Is he dead?"

"No. No, he's had laudanum."

"The officers drank Jack's brandy. They didn't let their men have any, though. They sent them through the house for plate, pictures off the wall, dishes, even my dresses. Others gathered the slaves in the drive. They put them in a neck coffle and left them there all day without water."

"Sally, please."

"They laughed and told jokes, with their feet up on Jack's desk. Your brother, Justin, made a joke about Jack dying a hero's death. He said Jack drowned in a ditch. How could he know that?" Gabrielle wanted to make her stop, but Sally held the knife higher now, her eyes glittering. "Tarletan said I was a rebel bitch, but he'd like to mount me anyway. But Justin said I was his, because he knew me, and he'd picked the plantation. Finally Tarletan said I wasn't worth an argument. They gave me to a lieutenant of Tarletan's legion. He took me aside and tore my clothes, but I hit him with a candlestick, and hit him and hit him. Then I ran out of the house, all the way to the woods. Some of the men laughed, but none tried to stop me until an officer ran out, yelling that I'd killed Lieutenant Owen. Tarletan kept shouting, 'hoy, hoy, hoy. Catch the vixen and every man jack of you can mount her till she can't twitch.' " She laughed jerkily. "But they didn't catch me. No. I hid. I hid. Finally they began to leave. The animals they didn't take, they killed, sabering and bayonetting pigs and sheep. They even shot some horses that ran. Then they set the fire and rode away, the green coats toward Charlestown, with the slaves and the stock, the red to the west. I sat up here and watched it. Everything he built, burning, burning."

James suddenly sat up on the cot, knuckling his eye with a small fist. "Who's the lady, Mama?"

Everyone except Sally jerked as if fearful of what the boy might have heard. "Such a pretty child," she said. "I never had—. I wanted Jack's baby so badly. There's an old wagon behind where the stables were, and I think some of the tackies made it into the woods. Look." Before anyone could move she darted into the bushes, the cracking and snapping of branches marking her trail.

Daniel started after her, but Gabrielle stopped him. "No. First we carry Michael down to that wagon. Get up now, James. You can walk that little way."

The boatman looked doubtful, but he took the front end of the cot wordlessly.

Sally had said the wagon was old, but it had been less than the truth. Every board was dried and gray, and many were split. The wheels were warped; when Daniel shook one the entire wagon rattled. He climbed under it, around it, and in it, and finally dusted his hands.

"It ain't much, ma'am, but maybe it'll get us some place near."

"Then you go find one or two of those horses. What's the matter, Daniel?"

He shifted under her gaze. "Ma'am, it's that lady, Mrs.

Hudson. It ain't right to leave her here like this.''

Gabrielle's face hardened. "At the first farm we come to,
I'll tell the people she's here. No, Daniel, that's all. If it were
just the rest of us, without Michael, we could take her. But
Michael is here. If we have her with us people will notice us
the more. They know her hereabouts. And if Michael's
taken, he'll be killed. Justin'll see to that.'' She held up her
hands like scales. "Her life against Michael's. It's no con-
test.''

''But—''

Martha poked him in the chest. "You hush up, Daniel. A
man don't know nothing about it. You go on and get them
horses. Go on with you. Here, Miss Gabrielle, you let me
take that.''

Gabrielle relinquished the bundle she'd been lifting into
the wagon gratefully, and sank to the ground. James ran to
her, and she hugged him. "We're going somewhere safe,
Martha, somewhere far away. We're going to Georgia.''

"Georgia! Lord's sake, Miss Gabrielle, them British got
every stick and lump of Georgia!''

"Exactly. The fighting's over there. We'll go just as far
into Georgia as we can, until we find a place where they don't
even know the fighting ever started, and that's where we'll
stay. That's where we'll be safe until it's over.'' They would
be, no matter what it took. No matter what.

Four months later, in September 1780, Gabrielle was
patching James' shirt carelessly. Her worried gaze was on
Michael, coat around his shoulders against the early chill of
the Georgia hills, limping toward the cabin on his walking
stick. She'd told him he was exerting himself too much, too
soon, but he wouldn't listen. And she didn't want to think of
what she hadn't told him.

With each piece of bad news that she gave him, Tarletan's
successes, and now the defeat at Camden, he pushed himself
harder. Camden. Horatio Gates, the new general sent by
Congress, had blunderingly lead his army to disaster. In the
middle of the battle he'd fled, leaving that giant Bavarian, the

Baron de Kalb, to die trying to hold the field with his Continentals. The survivors had fled north after the general.

Even that hadn't shaken Michael's resolve. He refused laudanum, despite pain that often kept him lying awake at night. He fought the pain as if it were the British he could no longer come to grips with.

He bent down to kiss her fingers. "You shouldn't have to prick these sewing patches, lass. It's not the life I promised you."

"I don't mind," she said, but he smiled disbelievingly and went inside. She followed. "Michael, it's true. You're all that's important."

He dropped into a chair and pulled her down on his lap. "It's this that I say is important."

"Michael, your leg!"

"It feels better for having you sit on it. Now then. Martha has the boy down to the creek for washing him and the clothes, and Daniel's gone to the store." He unfastened the first button on her dress, and the second. "We have the cabin to ourselves for at least two hours more." He began to rain kisses on her satin breasts.

"Michael, stop." She knew he was just trying to distract her. An hour after they rose from the bed his dark mood would be back on him—blacker if past experience was a guide. "Darling, this must be talked about. You must stop taking the whole blame for the way the war's gone."

"I'm not—" With a sigh he let his head fall against her shoulder, and she stroked his hair. "You don't understand, Brielle. I promised you the world, and I've brought you down to a dirt-floored log cabin. I should be finding James a pony—and a tutor. Instead all he has is one top and Daniel's carved horses and what little I can teach him. And you, doing work that no lady should have to. I've a right to be in a fey mood. It'll take a miracle to recover the things you should have."

"Darling," she said hesitantly, "it might not be that—"

Daniel rapped on the doorjamb, keeping his eyes on the floor. "Colonel Fallon, Ma'am. Visitors."

Two men pushed past the boatman. "Henri! Louis! Oh,

Lord!'' Gabrielle sprang up, bursting into tears as she hastily fastened her bodice. Joy and trepidation warred in her heart. They were her brothers, and she loved them, but she wished they'd never come. Now Michael would find out. She glared at Daniel.

Michael had bounded to his feet, and the three men were engrossed, laughing and handshaking and backslapping. ''Brielle,'' Michael called, ''quit hiding in the corner. It's your brothers have found us, lass. Bring us some glasses and that jug of rum. Wait till you taste this, Louis. I think they make it by fermenting tobacco, then strain it through some of that Georgia clay.''

Louis peered into the glass Gabrielle handed him. He took cautious sip, and his eyes squeezed shut. ''God,'' he gasped. ''I think you're right.''

''It'll grow on you. Now Henri, I can understand Louis here being free, but how did you get out of Charlestown? They're not giving passes to officers on parole, are they?''

''Hardly that.'' Henri stroked his new thin mustache with a forefinger and smiled. ''In fact, they barely let us walk the streets. Well, it wasn't quite that bad, except for having Justin trying to talk me into turning coat. Didn't try it too often, thank God. Didn't want it too well known he had a brother was a rebel officer. Stab me, he didn't.''

''Two brothers,'' Louis murmured.

''But how did you get out? And why? If you're retaken they'll thrown you in a cell. And if they claim you were fighting—. Well, they hang you for breaking parole, you know.''

''I know. But they were bound to anyway. They're not satisfied with parole any longer. Strike me blue, but they're not. Clinton left Cornwallis with instructions to bring South Carolina back to the crown, and Cornwallis gave Nesbit Balfour instructions to force Charlestown back. He demanded oaths of loyalty to the King from all the prominent citizens and all the officers on parole.''

''But that's in violation of any parole I ever heard of,'' Michael protested.

''Not according to Balfour,'' Henri said. ''He said our

paroles only encompassed service with the American army. Stab me if he didn't. When some protested, he had them shipped off to prison in St. Augustine. Christopher Gadsden. Edward Rutledge. Thomas Heyward. Many of the older men, like Charles Pinckney and Henry Middleton, agreed and were accepted back into the fold. But I could see what was coming then. If the paroles only applied to service against the crown, then they'd soon enough be demanding we serve for the crown. So I stole a boat and rowed across the Ashley. Just blundered around then, until I ran into Louis."

"It's all of a piece," Michael sighed. "Bit by bit they're crushing us. How many will risk hanging rather than join the winning side? Oh, the hell with it. How did you find us?"

"We found your traces. There was a widow named Johnson and her two daughters who were running messages and medical supplies to Francis Marion under their petticoats. Then there was a teamster who'd seen you in a rickety old wagon, crossing the Savannah at Hutson's Ferry. Well, we didn't have an idea of where to look when we got down here. But we walked into Grierson's store, and there stood Daniel, trading deerskins and foxhides for salt and sugar."

"Wait a minute, now. You said something about taking supplies to Marion. Where's he operating? I thought the British had the Carolinas in a sack." Daniel muttered about chores and scurried out of the cabin.

"Are you joking?" Henri looked amazed. "Don't you hear any news here?"

Michael stared at Gabrielle's back. She'd suddenly busied herself over dinner. "Of course I hear," he said slowly. "Brielle and Daniel—. Brielle and Daniel bring me all the news from the store."

"Well, stab me, if doesn't sound like it. After Charlestown fell, it was damn rough, I'll admit. Redcoats and Tory militia ran wild. Justin wasn't the only one to write his own laws. For a couple of months it seemed like they couldn't lose. Then, in the middle of July, the whole state exploded. South Carolina's aflame from one end to the other."

"What he's trying to say," Louis put in, "is people were pushed as far as they could go. Partisan bands formed all over the state. Marion isn't the only one. There's Andrew Pickens and Thomas Sumter and William Davie and—.

"But what kind of fighting are they doing? Did they take part at Camden?"

"Oh, no. As a matter of fact, Marion got started because Gates, the fool, didn't want him. He rode in with some volunteers, and Gates took them for ragamuffins. Finally, he told Marion to ride off and do whatever damage he could, just to get rid of him. So, Marion's men raid supply convoys, prisoner details, isolated outposts, in fact, anywhere they can catch the British by surprise. Between raids they hide in the swamps, and if the pressure gets too bad, they go back to being farmers for a while."

"Of course," Henri said, "the other side has partisans, too, though they organize like regular militia. They rob and burn out anyone who hasn't sworn loyalty to King George. Cunningham's back, and Browne. And then there's a fellow named Wemys, and M'Girth, and, of course, Tarletan and Huck. And Justin. We mustn't forget Justin."

"Brielle," Michael said. "Gabrielle, turn around and look at me. Look at me, I said."

His eyes seemed to drill into her. "Daniel was just doing what I told him," she said finally. "Don't look at me like that, Michael. Darling, I did it for your own good."

"My own good! God's teeth, woman, what are you talking about?"

She stiffened. "Yes, your own good. If you'd known there was even a spark of resistance left, you'd have already returned, to get in the fighting again."

He slammed his walking stick on the table. "And I damn well will."

"You can't. Don't you understand that? You can't." She fought back desperately. "Henri and Louis are putting the best face on it they can, but listen to them. The Tories are regular militia, the patriots just farmers hiding in the swamps. One American army has been lost at Charlestown, and another at Camden. Do you think they'll be a third? The Carolinas are done for. As far as we're concerned, the revolution is over."

"Damn it, Brielle, it isn't over, and it'll never be over so long as one man still believes in liberty."

"It's been a fine struggle, Michael, perhaps even a noble struggle. But it's over with. I don't want to see you hang for treason. I don't want to take my, my child to live on the charity of Papa and Justin. You say you want to take us back to Tir Alainn, but you seem bent on leaving James and me in poverty."

"If the revolution is lost, then Tir Alainn is lost, and the rest with it. God's blood, if you don't believe in what we're fighting for any longer, you still must see that we have to win. Or you and I and James will spend our lives running and hiding. Aye, and Louis and Henri, too."

"Once it's over the British will be ready to rebuild. They'll be pardons for everyone, except a few like John Rutledge. Full pardons, Michael. We'll be able to take up our lives, and our property, again."

"Do you know me so little, then? For this, you lied to me. You lied to me!"

"Michael, I—"

His face a mask of cold rage, he turned away from her. "Louis, how many men of the Legion can you gather?"

Louis hesitated, glancing at Gabrielle before speaking. "Not many, I'm afraid. They're mostly dead, or prisoners. I can find two or three hundred if you'll take volunteers."

"No, only men who were with us before. For one thing, there's no time to train them, and for another it's hard to tell who to trust."

"Whatever you say, colonel. Now, horses are going to be a problem, but Henri knows a man—"

Gabrielle stared at Michael's back. He'd shut her out. He wasn't going to listen. It didn't matter how much sense she made. He'd wrapped himself in his stubborn male pride, damn him. Well, she could be stubborn, too. There was a weapon she could use to get through to him, a weapon to force him to give up this mad idea of going back. She turned and blundered up the ladder to the loft before she was tempted to use it.

On the cornshuck mattress she shared with Michael, she wept bitterly. All she had to do was tell him she was with child again, and needed him until after the baby was born. So much could happen in that time. Then why didn't she? The answer leaped to mind. He wouldn't believe her. He'd assume it was just another lie, and instead of pulling him closer it'd be a wedge to force him away more quickly. She put her hands to her stomach and wondered how much longer it'd be before she could feel the stirrings of life. And whether the child would be born with a father still alive.

31

Michael straightened his uniform, patched and cleaned by Martha, before riding out to inspect the Legion. Gabrielle had refused to touch it—or to do anything else to help him leave. Their talk was limited to her attempts to stop him. And that always made him think of how he'd been kept there, and lied to. Lied to! Damn it, couldn't she realize how important the cause was? He mastered his anger before it built into another cold rage.

The uniform, and his presence, put a spark in the men. For the first time they sat their saddles as if they really were the Irish Legion again.

There were only bits and pieces of uniform among them, but their tack was well cared for, he noted, and he never found a speck of dust on saber or pistol or carbine. They weren't as pretty as they'd been so long ago at Tir Alainn, but these men were hard, the best of the Legion. Forty-seven men, ready to ride behind Louis and Henri. And the flag. He stopped in surprise.

Young Tom Jarvis had ridden forward. "I did like you said, colonel. I laid low till I heard the Legion was forming again." He lowered the flag toward Michael. "My mama did the stitching, sir."

He saw right away what the boy meant. Stars, a little cruder than the rest, had been added. The last had a jagged streak of red across it, as if it were broken.

"For Charlestown," Louis said. "Where the Legion died."

Henri laughed. "But the Archangel Michael raised his hand, and we are reborn. Stab me if we're not."

Louis moved closer and spoke quietly. "Michael, the boy

has a right to be here. For all his youth, is he less a man than those of years who've signed the King's oath from fear?"

"Very well, then. Back to your places." He glanced toward the cabin. Gabrielle showed briefly in the door. Deliberately she turned her back and went inside. Martha was outside, holding an excited James by the hand, but at a peremptory call from the cabin she carried the protesting boy inside. Oh, hell. He whirled his horse to face the troops. His voice cracked like thunder.

"We are the last unit of the American army in Georgia." Suddenly the October air seemed colder, and the group smaller. "And that might well go for South Carolina, and most of North Carolina. Now, you've heard of the partisans, Marion and the rest. They are no army. Oh, they're running the redcoats ragged, making them protect against raids instead of moving on a campaign, but it'll take ten years to chase the British out that way, and then only if they decide it's no longer worth the price to stay. It takes an army to defeat an army, and that's why we're not going to join the partisans. We're going to North Carolina. And if there's no army to be found there, then we'll become the cadre for one. Major Fourrier, prepare the Legion to move out."

He took a last look at the cabin, but the door was still empty. With a rigid face he rode to the head of the column, moving north.

In early December Michael found the American army, at Charlotte, in North Carolina. As he led his men down from the high ground around the town his heart sank.

The only sentries were in the camp down in the hollow, ragged, thin, and miserable in the sharp wind and icy, misting rain. The rude shelters, of canvas and half-burned boards, hardly deserved the name. Garbage littered the camp, and a heavy stench hung in the air. Weary men stared numbly into fires, not even looking up as the Legion rode past. The sentries, shifting on rag-wrapped feet, eyed them sullenly.

"Hell and death," Louis muttered. "They make us look ready for a dress parade."

Michael frowned, studying the sea of churned red mud. Only luck had kept it from already freezing into knife-edge ridges that'd slash the feet of men and horses alike. If the army didn't move soon, it'd die there.

A heavy-set officer in a white coat with blue facings, and a leather jockey-cap, rode toward them. "I'll be damned," Louis said. "If William Washington's here, things can't be as bad as they seem. Colonel Washington! Colonel Washington!"

Washington reined in. "Fourrier! By God, I thought you were dead at Camden."

"Not so, as you can see. Colonel Washington, let me present Colonel Michael Fallon, of the Irish Legion."

"Pleased to meet you, Fallon. Fine-looking bunch of men, and the good Lord knows we can use them."

Michael gripped a firm hand. "Thank you, colonel. If you'll forgive me, from what I can see you can use a whole army. I'm considering taking my men on, and try joining with the men who fought at King's Mountain in October. An army that's won one battle can win others; I'm afraid your men look ready to lose again."

Washington shook his head. "You won't find many if you do. They were overmountain men, you know, and they considered it a personal thing. Ferguson sent threats to them about what he'd do if they didn't swear loyalty to the King." He laughed. "Stupid thing to do. most of those men barely cared what was happening this side of the mountains. Then he threatened them. And once they'd killed him and wiped out his command, they went home. Or most of them did. The rest will be joining us right here. We've a new commanding general. Nathaniel Greene."

"Another one," Michael growled. "I wonder when Congress will tire of sending their political cronies south. First Howe, who lost Savannah and most of his army. Then Lincoln, who lost Charlestown and all of his army. Then Gates. He only lost his army, without losing a city. I thought they'd make a hero out of him. But you say they've replaced him. Who's this, Greene, do you say?"

"He was at Trenton, commanded a division at Brandywine, and then the main column at Germantown. Since then he's been quartermaster general for the army. Cousin George, I mean, General Washington, handpicked him for us. Conditions will improve now. You'll see. Come, I'll show you where to camp. You know, I wanted to meet you back when we were in Charlestown."

"And I'd hoped to meet you, Colonel." He followed Washington, holding up his end of the conversation without really thinking about it. So Greene had been quartermaster general. Being moved to that from a field command wasn't exactly a recommendation for a general. It seemed they were in for another long hard spell.

When Greene sent for Michael, two weeks later, he wrapped his blanket and his saddle cloth around his shoulders before trudging up to the red brick courthouse. He was morosely cursing frozen mud when the sentry let him in.

Greene waited until Michael had disposed of his wraps before gesturing to a chair. "Sit, Colonel Fallon." His florid face was dominated by bushy eyebrows, and the backs of his hands were scarred.

"Thank you, sir."

Greene pushed a paper across the desk as Michael sat. "That is from your Governor Rutledge, sent, I take it, as soon as he discovered you were hardy again. It's a promotion to full colonel in the South Carolina militia." Michael murmured his thanks. "Yes, yes. But I have something else for you, and I hope you'll take it instead. A Continental commission. Lieutenant Colonel. I have some good Continental officers with me, but I need more."

Michael kneaded his hands, still stiff from the cold, and shook his head. "I'm sorry, General, but I can't accept. If I'm a Continental officer, you can send me where you want, if it's all the way to New England. But it's here I think I'm needed, and so long as I'm militia, I cannot be sent elsewhere."

Greene limped to the fireplace and poked up the fire. "Would it change your mind if I told you I intend to make South Carolina the seat of the war?"

"Sir?"

"I intend to run Charles Cornwallis off his feet. I don't dare face him with what I have now, not unless I have to. So I will split my forces, sending Dan Morgan—you'll be assigned to him—to the west of Cornwallis, against Ninety-six. Ninety-six. It always strikes me odd to see such a prosperous village named for its distance from Charlestown. I will move down the coast trying to cut his supply lines. Whoever he turns against will run away while the other raises havoc. And when Cornwall turns against that one, the first will strike. In that way we'll dance him around the Carolinas until he's run down and we've had a chance to whip some of these farmers into soldiers. Well, Fallon, does that sound like we're going to New England?"

Michael was stunned. The plan was daring as hell, and twice as dangerous. Had he really thought that Greene would be timid because he'd been a quartermaster? "General, it sounds to me like we're going to run his damned legs off. Almost do you convince me. Not quite, sir, but almost."

Michael was watching a rabbit turn on a spit when the scouts rode into camp, but he quickly followed them to General Morgan's tent. A crowd had already gathered. Washington and John Howard, who commanded the infantry, represented the Continentals. For the militia there was Davidson, from North Carolina, and McDowell, from over the mountains, and Pickens, who'd brought in his partisans.

Morgan worked his hands against the pain of arthritis all the while he spoke. "Cornwallis has got Benny out after us."

That brought a buzz of "Tarletan, Tarletan."

"What does he have?" Washington asked.

"The scouts give him plenty. He's got his Legion, plus the 71st Highlanders, the 7th Foot, and the 17th Light Dragoons. And at least two field pieces. I want camp broken in thirty minutes. William, you and Michael get screens out between us and them. It's time to run, boys.''

Michael didn't even have to tell Jarvis to blow To Horse.
The alarm spreading through the camp already had the Legion mounted. Michael looked regretfully at the half-cooked
rabbit and left it. It'd go bad before he could finish it.

The next few days were frantic, the Americans running,
crossing rivers only hours before the British running to catch
them. Michael and Washington kept a close eye on them,
sometimes even close enough to hear Tarletan's foxhunter's
cry of hoy, hoy, hoy, as he pushed his men on. Fatigue ran
through both camps, but the British took no rest. They
crossed the Pacolet River in the dark, just six miles below the
American camp. Michael rode half asleep in the saddle as
they abandoned camp, leaving the first food in days on the
cookfires. That night they stopped six miles from the Broad,
in a large, grassy area used for gathering cattle. Hannah's
Cowpens, it was called.

False dawn brightened into first light. The cavalry sat their
horses calmly, waiting in reserve a few hundred yards behind
the ridge on which General Morgan stood. Except for him
they might well have been alone. There was no sound except
the creak of leather, and a horse stamping.

Morgan had explained his plan to every officer, down to
the rawest lieutenant, in a mass meeting, and he'd told them
to explain it to their men the same way. On the morrow, he'd
said, they'd be waiting for Benny.

But he hadn't let it go at that. Michael had seen him a
dozen times during the night, passing among the men, laughing and joking, calming fears, even stripping off his shirt to
show the knotted scars where he'd been flogged by the
British as a boy. More than one of the militia had calmed to
the point of offering a jug of popskull. Morgan would take a
modest swig, tell the man to take a swallow if he needed it,
but warn him that a man too drunk to shoot straight might
well get pinned to a tree by a bayonet. Generally the man
looked at his jug, then corked it and put it away.

From over the hill drifted shouting, and the scattered

rattle of musketry. Tarletan had arrived, and as hoped, he wasn't delaying a minute in his attack. The musket fire grew louder. Here and there a man in the cavalry coughed nervously, or eased his saber in its scabbard.

"Easy," Washington said.

Michael looked back at his men without speaking. They'd be ready.

Scattered militiamen were deployed as skirmishers before the ridge. Two shots, Morgan had asked. Two shots, and aim carefully. Then they could fall back, around the hill to the protection of the cavalry. Then it'd be up to the two lines on the ridge, the first militia who were time-expired regulars, the second Continentals. From the sound of the firing, some were shooting more than twice. And then the first running militia appeared coming around the ridge. But they weren't alone.

"Damn," Washington yelled. "Benny's cavalry is on them." He drew his saber. "Colonel Fallon, can your bugler give us a charge?"

Michael's saber came free. "Bugler!"

The notes rang in the morning air, and with a concerted roar the cavalry sprang forward. Militiamen scattered to let the horsemen through. The green-coated dragoons of Tarletan's Legion tried to swing their attention from hacking at fleeing men on foot to fighting mounted men with steel in their hands. The masses of cavalry merged.

Michael beat aside a descending blade and slashed at his attacker. The man screamed as blood poured down across his face. All around him was the clash of steel on steel, the grunts of men's efforts to stay alive, the truncated screams of those who failed. His horse reared, screaming as a saber gashed its shoulder, but he mastered it. A burning pain along his leg told him he hadn't entirely escaped the blow. He cut at a man in front of him, not knowing if that was his attacker or not.

Suddenly the British were streaming away. For the first time Michael could see they'd come forward onto the field before the ridge. The British infantry advanced, regiments abreast, with a measured tread, their bayonets sloped pre-

cisely. On the far side the brass helmets of the 17th
Dragoons gleamed. The field already had its first covering of
dead, a notable number of redcoated officers and sergeants
among them. From where the attack had started, two
fieldpieces pounded the American lines on the ridge.

Washington rode up cursing. Tossing down a broken saber
he bent from the saddle to take one from the ground. "I
almost had him. Damn it all, I almost had him, and the
damned blade broke."

"Who?" Michael asked.

"Benny, that's who. Tarleton himself. He was with that
lot. Look there. He's trying to rally them to come again. We
can take them."

"We'd better take those guns." The cannon belched fire
through the clouds of powder smoke drifting around them.

"I think you're right. Forward!"

Once more they roared forward. The artillerymen saw
them coming. Desperately they swung the guns around and
fired. The first round was the solid shot they were using
against the distant American infantry. A single man was
plucked from the saddle. They swarmed over their guns,
then, ramrods and sponges twirling and spinning. A blast of
cannister ripped gaping holes in the charging line, and then
they were on the guns.

Michael used the flat of his blade where he could. He knew
the Royal Artillery of old. They wouldn't abandon or surrender their guns, and there were too few of them to stand
against the charge. In an instant it was done.

Michael looked around. There was Louis, and there Henri.
And young Tom with the flag. Before he had time for more,
someone screamed, "The ridge!"

He wondered for a moment if he was seeing things. With
the British infantry bearing down on them, the first line of the
Americans had shouldered their muskets and was marching
up the ridge. Even as he watched, the second line did the
same. Morgan was riding frantically down from the ridgetop,
shouting and waving his arms. The British infantry sprang
forward, shouting. And the 17th Dragoons swung onto the

field in line to face the American cavalry.

"What in hell's going on?" Washington shouted. "I just sent a messenger to the militia saying if they'd hit the left flank we could roll them up."

"Maybe we still can," Michael replied. He took a quick look over his shoulder. "Tarletan hasn't got the others ready yet. If we can cut through, and hit the infantry in the rear—."

"And if the militia shows up. Well, it's a damned small chance, but it's all we've got. Form! McCall! Harris! Form line abreast!"

Michael awaited the order calmly. Everything seemed to move at a snail's pace, with infinite time for the smallest things. He adjusted the chin strap on his brass helmet, and checked the wrist cord on his saber. Washington's sword crept upward. From the British came the tinny notes of a bugle, and the Dragoons moved forward. The sword floated downward. With a roar, time returned to its normal course, and the American line rolled ahead.

The lines smashed into each other, and Michael was again in a tangle of flashing steel and desperate men. Barely was there room to hack, and none for cut and thrust. Some of the dragoons fell back, trying to reform where there was more space. Michael pressed forward, Legionnaires at his heels, and the dragoons were forced back again. And again. On the ridge the British bayonets were less than thirty yards from the backs of the American line, still marching away. Suddenly, as one man, the Americans turned. There was no time to shoulder muskets. They dropped them to waist level as if to use bayonets and fired. The redcoat line staggered under the blow. At once the Continentals were on them, pushing bayonets. At that instant the militia came howling around the ridge, stopping to fire as each man chose, and tore into the British left.

First one by one, and then in bunches, the British threw down their arms and cried for quarter. "Tarletan's quarter," someone screamed, and a hundred voices echoed, "Tarletan's quarter."

In an instant the American officers were on their men,

beating aside bayonets and knocking muskets up. Michael
booted one man before he could bayonet a prostrate redcoat,
and rode his horse into another with an upraised saber.
"They're surrendering, damn you. Put down that saber, or
I'll have your hide for breeches."

"He's leaving," Washington yelled. "He's running." He
put spur to horse, his Continental dragoons streaming after
him. Tarletan and his British Legion cavalry, perhaps two
hundred in number, were riding away to the south.

Michael hesitated only a moment. There wasn't a British
soldier left standing who didn't have his hands in the air.
Continentals were already moving some off under guard, and
the militia were already beginning to loot.

"Major Fourrier," he shouted, "form the Legion."

"Yes, sir. Bugler, sound assembly."

"Colonel Fallon!" General Morgan picked his way across
the field, wincing at almost every step his horse took. "Colonel Fallon, leave the remnants to Colonel Washington."

Remnants. Then it hit him. Excpet for those who'd fled
with Tarletan and a few stragglers, the entire British force
was dead or captive. It might not be as big a victory as
Saratoga, but it was every bit as complete. He said as much to
Morgan.

"Maybe so," the general said, "but we've no time to rest
on our laurels. Cornwallis still outnumbers us better than two
to one, and he'll burn down hell to get to us. He has political
ambitions, you know, and this won't shine in England."

"It looks fine from here, though, now doesn't it? What do
you want me to do, general?"

"Until Washington rejoins us, your Legion will have to be
both our eyes ahead and our eyes behind. Detach one rider for
me to send a message to General Greene, and put a patrol
across the river. I intend to have every man, prisoners in-
cluded, across the Broad before dark. It's time to run again."

Jean-Baptiste shuffled to the map on the wall of his study
at Les Chenes, leaning heavily on a walking stick. The three
months since the disaster at Cowpens had changed him. He

was always tired, of late, and he couldn't seem to find any appetite. Something was wrong inside, and he didn't need those fools of doctors to tell him. He could look in a mirror and see the shrunken face and the burning eyes. He could almost count the hours left there. But it wouldn't matter if he could bring his plans to fruition, if he could die knowing the Fourrier family was secure.

That was why, every time he looked at the map, he wanted to howl with rage. A year before, in May of 1780, he'd been sure it was all but finished. To the north, if there'd been no great successes, at least much of what had been lost at Saratoga had been regained. And in the south the King's forces were everywhere victorious. How could it all have changed so?

Pins traced the armies' movements. Morgan and Greene fled north, Cornwallis pursuing. Always the rebels fell back, and the King's troops advanced. All the way across the Dan River into Virginia. Then, unexpectedly, they'd recrossed. There'd been a bloody, all-day battle at Guilford Courthouse. The reports agreed: the British had held the field. The rebels were limping back into South Carolina after sneaking away in the night. The latest issue of the *Royal American* up from Charlestown called it a great victory. But Cornwallis wasn't pursuing any longer. The last intelligence had him moving down the river toward Cape Fear. What in God's name could he want at Cape Fear?

Justin pushed open the door, beating dust off his uniform. "I've got her."

"What in God's name does he want at Cape Fear?"

"Cape—?" Justin looked at his father in surprise, then frowned at the map. More reports, it seemed, and more worrying. The older he got, the more he worried. "Cornwallis? Maybe he's after supplies from the Navy, or maybe he wants to move the army by ship. It doesn't matter. The rebels were whipped badly at Guilford Courthouse, and we'll take care of what's left as soon as they cross into South Carolina."

Jean-Baptiste snorted. "It does not matter, he says. We have no idea what is happening or why, but he says it does not matter. Cornwallis will not be resupplied at Cape Fear, nor will he enship his army. The waters are too dangerous there. He must move north into Virginia or back into South Carolina before the Navy can aid him.''

"Well, there's no need for him to return here. We'll chew Greene up in one battle, what's left of him.''

"It is devoutly to be wished.'' Jean-Baptiste dropped into a chair with a heavy sigh. "Now. What have you discovered of Gabrielle?''

"That's what I was telling you. I've got her, her and Fallon's brats.'' He went back to the door. "Get in here.''

Jean-Baptiste coldly watched Gabrielle enter. The boy, close on five years old, clung to her skirts, and she had a newborn babe in her arms. One had been bad enough. Now his daughter had borne two of that scum's children. Justin must be blind. Even if he couldn't see Fallon in Robert, it should be plain that this boy was Robert's brother. "Leave the children outside. Did you take her maid? Leave them with her.''

Gabrielle tightened her grip. "No.''

"Here, give them to me. Damn it, I won't hurt them.''

"Because you won't touch them,'' she said, backing away. "I'm warning you, Justin, if you as much as touch my children, I'll kill you.'' There was a ring of determination in her voice that brought him up short. "I know what you did to people who helped me, for no more crime than that. You will not put those bloody hands on my children.''

Jean-Baptiste rapped his stick against the desk to get their attention. "Enough. They can stay. I do not usually allow children in this room, but I will make an exception for my, my daughter's children.'' He'd been about to say, my grand-children, but the thought of the Fallon blood in them stopped him.

"I'd like to go to my house in Charlestown,'' Gabrielle said with firmness. "If you'll have the coachmen take me—''

"Oh, no,'' Justin said. "You'll remain right here at Les Chenes, where we can keep an eye on you.''

Jean-Baptiste spoke before Gabrielle could open her mouth to protest. "We can keep an eye on her just as well in Charlestown." Certainly, considering the risk of Justin seeing James and Robert together. He couldn't give Justin time to protest. "The infant, is it a boy, or a girl?"

"A girl." She smiled at the child, and cooed to make her smile back. "Her name is Catherine," she added, and saw the arrow strike home.

"Your mother's name," Jean-Baptiste said finally. "And did Fallon approve of that?"

"He did," she lied. Michael had been gone for six months, but it seemed like six years.

Justin smirked. "Trying to ingratiate himself now that his damned rebellion's lost."

"No matter," Jean-Baptiste said. "It will do him no good." He examined Catherine carefully. "She may gain beauty; a useful quality." He turned away. "Send them on to the city, Justin."

Gabrielle felt a chill inside as Justin took her out to the carriage. A useful quality, her father said. What if he took the child, to raise under his care? She had to escape. Somehow, she had to.

The British officers riding by bowed with exaggerated courtesy, but the women pointedly turned their backs and fanned the hot August air vigorously, as if dispelling a bad odor.

"At least they didn't stop," Gabrielle said.

Lucy Mainwaring laughed. "Oh, my dear, they at least know by now that no decent woman in this city will associate with them."

"That hasn't stopped them from trying," she maintained angrily. It was silly to get so upset over a trifle. But then, trifles loomed large when nerves had been worn thin by life under enemy occupation. Hunger hadn't helped. With prices increased over a hundred times since the war began, no one without a British army requisition could afford to eat well.

And Michael. It was almost a year since she'd seen him. Even the letters had stopped when Justin took her from

Georgia. So long not to feel his arms around her, his lips and his hands on her. Damn him. Leaving her just when she needed him most. God, she had to get out. She had to.

She couldn't stand the small talk and the streets full of redcoats any longer. Making her excuses to Lucy, she hurried home.

Martha met her at the door, a big smile wreathing her face. "Daniel bring a letter from Mrs. Jackman. And Miss Gabrielle, he done found his wife. Mrs. Holmes, to Oldfield plantation, she took her in."

"Wonderful!" She handed Martha her parasol and tucked the letter in her pocket. "I'll read it while I'm with Catherine. Is she ready?"

"Yes, ma'am," Martha said disapprovingly.

Gabrielle smiled briefly as she hurried upstairs. Martha had protested long and vigorously about her nursing Catherine herself. She still maintained a silent disapproval.

In the nursery Catherine was making hungry sounds in her cradle, while James played on the floor with wooden horses. "No good, Mama," he said, slapping the floor with his hand. "Floor's no good."

"I know, darling." She bent to smooth his hair and kiss his forehead. What would Michael think if he knew his son preferred the cabin's dirt floor to wooden ones? "And have you been good while I was gone? Has he, Martha? Very well then, you may take him to the stables to watch the horses groomed."

She had to laugh as he bounded to his feet and scurried to the door. Martha opened it for him with a smile, then had to grab his hand as he tried to dart out. He tugged impatiently, more leading her than she leading him. Next to playing in the dirt, he liked horses best.

Gbrielle undid her bodice and lifted Catherine from the cradle. In a few moments the infant was suckling contentedly, clutching her breast with tiny hands, and she could open the letter one-handedly and read, hurriedly scanning for the most important news first. A sigh of relief escaped her. Michael was alive and well.

He'd been mentioned in despatches at Guilford Courthouse, Louisa Jackman wrote, and also for his actions in harrying the enemy before the battle. He'd also been at Hobkirk's Hill and the siege of Ninety-Six. He was making quite a name for himself, it seemed, in cavalry skirmishes. All that mattered, though, was that he was unhurt, and so were her brothers.

Now she could start at the beginning and read the general news and gossip.

> Food is now as scarce here in the country as it is in Charlestown, what with both armies foraging. The red-coats have stopped burning houses, but they *have* fired three churches. No one can imagine why. And they are still stealing slaves, in even greater numbers than before.

To that Gabrielle could attest. She'd seen them, hundreds at a time, being rowed out to ships for the West Indies. Some had come into the city on their own, after the plantations had been burned, only to find the British regarded them as fair game. Even free blacks risked being taken. It was as if the British knew they were going to lose and were taking as much as they could while they could.

Then she came to the last paragraph of the letter.

> The Tory partisans, I fear, have grown worse. They are running riot, burning and hanging as if to rid the state of all who haven't taken the King's oath. Their actions daily drive people, no matter their previous sympathies, to our cause. Wade and Henry Hampton have left the Crown to join their brother John with General Greene. Most painful for me to relate is that Justin is foremost among the looters and burners, and the quickest to hang on the slightest excuse.

Saddened, she folded the letter. It wasn't that she didn't know what Justin did. She'd seen what he left behind. She had dreamed about it. It had been a grief to realize that Justin was insane. It was imperative to get out, to get the children beyond his grasp.

Martha returned just as she was putting Catherine back in the cradle. "Miss Gabrielle, Daniel waiting in the stable to see you. And Mrs. Croft downstairs. I think she been crying, ma'am."

Gabrielle sighed. Rebecca Croft had reason to cry. Her husband was one of those exiled to St. Augustine. Now they were being exchanged, some of them, but not to come to Charlestown. They were being sent to Philadelphia, and their wives and families had been ordered to leave South Carolina as best they could. "Tell her I'll be right down. And tell Daniel I'll come to him as soon as I can."

Rebecca Croft rose as Gabrielle entered the drawing room. She was trying to keep a cheerful face, but her eyes were red and puffy.

"It's so good to see you, Rebecca." She motioned her back to her seat and reached for the bellpull. "May I offer you some wine, or herb tea?"

"No, thank you. I —. I came to see you about, about Colonel Hayne." It was so obviously not what she'd been going to say that she blushed in confusion. "I mean—. That is—. Do you think they'll actually hang him?"

Gabrielle sighed. They'd been over this a hundred times before. Whatever Rebecca was crying for, it wasn't Isaac Hayne. "Rebecca, we've all signed the petitions, and we all know they haven't done any good. Now tell me what's really troubling you. Has something happened to your husband?"

"To Thomas? Oh, no, he's—." She closed her eyes and took a deep breath. "I've tried to be strong, Gabrielle. God knows, I've tried. You know I've been told to leave. I've been trying to sell our horses for the money." She laughed bitterly. "That's engaging in trade, and as an admitted rebel I need permission for that. But when I went to Colonel Balfour, there was a man there with papers. They said Thomas's estates had been confiscated and the horses weren't mine to sell. I don't even know whether the children and I will be allowed to take our own clothes, and I've no idea how we're going to leave. I'd managed to scrape together enough to hold four places on a ship sailing this very afternoon, but now—. I don't know. I'm sorry, Gabrielle. I shouldn't burden you with my troubles, but I needed someone to talk to.''

Gabrielle rose without a word and went to the highboy between the windows. Her father gave her a small allowance to run the house, but she managed to save a bit of it. She took a purse from the drawer.

"Oh, no, I can't," Rebecca gasped.

"Don't be foolish." She took the other woman's hand and closed it around the purse. "How many people in this city have you aided, Tory and patriot alike, for no more reason than they needed it? And if you can aid strangers, why can't I help a friend?"

"I—."

"Think of your children. Think about going to Thomas. There won't be much left after four passages to Philadelphia, though."

"I have relations in Philadelphia." She seemed suddenly closer to tears than any time before. "Oh, thank you, Gabrielle. God bless you."

"You'd better hurry now, to secure those passages." She helped Rebecca out through streams of tearful gratitude. She prayed that when her chance came to leave, it would come more easily.

Daniel was pacing in the stable when she got there. "Ma'am, we got to hurry. I found me a man who sold me a pass, but we got to get you out of the city right now. Today."

The stablemen were showing James how to hold a currycomb; she drew Daniel a little more away from them. "Why, Daniel? Did he suspect something?"

"No, ma'am. But, ma'am, all he got to do is think about selling me on the dock. We can't risk waiting, ma'am. You got to get out today."

"Very well. Do you have everything ready?"

"Yes, ma'am. The clothes and the cart in a yard up the Bay." He paused, looking doubtful. "Ma'am, I could still send a boy to Mrs. Jackman. I send him now, her carriage could meet you the other side Clement's Ferry."

"That's the first thing my father's men will look for,

Daniel, a carriage. Consider walking the penance we do for an easy escape.'' She smiled. ''You fetch James, and I'll bring Catherine and Martha. We'll leave immediately.''

The shoulder straps of the small cart dug into Gabrielle's shoulders, and she stopped to ease them. It didn't help much. At least, thank God, she'd be able to abandon the cart once they were through the city gates.

Catherine slept in a sling across her chest, the way poor women carried their infants while they worked. Martha had wanted to carry her, but Gabrielle had refused. Catherine was a part of her disguise, like the coarse lindsey-woolsey dress and the dirt on her face.

She looked back at James, peeping over the edge of the cart. ''Remember now, not a word till we're out of sight of the soldiers.''

''Yes, Mama.'' He beamed through his dirt. He seemed to enjoy it, as well as the ragged clothes.

Ahead, she saw Daniel stroll past the guards. They hardly even looked at him. She started forward again.

Bit by bit the entrances to the city had been fortified by the British, and much of the old rebel defense lines redug. On either side of the gate was an emplacement with two cannon, and the single guard of the days when the country seemed secure had been replaced by a squad under a sergeant. He stepped into the road with an upraised hand as she approached.

''And where might you be going? Let's see your pass.''

''I'm going to gather firewood and kindling,'' she said in a coarse voice, as she handed him the pass. ''To sell.''

The sergeant's eyes strayed from the pass to her figure, and a leer came on his face. ''Fine-looking bit like you, I'll wager that ain't all you sell.''

A blush suffused her face. ''I'm a respectable woman, with a respectable husband. I don't sell nothing but firewood.''

''Respectable, ay? I hear all the respectable women are rebels.'' He tapped the pass against his teeth. ''Maybe I

ought to search you. You might be a spy, have our battle
plans under your petticoats. Not that you're wearing any as I
can see.''

The other guards guffawed. She was the center of attention, now. Desperation crept into her. ''I'm carrying nothing
but my baby.'' Daniel was far up the road, looking back, but
there was nothing he could do.

''Well, you can leave the baby here.'' He tried to make his
attitude at once inviting and threatening. ''You and me,
we're going in those bushes behind the number two gun, and
I'm going to search you, inside and out as it were. You
cooperate, and it won't take long. You don't—.'' There was
nothing in his look but threat, now.

She tried to swallow, and couldn't. God help her. All she
had to do was tell him who she really was. She'd be safe,
then. If she could convince him. But Papa would put her
under guard at Les Chenes. And Catherine. She opened her
mouth with no idea of what she was going to say.

''Trouble, sergeant?'' Gabrielle took one look at the officer coming out of the guardhouse and hurriedly averted her
face. She knew him.

''No trouble, Captain Mason. Just checking this woman's
pass. Going after firewood, so she says.''

''I know about your checking women's passes, sergeant. I
suggest you go to the Bay and find a whore. They abound
there. Let me see the pass.''

She studied him surreptitiously as he looked over the
paper. It was the same man. He was quartered in a house just
down the street from her. Oh, God. She kept her eyes on the
ground. Martha passed, looking frightened; the soldiers
never noticed one more black woman with a basket on her
head.

''This is in order, I be—.'' Abruptly he tilted up her chin.
She stared at him, wide-eyed and trembling. He nodded
slowly, and tucked the pass into the sling with Catherine. ''I
knew a girl, once, who looked very much like you. Her father
kept her a prisoner. We aren't all barbarians, miss. Good
luck. With your wood gathering, that is.'' He smiled when

she stood rooted to the spot. "Well, get on with you. You're blocking traffic."

She took a step, then paused. "Thank you," she said, and threw her weight against the shoulder strap.

Daniel and Martha were waiting together up the road. The road to Tir Alainn.

32

The British cavalry fled down the road through the morning hours of September 8, 1781. They were only fleeing as far as their camp, Michael knew, in front of the brick house by the springs that fed Eutaw Creek. But he was of no mind to follow. Not with thirty men. He told off two to escort the dozen prisoners they'd taken, unarmed and digging sweet potatoes, back along the road toward Burdell's Tavern and the approaching army under Greene.

Louis moved up beside him. "What do we do now, Michael? They'll warn Leslie, for sure."

"We wait. No one was thinking this would be a surprise." He paused as the first companies of militia moved up the road past him. Already the drums in the British camp rattled assembly. "It'll be another hour or two, yet. If we move over into those trees, we'll be just about in position."

"Sergeant," Louis called, "move the men off to the right, there. Dismount and post two sentries. Henri, if you still have those cards, I'll let you win back some of your markers."

Michael followed slowly, checking the ground. The scattered trees were going to break up infantry formations. Attacks would be disjointed, and defense worse. From where the creek flowed into the Santee, all along the bank was tangled myrtle. Impassable. If there was ever a good battle ground, this wasn't it. Dismounting among his men, he lay down to sleep, with his reins wrapped around his hand. As he drifted off he heard someone remark about him setting an example for coolness, and smiled. He just wanted some sleep.

Young Jarvis woke him with a shake. "Time, sir."

The Legion was already mounting, and so was Lee's

cavalry, next in line. Beyond them the American army stretched to within a few hundred yards of the river. And ahead of them were the British.

Both sides' artillery let go with a roar just as he swung into the saddle. He tightened his reins as his horse danced sideways, and loosened his saber.

Louis had his out. "We should be hitting their flank. It's hanging in the open."

Michael pointed to a hedge line that came almost to the British flank. "What do you suppose might be back there, waiting for us to swing against their flank so we can be hit in the rear?" He caught sight of the bugler with his horn at the ready. "Put that down, man. Not a sound till you hear the signal."

Cannon smoke drifted down toward the river as each side tried to dismount the other's guns before attacking. An American three-pounder suddenly flipped onto its back, the guncrew writhing around it on the ground. A British cannon spun into the air, and then another American gun was gone.

As if it were a signal a ripple ran down the British line. Bayonets dropped to the proper slant, and two regiments stepped off together. The cannon continued to pound. Michael drew his saber. Behind him he heard the rasp of others.

The regimental lines broke as they advanced, splitting as they flowed around trees and over uneven ground. In scarlet parcels of five and ten and twenty they came on. And the front lines of American militia fired.

As if practicing on a parade ground, they moved. Front rank, fire. Fall back and reload. Second rank advance to the front. Front rank, fire. Fall back and reload. Second rank advance to the front. The air in front of them thickened with a fog of powder smoke. Men hacked and coughed, and paused to wipe their eyes, but they continued the drill.

First came a grunting roar, heard above the shouted orders between volleys. Then the redcoats came wading out of the smoke, by ones and twos at first, dimly seen and disappearing in a hail of musket fire, then more and more, until

screaming hundreds plunged into the American line with
flashing bayonets. Instantly scores of smaller battles broke
out, a dozen men against twenty here, ten against ten there. A
militiaman slipped away, and then another. Suddenly it was a
flood, and the British howled after them.

Behind Michael his men moved impatiently. "Wait the
signal, damn you," he growled, but he leaned forward in the
saddle himself. Would the damn thing never come?

Drums beating the cadence, the blue facings of the North
Carolina Continentals appeared to meet the charge. They
halted to fire a volley, then rushed forward with a deafening
roar. Above the din three long bugle notes sounded.

At the third Michael whipped his saber down. "Forward!" And the Legion ripped into the British flank just as
the Continentals hit their front.

In seconds the entire breadth of the field was a maelstrom
of twisting, grappling men. There was no room or time to
load and fire. It was bayonet against bayonet, sword against
sword, bare hands against bare hands. A solid sheet of sound,
men yelling and weapons clashing, hung in the air.

In the crush there was no room for the intricacies of sword
play. Michael knocked aside bayonet thrusts with hand or
foot. He kicked men in the face. He hacked and slashed at
everything that came close. His horse screamed as someone
realized that it was easier to bayonet the mount than the man.
Another redcoat thrust into the horse, and it rolled to the
ground, screaming and thrashing.

Michael stepped out of the saddle as the horse fell, already
looking for another mount. One reared and plunged nearby
with trailing reins. Sidestepping a sword thrust from a
screaming young officer, he grabbed the man's sword wrist,
smashed his saber hilt against the man's head, and as he fell
thrust him through. Then he was stepping over the body and
into the saddle.

The battle had moved into the British camp. Redcoats
were falling back through the tents by companies, or even
platoons. A score of them, in buff facings, turned to form
ranks. It took a moment for it to register. Buff facings. That

was the 3rd. They'd been on the far side of the line. That meant they'd all been forced back. They must be kept moving.

Quickly he grabbed passing horsemen, a half dozen of the Legion, a handful of Washington's, a sprinkling of Lee's. They caught the Buffs unprepared. Wheeling by ranks the infantry turned to face the charge, but before they could fire, sabers were rising and falling in their midst. They scattered like leaves before the wind.

Ahead, the brass-fronted bearskins of the grenadiers and leather light infantry caps moved along the creek, heading for the palisade behind the house. The house. Damn, it'd be a natural strongpoint.

"Shall we charge them?" one of Lee's troopers shouted.

"No, the house, the house!" Michael shouted.

Even as he led the dash out of the camp he could see they were too late. Redcoats, many supporting or even carrying wounded, were crowding through the doors and climbing in windows. Green-coated infantry of Lee's Legion closed with a rush. The doors slammed shut and a withering fire poured from every opening at point-blank range. The charging line crumpled like wet paper.

Michael drew his men in. It was futile to send cavalry against that. Suddenly, with a rumble of caisson wheels and the jangle of harness, four six-pounders swept by. Before the horses were led away the guns had already been swung against the house.

"Too close!" Michael spurred toward them. Men swarmed around the guns, loading. "You're too close! Pull back!"

The hail of lead that had smashed Lee's infantry began to fall among the cannon. The guncrews tried to continue, but they fell in bunches, running forward with cartridges, in the act of ramming home the shot. Before a single gun had fired, there wasn't a man left standing.

"You there," Michael shouted at the men with the gun carriage teams, "come on. We'll get the guns off."

They followed reluctantly. Suddenly Michael felt a tremendous blow on his side. He swayed in the saddle and almost fell. At that the men scattered, leaving the horses to run free. There was no chance to bring even one gun away alone. Instead he'd better look to getting away himself. He gave his horse rein and let it run. Twice more musket balls tugged at his coat, and once his horse screamed as it was nicked in the shoulder.

On the other side of the road, out of range of musketry, he pulled up, hunching over against the pain. The wound was low on his side, almost on top of the scar from the splinter he'd taken at Charlestown. He felt a wild desire to laugh. The British must have picked out one particular place to shoot him, and meant to keep at it until they succeeded. At least it'd gone all the way through. There'd be no probing for Gabrielle to do.

The men from his Legion had followed him, he realized; the others had gone God knew where. He forced himself to straighten. He couldn't charge the house. That was a job for infantry. But other than Lee's, only scattered infantry parties were visible.

Suddenly redcoats poured out of the brick building. Others clambered over the palisade. Along the creek, the light infantry and grenadiers formed ranks. The unmanned guns were quickly pulled back close to the building. The redcoats looked tired and dusty in their bandages and torn uniforms, but they sloped bayonets precisely and stepped off toward the tents to the beat of a drum.

Michael pounded his fist against his thigh. God, for even twenty more men. He was in perfect position to strike their rear.

Louis galloped up, his helmet gone, wild-eyed. "We're pulling back," Blood was running down his face.

"Louis, get the rest of the Legion. We'll take this lot in the rear. Then the infantry can—."

"The infantry's looting rations," Louis snapped. "When they gained the tents half of them forgot everything but their bellies. We're to join what's left of the Legion, Michael. Greene's orders."

Beyond the tents, where the woods thickened short of Gaillard's Road, officers rode up and down rallying the Americans racing from the camp. "Turn and stand! Turn and stand!" The line was forming raggedly in the trees.

Michael saw his Legionaires approaching and immediately motioned them to the ground. "Dismount! Use your carbines!" He joined them, looping his reins around a nearby branch.

The British came out of the tents with their lines disorganized. The scarlet masses flowed and rippled as they tried to reform and press an attack simultaneously.

"Fire!" The command was repeated by a dozen American throats, and the woodline blossomed with smoke and the crash of muskets.

The carbine slammed back against Michael's shoulder. It didn't really have the range or accuracy, but even a ball far off target might find another in the tight-packed redcoat ranks. Smoke billowed up until he could see his targets only hazily. He bit open cartridges till his mouth tasted permanently of powder, fired till his ears rang and his shoulder was numb. He forgot all about the hole in his side, and the pain. He just loaded and fired like an automaton.

Some time later an officer stopped him as he was reloading. "The cease fire's come down. They've pulled back."

Michael stared at him dully in the sudden silence. "Who won?"

"God only knows."

Michael pulled himself wearily into his saddle as the officer ran off to a distant rattle of musket fire. His wound seemed to have stopped bleeding. Here and there a man on the field tried to lift himself up, and fell back. Someone screamed endlessly, and another sobbed for water. He found the clustered Legion. There were faces missing, more than he'd hoped for. But young Jarvis was there, and Louis, and—. "Louis, where's Henri? Louis?"

Louis shivered once. His voice and face were frozen. "Dead, Michael. He was hit when we charged into the camp. I saw it happen. He went down, and before he could get up again, two of them pinned him to the ground with bayonets. I killed them, but it was too late. He looked at me, and he screamed, and he died. The Legion is ready to move, sir.''

Michael wanted to say something, but Louis was too close to the edge. "Very well, major. Move out toward Burdell's Tavern. I'll find General Greene for orders.''

As the diminished Legion rode past him, he surveyed the field once more. Yes, he'd find Greene. And maybe Greene could tell him who'd won.

Cursing men, high-piled carts, and crowded carriages jammed the road into Charlestown. British soldiers, ragged and dirty, stumbled along, eyes fixed on the city ahead. The civilians kept gazing fearfully back.

Elizabeth leaned back worriedly, ignoring Solange, sniffling in the corner. She couldn't understand it. She'd been planning her party for the British victory of Eutaw Springs when Solange came to tell her what was passing on the road.

That doleful parade of fugitives had told the news. It had all been lies. There'd been no victory. The rebels were coming. And they'd surely come for the Fourriers. It took her thirty minutes to join the stream toward Charlestown.

She climbed out of the carriage at the Broad Street house wanting nothing more than a bath. "Take my things to my room, Solange,'' she said, and hurried inside.

The hall was unattended; someone was speaking in the drawing room, and she opened the door an inch.

Justin stood with his back to her, one arm around ten-year-old Robert's shoulders, Gerard, not yet six, held up in his other arm. All three of them looked down into a coffin laid across chairs. Justin spoke, his voice loud and cracking with anger and hate. "Yes, look at him well. Your grandfather. Jean-Baptiste Fourrier. His blood, my blood, your blood, all one. Murdered! By this damned trash that call themselves patriots. Rebel garbage against their King. Remember. Remember those dogs killed your grandfather. You must kill them. Kill them! Kill them!''

The rabid fire in his voice was terrifying. She backed away

from the door, and ran towards the stairs, bumping a chair in her haste. His voice cracked in the hall like a whip.

"So you've come back."

She turned slowly. The boys stood in the drawing room door, frightened. Justin moved toward her, his face a grim death mask. She backed away, one careful step at a time. "I, I saw the people fleeing, and I was afraid to stay at Les Chenes. The rebels may already be there."

"No, they aren't at Les Chenes, though I should thank them for sending you to me. They're all the way up in the High Hills of the Santee, licking their wounds. Oh, no. We flee, but they don't pursue."

"But I heard you say Papa Fourrier was dead. You said the rebels—. You said they—."

"They killed him. He traced our failures, their successes, and he aged years for every week of it. This morning, he couldn't be wakened. They killed him as surely as if they'd put a ball between his eyes."

"I see. I'll put on mourning—."

"No." He stopped, his black eyes boring into her. His words were as cold and brittle as ice. "You won't mourn him. I won't have a whore mourning my father."

The breath caught in her throat. What did he know? He looked like murder—. Frantically she ran for her room. Before she could get the door shut, he threw his weight against it and forced it open.

"Justin—."

His open handed blow knocked her across the room. "Be quiet, whore. Be quiet and listen." He took off his uniform coat and carefully folded it across a chair. "I overheard a man, it doesn't matter who, ask another man if he'd had the pleasure of Mrs. Fourrier yet. She was, he said, the hottest bit of flesh in the Carolinas."

"You should've challenged him. You should've killed him."

"I told you to shut up. The other man said, yes, he'd enjoyed Elizabeth Fourrier often, but she was a little too free with her favors for his taste. They didn't speak like men gossiping about a lady. They could've been talking about a girl at Sally Pritkin's house, or Mrs. Jennings'. I had to find out. I don't mind killing men to defend my wife's honor, but to defend a whore? I'd be taken for a fool as well as a cuckold.''

"It's all lies," she insisted desperately. "Lies."

"Men provided the information I needed. Did you actually spread your legs for every officer who passed through Charlestown, or does it just seem that way?'' He began kneading his hands. "I should have known. All the tricks you knew, all the special little—yes, Elizabeth, you're a whore.''

In a single step he was on her. One hand tangled in her hair and swung her around. The other caught her across the face, again and again and again. She fell sprawling across the bed. He began to pant. He slapped and punched, never caring what he hit, all the while ripping at her clothes. And when she lay there naked, bruised and whimpering, he opened his breeches and took her.

As she lay sobbing beneath his pounding he whispered in her ear over and over, "Like a whore. Like a whore.'' And the worst of it to her was that, even with the pain and the terror, she still found a thrill of excitement in it. When he was done he wiped himself on a piece of her dress and threw it in her face.

It was too much. Shrieking, she reared up clawing at him. She wanted blood. He fended her off easily, and slapped her back down on the bed.

"Damn you," she screamed. "You think I've bedded everything in breeches I could find? Well, you're right. And here's another name for you. Michael Fallon.'' She laughed hysterically at the look on his face. "Oh, yes. Michael Fallon. I should've married him, not you. And I would have if he'd been here when I found out I was—'' An edge of sanity cut into her. She licked her lips and pressed herself deeper into the mattress.

"When you found out you were—you gave me a bastard," he rasped.

Suddenly his hands were at her throat, lifting her, squeezing. She tried to scream; only a horrible gurgle came out. Everything was going black. She clawed at him, kicked, struggled desperately to hang onto consciousness, to hang onto life.

As abruptly as he'd begun, he released her.

"No." The word sounded like a snake's hiss. "I won't kill you. I have plans for you. Do you think you've paid enough? Not nearly. But your screams will pay a part of it. You'll scream, and you'll beg me to stop, but you'll have to pay." There was no sanity at all behind his glittering eyes.

"Please, Justin," she babbled. "Oh, God, please."

"Do you remember Sally Pritkin, Elizabeth? I see you don't. She's a procuress, though she looks like a lady. But then, if a whore can look like a lady, why can't a whoremonger? A few weeks ago I took Hamilton to her house. She was closed—to King's men. So we opened her up again, her house and her body. You should have heard her scream. It brought her scullery slave on the run. A scullery slave who was sometimes used upstairs when the clients were besotted." He raised his voice. "Come in, Samantha."

Samantha stepped silently into the room. Elizabeth's mouth dried from the look in her eye. She was thinner, and harder.

"She hasn't forgotten your kindness in selling her," Justin said drily. He picked up his coat, but paused at the door. "She's your new companion, Elizabeth. Day and night. She'll assist you in making your payments. If you leave her sight for five minutes, or if she tells me you've said more than hello to a man, I'll peel your hide." His look of anticipation froze her blood. The door slammed behind him.

Even after he was gone Elizabeth couldn't stop trembling. She was a welter of fear and hate. Justin was insane. She'd suspected, but now she knew. What would he do to Robert? More importantly, what would he do to her? Images of the ways he would make her scream danced in her head. And along with them, remembrance of his look of longing for it, and of the queer thrill that had shot through her even as he was raping her. Oh, God, he'd go further and further. And as afraid as she was of that, she was more afraid of her own reaction to it. She had to get away. She had to.

Suddenly she remembered Samantha's presence, and her own nakedness. She opened her mouth to call for a robe. The black woman's flat, hard gaze pinned her to the bed in silence. Those eyes were going to be on her for the rest of her life. A word from Samantha to Justin, and she would start screaming. She'll assist you in making your payments, he'd said. She wanted to scream, but instead she began hopelessly to cry.

Justin paused on the stairs, looking down at the boys waiting in the hall. How had he ever missed seeing it? All he had to do was know the boy's father, and Robert was a ten-year-old Michael Fallon, with his high cheekbones and his hooked nose and his damned blue eyes. Bile rose in his throat, but he managed to keep his face calm as he descended.

"Papa," Robert said, "do you—. Papa, what happened?"

"Come here, Gerard. Not you," he snapped as Robert started to lead him forward. He took a deep breath. "I want Gerard to come to me, by himself." Both boys watched him uncertainly, but Gerard ran to him when he held out his arms. The boy smiled as he swung him up to face level, and he had to smile also. Not in answer to Gerard, but for the proof of his eyes that this boy, at least, was a Fourrier.

"Papa—," Robert began hesitantly.

"Sit there," Justin said, pointing to a chair against the wall. "Don't move until I tell you to." He turned to the drawing-room door, still holding Gerard, and stopped. "I think you're old enough to stop calling me Papa. From now on you will call me sir."

"Yes, Pa—. Yes, sir," Robert said, but he said it to a closing door. It hadn't closed all the way. Through the crack he could hear Justin.

"Your grandfather, Gerard. Murdered. You must remember, and hate for it. You must hate the Americans, and most especially the Fallons. You must always hate anyone of the Fallon blood. They must be killed. All of them. They must die.'' The voice rasped on and on.

Robert began to feel very alone. And very afraid.

33

November of 1782 was bitterly cold, and there was little in the way of food or comforts in the camp of the Cooper River above the Charlestown Neck. Michael pulled his blanket higher around his shoulders and broke the governor's seal on a despatch. Probably more instructions regarding the split of authority between the governor and General Greene. Not the first time he wished John Rutledge was still governor. Matthews was more ready to bicker over details than anything else.

The operative phrase leaped off the paper at him:

You are hereby directed and required to assume the title, rank, and responsibilities of Brigadier General in the militia of the State of South Carolina.

Good God. A brigadier general with a command of one officer, thirteen men, and a boy. It was odd enough to be fitting for an odd anniversary. One year ago today they'd received word that the war was as good as over because Cornwallis had surrendered in Virginia. No one seemed to have told the British in the south, though. The fighting had dragged on, until one by one Savannah and every other town held by the redcoats had been abandoned. Except for Charlestown.

Before he could sink into bitter rumination he went on with his mail. The next was in a woman's hand. He checked the signature. Ann Thibodeau. That was one of Gabrielle's friends. He read hurriedly.

My dear Colonel Fallon,
As you must know, Gabrielle came to stay with me at

Riverview after her heroic escape from Charlestown. She is a dear friend of mine, and for that reason I dare to intrude in your and her private affairs. For the past year I have believed she was writing you, for I saw the letters. Then I saw her burn one after writing it. I confronted her, and she grew very angry. I fear she is pining because you haven't come to her. She is on the edge of a decision. You must come quickly, before she makes it, for once made, she will stick by it if it destroys all that she holds dear. Please, for her sake, come.

> I am, most respectfully,
> Ann Thibodeau

She was angry? He'd been lied to, and she was angry. When his anger had cooled enough for him to write, he'd worried when he hadn't received a reply to any of his letters. And now this. She was safe on the Santee, and angry because he didn't walk away from the war and go to her. Without knowing where she was. Damn it, he was forty miles from the Thibodeau plantation and didn't have two hours together to call his own. And what in hell had she been doing in Charlestown?

Louis pushed open the cabin door and broke in on his thoughts. "Foragers, Michael. They raided three farms above the Goose Creek Bridge." He paused as if waiting for someone else to speak, a habit he'd picked up since Henri's death. "They're running hard for the Neck, or so I expect."

Michael bit back an oath. Foragers again. The British penned in Charlestown needed food, and they got it by raiding farms. From small parties to hundreds of men at a time they came out. The Legion chased them almost every day. "Mount the men, Louis. We'll give them a run."

From Goose Creek the foragers would have to take the Wassamasaw Road to reach Charlestown. Michael brought his men to the road short of the turnoff to Clement's Ferry and waited. The rumble of approaching wagons came quickly. He motioned everyone back further into the trees. There were four wagons, each with a redcoat driver and two infantrymen with muskets. A half-dozen dragoons, along as guards, were driving a score of cattle ahead of them. All kept a wary eye behind for pursuers.

"They won't expect us from ahead," Michael said. "Now." He dug in his spurs and sprang into the road at a gallop, the others howling behind.

The dragoons, apparently thinking it a larger force, bent low over their mounts as if under a hail of fire and galloped toward the city. A few of the wagoneers fired, then they, like the rest, threw down their muskets and threw up their hands.

Michael slowed to a walk short of the wagons. "I'll tell you, Louis, there's been a time or two else I wish they'd given up this easy." He turned to look at his friend, and a riderless horse caught his eye, and a shape on the ground. "Oh, God, no. God damn it, no." He hit the ground running.

Louis looked up with a quizzical expression. A spreading red patch covered his waistcoat, and there was an ominous, pinkish froth at the corner of his mouth. "It—. It doesn't hurt. Always thought—. Always thought it'd hurt."

"Don't talk. We'll get you to a doctor in just a bit." He stuffed his handkerchief under the vest and felt it soak through immediately. "Get the best team turned around," he snapped over his shoulder. "You bloody-back bastards unload it at the double, or I'll hang every one of you."

Louis's chest heaved as if he couldn't quite catch his breath. "Thought—. Thought it'd be, big battle. Like Henri." He started to laugh, and a rivulet blood ran down from his mouth. "S-stab me if I—." He shuddered once, and was still.

Michael watched the eyes glaze, shaking his head. "No." He seized Louis's lapels and pulled him up. "No!" Louis's head hung back, sightless eyes staring at the sky. Slowly Michael put one arm around his shoulders, the other under his knees. He got to his feet and turned to the wagon. The British prisoners huddled at the back. "Your coats," he said, jerking his head at the wagon. They complied, hastily and fearfully.

He laid Louis on the piled coats gently. There was blood

on his hands, but he couldn't bring himself to wipe it off. Awkwardly he pulled himself into the saddle.

Tom Jarvis stared at the prisoners and bared an inch of saber. "Tarletan's quarter," he said grimly and an echo came from a score of throats. "Tarletan's quarter."

Michael paused and looked at the prisoners. One of them had pulled the trigger. One of them—. "No," he rasped finally. "Let them go. We're escorting Colonel Fourrier home."

He turned away, up the road, and after a moment Tom followed. A trooper whipped the wagon horses, and the rest of the Legion fell in behind. Not one man looked back at the British standing in the road.

Within two miles a lone rider approached. Michael raised his hand for a halt and waited. The rider resolved into a lieutenant of Continental dragoons, who reined in with a salute.

"General Fallon? I'm Lieutenant Carbell, sir, detached from Bland's Light Horse to courier duty for General Greene. I've been looking for you, sir. Been doing some foraging, I see." He jerked his head at the wagon.

"In the wagon," Michael said, biting off each word, "is Lieutenant Colonel Louis Fourrier, late of the Irish Legion. I am taking him to his family home, Les Chenes plantation. Now get out of my way."

"I'm sorry, sir. I didn't mean—. Sir, I have orders from General Greene, personally. You're to take command of McCary's Mounted Rifles and Waring's Dragoons, cross the Cooper River, and proceed against foragers along the Wando. There must be a dozen parties of them in that area, sir."

"A message to General Greene, lieutenant, from me, personally. Do we have to assault Charlestown, I'll be in the front rank, but I'll not kill another man to protect a cow. And not one more man of mine will bleed for a bushel of corn. Is that clear, lieutenant?"

"Yes, sir. Perfectly." Carbell shook his head. "It's funny, sir. That's almost the same message General Marion sent in yesterday."

Michael looked back at the wagon. "Would God I'd thought of it then." He rode on; the Legion followed in grim silence except for the rumble of the wagon wheels.

The morning of December 13, 1782 dawned crisp and clear over Charlestown.

Across the bay in a wide arc that stretched out of the harbor mouth the evacuation fleet lay, hundreds of sail to take the British army away from its last foothold in the south. And the thousands of civilians who refused to live under the new government. It was to be an orderly leavetaking, with the Americans moving in as the British fell back.

The British were leaving their redoubts near Shubrick's plantation on the Neck, marching down the road toward the King Street gate. A single bugle note sounded, and the Americans moved forward, close behind the British.

Michael slouched in the saddle, calmly watching the emplacements and trenches ahead. There'd been a good deal of talk about a trap, about being pulled into the open. He didn't believe the British would give up their forward redoubts for the few hundred men in the American advance party, but orders had come down. Every musket was loaded and had fixed bayonet, even if it was shouldered. He smiled as men ran into the redoubts and came out shaking their heads. Empty.

The old American lines were empty too, and so were the city streets, except for the British rear guard a few blocks ahead. Every window was shuttered, every door closed. The city seemed deserted.

Suddenly a window above his head banged open. Michael twisted in the saddle, a pistol appearing in his hand. With a sound like hundreds of metallic crickets musket hammers went back all along the street. The woman leaning out of the window froze, staring at the muzzles aimed at her. A slow smile appeared, and she blew a kiss to Michael. "God bless you," she called.

As if at a signal other windows opened, and other heads appeared, shouting and cheering, waving flags that must have remained hidden throughout the occupation. A torrent of jubilant sound washed over the street, and sprigs of pine and fern showered down. Girls ran out to bestow kisses and men offered bottles of wine.

Suddenly there was a shot, and total silence fell. A second clipped the horsehair plume from Michael's helmet. The street filled with a pandemonium of running, screaming people. A sharp movement at a window caught his eye. He moved toward the house, but his men were ahead of him, smashing down the door.

His attacker wouldn't wait, Michael realized. The rear of the house. He galloped around the corner; fleeing celebrants dashed screaming out of his way. He turned into the alley behind the house just as the back door opened and a man in a red coat ran out.

"Hold there, you," Michael shouted. The man whirled, raising a pistol, and a gun Michael didn't even realize he'd drawn went off in his hand. The red-coated man tottered two steps toward him and fell on his face.

The house disgorged his Legionaires, and they fell on the body, searching the pockets.

"He had two rifles back there, general. Didn't think them redcoats went in for rifles much, except for them Hessian jaegers."

"Not a regular," he mused half to himself. "That coat looks familiar, though. Of course. The King's South Carolina Horse, Justin Fourrier's band."

One of the searchers pulled a pouch from under the coat and upended it. Golden guineas showered across the corpse's chest. "God! What do you make of that, general?"

Justin Fourrier's man, with two rifles and a pocket full of gold, shooting at him. It added up to one thing. "A personal matter, lads. A man adding to the debt he owes me." How had he known Michael would be in the entering party, and with which column?"

A captain appeared at the head of the alley and saluted. "General Wayne's compliments, sir, and would you please inform him what the shooting's about."

"Just a man with a grudge against me, captain. Tell the general it's all under control." His men followed him back to the street, leaving the assassin with his gold spread around him.

The rest of the entry was uneventful. The cheering throngs returned, and the British continued their slow pullback until the last of them boarded boats from a wharf below Broad Street. Michael rode out onto the dock to watch the last boat go. A lone officer stood defiantly in the stern, facing the shore with a Union Jack in his hands. The last British flag to fly in South Carolina.

Michael's mind was on Justin. He was on one of the ships in the harbor, he'd wager. A wild impulse took him, and he whipped off his helmet and stood in the stirrups. "I'm here, you bastard," he shouted. "I'm still here."

Feeling a little foolish he dropped back and settled the helmet back in place. The wooden planks rattled as he cantered back to the street, and to the waiting Legion. It was time to see General Greene.

When they arrived at the State House, General Wayne was already welcoming General Greene, Governor Matthews, and the official party from the General Assembly who'd driven down from Jacksonborough to reestablish the state government in Charleston.

"Ah, General Fallon," Greene said, limping down the steps to Michael. "General Wayne tells us you had some trouble on the way in. A sniper."

"A private matter, general." Michael pulled a folded paper from his pocket, the seal on it visible. "General, I'm leaving you. The Irish Legion has been disbanded effective today, and I've resigned my commission. This is Governor Matthews' order to that effect."

"This is absurd!" Greene exploded. "The war isn't over, yet. There's still a British army in New York."

"The peace commissioners have been talking for weeks, general. A peace treaty may already be signed, for all we know. And as for that army in New York, the British don't hold a foot of ground south of there. If the northerners want help from us, we should send them the help they sent us. Little and slow.''

"Just a minute, Fallon," Wayne burst out. His men called him Mad Anthony, though Michael couldn't see the reason. "You seem to have forgotten quite a few Continentals, from Howard's Marylanders to my Pennsylvanians."

"Your Pennsylvanians came too late for all but marching into Charlestown," Michael snapped back. "The rest? The officers came from Maryland, Delaware, Virginia, most of them, but you check their rolls. Nine men out of ten or better signed on in the Carolinas. And there were more than a few in Congress didn't want to send the little they did. It's been the same from the beginning." His temper had a grip on him, and it forced him on when he knew he should stop. "When the port of Boston was closed, South Carolina sent more money and more food than any other state, *including* Massachusetts. We consistently overpaid our assessments for the American armies, and we sent troops wherever Congress or the generals asked, from Florida to Virginia. And what did the north send us? As little as possible, and grudgingly given." They stared at him, Greene and Matthews open-mouthed, Wayne white-faced with anger. He smiled. "I think, gentlemen, that you understand me now. I've a wife I haven't seen in two years. So, if you'll excuse me." He saluted and turned his horse up the street that led out of town. Once he thought he heard General Greene call after him. He didn't look back.

With an angry snort Justin snapped the spyglass shut. Soon Faydon would row out to the ship, and tell him Marston had shot the bastard down. God, but he wished he could have seen Fallon's face when he died. It was why he'd told Faydon to wait nearby and watch, so he could describe it. There wasn't a chance Marston had escaped.

His eyes darted, seeking Robert. The boy was forward, watching sailors splice line. A fine place for him, Justin thought, well away from Gerard, as he'd ordered. Like his bastard of a father, he'd associate with anyone.

A boat bumped against the side, and Faydon climbed over the rail. The weaselly little man sidled to the foot of the quarterdeck ladder.

"Marston missed," he hissed. His eyes flickered nervously.

Justin descended coldly. "Missed? With a rifle? At twenty yards at most?"

Faydon pulled his head in under Justin's gaze and lowered his voice still more. "Maybe he got excited. Maybe—. I don't know. He missed. Then Fallon got him running out the back door. God, I wasn't more than ten feet from him. They dumped the gold over the body, and Fallon said it was personal, and they all went away, leaving him there. God. And Fallon knew the uniform. I guess Marston didn't want to hang was he caught. A lot of good it did him. What are you looking at me like that for?"

"Ten feet from him," Justin said quietly. His voice was level. "Ten feet, and you didn't shoot. I know you had a pistol. At that range even you—."

"But I—. I wasn't paid for that. Twenty guineas don't buy murder." His voice rose with every word. "Besides, there were people all around, people watching. I—."

"Captain Mill," Justin called, "I have a thief here." Faydon's mouth gaped.

Mill, at the head of the ladder, looked down at Faydon like the wrath of God. "A thief you say, Major Fourrier?"

"Yes, a thief. He was in my command, but deserted after he was seen rifling my quarters. He took"—Justin weighed his man quickly—"one hundred and twenty guineas. And an enameled gold watch. Now he comes to me with some story about catching the real thief. As I said, however, he was seen."

Mill gestured; two brawny sailors closed in on Faydon. He writhed in their grasp. "It's a lie! He gave it to me! The watch was part of the price. Get your hands out of my pockets!"

"The price?" Justin sneered. "The price for what?" Faydon froze as Justin's deadly gaze grasped him. One of the sailors held up a bulging purse and a watch.

"Enough," Mill snapped. "Take him below and confine him to the cable locker. And if he mentions Major Fourrier's name again, gag him. Thieves, on my ship." He stalked away.

Outwardly Justin appeared satisfied. Inside, he burned. God strike Fallon dead. The whoreson dog had the devil's hand to shield him. And through Marston's uniform he wouldn't have any doubts as to who wanted him dead. Fallon must die, and now—before he could send his own assassins.

Fallon had escaped him. For the moment. But Elizabeth was still in his hands. That whore! She could pay a little more. The gag would stifle her screams, and Samantha could hold her for the strap. Those white breasts would redden till the black heart beneath them burned. His breath quickened in anticipation. He hurried below.

Ann Thibodeau turned the page and droned on: "I do not myself, in spite of what others may say, and I do not exclude learned churchmen and our most worthy political leaders, believe that this affair, if it may be called by so light a term—" Gabrielle let herself drift out of the present, back to that earlier reading circle, back to Michael.

She did that too much of late. Everything led her to him. Dinner plans became his favorite dishes, and dressing a choice of what he'd like to see. At times she had the feeling if she could only turn quickly enough, he'd be standing behind her. She smiled as she saw him behind Ann's shoulder. Yes, like that. He'd stride through the garden in just that manner, with the smile that flustered her as no other could. But why would she think of him in a plain black suit? And there were no streaks of gray at his temples. The air froze in her throat as the image put its hand on Ann's arm, and Ann looked up in surprise.

"I beg pardon, ladies," he said, his burning eyes never leaving Gabrielle's, "for not letting the butler announce me. I've come a long way to see my wife."

Ann's gaze went from Gabrielle, frozen in her seat, to Michael, oblivious of the reading circle crowding about him.

"Come, ladies," she said. "Come along, now. Come along." Herding her reluctant covey down the path, she stopped for a moment with a roguish grin. "General Fallon, the garden is yours for the next hour. The grass is very soft over behind those dogwoods." She swept away with a trilling laugh.

"Why didn't you write, Brielle?" He'd told himself it was time to be conciliatory, but he couldn't bridle his tongue. "I kept telling myself you had to be all right, but I didn't know."

She pulled away from his cobalt gaze. "I haven't had any letters from you, either. Why didn't you write to me?"

"But I did! I sent them to Georgia, where I thought you were. It wasn't until I got Ann's letter, not a month gone, I'd any idea you were here."

"If you'd stayed with me, as you should have, then you'd have known where I was."

Her eyes were burning, and her color was high. She was making an effort to hold her temper, he realized, and that made him lose his. "Stayed with you? As I should have? God's blood, woman! There was a war to be fought. I'm a soldier and a man, not a child to hide my head in your apron."

"Strange that you should mention children," she said coldly. "By leaving, you missed the birth of your daughter. That's right, your daughter. Her name is Catherine, and she's not quite two."

"I, I didn't know." A daughter. God send she was as beautiful as her mother. "But it wouldn't have changed anything. I still would've had to go. Can't you understand that?"

"No, I can't. I'll wager you didn't know Justin found us and took us to Charlestown. Your children were going to be raised by Papa." His face went white; involuntarily she took a step toward him. He pulled her to him, and after a moment she relaxed.

"Oh, God, I'm sorry," he said, and was surprised at the intensity of his own fear. The danger was past, but that they should have been in it—. "If only you'd told me. If only you hadn't lied."

Angrily she tried to push out of the circle of his arms. "You still throw that up to me? After what you did? You—."

He held her close, stroking her hair and riding over her protests. "No, Brielle. No. That doesn't matter any more. It doesn't matter." He lied. It did matter. She'd lied to him about something that was desperately serious. But it didn't matter nearly as much as she did. "You're all that matters to me now, Brielle."

She hesitated. Oh, damn, she did want him back. "Michael, the grass *is* soft."

With a joyous laugh he swept her up in his arms, and laid her down behind the dogwoods. His hands trembled with eagerness as he undid her bodice laces and bared her breasts. Her breath quickened as her nipples stiffened against his palms. His kisses covered her face, her neck, her breasts, till she moaned. His hands gently raised her skirts, slid across her silken belly, played in the curls between her legs.

He wanted it to be good for her, but his own eagerness led him to enter her in one thrust. Before he could speak a word she wrapped her arms and legs around him hungrily. She writhed against him with an urgency that swept him along. His breath rasped in his throat, and hers gasped past his ear.

"I'll never let you go," she whispered fiercely. "Never."

And they both came.

The old foundation at Tir Alainn had been cleared of charred rubble and was being enlarged to hold the new, brick manor that would rise there. Larger and grander in every way, Michael liked to joke, and harder to burn. Usually he stopped to watch the work whenever he passed.

This time he rode straight from checking the clearing of fields that'd lain fallow for almost four years to his four-room cabin. Daniel called to him, but he rode on without hearing. Dismounting, he hurried inside and began hunting through the plantation books piled on his desk.

Gabrielle looked up from her newspaper in surprise when

he didn't speak. James maneuvered his toy soldiers by the fireplace with a seven-year old's complete absorption. Catherine napped in her cradle.

"Have you seen this?" Gabrielle asked, watching curiously as Michael searched. "The new city charter gives the name as Charleston. I know some people say it that way already, but do you think that's reason enough to—. Michael, what *are* you looking for?"

"The list of slaves who've been freed. I'm certain I saw two men who were freed years ago. It's a good thing Sarah put all the papers in with the plate, or—." Her silence finally penetrated. He turned to look at her. "Brielle, where's the list?"

"There isn't one," she said levelly.

"Nonsense. You've always kept perfect records. You wouldn't—."

"Michael, no slaves have been set free."

"The war—," he began numbly.

"Had nothing to do with it. I didn't free any slaves because we couldn't afford it." He stared; she hurried on. "Yes, Michael, we couldn't afford it. If—."

"I said I'd free them. I said it. After eight years' service they'd get a mule, and tools, and fifty acres. And freedom. Just like any indentured man."

"Are you going to free the slaves, Papa?" James piped up suddenly. "Why? Slaves are slaves."

There was a moment's silence. It had been a long time since they'd lived as planters did. They'd gotten used to having the children under foot, like a farm family. But this was no time for James to be there, listening.

Gabrielle went to the door and called Martha. The black woman sensed the tension in the air and hustled the boy out quickly. Gabrielle hesitated a moment over the sleeping Catherine before speaking.

"He's right. Slaves are slaves. Not indentured men, Michael. They're slaves. If you free them you'll ruin yourself. You know what a field hand costs. How are you going to replace them, especially if the Assembly cuts off the slave trade?"

"I'll hire men."

"If you could find them, which you can't, and if they'd work for a wage that'd allow you a profit, which they won't, what'd you pay them with?" A stab of pain went through her at the look on his face, but she forced herself to go on. "Michael, you are very nearly bankrupt. Do you think I don't know the debt you took on just to start the house?"

"I wanted to give you back your home," he said stiffly.

"All right, then. I'll stop construction and send you and the children back to the city. The house there can be repaired."

"Michael, it isn't just the house, and you know it. You can't hide it from me. I learned how to read those books. And I have read them."

"It's not as bleak as it seems."

"Let *me* tell *you* how bleak it is." He tried to speak, but she rushed on. "Of the merchant ships—yours and Mr. Carver's—two are left, bogh needing rebuilding. Four vessels were lost with cargoes, cargoes that were uninsured because of the war. The shippers have claims before the courts, charging that you are responsible for their losses. And in the end, you'll have to pay. You loaned money to the state, to the militia, to the army. And they're as slow paying off those loans as they were in winning the war. And the prizes you took? The agents in France have stolen your proceeds. You have one thing. We have one thing. This plantation. If you can make a rice crop, we have a chance, a small one. Even so, it will take us years to recover. But if you let those slaves go, the wolves will close in. For the rest of our lives, every dollar we see, there will be two men fighting over which one gets it."

He went to the window and leaned a hand on either side. She was right. He'd tried to keep it from her. Hell, he'd barely admitted it to himself. If the worst came, there'd be nothing left, less than nothing. He'd had nothing before, but this time there was Gabrielle, and the children.

"I wasn't yet five," he said, "when my father died on Drummossie Moor, at the battle they call Culloden, going down with Stapleton's Irish Pickets. I was too young to know why my father didn't come home, or why that meant we had to leave our farm, but I learned other things. I learned about hunger, and watched my mother grow gaunt from giving me food she should've eaten. Every night, for the three years till she died, I went to sleep with the sound of her sobbing in my ears. Was a man named Grogan took me in, once she was laid to rest. To him a boy was meant to be worked, seven days a week, from before dawn to after dark, with a bit of time on Sunday for church. If that wasn't enough to save my soul, there was always his strap. I fought him. God knows how, but I fought him. The village folk said I was a wild, ungrateful child, born to hang, and when I ran away at fifteen, it was good riddance. I swore that no child of mine would ever go to bed hungry or cold. Well, there's no way back. Only forward, or down. If I must be foresworn on something, my children will not suffer for it."

"Michael—." Her voice caught, and she strove to keep the tears gathering in her eyes from falling. In the strong man who stood before her she could see no sign of that frightened, hungry boy. But how she wanted to find him and comfort him. "Michael, I never knew."

"The war hasn't given us much time for learning each other. But we have years, yet. Come now, no tears. Even Daniel thinks I'm out of step with the rest of the world. He keeps telling me to buy more fieldhands while the import's still allowed. So just you dry your eyes. I'm simply recognizing facts."

She caught the hidden despair. "I love you, darling. Now and for always, I love you."

He forced a light-hearted tone. "Of course you do." But above her head his eyes mourned something gone that could never be regained.

34

The plantation house went up, and Michael slowly fought his way from the brink of bankruptcy. It never ceased to amaze him how quickly Charleston recovered from the war. Almost as the last British ship cleared the harbor, the first vessel entered for trade. In a year the port regained its old eminence. Rice began to boom again, and a new crop, cotton, appeared. Despite the efforts of many, the end of the British bounty brought an end to the indigo market, though it took years to finally fade.

With the passing of the war other struggles had come. Revolution in France brought an outpouring of ardor, but the discovery of wholesale executions and the suspicion that slave revolts in the Caribbean had been French-incited cooled it. In Massachusetts a rebellion was begun under Daniel Shay over taxes, and there was talk of New England seceding. Arguments only slightly less fierce than those over independence were put forward over ratification of the Federal Constitution. It was barely saved by inclusion of a Bill of Rights. By June of 1796, with George Washington refusing a third term as President, there was burning debate over who would succeed him, and as to whether the nation could survive without him.

Michael tugged on his coat, cursing for the thousandth time the new, tighter fashions. They were damnable, especially in the June heat. Gabrielle always laughed and said he was just putting on weight. He snorted. He didn't weigh a pound more than the day he met her.

He slipped a box-lock pistol into his waistcoat, took his hat and walking stick from Caesar and hurried outside. He couldn't resist a look over his shoulder at the house as he

trotted down the steps to the carriage drive. That was another
thing Gabrielle twitted him about, but he thought his pride
was justified. When President Washington had stopped here
on his way to visit Charleston, he'd called Tir Alainn the
finest plantation house in the Carolinas.

Daniel, his gray hair the only sign of aging, waited at the
bottom of the stairs with his wife Callie, a slender woman
with dark, liquid eyes. Jeremiah, his oldest son at ten, and his
daughter Esther, seven, hid behind their mother's skirts.
Billy, the youngest at four, rode his father's shoulders.

"Good morning, Daniel," Michael said. "Good morning, Callie."

"Good for some folks," she muttered grimly.

Michael looked at her in surprise. Daniel quickly pushed
Billy into her arms. "You take the children on down to the
house, Callie. Go on, now. Go on." He waited until she'd
herded the children down the drive, shooting a last dark look
at Michael as she went, before he spoke. "I'm sorry, Mr.
Fallon. I don't know what's got into her lately. Since them
slaves rose up down to Santo Domingo and killed all them
white folks—. Well, she been filling them children's heads
with all kind of foolishness. Not that it mean anything," he
added quickly.

"I understand, Daniel. Now tell me. How's the problem at
the rice mill?"

"All fixed, sir." Slowly Daniel had become a kind of
overseer, at Tir Alainn. "We had to put a whole new shaft in
for the water wheel."

"As long as it's fixed. Look you, now, I have to go down
to Charleston. See that the barges are finished loading, and
start them downriver as soon as possible."

"I see to it, sir." Michael started to turn away, and Daniel
spoke again. "Mr. Fallon, you got your gun?"

Michael smiled grimly and touched his coat over the pistol
before climbing into the carriage. Saul, the driver, cracked
his whip, and the six-horse team swung down the drive.

Michael touched the gun again, and looked at the brace of
others in their holsters by the doors. For robbers, he told

Gabrielle. She must never learn that since the war there'd been over a dozen attempts on his life. And, with the memory of a dead assassin with gold spilled across his chest, he had no doubt they'd been incited by Justin.

What he'd do if he ever found Justin, he didn't know. He wasn't the sort to hire killers of his own. And the idea of seeking out Gabrielle's brother, to kill him himself, didn't appeal. No matter what Justin had done, he was her brother. But what else could he do? Until he found an answer he could only try to stay alive.

He'd just climbed out of the carriage in front of the Queen Street house when James came bursting out of the front door. At twenty he was taller and more slender than his father, his nose less hooked, and his cheekbones less pronounced. He had his mother's hazel eyes. It was the softening of Michael's features by Gabrielle's that made him more handsome and less rugged. "Sir," he called as soon as he touched the ground. "Sir, you must speak to Catherine."

"And what's she done now? Nothing to warrant this fuss, I'll wager."

"It's Thunder, sir. She wants to ride him. Even if riding to hounds is proper for a woman, and I'm not sure it is, Thunder is no horse for her."

The door banged open again, and Catherine rushed out. "I heard that. Riding to hounds *is* proper for a woman. And I can handle Thunder as well as you can." At fifteen, only slightly over five feet tall, she already showed signs of an exotic beauty. The hint of high cheekbones in a face framed by silky black hair made young men look again. Now she turned melting hazel eyes on Michael. "Oh, papa, do say that I can. I do so hate these fat, tame sluggards the groom saddles for me."

Michael frowned. "That horse is as much as a man can handle, and he's more than too much for you. If you so much as curry Thunder, you'll not be able to sit a chair, much less a saddle." She gave him the smile of an indulged daughter who knew herself safe from her father. "I'll tell your mother," he added, and her smile faded.

"You can't twist Mother around your finger," James laughed.

Michael rounded on him. "Since I'm laying about me, I might as well lay into you. I've no objection to you racing for wagers, or gambling at cards, or visiting Mrs. —" He suddenly realized Catherine was an interested listener. "Well. I wouldn't expect different from a son of mine at your age. But I don't expect you to be carousing when you're supposed to be at the Bridge."

James scowled. "That one-armed old—. Petrie told you, didn't he? Do you know, he wants to turn me into a book-keeper!"

"And well that he does. The Bridge will be yours one day, lad. How shall you keep it if you don't know the trade?"

"I shall deal only with gentlemen," James said stiffly, "and trust to their honor."

Michael winced. "God, you'll be stolen blind in a week. And as for Petrie, that one-armed old whatever-you-were-going-to-say was fighting battles before you were born, and he lost that arm while rotting in prison for doing what I told him. Now, down to the Bridge. Go on with you."

Michael shook his head as the young man muttered a sullen goodbye and stalked away. Maybe the lad was spending too much time with those fine friends of his. More and more he seemed to think what made a man was his birth rather than what he was. Perhaps—

"Papa, now that James has left, I wish to speak with you on a matter of some importance. I wish you to discharge Mr. Jarvis."

He looked at her in astonishment. She had her mother's will and his temper, and it was all in her face now. "Lass, what's Tom done to put you in such a lather?"

"He gets above himself."

"Above himself! And when did you start speaking of men getting above themselves?"

She realized she was on the wrong tack and shifted in an instant. "He isn't very responsible. And he's very young to be your chief clerk."

"Young! The man's twenty-seven! Catherine, look at me."

Catherine looked around, suddenly wide eyed and ingenuous. "Oh, Papa, it's getting late. I'm supposed to be in the kitchens. Bye, Papa." Brushing a kiss against his cheek, she darted away.

"Catherine? Catherine!" Muttering to himself, he went inside.

Gabrielle, sweeping down the stairs, made him forget everything else. "Darling," she said, and was in his arms.

He lost himself in kissing her. Each passing year seemed to add more fire to her kisses. Every time he was away from her, he missed her more than the last, and every homecoming was the best yet.

"Michael," she gasped finally, "the servants might be watching."

"Let them," he growled. "You're a witch, woman. Do you know that?"

"And how so?" She spoke idly, studying him as she loved to do. The iron-gray was heavy in his hair, now. But the added lines on his face made him seem, not older, but stronger in some way. Like a rock, she decided, that had weathered a thousand storms and would weather a thousand more. She tenderly noted the slight stoop that had come to his shoulders. But he could still swing her in the air with ease.

"I look at your portrait at Tir Alainn, and when I look at you, there's no difference." The sweet lie was comfortable on his tongue. "In fact, you haven't aged a day since I married you. And don't deny it."

She laughed throatily. He could *still* make her feel like a girl. "Oh, can't I, just once, so I can hear you say it again? No? Well, come into the drawing room anyway. I'll have you for a few minutes before you go."

"Where am I going?" he asked.

"To the City Tavern. There's a meeting this afternoon to rouse support for Thomas Pinckney for president, since General Washington won't run again."

His face darkened. "Damned Federalists. Yes, I'll go.

And I'll tell them—"

She pulled him down on the divan. "You can curse Alexander Hamilton later. For now, kiss me."

Some time later he stopped to catch his breath. Idly he toyed with one of her curls. "Brielle, what's afoot with Catherine? She said something about Tom Jarvis being too young for chief clerk, then ran off to the kitchen. You know how she hates the kitchen."

Gabrielle sighed. "You mustn't let her know I told you anything, Michael. She came in yesterday, furious. It seems she had an argument with Mr. Jarvis. Over what, I have no idea. He told her she was spoiled and arrogant, and being pretty was no pardon. That much I pieced together."

Michael chuckled. "Well, she is, and it is not. He said she was pretty, did he? Well, I've known more than one marriage began with less."

"Oh, not that, I hope." She bit her lip and frowned. "If anything comes of it—send him to London, Michael. You've been saying you needed an agent there."

"God's teeth, Brielle. What's wrong with him? It's not because he's a clerk, is it? Remember, I was a clerk, and less. I was a bound man." A stubborn look came on her face. He sighed. "All right, then. I'll make him a partner."

"Michael, no. She has to marry the man, not the position he holds. If Tom was like you, and she wanted him, I'd say make him a partner, and I'd help her catch him. But there's no force in him. She probably had to drive him cruelly to bring that anger out of him. He's no match for her. If she married him, she'd manage him so easily that inside of a year, she'd hate him." She laughed suddenly. "It's one of the things I love about you. You're such a challenge to manage."

"Oh, I am, am I? Do you realize we're talking as if she's old enough to marry? She has years yet. She's a child. Well, not quite a child. I think she's old enough not to be treated entirely as a child. In fact, I'm buying her a horse, a hunter, a good one. What are you smiling at?"

"Nothing. I thought you'd be buying her a horse soon."

"You did no such thing. I never thought of it myself till a little while ago."

"But someone else did. No, I can't tell you unless you promise to buy the horse. Promise, now." She waited for his grudging nod. "I can only deduce how Catherine tricked you into it. No, Michael, you promised. Sit still and listen. I was suspicious as soon as I discovered she was trying to make James believe she wanted to ride Thunder."

"Make him—," he exploded. "Are you telling me she never wanted to ride the horse?"

"Of course not. She's too intelligent to ride a horse that's as much as James can handle. But surely enough, James went to you, not me, with his complaint. Once the seed was planted with you, it was only a matter of time. You will buy her the horse? You did promise."

"Yes, I promised," he said sourly, but a sudden chuckle broke through. "I'll buy her the horse, the best one I can find. Now before the two of you manage me out of anything else, I'd better change for that meeting."

She trailed him out into the hall, and put a hand on his sleeve as he started up the stairs. "Michael, be careful."

He looked at her. "Careful? Of what?"

"Oh, just be careful," she said with strained lightness.

"It's just a political meeting," he laughed, "not a fight in an alley." And he ran up the stairs without seeing her wince.

The meeting was already under way in the Green Room of the City Tavern. It was a long time since it had been Dillon's. Tobacco smoke hazed the air, and some thirty men listened to George Helm orate. "And I tell you again, gentlemen," he was saying, one bony finger raised, "that the northerners are split. Some want Massachusetts' John Adams. Some want Connecticut's Oliver Ellsworth. We can ride right into that split, and make a South Carolinian, Thomas Pinckney, the second President of the United States."

As an approving murmur rose, Thomas Ollender hurried to the back of the room, his normally smooth face creased with worry. "I'm glad you're here, Fallon. They've just about swung everyone here to Pinckney." He raised his voice. "Gentlemen. Gentlemen, Mr. Fallon has arrived."

Everyone turned to look. "We welcome Mr. Fallon," Helm intoned, "both for his distinguished record in our glorious revolution and for his contributions to our great state since. He, gentlemen, will rally behind the cause of our state and—."

Michael's voice cut him off like an axe. "I wouldn't vote for the Federalists and their damned Constitution if the other choice was the devil himself."

William Jordan thrust his fat head forward like a bulldog into the silence that followed. "Come, sir. Come. You fought the Constitution as hard as anyone, with the possible exception of Patrick Henry, but you accepted it once a Bill of Rights was added."

"I did, sir, and the more fool I. We were betrayed. That so-called Bill of Rights clearly states that all powers not specifically, specifically, mind you, given to the Federal government are reserved to the states. And what did Alexander Hamilton do? He puts his Bank of the United States under way. The Constitution doesn't give the Federal government any such right, but Mr. Hamilton claims it's implied. Likely it's *implied* he should be King Alexander I!"

Helm broke in over the hubbub, trying to regain control. "Really, Mr. Fallon, the bank and your opposition to it are old news. We're here to put a South Carolinian in—."

"Is the last year new enough for you?" Michael grated. "I didn't hear so much rallying to support a South Carolinian when a Federalist Congress refused to confirm John Rutledge as Chief Justice of the United States Supreme Court. So who do we have instead? Your good Connecticut Federalist, Oliver Ellsworth. And have you heard the latest outrage he's committed? He and his cronies have declared that any treaty made by the Federal government has the force of law, and supercedes any state law."

For the first time Helm lost his own composure. "Good God, Fallon, you don't believe one state should be able to upset a treaty agreed to by the rest?"

"Of course not. But you'll note you spoke of being agreed to by the states. This wasn't agreed to by even one state. It was just announced by the Surpeme Court. And all they represent is the Federal government and the Federalist party."

A small shipowner named John Ott bounced to his feet. "You know me, Fallon. You know I'd like to go with Tom Jefferson. But with the Federalists we'll get a navy, and God knows we need one. The English seize our ships. The French seize our ships. The God damned Dey of Algiers seizes our ships. We must have a navy to protect us. And the Federalists will give it to us."

"But what kind?" Michael said before Helm could jump in. "We're poor, as nations go. Unless we let them tax us out of existence, they can't afford more than three or four ships-of-the-line and a handful of frigates. England or France put more than that under a single admiral!"

"A navy could seize their ships the way they seize ours," Helm snapped.

"So they could. But why make ourselves slaves to the Federal government, and through them to New England, just to get a navy, when the one thing it'd be good for can be done better and cheaper by privateers? Why, during the revolution—."

"We're all aware of your war record, General Fallon," Henry Tyree said with barely veiled sarcasm.

Everyone broke off talking to stare at them. The tension was palpable. "I haven't been a general for a long time," Michael said levelly.

"Exactly," Tyree said. He smiled nastily. "And the revolution's over long since. There won't be any privateers because we're not at war with anyone. Some men prefer to live in the past." A concerted gasp rose, but Tyree sensed only that he was the center of attention. "It's a new day, and time for new ways. There's a new capital being built for our country. We've already built a new one for our state."

"I seem to remember you own land up there," Michael said quietly, but the words rang like a shout. "Strange that so many of the men involved in choosing the site for Columbia turned out to have land right around the site they chose.''

"What are you saying? Are you implying—?''

"I'm *implying* nothing. I'm saying you're a crook. You've been wanting to try my measure since I walked in. Now you have your excuse. Say the word, and I'll name my seconds, and the state'll be rid of one of us by tomorrow night.''

Total silence filled the room as everyone waited for Tyree to say the fateful words. He opened his mouth, and realized with a sudden shock that he was making a deadly mistake. He's been thinking of Michael as an old man, but the icy blue eyes that regarded him were steady. They'd look the same over a pistol barrel. In that moment he knew if he challenged Michael Fallon, he'd die.

The moment stretched on, too long. Jordan stepped into the embarrassing breach. "Come, gentlemen. Come. Things are often said in the heat of political debate that aren't really meant. If I might suggest, let's forget anything's been said.''

There was another moment of uncomfortable silence. Then, slowly, men broke off in small groups, talking quietly. No one looked at Tyree. He sat staring at the floor. Suddenly he dashed out. The conversation faltered and resumed a steady drone. In the corner Helm and Jordan argued furiously, if quietly.

Michael walked to the table against the wall and poured a glass of flip. Ollender joined him, laughing. "What got into young Tyree, anyway? He seemed to be seeking a fight with you. Well, I was hoping you'd break this meeting up somehow, even if I didn't expect this. How's the flip?''

"Um? Fine, it's fine. Tell me,'' Michael said casually, "does Tyree have any financial troubles? Or has he paid off any debts lately?''

"Well, he gambles a good bit, of course, but—. Why would you want to know?''

"Just curiosity. No reason.'' Michael shook his head ruefully. He was becoming obsessed. It was entirely possible for a man to dislike him enough to want a duel without being in the pay of Justin Fourrier. "I'm sorry. I didn't hear that last.''

"I asked if you had any relations visiting the city. I was told there's a young man off a ship who looks a lot like you. I believe his name is Robert Carver Fallon. Any relation?"

The names hit Michael like a hammer. If he wanted something that smacked of Justin's touch, this was it. The names Carver and Fallon together, along with a man who looked something like him, would be sure to draw him. But for what? There was only one way to find out. "That does sound like a relation," he said carefully. "What ship, did you say?"

35

Rahman's Tavern wasn't the sort of place he'd expected this Robert Carver Fallon to be. It catered to ship's officers, and those off the better class of ship at that.

Michael eased his pistol in its waistcoat pocket, hefted his sword-cane, and went in.

He'd never seen the man behind the bar before, but the barman looked at Michael with the flash of recognition. Michael was getting tired of that. He'd experienced it too many times on the path to Rahman's, from people he'd never met. He tossed a gold eagle on the bar, and the tapster's eye jerked from him to the spinning coin.

"I'm looking for a man who calls himself Robert Carver Fallon."

The coin disappeared into the barman's apron. "Private room in the back. Second on the left." He worked his mouth, and seemed to decide he owed more for the money. "He's stayed here maybe twice before. Stays to himself. He's first mate on the *Argus*. He—" His mouth snapped shut abruptly as if he'd reached ten dollars' worth.

Michael didn't knock at the second door on the left. Easing the knob, he pushed it open with the sword-cane and stepped in. Immediately he stopped in shock, staring at the man reading at the table. Six feet tall and stocky, he had the hooked nose, high cheekbones, and coloring of the Black Irish, belied by cobat blue eyes. Michael was staring at himself in his mid-twenties.

The other man seemed shocked as well, not at seeing Michael, but at seeing him there. He closed his book and poured two glasses of brandy, pushing one across the table.

Michael sat, never taking his eyes off the other's face. Finally he said, "My name is Michael Fallon."

"I know," his young double said. "I use the Fallon name myself, though I've no right to it."

"No," Michael said softly. "I came here thinking the same thing, but I was wrong. And so are you, else my mirror lies to me. Lad, don't take this wrong; what is your mother's name?"

"She was born Elizabeth Carver, though she married Justin Fourrier. I was called Robert Fourrier till I knew better."

Michael nodded. He knew it was true, and it answered a hundred questions more than twenty years old. But it posed a hundred more. "I never knew, Robert. You must believe that. Lord, I know you for my son, but I don't know another thing about you. How did you find out, and when? And why didn't you come to me? The man said you've been here before."

"I didn't come to make a claim on you." Robert paused. "I'll be leaving in a few days; I won't trouble you."

"You listen to me. I mean to acknowledge you as my son. You can give me the lie if you want, but your own face will give it back to you."

Robert sighed and shook his head. "You have a wife, children. How do you think they'll feel even knowing I'm alive, much less you acknowledging me?"

"There'll be some shock," Michael admitted. Lord, but wouldn't there. "But it's either shock part of my family, or deny another part. Robert, you're no less my son than James."

"I don't know," Robert said doubtfully.

"Look you, I'll give you a little time to think. For now, tell me how you came to discover who you were. Did Justin know?"

"Not until just before we left America, I think. It was then he changed toward me. I didn't know why until mother told me on her death bed, nine years ago, now. It was then I ran away to sea."

Elizabeth dead. Michael couldn't believe it. She'd always been so alive, so greedy for life. He didn't realize he'd spoken the last thought until Robert answered him.

"Yes, she was. And I think she gave a lot of it to me. She and Justin fought a war over me. He'd mistreat me just to see the look on her face when he did it, and she fought to get me proper food, clothing, an education. I often thought it was more to fight him, than for—" He broke off, then began again. "He'd have killed me when she died, if I hadn't run away. I went back a few years later. I'm not sure why. Gerard had learned to hate me for a Fallon before I left, but I thought Marie and little Lucian wouldn't. Well, it doesn't matter. The servants turned me away; before I got back to town I was jumped by men who stabbed me and left me for dead. Since then there've been other attempts."

"He's a lot to answer for," Michael said grimly. "There's one question I must ask. Where *is* Justin? He has tried to kill me, too, more than once. I've tried to find him, but there's been never a glimmer."

"With him there wouldn't be. He has a big house in Jamaica, outside of Kingston. I don't suppose twenty people on the island know who owns it. The servants keep to themselves, and no one ever visits except the governor, or a visiting admiral or general. They think his wealth comes from noble connections. I wonder how they'd feel if they knew he was just another slave trader?" He hesitated. "Now that you know, what will you do?"

"It's not my way to send hired murderers, just as it's not yours, or you'd have done it already. But knowing where he is, maybe I can find a way to stop him." He laughed suddenly. "Anyway, we'll survive him. We're Fallons, lad; we survive. Now, will you at least come to my house, meet the rest of my family? At least you can do that."

Robert gazed at him eye to eye. Slowly he nodded. "I'll promise no more for after, but I'll come."

Gabrielle listened carefully to Michael's news. It took a great effort to keep her face composed, but she did it. When he finished she took a deep breath before speaking.

"Michael, hasn't it occurred to you that this may be another of Justin's attempts to kill you?"

"With my own son?" he asked incredulously.

"Yes. Justin is insane. And despite what Robert says, you've no proof he hasn't come straight from Justin, that Justin hasn't raised him all along with the purpose of killing you."

"That's—." What she'd been saying penetrated in its entirety, and he stared. "You know? For how long?"

"For some time," she sighed. "How many 'accidents' did you think I'd accept? Once I realized what was happening, it was no trouble to decide who was the only living man who hated you enough. And Justin certainly hates you enough to use this, this man against you, and delight in doing it."

"This man, Brielle? He's my son!"

"Your son!" She jerked out of her chair. "Your son is upstairs, sleeping. This byblow appears with his touching tale of a mother's death bed, and you lose all sense of proportion. God, Michael, if you saw it at the Dock Street Theater, you'd say you were cheated the price of a ticket. I'll wager she's not dead at all. She's with Justin right now, laughing over how you've been duped."

"With him knowing she bore my child?"

She winced. She didn't even want to think of another woman bearing Michael's child. Still, she had to admit the truth of what he said. If Justin knew, it would be better for Elizabeth if she were dead.

"Brielle, how much of this is because you're afraid Justin is using him against me, and how much is because of who his mother was?"

It was too close. Robert would be a constant reminder that Michael had once come to her bed loving another woman, thinking of another woman while he made love to her. "I don't want him in my house. I don't want him under the same roof with my children."

"It's my house, too," Michael said levelly.

"Dear God. Most men would pay their bastards to go away, not invite them into their homes."

"He's my son, damn it. My son, and no less my son for the accident of his birth. Now I've said my last word on it."

"As have I. You'll want to use a spare bedroom tonight."

Her back eloquently rigid, she glided out of the room.

With a snarl he poured a glass of brandy, gulped it down and poured another. By God, he'd use no bedroom tonight. Nor any bed. The brandy level in the decanter went down, and every swallow further solidified his determination.

Friday afternoon was sunny outside, but grim inside the Fallon house. Michael had announced in a voice like thunder that he was expecting a visitor, and that every member of the family would be expected to meet that visitor. And he told them the visitor's name.

James spent the day casting incredulous glances at his father. Such things just weren't done in the world he knew. Catherine, eyes blazing, was furious. Gabrielle waited quietly, but Michael noted the glitter in her eyes. He'd ridden rough-shod over her objections, and she was ready to explode. Damn it, it was his son he was bringing to his house, and no one would deny him that.

As the hours passed, they gathered silently in the drawing room, waiting. At precisely four, Caesar announced Robert Carver Fallon.

Then Robert entered. James and Catherine gasped, and Gabrielle stirred uneasily. This was no imposter. It was Michael as she'd first seen him. And that made it worse. There was no chance of his being other than Michael's bastard. With Elizabeth.

Michael hurried forward with an outstretched hand and guided him to a chair. "Welcome, lad. Welcome. Sit, and I'll pour you some wine. No?" He took a deep breath and turned. James and Catherine had moved close to Gabrielle's chair, standing on either side of her. "Gabrielle, may I present my son, Robert. Robert, my wife, Mrs. Fallon. And these are my other children—." Gabrielle, James, and Catherine gave not so much acknowledgment as a nod. Robert had a smile of sardonic amusement. "Are you certain you'll not have a glass of wine?" Michael asked as he finished. He had begun to sweat.

"No, thank you, sir," Robert answered.

"It won't do to pretend abstemiousness," James snapped. "My father's not taken in by that."

"Watch your tongue," Michael barked.

"To your bastard?"

"In front of your mother and sister." Michael's words cut James short for the moment, but Catherine leaped in immediately.

"I'd think you'd go away, instead of flaunting your shame. In fact, I don't think I've ever met a bastard before."

Her parents and brother gasped to hear that word from her mouth, but Robert only gave a deep laugh. "Of course you have," he said. "But they worked their way to it. I was born in it."

"It's not a thing to be proud of!" James said.

"I told you, James—," Michael began, when Gabrielle broke her silence.

"Why did Justin Fourrier send you?"

It was Robert's turn to be shaken. "Justin—? Mrs. Fallon, of all the men who might send me, Justin Fourrier is the last."

"Then why did you come here? What do you want?" Her voice was quiet, but her eyes glittered like bits of tiger's-eye.

"I come to Charleston often, Mrs. Fallon. My ship—."

"Do you want to harm Michael, or us? Or are you after money?"

"I want nothing from you, or your family. That I swear on my honor."

"Only gentlemen have honor," James said nastily. With a pointed look at Robert's coat of dark green superfine, he added, "And it takes more than a tailor to make a gentleman."

"I'd noticed," Robert said drily, casting his own glance at James' attire.

James bristled, but Michael stepped in quickly. "Stop this bickering, all of you!"

Robert rose smoothly. "I fear the bickering is my fault, sir. It will be better if I remove myself."

Michael hesitated, glaring at the others. "All right, then.

But there *will* be other meetings. We will all come to know one another. But if you're minded to go, now, I'll walk you to the door."

Catherine hurried from the room before them. By the time her father shook hands with Robert at the door, she was waiting by the front gate, hidden from the house by the great oak tree. It was disconcerting to watch Robert walk toward her. He looked so much like Papa that it seemed unnatural. He'd no right to look so much like Papa. And that was a foolish thought!

She spoke as he reached the gate. "I want to speak with you, Mr—. I want to speak with you."

"Do you?" he said with an infuriating smile. "Very well. You've my permission. Speak to me."

"Your permission? Permission! Damn you, what right have you to give me permission for anything?"

"Why should I not? You seem to think I need your permission to be alive."

She controlled her temper with an effort. "If you're telling the truth about wanting nothing from this family, then go. It must be plain that you're not wanted. Leave Charleston, and don't come back."

He smiled again. A tiger, this one was, as fierce as any man twice her size. "Madam, I congratulate you on your spunk." And with a tip of his hat he was gone.

She frowned furiously. He was altogether too insolent. Even if he hadn't been Papa's bastard she'd have wanted to get rid of him. There must be a way. There must be.

Michael returned to the entry hall to find James waiting, a frown on his face. "You wipe off that frown, lad. I'm your father, not one of your feather-brained friends."

James started. "I'm sorry, sir. It's just that your—." He checked his father's stormy face again and changed what he had been going to say. "That man is up to no good, sir. He came to our house for a purpose. Likely he wants money."

"He came because I asked him to," Michael said levelly. "You might as well get used to it. He's your brother."

"With all due respect, sir," James said rigidly, "I resent having this forced on me, not to speak of Mother and Catherine. What you should do—."

"I'll not be lectured. Not by my own son." Michael forced himself to moderate his tone. "I think we'd better end this conversation, James. We'll talk of it again later."

For a moment James hesitated. Then he hurried up the stairs, his back stiff. Michael muttered a small oath and mopped his brow. They *would* accept Robert, damn it. They—. Gabrielle stalked silently from the drawing room toward the stairs, without even a glance at him. "Brielle, I wish to speak with you."

"But I do not wish to speak with you."

"Damn it, Brielle!" He took a deep breath. "You didn't give him much of a chance."

Gabrielle whirled at the foot of the stair, her face as furious as his. "Much of a chance! You bring your bastard into my house, your bastard by another man's wife, by a whore, by—."

"He's my son. Please, Brielle. The rest doesn't matter beside the fact that he's my son. Can't you understand that?"

"No," she said simply. Until he leaves Charleston, I see no reason for us to be under the same roof. I would prefer to stay here, but if you wish to remain, I will pack and—." For the first time her voice faltered.

Michael's face grew stony. "Pack be damned. I'll be gone as soon as my horse is saddled."

She stepped forward with an outstretched hand, but he whirled with a snarl and slammed the door behind him hard enough to rattle the windows. Her face twisted on the edge of tears. This wasn't what she wanted. But she was right, and she had to make him see it.

By Sunday night Robert had reached a decision. A visit to the Fallon house the day before had gained him the intelligence that Mr. Fallon had left on Friday. For Tir Alainn, on a saddle horse, hurriedly. Mrs. Fallon was receiving no one, the butler'd said. James, white-faced and gripping the bannister as if he were going to tear if off, glared silently down at him from the second-floor veranda as he left.

For Robert there was no doubt as to what had happened. In spite of Michael's assurances, his presence had proved explosive. He would have to leave. He didn't want to go; he'd spent two days trying to think of a way to stay. The conclusions stayed the same, though, and the solution stayed the same. On Sunday night he told the innkeeper he'd be leaving first thing in the morning. Then he began to pack, and turned restlessly all night.

At a rap on the door early on Monday he turned from the open sea chest. "Who is it?"

"It's——. It's James Fallon. I want to speak to you."

Robert frowned. He didn't want to speak to any Fallons, James perhaps least of all. He opened the door. "Listen, James——."

James' fist caught him in the mouth. He stumbled back, falling to one knee by the bed. James closed the door, and stared down at Robert contemptuously. "Leave Charleston. We don't like bastards here. Leave, and don't come back, or you'll get worse."

Robert tasted the blood in his mouth and shook his head. "I suppose, for your being my half-brother, I should accept that."

"I thought you would," James sneered.

"But I won't." Robert surged to his feet, and his left caught James flush on the mouth.

James staggered back against the door. Incredulously he wiped at his mouth and stared at the blood on his hand. Robert stood in the center of the room, waiting. With a yell James rushed forward, fists flying. Robert met him almost joyously, and they stood toe to toe, hitting as if each blow were meant to knock the other man out.

It had lately become the fashion for young gentlemen to study boxing along with their fencing, and James had studied under Jem Tyler, who had fought two hundred matches in England. He fought with skill and science. But Robert's school had been the docks and the forecastle, where a man's authority depended as much on the power of his fists as his rank. He blocked what blows he could, took those he had to, and delivered a rain of short, sharp, murderous punches to the midsection and ribs.

Finally the cumulative effect told on James. His knees buckled, and he crumpled to the floor. Unbelieving, he stared up at Robert. He'd never been beaten; it was impossible that this byblow had put him on the floor. Laboriously he got to his feet, and launched another blow.

Easily Robert blocked it, and hooked a wicked right into James' belly. As the taller man doubled over, he raised his fist high, and halted. He'd been about to deliver a finishing punch, a fist into the socket behind the jaw, breaking the jaw and bringing unconsciousness. This was his half-brother he was fighting, not some drunken boatswain. Angry at himself, he pushed the still doubled James away and turned to dig a bottle out of his sea chest.

A scrabble at the door brought him round; James was darting into the hall. Robert muttered a curse. Well, what did it matter? He examined himself in the mirror. Aside from a small cut at the corner of his mouth, no one would know he'd been in a fight. But there'd be a mouse under his eye by nightfall.

In spite of himself he couldn't keep his mind off the Fallons. He'd planned to go at once. But he could not do it. The family was tearing apart. He had to tell them he was going, let them begin to knit themselves back together. With an oath he snatched up his hat and walking stick and left the room.

Halfway down the stairs to the common room, he saw James at the bar, pouring brandy with a shaking hand. James turned at his footsteps. When he saw Robert the glass dropped from his hand. He wet his lips slowly, then suddenly grabbed the bottle and dashed out into the street.

Outside, Robert saw him once, far ahead in the crowd. He looked back, and when he saw Robert, began to run. Probably thought he was being pursued, Robert thought. It was no more than he deserved.

He quickly lost sight of James in the early morning throng, mostly street peddlers claiming a good spot and sellers headed to the beef or vegetable markets. He'd no doubt they were going the same place, though, even before the butler opened the door and he heard the tag of a conversation inside.

"Well, just you keep knocking at his door until he comes out," Gabrielle said. "The idea of him running past me like that."

"But Mama," Catherine protested, "I'm supposed to go shopping with Alice and Mary, and then we're going to Mary's house to look at patterns. Besides, I don't think he'll come out. I think I saw a bottle in his hand."

"A bottle?" Suddenly Gabrielle became aware of Robert standing in the door. "What do you want?"

His stubborn streak ignited. "I've something to tell you, ma'am, but I'll not say it standing here."

"Why you—," Catherine began indignantly, but her mother shushed her.

"You run along, dear. I'll tend to this. Mr—." Her mouth tightened. She couldn't call him Mr. Fallon, but she had to call him something. And she couldn't have an argument on the doorstep. "Come into the drawing room, Robert."

Robert followed. "Ma'am, I apologize for speaking the way I did. You have every right not to want me in your house, so I won't stay long enough to take a seat. I'll just say what I have to, and go."

She turned from closing the door and looked at him in exasperation. "Robert, you're already in the house. Sit down."

"No, thank you."

"God, you're as stubborn as your fa—. I mean—. Oh, do sit down. I've no intention of standing until you're through, and I don't want to look up at you the whole while." She sank into a chair, and after a moment he took a seat across from her.

"I suppose I *can* be stubborn. All I wanted to say is, I'm leaving Charleston, and I won't be coming back. I'd appreciate your telling the family that I won't trouble them again."

Gabrielle found herself almost at a loss for words. "I don't understand. Why? You've gotten nothing you could've hoped for when you came here."

"I didn't come here for anything from the Fallon family. Remember, I didn't find my—Mr. Fallon. He found me."

"Then why? Why are you going, and why did you come in the first place?"

"I'm going because my being here is having an effect on this family I don't like and didn't want. And I came for the same reason I've come to Charleston before. The only really happy times of my life were spent as a child in and around this city."

She nodded thoughtfully. The man was a skillful liar; she'd find out just how skillful.

"Your only happy times, you said. Weren't you happy wherever you went when you left here? Jamaica, I believe Michael said."

"Your brother found out who my father was before we left," he said flatly.

She pushed aside the thought of what Justin would've been like to such a child. "But you found out when your mother died? And she told you to go to Michael?"

"No, she didn't tell me to go to him. In fact, I don't think she'd have mentioned him at all if she hadn't had to. You see, Justin used me against her, hurting me and letting her know it. It was the only reason he let me live. But she knew that when she died he'd kill me. I didn't want to believe it, then, even after everything. So she told me about my father. Just his name. Not even where he was from. I didn't discover that till I came here years later. But even at sixteen I knew that if I were a Fallon, Justin would certainly kill me. I stayed by her bed until she died, and then I ran."

Bit by bit she drew his story out, jumping now forward in years, then back, searching for discrepancy. And finding none. Slowly she was coming to believe him. And she realized something else, too. When she thought of him as Michael's bastard and Elizabeth's son, she hated him with a passion. But when she thought of him as Michael's son, she didn't know how she felt.

She didn't want to throw open her arms to him, but she could feel sorrow for the boy trapped under Justin's insane mercilessness. And he looked so much like Michael; there was nothing of Elizabeth in his face.

"I must be going, ma'am," he was saying.

"No. Stay awhile."

He shook his head. "I haven't talked this much about myself in the last five years together. I really have to go, though. Captain Byles promised to hold my berth, but if I don't leave now, I'll miss it. He's sailing with the tide."

"I meant don't go with the ship, Robert." She was surprised to realize she really did mean that. "Stay here in Charleston."

He stared at her in utter confusion. "I don't understand you at all. From the beginning you've made no secret that you couldn't wait to see the last of me. Now you just change your mind?"

"I haven't changed. At least, not entirely. But I suddenly realize I've been against you for all the wrong reasons. You *are* Michael Fallon's son." She took a deep breath. It didn't get any easier as she went on. "I'm not saying everything's going to work out overnight. It may not work out at all. I want to try, though. For you, for Michael, maybe for me. Robert, will you stay in Charleston?" The last sentence left her feeling as if she'd run for miles.

"I—." She looked at him, and her eyes were truly asking. "I'll stay," he said. The smile that blossomed made him think of sunshine.

"Good. Good. Can you ride, Robert? Then I'll have the best horse in the stable saddled. Ride to Tir Alainn and bring him back. Tonight we'll sit and find a way through this. But for now, bring Michael to me."

The burning afternoon sun was beating down as Robert galloped up the drive at Tir Alainn. He hadn't stopped except to ask directions, and he and the horse both were lathered and tired. He leaped down, tossed the reins to a staring black man, and raced up the stairs. A shout spun him around.

Michael, his shirt clinging to him with sweat, raced up the path from the rice fields, flogging his horse. "What's the matter, lad? You came in here like the devil was at your heels. It's not Gabrielle? She's all right? She's—."

"She's all right. She sent me for you. Bring Michael to me, she said."

"She said that, did she? And to you?" Michael put back his head and shouted for pure joy. "We'll need fresh horses first. Kip! Lucifier! Get Hawk and Strider saddled! Stir your stumps!"

Twenty minutes later they pounded down the drive. They kept the horses at a gallop, slowing occasionally to breathe them. But always Michael was impatient to push on, to resume the gallop and hold it as long as possible. The lowering summer sun baked them, and powdery dust hanging in the air coated their lips and filled their nostrils.

Every wooden bridge they crossed rattled and drew the eyes to water, but they stopped only twice. A swallow for the horse, a swallow for the man, and they were gone. Darkness came, but the heat was still there, and worse for the air's heaviness. Short of Clement's Ferry they saw the ominous red glow in the sky toward Charleston. They looked at each other, fear hanging between them. It looked like fire. Without a word they leaned low over the tired horses, whipping them back to a gallop. They'd run them into the ground now, before they'd draw rein.

The glow grew brighter as they drew nearer. A bar of fire stretched the length of the city, flames clawing at the night sky like a madman's vision of hell.

The streets were choked. People who lived away from the blaze struggled to get closer and see. Those who lived close fought to get away and live. Michael and Robert forced a way through, ruthlessly whipping aside men who grabbed their reins or tried to hinder them. More and more they found streets leading toward the fire too clogged to use. They began to head down the peninsula, toward Broad Street. They'd circle around the lower end of the fire.

A numbness grew in Michael's brain. There was going to

be no circling around. He knew that now. The house on Queen Street was in the midst of the devil's bonfire. Desperately he searched the throng for a familiar face. They all looked alike, painted with fear and washed with the glow from the fire.

Suddenly he leaned from the saddle; he had seen a maid from his house. "Miriam, where's Mrs. Fallon? Where's my wife?"

"I don't know," the woman screamed. "She send me on a errand. She send most everybody out. I don't know where she be." Tears ran down her face, and she began sobbing.

"When did it start? Do you know if she knew about it? Stop that and answer me, damn it. When did it start?"

"Before I leave," she wailed. "It start before I leave. Mrs. Fallon, she say it way off. She say one time she get scared by fire, but she ain't scared this time."

"Papa!" He jerked around. "Papa!" He saw Catherine, standing on the seat of his carriage and waving.

He forced his way to her, coughing as the wind shifted to carry smoke down on them. "Thank God, you're all right. Where's your mother? And James?"

"I don't know, Papa. I don't know." Tears streamed down her face; her body quivered with tension. "Papa, she always reads in the evening. And I, I think James was drinking in his room. Oh, God, Papa, I don't know." The tension broke; she sank down on the seat, her body wracked with sobs.

Michael slipped out of the saddle and pushed his way through the edge of the crowd. From a block away he could feel the heat, and it grew hotter with every step. Firemen heaved on the handles of their pumps, but the hoses were directed at buildings not yet aflame. They'd already given up on everything in the blocks on fire. One of them loomed in front of him.

"Go back! There's nothing—."

He backhanded the man out of the way without breaking stride. Nothing he could do? Gabrielle was in there.

Someone grabbed his arm, and he whirled with raised fist. Robert backed away, holding up his hands, his arms full of blankets. ''We'll need to wet these, and us, in the water trough over there.'' He saw the protest forming. ''Or did you expect to carry both of them out by yourself?''

Michael nodded jerkily and took one of the blankets. He jumped into the trough, barely waiting for clothes and blanket to soak before leaping out. The blanket wrapped around his head, he ran into the fire. Robert followed at his heels.

The wetness didn't reduce the heat. It just kept the cloth from burning. Steam quickly began to rise, and breathing was impossible except through a fold of the blanket. Through shoe leather the pavement felt like hot coals.

Only one thing gave Michael hope. Here and there a house, with all around it blazing, merely smouldered, or only the roof burned. It would be so at his house. It would be so. Then he could see his house. Flames already roared from the windows of the upper stories, but the ground floor was still intact. There was yet a chance.

He raced forward and reached to swing open the gate. And jerked his hand back with the red bar of a burn across it. Without a pause he kicked the gate open and ran through. The oak in the front yard had no more leaves, and even some of the heavier branches were beginning to show flame. He took the steps two at a time, threw his weight against the door, and smashed it open.

Gabrielle lay sprawled in the entry hall as if she'd collapsed trying to get to the door. Frantically he rolled her over. She stirred slightly, murmured. He wanted to cry with joy. Then he looked up.

Half-way up the first flight the stairs became a wall of flame, and two burning timbers blocked the way. Robert was fighting to get through. He tugged his coat off and managed to loop it around one of the timbers. He strained, trying to pull it out of the way before the coat burned through. Suddenly the timber shifted. It slipped, then more. And fell against him. He leaped back, shirt sleeves ablaze. Frantically he managed to beat them out, then started back up the staircase. Snatching his blanket he swung it preparatory to looping it around the timber.

"No!" Michael shouted. "You'll never get out without that around your head."

"James is up there! Your son—!"

"I know it! God, don't you think I know it? But I can't get to him, not if I stay here till it burns down on top of me! And if I stay much longer, she'll die! Oh, God, I hope he's dead! Please, God, let him be dead!" He realized he was shaking uncontrollably. It wouldn't stop. He grabbed hold of Gabrielle, and calmness came to him. He had to be calm, because he had to get her out.

He motioned Robert toward the door. "Go. I'll follow with her when you're clear. Go, damn it, and don't forget the blanket."

Robert hesitated, then ran out. Michael watched him splash into the trough by the gate, then dart away down the street, the blanket like a shawl around his head and shoulders. He picked Gabrielle up and followed, trying to ignore that everything was burning as far as he could see, that buildings were collapsing into the street.

Carefully he lowered her into the water trough. It was hot, too, but it could still save her. He splashed water over himself, soaked the blanket. Tenderly he kissed her eyelids. Then he arranged the blanket around her, carefully positioning an edge to filter her air. Squinting his eyes against the heat he picked her up and turned down the street. All he had to do was keep moving forward.

Within half a dozen steps his nose and mouth were dry. Not dry as thirst, but swelling, skin-cracking dry. He felt the burning of it deep in his chest. Blisters formed on his face and hands, and his eyebrows singed. The heat through his boot soles blistered the bottoms of his feet. They broke as he walked, and new blisters formed. But he kept on moving. That was all he had to do, the only thought he allowed in his mind. Keep moving forward, and he'd get her to safety. That

was all that was important. For endless steps that thought
kept him moving.

Something touched his arm. He looked around in bewilderment. Someone took Gabrielle from his arms, and he
realized they'd made it. There was Robert, and Catherine,
too. "Doctor," he croaked. "She needs. Doctor." A man
was in front of him, peering into his eyes. "Not me. Her."

"I've looked at her," the man said. "She's dead."

Michael pushed him aside and stumbled to where Gabrielle lay on the pavement. Someone had put a coat over her
face. He ripped it aside with an oath. The soft brown hair still
framed her face, auburn highlights glinting from the firelight. Her satiny skin still had the glow of life. She looked as
if she were sleeping. She even had that slight smile she had
when she was—

The doctor stopped behind him. "There was nothing you
could have done. When you reached her, it was already too
late. Once a certain amount of smoke gets into the lungs, I'm
afraid—"

"Shut up, " Michael said tonelessly. He managed to get
his arms under her and stand erect. He looked around for the
carriage. The crowd parted in front of him as he walked
toward it, staring straight ahead.

Suddenly there was a shot, and the people in front of him
scattered. Something brushed his head, and wetness dripped
down his cheek. In front of him, Henry Tyree appeared,
throwing one pistol aside and pulling another. Michael kept
walking toward the carriage.

"Damn you," Tyree shouted. "I don't care about the
money. I just want you."

Robert had just taken his hat and pistol from Catherine
when the shot rang out. Instinctively he turned, arm coming
up to the duelist's ready. And suddenly there was a clear path
from him to Michael to Tyree. He stepped to one side to clear
Michael and shouted. "You!"

Tyree paused in the act of raising his gun. His eyes darted
from Michael, still walking steadily toward him, to the

waiting Robert. He snarled, and his pistol came up. Toward Michael. Robert fired on the instant.

Tyree was hurled back, his unfired gun lying beside him, still cocked. Michael walked past him without even looking down. He climbed into the carriage and put Gabrielle on the seat beside him, his arm around her so she could lie against his chest the way she liked to. Saul, weeping on his perch, peered at him wide'eyed.

"Home," Michael said, and when Saul didn't move he snapped, "Tir Alainn, damn you!"

The driver spun around, and the carriage rolled into the night. Michael held Gabrielle close, his tears falling onto her hair.

36

Michael's study as Tir Alainn was dark. The curtains kept
the darkness in. Only two candles were lit, one on either
side of Gabrielle's portrait. The portrait was in the only pool
of light in the room.

Michael sat at his desk in the darkness. He didn't drink. He
just sat, watching the portrait. He didn't eat, either. Regu-
larly, trays were set outside the door. They grew cold, and
were replaced by fresh trays that in turn grew cold. Un-
touched.

He sat, and looked at the portrait. Seeing Gabrielle.
Laughing. Raging. Lost in love. There were so many
memories. But sometimes another would sneak in. Gabrielle
lying in the street. The long walk from the house after the
minister spoke to the new-cleared ground—the first two
graves to hold Fallons in the New World.

There'd been more people than he wanted. All he wanted
was Robert and Catherine. But they said they wanted to pay
their respects. They said they wanted to honor her memory.
They couldn't understand a private grief, so they poured in
by dozens, with flowers and black crepe.

He'd watched the wooden coffins with their shiny brass
handles lowered into the ground, trying not to think of the
stones added to one to bring what was in it up to the weight of
a man. He'd watched the dirt sprinkled, as required, impassively, and stayed with cold eyes and a cold heart after
everyone else was gone, until the last spadeful of earth was in
place. Then he'd walked back to the house, to his study,
closed the door and pulled the curtains.

They said he was cold. They said he was unfeeling. He
didn't care enough about what they thought to explain. He

just wanted to look at her portrait, and remember the good times.

There was a rap at the door, but he didn't look around. Catherine stuck her head in hesitantly, then entered determinedly. "Papa, I must talk with you."

Michael gazed at her. She was a beautiful child. As beautiful as her mother, perhaps. His eyes drifted back to the portrait. Thank God he had had St. Memin paint it.

Catherine walked to the window and threw open the curtains. The sunlight hurt his eyes after so long. She stood staring out before speaking. "Charles Manigault has asked me to marry him."

He jerked erect. "You told him he'd stepped beyond the bounds, of course."

"I'm thinking of accepting," she said slowly. "He says we should spend a year or more touring Europe for our honeymoon. I'd like that."

"Honeymoon!" he roared. "Damn it, girl, you're fifteen. A child. You'll not even think of marriage for years yet!"

"But, Papa—."

"No, don't smile at me like that. You'll bend me around your finger no more. With—. With your mother gone— Within the hour you'll bring me a note to young Manigault, telling him you'll not be seeing him again. Within the hour, mind, or you'll not sit down for a week. Marriage, at your age. Go on with you, now."

Catherine hurried out of the room. Thank God! But, drat it, now she wouldn't be able to see Charles. He'd be totally baffled as to why. But Papa was alive once more.

Robert, waiting in the hall, looked at her expectantly. She nodded with a bad grace, and pointedly turned her back as he knocked on the door.

Michael was on his feet when Robert entered, still looking at Gabrielle's portrait, but wondering how he was going to handle Catherine. "At least you aren't aching for an early marriage," he said.

"I beg your pardon, sir?" Robert replied innocently.

"Nothing, lad." He stepped closer to the mantel. It was

good the curtains were open. She'd always been beautiful in the sunlight.

"Sir, I hesitate to come to you with this, but I need your help."

"Um?" Michael pulled his attention from the portrait with an effort. "My help? Of course. Whatever you need."

"I want to buy a half interest in a brig, but I've only money for a quarter. I'm not known in Charleston, and—."

"And bankers are loath to lend to strangers. No matter. I'll give you the money."

"I can't take it, sir," Robert said quickly. "I mean no offence, but I've been my own man for too long."

Michael nodded slowly, as if seeing Robert clearly for the first time. "Yes. Yes, I see. Well, I'll take no offence at a statement of fact. Will you accept an introduction to William Kershaw, the banker?" At Robert's nod he bent over his desk and began to write rapidly. "This will get you your money."

"There's one other thing, sir. I'd like you to take a look at the brig. She's the *Curlew*, lying at Motte's Wharf. I need your opinion of her."

Michael stopped sanding the introduction. "My opinion? You know a good ship from a bad by now. You've worked the sea nine years."

"I still have doubts of this one, and I've heard it said you have a natural eye for ships. Will you come to Charleston and look at it? I need that as much as the introduction."

Go to Charleston? He didn't want to leave that room, or Gabrielle's portrait. But he couldn't look at Robert's brig from his study. And he couldn't keep Catherine in order from there. God, she might just run off with Manigault if her temper was roused.

"All right. I'll come down tomorrow and look at the *Curlew*."

Robert smiled broadly. It was done. "Thank you, sir. I'd better get this note to Kershaw before the ship's sold. And thank you again."

Michael found himself smiling as Robert made his good-byes. He seemed entirely too overjoyed for just a ship.

Perhaps there was a girl in Charleston as well. Wouldn't that be a fine thing. His grief for James brushed him like a dark wing, then was gone.

Now for Catherine. On his way out of the study, he stopped just inside the door. Sunlight bathing the portrait made the flesh seem warm and alive. Gabrielle had been full of light and life. He'd been wrong to shut her up in darkness. She'd never accepted darkness, for herself or for him, never surrendered, never accepted an ending. If this was the ending of his story, it was the beginning of Robert and Catherine's. And they needed him still, to help their story begin well.

He poured a glass of wine and raised it to her portrait, tears in his eyes and a smile on his lips. "To us, Brielle. To life. To America and the Fallon blood, for a thousand years to come."

There are a lot more
where this one came from!

ORDER your FREE catalog of ACE paperbacks here. We have hundreds of inexpensive
books where this one came from priced from
75¢ to $2.50. Now you can read all the books
you have always wanted to at tremendous
savings. Order your *free* catalog of ACE
paperbacks now.

ACE BOOKS • P.O. Box 690, Rockville Centre, N.Y. 11571

1A